Unfinished Paths

Fiona Sterling

Published by Fiona Sterling, 2024.

This is a work of fiction. Similarities to real people, places, or events are entirely coincidental.

UNFINISHED PATHS

First edition. October 9, 2024.

Copyright © 2024 Fiona Sterling.

ISBN: 979-8227372369

Written by Fiona Sterling.

Chapter 1: Whispers of the Past

The air was thick with nostalgia, and as I parked my car in front of the bakery, the sweet scent of vanilla and freshly baked bread wafted through the open door, wrapping around me like an old sweater. It was just as I remembered—cozy, cluttered, and filled with the chatter of locals who looked up from their pastries as I walked in, their faces flickering with recognition and surprise. It had been so long since I'd allowed myself to step into this world, to bask in the warmth of a place that once felt like home.

"Clara!" Mrs. Fitzroy called from behind the counter, her hands dusted with flour. She was as much a fixture of the bakery as the glass display case filled with gooey pastries. "Is that really you? You've grown into such a lovely woman!"

I forced a smile, my heart squeezing at the memory of her soft hugs and endless supply of cookies. "Thank you, Mrs. Fitzroy. It's good to be back."

The townsfolk resumed their conversations, but I could feel their curiosity prickling at my back like the autumn breeze that swirled through the open door. I grabbed a chocolate croissant, its flaky exterior crumbling as I took a bite, each morsel a sweet reminder of simpler times. I couldn't shake the weight of what had brought me back. The invitation, delivered by my estranged brother's trembling hand, had felt like a ghostly whisper from the past, beckoning me to face the shadows lurking in the corners of my memories.

As I chewed, I caught sight of the park through the bakery window. The old swing set, painted a chipped red, still swayed gently in the wind, just as it had five years ago. I could almost hear the echoes of laughter, the sounds of children running around, playing tag while I tried my best to ignore the insistent tugging at my heart. With a heavy sigh, I left the warmth of the bakery and made my way toward the park, my footsteps soft against the cracked pavement, each step stirring up dust and long-forgotten dreams.

The park was quiet, save for the rustle of leaves whispering secrets above me. I settled onto a weathered bench, its slats warm from the afternoon sun. It was here that I had spent countless hours, daydreaming of far-off places and inventing tales of adventure with my childhood friends. But the memories were laced with shadows, the kind that linger when laughter fades into silence.

"Clara? Is that you?"

I turned at the familiar voice, heart jumping into my throat. It was Jason Blackwood, standing at the edge of the park, looking as handsome as ever. His dark hair tousled by the wind, his hazel eyes filled with a mix of surprise and something else I couldn't quite place.

"What are you doing here?" I managed to ask, though my voice was barely above a whisper, caught in the web of our shared past.

"I could ask you the same," he replied, a half-smile playing on his lips. "It's been a while."

"Five years, to be exact," I said, trying to keep my tone light, though my heart betrayed me, racing at the sight of him. "I didn't think I'd ever come back."

"Guess we're both full of surprises," he said, taking a step closer, the afternoon sun casting a golden glow around him, making the moment feel surreal, like something out of a movie.

"I suppose we are," I replied, heart pounding in my chest. "Are you still working at the distillery?"

Jason's smile faltered, a shadow crossing his face. "I left a while back. Decided it was time to forge my own path. Family businesses can be... complicated."

His words hung in the air, heavy with unspoken truths. We stood there, suspended in the moment, the park alive with the sounds of rustling leaves and distant laughter, yet it felt like we were encased in a bubble of our own making, one where time stood still. I remembered the warmth of his hand on my back, the way he had always known how to make me laugh, how to peel away the layers of anxiety I'd worn like armor.

"I didn't know," I said, feeling a pang of sympathy for him. The Blackwoods had always been at the center of town gossip, their family drama splashed across newspaper headlines like a scandalous reality show. "I'm sorry to hear that."

"It's not all bad. I'm just figuring things out. This town... it has a way of keeping you tethered." He glanced around, a flicker of frustration crossing his features. "Sometimes, that's not what you need."

"Or maybe it is," I said, surprising myself with my boldness. "Maybe we both need to confront our pasts to move forward."

He met my gaze, and for a heartbeat, the world around us faded, leaving just the two of us, our shared history whispering in the background like an old song. "Are you staying long?" he asked, his tone softer now, the walls he had built beginning to crumble.

"I'm not sure yet," I admitted, my heart caught in the web of possibility. "I have some things to settle, a family to reconnect with."

"Family," he echoed, his voice laced with a bittersweet note. "A loaded word for both of us."

Before I could respond, laughter erupted from the direction of the swing set. A group of children were chasing each other, their bright giggles mingling with the rustling leaves, a perfect snapshot of innocence. I felt a pang of longing for that carefree spirit, a yearning for the simplicity of childhood when our biggest worries were scraped knees and schoolyard crushes.

"I guess some things never change," Jason said, glancing at the children. "Ever think about what life would be like if we'd never left?"

"More than I'd like to admit," I replied, the truth spilling out with surprising ease. "I often wonder how different things would have been if we hadn't gotten caught up in our families' drama."

"We were just kids, Clara," he said softly, his eyes searching mine. "But it feels like we're still living in the aftermath of that night."

His words hit hard, a palpable tension crackling between us. I nodded slowly, the weight of unspoken words heavy in the air. Perhaps it was time to unravel the threads of the past, to confront the ghosts that had haunted us for far too long.

As the sun dipped lower in the sky, painting the horizon in hues of orange and pink, I felt the pull of something deeper—an uncharted territory waiting to be explored. The decision lay heavy on my shoulders. Would I embrace the past, the bittersweet memories, and the possibility of rekindling old flames? Or would I let them linger as specters in the corners of my mind, forever haunting my dreams?

A light breeze stirred the fallen leaves, sending a flurry of crisp, gold and crimson spirals dancing across the pavement. I stayed on the bench for a moment longer, watching the children play and hoping the memories of laughter would drown out the ghosts that lurked in the shadows. But the ghosts had a way of creeping back in, slipping through the cracks in my carefully constructed facade. Jason's presence lingered, a warmth against the chill that began to settle in the air, and I couldn't shake the feeling that our paths were intertwined once again, as if the universe was nudging us together for a reason.

"I should probably get going," I finally said, my voice tinged with reluctance. "I have... things to do."

"Things?" Jason raised an eyebrow, that teasing glint back in his eyes. "Like standing in the park reminiscing about the good old days, or something a little more exciting?"

I couldn't help but laugh. "Believe it or not, I have an appointment at my family's old home. It's been a while since I've seen the place."

"Your family home?" His expression shifted to something more serious. "Isn't it...?"

"Haunted? Yes, in more ways than one." I took a breath, willing myself to be brave. "It's still standing, though the memories could probably use a good haunting of their own."

He nodded, the understanding flickering in his gaze. "Want some company? I could use a little distraction from my own ghosts."

"Is that a generous offer or a ploy to ensure you have a front-row seat to my potential emotional meltdown?"

"Let's go with generous," he shot back, the corners of his mouth turning up in a smirk. "I promise to only laugh at you if you trip over your own feet."

I rolled my eyes, but I felt a tug of relief, realizing how much I appreciated his presence. "Fine, but only because I'm pretty sure I'll need someone to help me wade through the memories. Plus, I could use a strong arm to fend off any vengeful spirits."

Together, we walked through the park, side by side, the laughter of children trailing behind us like a happy echo. The path wound through towering oaks and sprawling maples, their leaves vibrant against the backdrop of an overcast sky. I couldn't help but steal glances at Jason, his familiar features painted with the light of the setting sun, stirring a bittersweet blend of nostalgia and longing within me.

We reached my family's home, an old Victorian with peeling paint and a sagging porch that creaked under our weight. I had always thought it had a certain charm, even in its disrepair. But now, standing in front of it, the memories hit me like a tidal wave. "Welcome to my personal museum of regret," I muttered, taking in the cracked windows and wild overgrowth.

"Not quite the welcome I expected," Jason replied, stepping closer to inspect the porch railings. "Are you sure it's safe to go in?"

"Safer than my emotional state right now," I shot back, a hint of sarcasm escaping my lips. "But you're welcome to run away if you're feeling brave."

"Bravery is overrated," he said, chuckling. "I'll stick around to witness your bravery in action."

With a deep breath, I pushed open the creaking front door, the hinges protesting loudly as I stepped inside. Dust motes danced in the fading light, and the scent of mildew hit me like a wave. Every inch of the place seemed to exude memories—some sweet, others sharp and painful.

"Wow," Jason said, glancing around the dimly lit foyer. "This place is like stepping into a time capsule."

I nodded, gesturing toward the parlor, where faded photographs hung on the walls, depicting moments that felt like they belonged to someone else. "This was my mother's favorite room," I murmured, tracing a finger over the mantelpiece, where a long-ago extinguished fireplace still held the remnants of charred wood. "We used to have tea parties here, pretending we were royalty."

"Did you wear fancy hats?" he teased, a glimmer in his eyes.

"Of course! A girl must have her princess fantasies," I replied, feigning indignation. "Though I quickly learned that reality doesn't come with a tiara."

As we moved further into the house, I led him to the kitchen, which still retained a hint of the cinnamon and sugar that used to linger in the air during my mother's baking marathons. "She always insisted on making cookies from scratch," I said, memories rushing back. "No store-bought nonsense in this kitchen."

"I get it; it's a sacred space." He paused, surveying the kitchen as if he were taking in a historical artifact. "What do you plan to do with it?"

"Honestly? I have no idea." I ran my fingers over the countertop, feeling the cold, smooth surface beneath my touch. "Part of me wants to preserve it, to honor what was, while the other part just wants to forget it ever existed."

Jason stepped closer, a thoughtful look crossing his face. "You can't just erase your past, Clara. It's part of who you are."

"Easier said than done," I shot back, frustration bubbling beneath the surface. "Sometimes it feels like the past is a heavy backpack I'm lugging around, and I'm just tired of the weight."

"Maybe it's time to unpack it," he suggested gently, his voice low and steady. "You don't have to carry it all alone."

His words hung in the air, and for the first time, I let the tears I'd been holding back shimmer in my eyes. "I thought I could just close the door and walk away."

"Sometimes, the only way out is through," he said, his expression earnest. "And I'm here, whether you want company or just need someone to listen."

I swallowed hard, the lump in my throat threatening to choke me. "You really mean that?"

"Of course." He took a step back, giving me space. "I know this is hard for you, but you're not in this alone. Not anymore."

The warmth of his sincerity seeped into the crevices of my guarded heart, and I realized that maybe, just maybe, I could let him in. "Thanks, Jason," I murmured, grateful for his presence, for the safety net he was offering. "I didn't think I'd be able to confront this place without losing my mind."

"Good thing I have a reputation for saving damsels in distress," he replied, that teasing glint returning to his eyes. "Shall we explore further? Or should I start prepping for our dramatic escape from the past?"

"Let's see what else we can find," I said, a spark of determination igniting within me. "Maybe there are some hidden treasures lurking around."

As we ventured deeper into the house, I felt the first flutter of hope amidst the cobwebs of despair. Perhaps facing the past wouldn't mean banishing it forever, but instead, finding a way to carry it with me—something lighter, more manageable. After all, if there was anything Jason Blackwood had taught me in the past, it was that sometimes, the right company could turn even the darkest memories into something beautiful.

As Jason and I explored the dimly lit corners of my family home, I could feel the air grow thick with tension and unspoken words. Each room held its own stories, whispering secrets I had long tried to bury beneath layers of time. Dust motes floated lazily through the shafts of light, almost mocking the turbulence swirling within me. I opened a door to what used to be my bedroom, half-expecting to see the familiar chaos of childhood strewn across the floor. Instead, I found it mostly empty, save for a bed frame draped in ghostly white sheets and the faint outline of faded pastel wallpaper peeling at the edges.

"I can see your childhood self painted all over this place," Jason remarked, leaning against the doorframe, arms crossed. "Did you really have that many stuffed animals, or did they just reproduce when you weren't looking?"

I rolled my eyes but felt a smile tug at my lips. "It was a family of them, and I can assure you they didn't reproduce. They were my confidants, my partners in crime." I stepped inside, running my hand along the edge of the desk that had once held my dreams, wishes, and a fair number of failed science projects. "And now they're just a bunch of sad fabric remnants."

"Sad, but at least they were soft," he replied, the corner of his mouth lifting in that infuriatingly charming way that made my heart skip a beat. "What do you want to do with this room?"

"I don't know," I admitted, pulling back the sheets to reveal the faint imprint of a pillow. "Part of me wants to turn it back into a sanctuary. A place where I can remember what it felt like to be carefree."

Jason stepped into the room, glancing at the small bookshelf crammed with dust-covered novels. "Or maybe it's just a storage unit for emotional baggage."

I chuckled, then sighed. "Both, I suppose. But it's a bit hard to unburden when the baggage feels heavier than ever."

He studied me, his gaze searching, and I could feel the weight of his concern. "You can talk to me, you know. I'm not just here for comic relief."

"I know," I said, surprised by the vulnerability in my voice. "It's just... complicated." I wanted to tell him everything—the family rift, the long nights spent wondering what could have been, but the words got caught in my throat, like an unplayed note in a song.

"Complicated is my middle name," he said, the teasing tone lightening the mood. "Well, not literally, but you get the idea. Let's keep digging. Who knows what else we might find?"

We rummaged through drawers filled with long-forgotten treasures—doodles from my younger self, a collection of birthday cards, and a diary with pages faded from time. Each discovery felt like a small piece of a puzzle, a glimpse into the girl I used to be. And with each moment, the tension between us simmered, crackling with the potential of what could be.

"Wow, look at this," Jason said, pulling out a photograph. It was one from a school field trip, a candid shot of me with a giant smile, arms thrown around my best friend Lily, with Jason himself scowling in the background. "You were quite the overachiever."

"Clearly, my charisma was just too powerful for him to handle," I said, snatching the picture from his hands. "Lily was always the star of the show. I was just... there."

"Everyone has their role to play," he replied, stepping closer, the warmth of his presence wrapping around me. "You were an important piece of the puzzle, even if you didn't realize it then."

"Are you just saying that to make me feel better?"

"Of course not," he said, a hint of laughter in his eyes. "But I think it's time you started seeing yourself the way others see you."

As his gaze lingered on mine, I felt a swell of emotions that threatened to spill over. He leaned in slightly, the air thickening between us, and I could see the memories reflected in his hazel eyes—the shared laughter, the stolen kisses, the moments of silence where the world fell away.

"Maybe it's time for a change," I said softly, the words almost a whisper. "To make this place something new."

"New beginnings," Jason echoed, the weight of his gaze heavy and hopeful. "I like the sound of that."

Before I could respond, the floor creaked ominously beneath us, pulling my attention to the hallway beyond. "Did you hear that?"

"Yeah, it sounded like the house just exhaled," Jason replied, amusement threading through his voice. "Maybe it's trying to tell us something."

"Or maybe it's warning us to get out," I quipped, though my heart raced at the thought of what else might linger in the corners of this house. "What if there really is something—"

Before I could finish, the sound came again, this time louder and more insistent, echoing through the empty spaces like a heartbeat. I glanced toward the hallway, a chill skimming down my spine.

"Okay, now that's not just the house settling," Jason said, his voice dropping to a cautious murmur. "I think we should investigate."

"Investigate? Are you out of your mind?" I shot back, half-laughing, half-serious. "I'm not here to play ghost hunter!"

"C'mon," he urged, his eyes gleaming with a mix of curiosity and mischief. "What's the worst that could happen? We find a raccoon that's made this place its new home? Or maybe a ghost that just wants to share a few secrets?"

I rolled my eyes but felt the thrill of adventure stirring within me, battling the fear that lingered just beneath the surface. "I guess we could just take a quick look."

"Quick look it is!" he said, gesturing for me to lead the way.

With Jason trailing closely behind, I took tentative steps down the hallway, each creak of the floorboards echoing louder in the oppressive silence. The house felt alive, as if it were holding its breath, waiting for us to uncover its secrets. I paused outside a door that led to the basement, the source of the strange sounds. My heart raced at the thought of what lay beyond.

"Do we really have to go down there?" I whispered, suddenly regretting my decision to explore.

"Unless you want to turn back now, I think we owe it to ourselves to see what's happening," he said, his tone reassuring yet filled with excitement. "You might just find your inner Indiana Jones."

With a shaky breath, I nodded, the mix of trepidation and intrigue pulling me forward. I reached for the doorknob, feeling a chill that had nothing to do with the temperature.

As I turned the knob, the door creaked open, revealing darkness that stretched beyond the frame. I swallowed hard, the anticipation hanging thick in the air. "Okay, let's do this."

With one last glance at Jason, I stepped into the abyss, my heart pounding with every step. But just as I crossed the threshold, the lights flickered overhead, plunging us into darkness. I heard Jason's sharp intake of breath behind me, and then—

A low, guttural sound echoed from the depths below, reverberating through the floorboards like a warning.

"Clara," Jason whispered, his voice laced with urgency. "We need to get out of here. Now."

But it was too late. A shadow flitted across the darkness, and as the lights buzzed back to life, I found myself staring into the abyss, where something ancient and malevolent seemed to stir, awakening after years of silence.

Chapter 2: A Chance Encounter

Arriving at my childhood home, I was greeted by a scene that felt both familiar and foreign. The faded paint, peeling at the corners like the memories I'd long buried, had lost its once-vibrant hue. The garden, once meticulously tended, had surrendered to a tangle of wildflowers and weeds, an unruly testament to the years that had slipped away in my absence. It was a stark reminder of the life I had crafted in the city—a polished existence filled with high-rise offices and coffee shops where the baristas knew my name but never my story.

Determined to face the ghosts of my past, I stepped out of my car, the gravel crunching underfoot as I took a deep breath of the crisp, earthy air. This place had been a sanctuary once, filled with laughter and late-night whispers under starry skies, but the weight of unspoken words hung heavy in the air now, thickening with every step I took toward the old bookstore on the corner. It stood as a relic of my childhood, its wooden sign swaying gently in the breeze, inviting me in with the promise of dusty shelves and stories waiting to be discovered.

As I pushed open the door, a little bell tinkled above, announcing my arrival. The smell of old paper and leather binding enveloped me, wrapping me in nostalgia. My fingers grazed the spines of the books lining the shelves, each one a portal to a different time, a different world. This had been my haven, a place where I could escape the tensions of my reality. But today, I felt like a trespasser in my own history.

It was outside, just as I was about to step back into the world I had known, that fate had other plans. I collided with someone, nearly spilling my coffee as I looked up, startled. My heart raced as I recognized him—Jason. The boy next door who had once filled my days with mischievous laughter and shared secrets. Now he stood before me, taller than I remembered, with his dark hair falling across his forehead and an intensity in his deep-set eyes that sent a shiver down my spine.

"I didn't think you'd come back," he said, his voice a low rumble that stirred something deep within me. There was disbelief etched on his face, mingling with an emotion I couldn't quite place.

I swallowed hard, torn between the twin emotions of anger and longing that threatened to spill over. "I didn't think I'd want to," I replied, trying to keep my voice steady despite the rush of memories flooding my mind. The way he used to tease me, the way we'd plotted our little adventures like secret agents on a mission, the summer we were inseparable—everything felt so vivid, yet so far away.

He stepped back slightly, as if to give me space, but the distance only amplified the tension between us. Our families had been close once, bound by friendship, but the rivalry that had developed over the years twisted everything into a messy knot of animosity. "It's been a while," he finally said, his gaze drifting to the cracked pavement beneath our feet, as if he were searching for the right words.

"Six years," I replied, my voice softer now, the walls I'd built around my heart starting to crumble. "Not that anyone was counting."

Jason chuckled, a sound that was both warm and bittersweet. "I think a few people around here were. You left quite the impression." He looked back at me, and in that moment, it was as if the years melted away. I could see the boy I had known, the one who could always make me laugh, hiding behind the man he had become.

"I guess I didn't leave quietly," I said, my tone wry, trying to mask the flood of emotions churning within me. "I suppose that's what happens when you escape a place like this."

His expression shifted, a flash of understanding crossing his face. "Escape or run away?" he asked, a hint of challenge in his voice.

"Does it matter?" I shot back, a little too quickly. The sharpness of my words surprised even me. "Either way, I'm here now."

He nodded, a small smile playing at the corners of his mouth. "Welcome back, then. The town's just as charming as you left it."

"Charming? That's one way to put it," I replied, allowing myself a chuckle. "More like a time capsule."

"Some things never change," he said, leaning against the wall, a casual posture that somehow felt inviting. "But it's not all bad. You might find a few surprises."

A challenge laced in his tone caught my attention. "Surprises? Like what? More rivalries? Or just more of the same?"

He raised an eyebrow, his expression shifting to something more serious. "You might be surprised at how people have changed—maybe even how you've changed."

I wanted to dismiss his words, to brush them off as just another jab, but there was truth in them. Coming back was a journey into the past, a confrontation with the choices I'd made and the person I had become. I had carved out a life in the city, one where I had learned to embrace my independence, but here, in this place that cradled my childhood dreams and heartbreaks, the weight of nostalgia threatened to pull me under.

"Maybe I'm not the only one who's changed," I said, locking eyes with him again, feeling the spark of our history crackle in the air between us. There was something raw and unfinished between us, an energy that begged to be explored, and I felt a flutter of excitement mixed with trepidation.

"Maybe not," he replied, his gaze steady, a smirk dancing on his lips. "But you can't deny that we had some pretty epic moments together. How many secrets did we share on this very street?"

His playful tone was infectious, drawing me in. I couldn't help but smile, despite the layers of tension lingering just beneath the surface. "Too many to count. And don't forget all those times we got into trouble."

"Ah, trouble," he mused, leaning closer, the playful gleam in his eyes making my heart race. "Trouble always finds a way of catching up with us, doesn't it?"

"Or it leads us right back to where we started," I replied, my voice barely above a whisper, the realization of our shared history hanging in the air like an unspoken promise.

As the sunlight dipped lower in the sky, casting golden hues over the street, I could feel the threads of our past weaving together once more. The world around us faded, and in that moment, it felt as if everything else had fallen away, leaving just the two of us standing on the cusp of something new, something that had the potential to break free from the confines of our tangled past.

Jason leaned against the weathered bricks of the bookstore, arms crossed, as if guarding the memories we'd shared, both sacred and tainted. A breeze ruffled his hair, framing his face in a way that made him look both rugged and somehow familiar. I could feel the weight of our history pressing in on us, the silent stories we had woven in the spaces between our words.

"Why did you really come back?" he asked, his tone shifting slightly, as though he were digging for something deeper, something buried beneath the surface of our carefully crafted small talk.

I hesitated, caught off guard. The question hung between us like the low-hanging clouds threatening rain. "Isn't it obvious? Family obligations. You know how it is." I attempted a light laugh, but it sounded more brittle than I intended, cracking under the weight of unspoken truths.

"Obligations," he repeated, his gaze narrowing. "That's one way to put it. Are you sure it's not more about facing the music? Or maybe facing the people you left behind?"

I could feel my pulse quicken, his words piercing through the veil I'd constructed around my return. "A little melodramatic, don't you think?" I countered, managing a smirk, but inside, my heart thudded in a rhythm that echoed the conflict simmering just beneath the surface. "I didn't come here to debate my motives, Jason."

"Then what did you come here for?" he shot back, the playful banter morphing into a challenge. "To find closure? Or to reopen old wounds?"

The air between us crackled with an intensity that was both invigorating and terrifying. I shifted, feeling the weight of his gaze as it searched mine for answers. "Maybe a little of both. Or maybe just to figure out what this place means to me now."

"Sounds like a noble quest," he said, his expression softening slightly, the challenge giving way to curiosity. "What if I told you this town has a way of surprising you? Maybe you'll find more than you bargained for."

"Like you?" I quipped, raising an eyebrow.

"Touché," he laughed, the sound easing some of the tension. There was something about that laugh that reminded me of endless summer days, the kind that lingered just long enough to steal your breath away. "But seriously, what if we both need to dig a little deeper? Maybe what you're really looking for is just a good old-fashioned adventure."

"An adventure?" I echoed, feigning disbelief while my heart raced at the thought. "What kind of adventure can one have in a town that hasn't changed since the last century?"

"You'd be surprised," he said, his voice dropping to a conspiratorial whisper, eyes gleaming with mischief. "I happen to know a few spots that are off the beaten path, where memories linger in the shadows and secrets hide in plain sight."

"Is this some kind of elaborate ploy to win me over?" I teased, crossing my arms in a mock defense.

"Maybe," he replied, his smile widening. "Or maybe I just want to see you embrace the chaos you once thrived on. We used to have fun together, remember? Before everything got... complicated."

"Complicated is putting it mildly," I said, a hint of bitterness creeping into my voice. The memories of our families' falling out danced at the edges of my consciousness like fireflies in the dusk. "It's not easy to forget that."

He nodded, a flicker of understanding passing between us. "No, it's not. But maybe it's time to start rewriting the narrative. We could start with a cup of coffee at that little café down the street. You remember, right? The one with the terrible pastries but the best conversations?"

A laugh escaped me before I could stop it. "How could I forget? We used to argue about their coffee being the worst in the state."

"And yet, we still went there every day," he replied, the warmth in his tone making me reconsider. "So, what do you say? Just for old times' sake?"

There was an irresistible pull to the idea. Perhaps this was exactly what I needed—a chance to sift through the remnants of my past while being swept up in a familiar thrill. "All right," I finally said, surprising myself. "Lead the way."

He stepped aside, gesturing dramatically as if he were welcoming me to a grand adventure. "Prepare yourself. The nostalgia will be overwhelming."

As we walked side by side, the air around us buzzed with an electric energy, the kind that only comes from unearthing old memories and mingling them with fresh possibilities. The streets seemed alive with our shared laughter, echoing through the quaint little town like a long-lost song. I was surprised at how easily it flowed between us, each teasing quip and playful jab bringing back a sense of camaraderie I thought was lost to time.

We strolled past familiar storefronts, my senses tingling with the scent of blooming lilacs and the faint sound of distant laughter wafting through the air. The sun dipped lower in the sky, casting a golden glow that made everything feel a little more magical. "You know," I mused, "if I didn't know any better, I'd think you planned this whole thing just to get me back."

"Maybe I did," he replied, a glimmer of mischief in his eyes. "Or maybe you just can't resist a little chaos."

"I never could," I admitted, my heart fluttering at the thought of what lay ahead. "But I'm still cautious. Remember, chaos has a way of biting back."

"Only if you let it," he countered, a knowing smile gracing his lips. "But don't worry. I'll be here to catch you if you fall."

That was the moment I felt it—the unspoken promise nestled between us, like the soft rustle of leaves heralding a summer storm. The weight of our shared history faded, replaced by a sense of possibility. I might have returned to a place filled with memories and ghosts, but perhaps it was also a chance to reclaim a part of myself I had left behind. As we reached the café, I realized this was more than just coffee. It was the beginning of something new, a chance to embrace the tangled threads of our past and weave them into a narrative that felt whole.

The café stood like a time capsule, adorned with mismatched furniture and walls lined with quirky artwork that looked like it had been sourced from garage sales across the county. The old sign out front creaked slightly in the breeze, its paint peeling yet somehow charming, just like the town itself. As we stepped inside, the comforting aroma of burnt coffee and freshly baked pastries wrapped around us like an embrace. I could feel my pulse quicken, both from the caffeine cravings and the thrill of being back in this familiar territory.

"Prepare for the worst coffee in the universe," Jason said with a conspiratorial grin, his eyes dancing with mischief. "But it's all part of the experience."

"Experience, huh? That sounds like a euphemism for 'you'll regret this,'" I shot back, pretending to consider my options on the menu. "You know, I've had coffee in places that would put this place to shame."

"Sure, but can they compete with the ambiance? Or the wild stories that come with every sip?" He leaned closer, his voice lowering as if he were about to reveal a great secret. "Last time I was here, someone mistook a muffin for a cat and tried to adopt it."

I laughed, the sound bubbling up unbidden, surprising even myself. It was a simple moment, yet it felt so good to ease into the banter, as though we were trading fragments of a time capsule, piecing together the memories we both shared. "Only in this town could a muffin earn its own fan club," I replied, shaking my head. "You realize this place is still a total wreck, right?"

"It's a beautiful wreck," he insisted, gesturing around with exaggerated flair. "The heart of the community, where dreams are brewed and secrets are spilled."

As I moved to the counter to place my order, I noticed the barista—an elderly woman with a cascade of silver curls and a smile that could light up the darkest corners of the café. "Well, if it isn't the prodigal daughter!" she exclaimed, her eyes sparkling. "We thought you'd abandoned us for good!"

"Not quite," I replied, suddenly feeling the warmth of nostalgia wash over me. "Just took a little detour. This place still looks the same."

"Some things never change," she said knowingly, her gaze flicking between me and Jason. "You two always had a knack for stirring things up."

"Guilty as charged," Jason quipped, leaning casually against the counter. "But we're just here for some coffee and maybe to save the town from culinary mediocrity."

I raised an eyebrow, stifling a grin as I returned to the table with our drinks. "That's quite the mission statement. I didn't realize we were on a quest."

"Every good adventure requires a quest," he replied, his tone serious but his eyes glimmering with playfulness. "And we're just getting started."

As we sipped our lukewarm coffee—an unfortunate truth of small-town brews—conversation flowed effortlessly between us. We exchanged stories about the years apart, the cities we had explored, the people we had met. I told him about my hectic life in the city, filled with deadlines and ambition, while he shared tales of his escapades in the same town that had once seemed so small and limiting. I realized how much I missed having someone who understood me, someone who could match my sarcasm and wit beat for beat.

"So, what's the big plan now that you're back?" he asked, his gaze steady and probing. "Are you really just here to patch things up with family, or is there more?"

"Honestly? I'm not entirely sure. It feels like I'm treading on thin ice. This place is filled with memories, good and bad, and I have no idea how to navigate it all." My voice dipped as I leaned closer, the weight of my vulnerability creeping in. "It's like I'm trying to rediscover who I am here."

He studied me for a moment, his brow furrowing slightly. "You're still you, no matter how far you roam. You just might have to sift through the layers to find that version again."

"You make it sound so easy." I shrugged, an attempt to lighten the mood. "What if I just want to throw my hands up and declare a new identity? How about 'Queen of Coffee'?"

"King of Chaos," he shot back, smirking. "Your court awaits."

Just then, a loud crash from the back of the café jolted us both. We turned our heads in unison, eyes wide, to see a couple of teenagers hastily gathering their things after bumping into a table. "This is why we can't have nice things," Jason muttered, shaking his head with a grin.

Laughter bubbled up again, but beneath the surface, I felt a ripple of tension. The chaos in the café reminded me of the life I had left behind, the uncertainty I had fled from. "You know," I said slowly, "I didn't think coming back would stir up so much... everything."

"Everything?" He leaned forward, genuinely curious. "What do you mean?"

"Like the past and the present colliding. The memories of us and the potential for... whatever this is." I gestured between us, feeling my cheeks heat at the admission. "It's all a little overwhelming."

"Good," he replied, his expression serious for a moment. "Overwhelming means you're feeling something. Better than the numbness that comes with complacency."

Before I could respond, the door swung open, and a gust of wind swept through the café, carrying with it the unmistakable scent of rain and something else—a tension that made the hairs on the back of my neck stand up. I turned to see a figure standing in the doorway, silhouetted against the gray sky.

It was a familiar face, one that sent a jolt of recognition coursing through me. My heart dropped as I realized who it was—the last person I expected to see. Someone from the past I had hoped to leave behind, a reminder of everything I had tried to escape.

Jason noticed my sudden stillness, following my gaze. "You okay?" he asked, concern etched in his features.

But I couldn't answer. The figure stepped further into the light, revealing a face that made my breath hitch. My mind raced, processing the implications, and I suddenly felt like I was standing on the edge of a cliff, ready to plunge into the unknown.

"Looks like we have company," Jason said, a hint of apprehension creeping into his voice.

"Company?" I whispered, dread pooling in my stomach. "That's putting it mildly."

As the figure stepped closer, my pulse quickened, anticipation mingling with fear. The world around us faded, and all I could think was that the past was not done with me yet.

Chapter 3: Brewing Tensions

The morning sun slipped through the lace curtains, casting delicate patterns on the wooden floorboards of my childhood home, a place where echoes of laughter intertwined with the scent of lavender that my mother had cultivated in the garden. I stood at the kitchen counter, absently stirring a pot of simmering apple cider, my mind drifting like the steam rising from the surface. Evergreen Hollow had always been a tapestry of sweet memories and bitter legacies, and as the familiar warmth wrapped around me, I felt the heaviness of my family's history. The Blackwoods were always a shadow lurking just beyond our doorstep, their presence as omnipresent as the trees lining Main Street.

"You're really back, huh?" My brother, Jamie, strolled into the kitchen, his voice teasing yet laced with an undercurrent of concern. He leaned against the doorframe, arms crossed, a smirk playing at the corners of his mouth. "Thought you'd run off to the city and forget about us small-town folks."

"I did forget a little," I admitted, flicking a glance his way, "but only because someone had to remind me how to make apple cider without burning it." I reached for the cinnamon, the spice mingling with the sweetness of the apples, creating a scent that danced in the air, a reminder of simpler times. Jamie rolled his eyes, the camaraderie between us palpable, yet I could sense the tension building outside our quaint little bubble.

"Seriously, though," he said, pushing off the doorframe and stepping closer, his expression sobering. "You know what's happening with Carter, right? He's been stirring up trouble ever since you left. It's like he's taken it as a personal challenge to make our lives miserable."

The name sent a shiver down my spine. Carter Blackwood, the youngest heir to the family empire, had always been trouble with a capital T, wrapped in an irresistible charm that could make even the most cautious hearts flutter. His dark hair and piercing blue eyes often caught the light in a way that made him seem almost otherworldly. And yet, beneath that allure lay a competitiveness that could turn friendships into rivalries with a mere flick of his wrist.

"Don't tell me he's plotting something ridiculous," I groaned, feeling the weight of inevitability settle in my chest. "What is it this time? Another race down Old Mill Road? Maybe a prank involving the distillery?"

Jamie chuckled, but it was a hollow sound. "Worse. I overheard him at the diner last night. He's got some plan to confront you about... well, you know what happened between our families. He's been rallying some of his friends to get involved."

I paused, the apple cider forgotten, my heart racing at the thought of Carter facing me again, and this time with an audience. Memories of our shared past flooded my mind—how we'd spent lazy summer afternoons fishing at the lake, the thrill of our youthful competition as we battled it out in go-karts, the camaraderie that had once existed before the rift widened between our families.

"Carter has no idea what he's getting himself into," I murmured, more to myself than to Jamie. My protective instincts flared, an urge to defend my family igniting a fire within me. "I can't let him turn this into a spectacle. This is our home."

Just then, the front door swung open with a flourish, and our neighbor, Mrs. Thompson, bustled in as if she owned the place. She was a whirlwind of energy, her gray curls bouncing around her head like a halo. "Oh, dear, I just heard the news! You're back! How wonderful!" she exclaimed, her eyes sparkling. "You know, the whole town has been buzzing like a beehive since you returned. They say the Blackwoods are plotting something, and you might want to keep your head down."

"Thanks for the heads-up, Mrs. Thompson," I said, forcing a smile, though my heart sank at the thought of becoming the center of a new drama. "I'll be sure to steer clear of the Blackwood family drama."

"Oh, sweet girl, you can't avoid it!" She waved her hand dismissively, a glint of mischief in her eyes. "You're part of this town's story now, and the Blackwoods are a chapter you can't skip over."

As she spoke, the weight of her words settled heavily on my shoulders. I glanced out the window, where the shadows of the mountains loomed like ancient sentinels, watching over our lives. The world outside seemed quieter now, a deceptive calm before the storm I could feel brewing in the air.

"Carter's not just going to roll over," Jamie warned, his voice a low rumble, pulling me back from my spiraling thoughts. "You know how he is. He thrives on this kind of chaos."

"Then I guess I'll have to show him that I'm not afraid of a little chaos either," I replied, determination hardening in my chest.

As the cider continued to simmer, a plan began to take shape, unwinding like the fragrant steam curling through the air. I could almost see the path before me, lined with the memories of my past, leading toward a confrontation I both dreaded and craved. If the Blackwoods wanted a fight, I would meet them head-on. The weight of my family's legacy hung over me like a shroud, but I refused to let it stifle me.

With a deep breath, I turned back to the simmering pot, the rich aroma enveloping me like a warm embrace. I was ready to reclaim my place in Evergreen Hollow, and if that meant facing down Carter Blackwood, so be it. The world outside may be whispering about brewing tensions, but within me, a fire sparked to life, igniting a resolve that would not easily be extinguished.

The following days unfolded like the vibrant petals of a blossoming flower, yet beneath their beauty lay a dangerous undercurrent. Evergreen Hollow buzzed with whispers, each exchange a thread in the tapestry of small-town life, woven together by the looming shadow of the Blackwood family. My childhood friend, Sarah, stopped by unannounced one afternoon, her usual cheerful demeanor dimmed by the weight of the town's unease.

"Have you heard?" she asked, her voice low as she perched on a stool at the kitchen island. "Carter is planning a gathering at the distillery this weekend. It's supposed to be a big deal. He's got some kind of announcement."

"An announcement?" I echoed, curiosity piquing despite the tension that wrapped around my heart like a vice. "What could he possibly announce? His latest scheme for world domination?"

Sarah rolled her eyes, a playful smile breaking through her worry. "More like his latest attempt to stir the pot. But you should know, everyone's been talking about it. You're the topic of discussion, and I'm not sure it's good."

I leaned back, crossing my arms. "What does Carter want from me? He knows I just got back. This is the perfect time to let sleeping dogs lie." The rhythm of the apple cider I had prepared earlier still echoed in my mind, a comforting reminder of my resolve.

"Sometimes I think he thrives on chaos," Sarah said, her eyes narrowing with concern. "And you, my friend, are the perfect catalyst."

"Great, just what I need—a starring role in his dramatic production." I sighed, stirring the remains of my cider, which had long since cooled. "Maybe I should just stay home and bake pies or something. You know, avoid the whole family feud scene."

"Not a chance," Sarah replied, her laughter infectious. "You're not getting out of this that easily. You need to show Carter you're not afraid, and trust me, everyone's going to be watching. It's not just about you and him; it's about our families."

As I mulled over her words, the determination I had felt earlier began to rekindle within me, burning brighter than before. Perhaps it was time to confront the ghosts of my past, to unearth the skeletons that lingered in the shadows of my family's history. The thought sent a shiver down my spine, but it also ignited a spark of excitement.

"Fine. I'll go," I declared, surprising even myself. "But only if you promise to come with me. I'm not facing the Blackwoods alone."

Sarah grinned, her eyes alight with mischief. "Deal. Just remember, no throwing pies at Carter's face. That'll only make him more charming in his misguided attempts to win you over."

The weekend arrived faster than I anticipated, the sun rising with a warm golden glow that seemed to herald the day's events. The distillery loomed in the distance, its brick façade a testament to the Blackwood legacy. As we approached, the aroma of aged whiskey and sweet corn wafted through the air, both enticing and nauseating in its familiarity.

"Are you sure you want to do this?" Sarah asked, her fingers brushing nervously against her jeans. "We could always fake an emergency and escape."

"Not a chance," I replied, squaring my shoulders and summoning every ounce of courage. "If I let him dictate my actions, I might as well pack my bags and leave again."

We stepped inside, the spacious interior filled with laughter and chatter, the clinking of glasses resonating against the wooden beams overhead. Carter stood at the center, his smile charming the room like a well-practiced actor taking the stage. The crowd, a mix of townsfolk and curious faces, leaned in closer, hanging on his every word.

"Welcome, everyone! Thank you for joining me for this special occasion," he declared, his voice smooth and confident. "Today, I have something exciting to share that will change Evergreen Hollow forever."

A ripple of anticipation coursed through the crowd, and I felt the urge to step back, to blend into the shadows where I could observe without being noticed. But Sarah nudged me forward, a reminder that retreat was not an option.

"Does anyone else feel like we're about to witness a dramatic reveal?" I whispered to her, rolling my eyes.

"I think you mean a dramatic disaster," she replied, stifling a giggle.

Carter continued, his words weaving a tale that pulled the audience in. "As many of you know, our family has always prided itself on its contributions to this town. But it's time for a new chapter. I'm thrilled to announce our latest venture—a brand-new line of spirits that will redefine craftsmanship in Evergreen Hollow!"

A cheer erupted, but I felt a jolt of disbelief. Did he think a new product could overshadow the animosities between our families? Carter's gaze shifted, catching mine in the crowd. His smile faltered for a fleeting moment, a flash of something unreadable dancing in his blue eyes before he quickly masked it with charm.

"Let's toast to the future," he declared, raising a glass high. "And to the power of community, which unites us all!"

The crowd erupted into applause, and I could feel my heart pounding in my chest. As glasses clinked, I remained rooted in place, torn between admiration for Carter's charisma and the urge to confront him about the damage his family had wrought.

"Do you think he's serious?" Sarah asked, tilting her head as she observed the scene. "Or is this just a cover for something else?"

"I suspect it's a cover for something far more sinister," I muttered under my breath, keeping my eyes locked on Carter. "He wants to maintain the façade of unity while secretly plotting his next move."

Just then, he caught my gaze again, and this time, his expression shifted to something more genuine—an unmistakable challenge. I could feel the air between us crackling, as if a storm was brewing just beneath the surface. The tension hung heavily, drawing me in like a moth to a flame.

As the crowd cheered, a part of me felt exhilarated. Perhaps this gathering was not just about the Blackwoods and their latest marketing gimmick; it was about me reclaiming my place in this town, setting the stage for my own story. The brewing tensions would not end tonight; they would only sharpen the edges of what was to come, and I was ready to embrace whatever chaos lay ahead.

With that thought in mind, I stepped forward, my heart pounding in sync with the rhythms of Evergreen Hollow, determined to confront the past and forge my own path amid the brewing storm.

As I moved through the crowd, the laughter and clinking glasses became a blurred hum, the air thick with the mingling scents of polished oak and aged spirits. My pulse quickened with each step I took toward the center of the room, where Carter stood like a dark star, magnetic and troubling. The chatter ebbed and flowed around him, wrapping him in an aura of power that both fascinated and infuriated me.

"Didn't expect to see you here," Carter called out, his voice cutting through the noise like a knife. He leaned casually against the bar, his posture relaxed, yet I could sense the tension simmering just beneath the surface. "I thought you'd want to avoid the family drama."

"Wouldn't dream of it," I shot back, injecting a lightness into my tone, though my heart raced. "What's a little drama between families? It's practically a rite of passage here."

His lips quirked into a half-smile, one that was both alluring and dangerous, and I could feel the eyes of the room shifting between us, a charged energy crackling in the air. "Ah, I see you've come to play. But tell me, what's your strategy? I mean, avoiding the pie-throwing contest is a solid start."

"Very funny," I retorted, folding my arms, trying to project confidence. "I'm not here for games, Carter. Just trying to make sense of your latest venture before I decide whether to support it or throw my own cider in your face."

"Such hostility," he remarked, feigning offense, his blue eyes glinting with mischief. "I was only trying to make a connection, you know. Just because our families have a history doesn't mean we can't—"

"Please spare me the pleasantries," I interrupted, not wanting to dance around the topic any longer. "You know what this is really about. Your family and mine have been at each other's throats for years. A new spirit isn't going to change that."

He studied me, a flicker of surprise crossing his features. "You're right. But what if I told you that this project is about more than just business? It's about bridging gaps, starting anew. Maybe even bringing our families together."

"Is that so?" I raised an eyebrow, skepticism thickening my tone. "A new brand of whiskey will solve our centuries-old feud? Sounds a bit too good to be true."

"Maybe it is," he conceded, leaning in slightly, his voice dropping to a conspiratorial whisper. "But don't you want to see if it can? Wouldn't it be worth checking out?"

His audacity was both frustrating and captivating, like a flame flickering against the darkness. The atmosphere buzzed with curiosity, and I could feel the weight of the onlookers' gazes, their anticipation palpable. I had no intention of letting him turn this into a spectacle, a platform for his charm to win me over.

"Perhaps," I said, "but I think you owe it to everyone here to be honest about your intentions."

Just then, the doors swung open, a gust of wind billowing in, rustling the edges of our conversation. An unexpected figure stepped through: Jason, Carter's older brother, who had spent the past few years distancing himself from family affairs. The room fell into an uneasy silence, all eyes darting toward him as he strode forward, his presence commanding.

"Carter," Jason said, his voice like gravel, laced with authority. "Can we talk?"

Carter's smile faltered, and I caught the fleeting tension that rippled through him, like a dark cloud passing overhead. "Can't it wait, Jason? I'm in the middle of something important."

"No, it can't," Jason replied, his tone hardening, his gaze cutting through the jubilant atmosphere. "This isn't just about you. You're putting the family at risk with your antics. You know what Father would say if he were here."

I felt a chill run down my spine. The mention of their father hung heavily in the air, a specter that cast a long shadow over our families. The Blackwoods had always had a fierce reputation, and the thought of being caught in the crossfire of their internal struggles sent an uneasy flutter through me.

"Look, we can't just pretend everything is fine," Carter snapped, his earlier bravado cracking. "This is about the future of our family, our legacy."

"Then act like it," Jason shot back, his frustration evident. "You're drawing attention to yourself, and not the good kind. It's time to think about the consequences of your actions."

The tension was palpable, an electric current that danced in the air. I glanced between the brothers, sensing the rift widening before me. My instincts kicked in, and I edged closer to the bar, unwilling to be an innocent bystander any longer.

"Hey, maybe we should all take a breath," I suggested, forcing a lightness into my voice. "It's a celebration, after all. Let's not ruin it by bringing family drama into the mix."

Carter shot me a grateful look, while Jason's brow furrowed, suspicion etched across his features. "What's your angle?" he asked, scrutinizing me. "You're not one to back down from a fight, especially when it comes to our families."

"Maybe I'm just here for the free drinks," I quipped, a hint of defiance in my tone. "Or maybe I'm tired of our families acting like feuding titans while we're all stuck in the middle. Isn't it time we figured out how to coexist?"

"Easier said than done," Jason replied, crossing his arms as he regarded me with a mix of skepticism and curiosity.

"I agree," Carter added, his gaze shifting between us. "But if we can't start here, when can we?"

Before Jason could respond, the door swung open again, this time revealing an unfamiliar figure, a man cloaked in a dark coat, his eyes scanning the room with an intensity that sent a ripple of unease through the crowd. He wasn't from around here; I could tell that much. Something about him felt out of place, like a rogue wave crashing into calm waters.

The chatter faded, and a silence fell as he strode toward us, his demeanor unyielding. "Carter Blackwood," he called, his voice steady and commanding. "We need to talk."

Carter's expression shifted to one of alarm, the bravado draining from his face as the air thickened with tension. "Who are you?"

"Someone with a message," the man replied, stepping closer, his eyes never leaving Carter's. The crowd murmured, curiosity turning to concern as everyone held their breath, caught in the web of uncertainty.

The atmosphere crackled with unspoken words, and I felt the ground shift beneath my feet. Whatever this man had come to deliver was going to change everything. As I stood there, poised between the two families and the unfolding drama, I couldn't shake the feeling that the storm was only just beginning, and I was right in the eye of it, caught in a whirlwind I hadn't anticipated.

The man's gaze finally turned toward me, an intensity in his eyes that left me breathless. "And you, too," he said, locking his stare with mine. "You're going to want to hear this."

And with that, the air thickened with foreboding, the tension coiling tighter around us, as secrets long buried began to claw their way to the surface.

Chapter 4: An Unexpected Invitation

The air inside the Brewmaster Distillery was alive, a palpable energy swirling around the room like the golden spirits that glistened in the low light. The walls, lined with oak barrels, whispered stories of time and craft, each echo of laughter or clink of glass a reminder of the joy trapped within their stout frames. As I stepped across the threshold, the scent of caramelized wood and earthy undertones wrapped around me, beckoning me further into a space that felt like both a haven and a battleground.

I stood awkwardly by the entrance, my heart racing beneath the thin fabric of my dress, a whirlwind of emotions churning within me. Memories of Jason flashed through my mind, vivid snapshots of sun-drenched afternoons spent laughing, our hands brushing as we navigated the uncertain terrain of young love. But shadows lingered—my family's disapproval, the whispered judgments, the aftermath of that last painful conversation. A tangle of loyalty and desire gripped me tightly, leaving me breathless as I scanned the room.

Then I spotted him. Jason stood near the bar, a glass in hand, laughter spilling from his lips like the whiskey he poured. His tousled dark hair caught the light, framing a face that had haunted my dreams for too long. Time had carved new lines around his eyes, adding depth to the boyish charm I once knew. He hadn't changed so much, yet everything felt different—the air crackled with unspoken words, a tension simmering beneath the surface. As his gaze found mine, his smile widened, instantly igniting the familiar flutter in my chest.

"You came," he said, moving towards me, his voice rich and warm. It was as if the world around us faded, leaving only the two of us in that crowded room. I could see the flicker of hope in his eyes, a spark that mirrored my own curiosity and confusion.

"Yeah, I—" I stumbled over my words, unsure if I was about to explain my presence or apologize for my absence. "I thought I'd check it out."

He raised an eyebrow, the corner of his mouth quirking up in a teasing smile. "Just check it out? You make it sound like you're window shopping at the hardware store."

The playful jab drew a reluctant smile from me, and for a moment, I allowed myself to lean into the lightness between us. "Okay, fine. I'm here because I have a weak spot for artisanal spirits and a slight inclination towards questionable life choices."

"Ah, a connoisseur of bad decisions," he grinned, his laughter infectious. "I knew there was something special about you."

As we fell into easy banter, the weight of my family's expectations began to lift, if only slightly. Around us, the hum of conversation swelled, laughter weaving through the air like a familiar tune, and for a moment, I felt like I had been transported back to simpler times—before everything had become so complicated.

"Come on, let me show you the good stuff," Jason said, his eyes sparkling with mischief as he gestured towards the tasting room, where an assortment of whiskey bottles stood proudly on display. "You've got to try the aged rye. It'll change your life."

"Or ruin it," I quipped, but my feet followed him willingly as he led me deeper into the heart of the distillery. Each step felt like a leap into the unknown, the rush of nostalgia mingling with a thrill I hadn't expected.

The tasting room was intimate, a warm glow illuminating the rich mahogany bar where a few patrons engaged in spirited discussions. A couple at the far end raised their glasses in a toast, the light catching the amber liquid and refracting into a kaleidoscope of color. As Jason slid onto a barstool, I took a seat beside him, feeling both exhilarated and vulnerable.

"Two glasses of your finest aged rye," Jason ordered, his voice smooth, filled with confidence. I watched him, captivated by the way he commanded the space, and the bartender poured two generous servings, the liquid swirling and dancing as if it shared in our excitement.

"Cheers," Jason said, raising his glass. I met his gaze, and for a heartbeat, it felt like we were the only two people in the universe.

"Cheers," I replied, clinking my glass against his with a tentative smile, the sound echoing like a promise between us.

As we sipped the whiskey, warmth spread through me, both from the drink and the undeniable chemistry crackling in the air. "So, how's life treating you these days?" he asked, genuine curiosity etched into his expression.

"Busy, mostly," I replied, swirling the whiskey in my glass as if it would reveal secrets. "Work, family, the usual chaos. And you? Still charming the locals with your magic potion?"

He chuckled, shaking his head. "Something like that. I've been working on a new blend, actually. It's a bit of a gamble, but if it pays off, it could change everything for the distillery."

"Ambitious. Just like I remember you."

He leaned closer, a conspiratorial glint in his eyes. "You know me too well. But it's more than just ambition; it's about proving that I can carve my own path, despite what everyone expects."

There was a shared understanding in that moment, a silent acknowledgment of the struggles we both faced—his fight against the weight of family legacy, my battle with loyalty and self-discovery. Just as I felt the walls of my reservations crumbling, the atmosphere shifted.

A group of loud patrons burst into the room, laughter spilling over like the whiskey they held. I turned, momentarily distracted by the chaos, but when I turned back, Jason's expression had changed.

His gaze flickered past me, the warmth replaced by something colder, more guarded.

"Looks like the night just got more interesting," he murmured, and I followed his gaze, my heart sinking as I recognized the familiar faces. It was my brother, Jake, accompanied by his friends—the very people I had hoped to avoid tonight.

"Great," I muttered under my breath, feeling the tight knot of anxiety return. The laughter of the group echoed around me, laughter that had once been carefree now felt like an impending storm.

"Do you want to go?" Jason asked, his concern cutting through the tension in the air.

I hesitated, caught between the thrill of rekindling our connection and the looming reality of my family's expectations. "I—"

Before I could finish, Jake's voice rang out, buoyant and teasing. "Well, well, if it isn't my little sister, getting cozy with the enemy."

Jason stiffened beside me, the easy warmth of our earlier connection dissipating in an instant. The air thickened with unspoken words, and I could feel the storm brewing, my heart pounding as I braced myself for the clash of loyalties that was about to unfold.

The moment Jake's voice sliced through the atmosphere, a chill danced down my spine. Jason's expression shifted, the warmth in his eyes giving way to an unreadable tension, as if the air had suddenly thickened with unspoken words. I turned slowly to face my brother, who stood at the bar's edge, flanked by his friends like a general surveying his troops.

"Seriously, Jake?" I shot back, attempting to keep my voice steady. "Can't you pick a better time to stir the pot?"

He smirked, his confidence radiating off him like a beacon. "What? I can't help it if I'm shocked to find you flirting with the enemy. Thought you had better taste."

"Flirting? Is that what you call two people sharing a whiskey?" I retorted, crossing my arms defensively. But deep down, I could feel the warmth rising to my cheeks, fueled by more than just indignation.

Jason leaned back slightly, tension creeping into his posture as if he were bracing for impact. "I just invited her to the tasting," he said, his tone cautious, almost measured. "No need to make a scene."

"Right, because nothing says 'good taste' like mixing family drama with artisanal spirits," Jake shot back, laughter spilling from his friends, each one leaning in, eager for the unfolding spectacle.

I felt the heat of embarrassment wash over me. "Jake, this isn't high school. I'm not some trophy you can show off to your friends."

His laughter subsided for a moment, but the glimmer of mischief in his eyes remained. "And yet here we are, playing out the classic love triangle. It's almost poetic."

"Hardly a triangle when there's only one person interested," I muttered, shooting a sideways glance at Jason, who was now carefully studying the condensation on his glass, a veil of silence stretching between us.

Jake stepped closer, the crowd parting around him as if he were a magnet. "Come on, sis. Let's just be real for a second. You don't actually think he's good for you, do you? You know what he did."

There it was—the unearthing of old wounds, the reminder of choices that had shattered us both. I could feel Jason stiffen beside me, the weight of my brother's words hanging heavy in the air. "That was years ago, Jake. People change."

"And yet here you are, still tied to the past," he replied, his voice a mixture of concern and challenge.

"Maybe it's time to cut those ties," Jason said quietly, his gaze finally meeting mine, and for a brief moment, I could see the hurt lingering beneath his guarded demeanor. The air crackled between us, a mix of unresolved tension and hope that hung like a thick fog.

"What's it going to be, little sister?" Jake's challenge was unmistakable. "Are you really going to let him pull you back into the depths of his mess?"

"Enough," I snapped, my voice louder than I intended. A few heads turned, the room quieting momentarily, and I took a deep breath, trying to rein in the tempest brewing inside me. "I'm here because I want to be. Not because I owe you an explanation."

Jason's lips quirked into a faint smile, and for a second, I could feel a sense of solidarity return. But the moment was fleeting, and I could sense the storm building again.

"Look, it's just whiskey, okay? Just a drink," I said, my voice softer, trying to bridge the gap that had opened between us. "It doesn't mean anything."

"Is that so?" Jake challenged, his brow raised in disbelief. "Because it looks like a lot more than just whiskey to me."

I turned my attention back to Jason, who appeared caught in a web of conflicting emotions, and I could see the flicker of frustration dance in his eyes. "You know what? Maybe it is a lot more. But it's my decision. Not yours."

His expression shifted slightly, a glimmer of admiration breaking through the tension. "Well said."

"Are you really siding with him?" Jake said incredulously, looking between us as if we had conspired against him.

"No, I'm not siding with anyone. I just want to enjoy my night," I replied, feeling the pressure of judgment looming over me. "Can you not make this harder than it has to be?"

Before Jake could respond, one of his friends interjected, clearly eager to divert the tension. "Hey, let's just grab another drink! How about a round of shots to lighten the mood?"

"I'm in!" another voice chimed in, and soon the group began to gather around the bar, excitement shifting the focus away from the simmering conflict. I took a moment to breathe, grateful for the distraction, but a part of me still felt the weight of Jake's words pressing down on my chest.

"Come on, let's get out of here for a minute," Jason said quietly, his eyes fixed on me with a hint of urgency.

I nodded, relieved to escape the scrutiny of my brother and his entourage. As we maneuvered through the crowd, the noise of the distillery enveloped us—laughter, the occasional burst of music from a nearby speaker, and the intoxicating aroma of whiskey hanging thick in the air.

Once outside, the cool night air hit my face like a splash of water, grounding me in reality. The stars twinkled above, a vast canvas that seemed to echo the turmoil of emotions swirling within me. Jason leaned against the wooden railing of the distillery's porch, the soft glow of lanterns illuminating his features, casting a warm light on the shadows of his past.

"Thanks for standing up for yourself," he said, breaking the silence that hung between us. "Not many people would have the guts to do that."

I shrugged, trying to downplay the compliment, but the heat in my cheeks betrayed me. "It's not easy having family around. They can be... intense."

"Intense is one way to put it," he replied, a wry smile playing at the corners of his mouth. "But I admire how you handled it."

"You're just saying that because you were the one stuck in the middle," I teased, nudging him lightly with my elbow. "I didn't see you jumping in to defend my honor."

His laughter was a melodic sound, warm and rich. "Maybe I'm just more of a coward than you."

"Coward? Not with that charm." I grinned, and for a moment, the heaviness of the night seemed to lift, replaced by a flicker of the connection we had once shared.

But the moment was brief. As I glanced back at the entrance of the distillery, the sounds of the party faded, leaving us in a bubble of intimacy tinged with uncertainty. "Do you really think people can change?" I asked, the question lingering like the smoke from the whiskey barrels behind us.

"I think they can try," he replied, his gaze steady and sincere. "It's not always successful, but it's the effort that counts."

"I want to believe that," I said, my voice barely above a whisper. "But what if they're just the same person, pretending to be different?"

"Then you learn to be stronger than them," he said, his eyes searching mine. "You take their past and use it as a shield. It's how you protect yourself."

We stood in silence, the weight of his words settling around us like the cool night air. There was something in his gaze—an understanding that passed between us, an unspoken acknowledgment of our histories, both entwined and apart.

I could feel the tension in my chest, a mix of hope and fear, of longing and uncertainty. Would we be able to bridge the chasm of our pasts, or were we destined to remain on opposite sides of an ever-widening divide?

Before I could articulate my thoughts, Jason took a step closer, the warmth of his body radiating towards me. "You know, despite everything, I'm glad you came tonight. It's nice to see you."

"Likewise," I replied, my heart racing as our eyes locked, the world around us fading into a blur. The space between us felt charged, a tangible force that pulled me closer, and for a heartbeat, the weight of our shared history began to lift.

But just as I felt the dam of my resolve start to crack, the sound of laughter erupted from the entrance, drawing my gaze back to the chaos of the distillery. Jake and his friends were stepping outside, their energy spilling into the night, and I felt the moment shift, the fragile connection between Jason and me slipping away, replaced once more by the harsh reality of my brother's disapproving gaze.

"Looks like the party's not over yet," Jason said, the hint of disappointment in his voice.

"No, it's just getting started," I replied, steeling myself as I turned back toward the noise. The night stretched ahead, filled with promise and peril, and I was left wondering if I could navigate the tumult of my past while forging a new path into the uncertain future that lay ahead.

I turned away from the approaching chaos, absorbing Jason's warmth as the cool night air settled around us like a comforting blanket. The laughter and banter that had once felt like a vibrant song now threatened to drown me in dissonance. Yet here, under the soft glow of the distillery's lanterns, the world felt momentarily balanced—like the perfect blend of spirits, all rich and complex.

"Hey, what's your poison tonight?" he asked, a playful glint in his eyes that stirred something deep inside me. "Whiskey or just a shot of sibling drama?"

"Ah, the age-old dilemma," I replied, attempting to feign nonchalance. "I'll take a double of the whiskey, hold the drama, please."

He laughed, a rich sound that sent a ripple of warmth through me. "You know, they say life is too short to drink bad whiskey or engage in pointless family feuds."

"Wise words from a master distiller," I said, rolling my eyes. "What else do you have, a fortune cookie?"

He leaned closer, the space between us charged with an electricity that made my breath hitch. "I'd say it's more like a personal motto, but a fortune cookie could work too. I could use a good laugh."

Our moment hung in the air, the distance between us shrinking with every heartbeat. I could almost taste the heady mix of anticipation and nostalgia. Yet, just as I felt myself leaning into that comfort, the shouts from the entrance pierced the moment like a knife. Jake's voice, full of bravado and mischief, broke through the quiet.

"Come on, everyone! Let's take this party to the next level!"

I turned, my heart racing as Jake strutted forward, followed by his friends, their raucous energy flooding the porch like a wave. They were loud and unrelenting, the very essence of chaos, and I felt my own emotions twist into a tight knot.

Jason's gaze darted towards them, his expression shifting from warmth to something more guarded, more aware. "So, is this what you meant by sibling drama?"

"More like sibling overkill," I muttered under my breath. Jake and his entourage approached with all the subtlety of a freight train, the exuberance radiating off them like the heat from a bonfire.

"What's this?" Jake called out, spotting us together. "Sister and Jason, sharing a moment? I didn't know we were having a romance novel moment tonight!"

"Very funny, Jake," I shot back, trying to keep my voice steady. "This isn't a scene from a cheesy film."

"Right, because we all know how well your last romance ended," he replied, his words laced with sarcasm. "So, what's next? A passionate embrace in front of the barrels?"

"Oh, please," I groaned, pinching the bridge of my nose. "Can you not be a total jerk for five minutes?"

Jason chuckled, easing the tension slightly. "You know, I've always found that dramatic entrances are best paired with excellent whiskey."

"Great! You're already a hit at the party, my man!" Jake quipped, oblivious to my need for a moment of reprieve.

The group of friends started to mingle, their laughter blending into the ambient music spilling from inside the distillery. I could feel the energy shifting, the playful atmosphere blending with an undercurrent of chaos that churned in my stomach. As they drew closer, my brother's smirk transformed into an all-too-familiar expression of scrutiny.

"I thought you were above this kind of nonsense," he said, gesturing to Jason, who was still leaning casually against the railing.

"What nonsense? Having a good time?" I shot back, folding my arms defensively.

"Looks like you're having a moment, and I'm just here for the comedy," he retorted, the glint in his eye suggesting he was reveling in the discomfort he had stirred.

The others chimed in, egging him on with their playful jabs and laughter. My face burned, caught between the urge to defend Jason and the desire to retreat into the shadows.

"Are you two planning to discuss the nuances of whiskey or just flirt behind the barrels?" one of Jake's friends chimed in, winking at us as if we were the stars of a romantic comedy.

"Does it matter?" I replied, attempting to maintain my composure. "Flirting is just as good a pastime as whatever this is."

Jason gave me a sidelong glance, amusement flickering in his eyes. "I'm all for flirting, but it would be nice if the audience didn't ruin the mood."

"Duly noted," I said, grateful for his lightheartedness. The laughter from the group continued to swirl around us like a thick fog, and I could feel my brother's gaze piercing through the levity, probing for weaknesses.

"Maybe I should take you both back to the tasting room before things get too steamy out here," he suggested, feigning innocence.

"Right, because nothing says romance like a room full of whiskey enthusiasts," I shot back, my frustration bubbling over.

"Just looking out for my little sister," Jake replied, his tone dripping with mock sincerity. "Wouldn't want you to be caught in a scandal, now would we?"

"Honestly, I think you're the one creating a scandal here," I countered, my voice rising in irritation.

"Touché," he conceded, but his smirk remained, unfazed by my irritation.

As if sensing my mounting frustration, Jason stepped forward, his demeanor shifting slightly. "Look, how about we all just enjoy the night? No drama, just whiskey and fun."

The tension hung heavy, but it was met with an unspoken agreement among Jake's friends. They cheered in playful camaraderie, their focus momentarily shifted away from our charged exchange.

"Fine," Jake relented, raising his glass in mock surrender. "But I'll be watching you two. You know how I feel about this... arrangement."

I clenched my jaw, but Jason interjected smoothly, "We can handle ourselves, trust me."

As the party continued to swirl around us, I found myself increasingly caught between two worlds—one tethered to my brother's expectations and the other pulsating with the thrill of rekindled feelings. The whiskey began to blur the lines, and laughter echoed like a distant memory, reminding me of what had once been.

Then, as if to punctuate the evening's absurdity, a loud crash echoed from the tasting room. The door swung open, and a figure stumbled out, a flash of vibrant colors and sheer chaos colliding with the carefully crafted atmosphere.

"Party's over, folks! Get your shots while you can!" a voice bellowed, and the crowd turned in shock.

I squinted through the dim light, trying to catch a glimpse of what had just happened, but before I could process the scene, chaos erupted. People surged toward the entrance, laughter turning into confusion, glasses clinking as drinks threatened to spill.

Jason and I exchanged a glance, the tension between us suddenly igniting again. "What the hell is going on?" he asked, moving toward the fray, and I followed closely behind, adrenaline coursing through me.

As we pushed through the crowd, the figure at the door came into focus—a disheveled woman with wild hair and a streak of something dark across her cheek, panic evident in her eyes. "They're coming! We have to go now!" she shouted, and the atmosphere shifted from jovial to tense in an instant.

"Who's coming?" I pressed, anxiety tightening my throat.

Before she could answer, the door flew open wider, revealing a shadowy figure silhouetted against the light, a look of intent etched across their face. Time seemed to freeze, the joyous atmosphere of the distillery collapsing under the weight of impending danger.

In that moment, I felt the thrill of uncertainty—my heart raced as I took a step back, caught in the spiral of chaos that threatened to engulf us all.

Chapter 5: Secrets and Lies

The air in the distillery was thick with the mingling scents of aged oak and sweet caramel, each breath a reminder of the rich legacy that surrounded us. The golden amber of whiskey glimmered under the soft glow of antique chandeliers, casting flickering shadows that danced across the weathered wooden walls. I leaned against the bar, my glass cradled in my hands, the cool surface grounding me as the tension wrapped around us like a suffocating blanket.

Jason was seated next to me, a hint of mischief sparkling in his deep blue eyes. He had a way of drawing me in with his stories, each word dripping with both charm and vulnerability. As he recounted tales of the distillery's early days—his father's relentless pursuit of perfection and the family's struggle to maintain their place in an industry that shifted like quicksand—I felt a stirring within me. His passion was palpable, and it filled the space between us, electric and alive. I found myself leaning in, desperate to hear every detail, as if his words were the lifeblood of a world I longed to be part of.

"Sometimes, it feels like I'm just a ghost in my own family," he said, his voice barely above a whisper. "Everyone has these grand expectations, but I just want to breathe, to be more than a name on a label." He turned to face me, those blue depths filled with an earnestness that tugged at my heart. The storm cloud of tension shifted, replaced by the warmth of shared understanding.

Before I could respond, a loud crash shattered the moment. The barroom door swung open, slamming against the wall, and in staggered Carter, his eyes wild and unfocused, the unmistakable scent of whiskey trailing behind him like a dark shadow. He was a storm unleashed, his presence electric with rage. "What the hell are you doing here?" he bellowed, pointing a finger that trembled with indignation at Jason.

I froze, heart pounding like a drum in my chest. The room turned silent, every head swiveling to take in the scene. Jason straightened, a mix of confusion and irritation flaring across his face. "What's your problem, Carter?"

"My problem?" Carter sneered, the harshness of his voice echoing through the distillery. "You think it's just fine to cozy up to her? To our family's sworn enemy?" His gaze locked onto mine, a storm brewing in the depths of his hazel eyes. "You're just as bad as he is."

"Stop it!" I shouted, a burst of courage swelling within me. I didn't know where it came from, but the anger bubbling up inside demanded to be heard. "This isn't some game, Carter. You don't get to dictate who I spend time with."

Jason looked between us, his expression a mix of concern and admiration. It was as if my words had reignited something within him, a spark of defiance against the chaos of our families' history. "Carter, this isn't about you. It's about what we want, what we—"

"Want?" Carter interrupted, laughter laced with bitterness. "You want to betray everything our families built? You want to risk it all for her?" He gestured wildly, frustration radiating off him like heat from a fire.

The room was tense, breaths held, eyes darting between us like moths drawn to the flame of confrontation. I felt the weight of the accusations hanging over us, each one a dagger aimed straight at my heart. What did it mean to be caught in the crossfire of this rivalry?

"Carter, this isn't betrayal," Jason said, voice steady despite the chaos. "We're trying to figure out what this—what we—mean in the grand scheme of all this."

"Figure it out? You mean wallow in your own selfishness?" Carter spat, taking a step closer, his hands balled into fists at his sides. "You're both so blinded by whatever this is that you can't even see the consequences."

With a calm I didn't quite feel, I stepped between them, feeling the heat radiating from their confrontation. "We're not enemies," I said, forcing my voice to remain steady. "This rivalry has gone on for too long. What if we could change that?"

Carter's expression faltered, a flicker of uncertainty crossing his features. "Change what? The fact that our families have been at each other's throats for generations?"

"Yes! But it can start with us. With understanding." I didn't know where my words were leading, but they felt right, a call to break the cycle of hatred that had entangled our families for so long.

Jason's eyes met mine, the warmth from earlier reigniting, but Carter remained skeptical, the tension palpable between us. "And what do you suggest? A reconciliation? A family dinner?"

I couldn't help but chuckle at the absurdity of it. "Why not? It's a start. It's ridiculous that we're here, trapped in this cycle, all because of things that happened before we even took our first steps."

Carter glanced at Jason, then back at me, clearly torn. "And what if it doesn't work?"

"Then we deal with it. Together," I said, a conviction blooming within me. "But at least we'll know we tried."

The silence stretched between us, charged with the weight of unspoken words and buried emotions. The air was heavy, thick with possibilities, yet as Jason opened his mouth to respond, Carter cut in, his voice lowering, simmering with restrained anger.

"I won't let you drag our family down with your choices, Jason. Just remember that." With that, he turned on his heel and stormed out, the door slamming shut behind him, leaving a palpable void in his wake.

The tension hung thick, but the resolve between Jason and me had shifted. We stood there, on the precipice of something undefined, a new chapter waiting to be written in the pages of our intertwined lives.

The door swung shut with a heavy thud, leaving a charged silence in its wake. I turned to Jason, who was still processing the whirlwind of emotions that had just erupted. His jaw was tense, and the flickering candlelight reflected a blend of frustration and something else—a fierce determination that stirred something deep within me.

"Great," he muttered, running a hand through his tousled hair. "That went well."

I couldn't help but smile at the absurdity of it all. "If by 'well,' you mean a textbook example of family dysfunction, then absolutely." I took a sip from my glass, the whiskey smooth against my tongue, calming the tumultuous waves of emotion that threatened to overwhelm me. "But we can't let him dictate our choices forever, right?"

He met my gaze, a hint of a smile breaking through his earlier tension. "Right. Besides, I'm not about to let my brother's drunken outburst ruin my night. Or our chance at figuring this out."

There it was again—the spark of connection, the understanding that shimmered in the air like the golden liquid in our glasses. It was intoxicating, the way we were drawn to one another despite the chaos surrounding us. I leaned closer, eager to hear more of his thoughts. "So, what's the plan, then? Do we start plotting a revenge strategy against Carter's insufferable ego?"

Jason chuckled, the sound warm and inviting, and I felt my heart flutter. "You're thinking too small. We should come up with a way to take the distillery to the next level. Get everyone onboard. Show them we're more than just the sum of our families' grudges."

I tilted my head, intrigued. "And how do you propose we do that? Turn the distillery into a hip, millennial hangout spot?"

His eyes danced with mischief. "Why not? Picture it—a tasting room with art installations, maybe live music on the weekends. We could even host whiskey-making classes. I mean, who wouldn't want to learn how to create their own unique blend?"

"Now that," I said, "is a concept I can get behind. But, what if your family refuses to play ball? This isn't just a cute idea; it's a huge leap."

Jason's gaze softened, and I could see the gears turning in his mind. "It's true. My parents can be stubborn. They cling to tradition like it's a lifeboat in a storm." He took a deep breath, his expression shifting to one of resolve. "But maybe they just need a little push. If they see that I'm serious about this—and that you're a part of it—maybe they'll come around."

"Serious? You mean, like bringing me into the family business?"

He leaned closer, the warmth radiating off him creating a bubble of intimacy in the midst of the chaos. "Absolutely. You have this energy, this passion that can breathe life into the distillery. Plus, you've got ideas that are fresh and innovative. I can't think of anyone better to help me."

A rush of excitement surged through me, but I fought to temper it. "And what about Carter? He's not going to sit idly by and watch his brother forge a new path without trying to undermine it."

"Let him try," Jason replied, a determined glint in his eyes. "This is about breaking free from the expectations and stepping into something new. I'm tired of living in the shadow of what's always been."

As we sat there, our conversation bubbling with potential, a server approached, her tray loaded with more whiskey and fresh glasses. "What are you two conspiring about over here?" she asked, her tone playful, and I couldn't help but laugh.

"Just plotting world domination," I quipped, earning a raised eyebrow from Jason.

"Ah, the classic whiskey-fueled plot," the server said, grinning as she set the drinks down. "I'll let you know, I'm available for hire if you need backup."

"Thanks," Jason said with a smirk, "but I think we'll manage. For now."

As she walked away, I turned back to Jason, our plans swirling in the air like the aromas of whiskey around us. "Okay, so we push for innovation, but how do we get everyone on board? Especially your parents?"

He considered this, tapping a finger against his chin thoughtfully. "What if we host a family event? Something that showcases your ideas in action? A mini-festival where we invite local distillers and artisans. It could be a way to highlight community and collaboration."

"Now we're talking," I said, feeling my enthusiasm build. "A festival could draw people in, shift the narrative. But your parents might see it as a gimmick."

"Then we prove it's not. We show them that evolution doesn't erase tradition; it builds upon it."

"Wow, look at you, Mr. Deep and Philosophical."

He grinned, his confidence infectious. "I've been known to surprise people."

Before I could respond, the door swung open once more, and in walked Carter again, though this time he seemed more composed, a shadow of embarrassment lingering in his expression. He took a moment to scan the room before his gaze landed on us, suspicion etched across his features.

"Back so soon?" I asked, unable to resist a cheeky smile.

"Don't start," Carter shot back, crossing his arms. "I'm not in the mood for your sarcasm."

"Good thing I was about to give you a lecture on the benefits of humor in times of conflict," I replied, taking a sip from my glass.

Carter rolled his eyes but stepped closer, clearly still on edge. "What's going on here? I don't like the look of this."

"Just discussing the future of the distillery," Jason interjected, his tone carefully neutral.

Carter's gaze flickered between us, his jaw tightening. "And I'm sure your plans don't include me, right?"

"We're brainstorming ideas, Carter," I said, trying to defuse the tension. "You might be surprised at how much we need your input."

"I doubt it," he muttered, taking a step back, defensive.

"Let's not turn this into another confrontation," Jason said, his voice steady. "We're not enemies, Carter. This is about all of us."

But as Carter's expression hardened, I felt the air grow thick once again. It was a delicate balance, one wrong move could send the entire conversation spiraling. In that moment, I knew we were teetering on the edge of something monumental, the weight of our families' legacies pressing down as we all tried to forge a new path forward.

Carter's voice sliced through the air, laden with tension. "You think you can just sit here and plan your little festival without involving me? Like I'm not even part of this?" The sharpness of his tone was like a whip crack, echoing in the silence that had enveloped the distillery after his return.

Jason's expression shifted from surprise to exasperation. "This isn't about excluding you. It's about trying to move forward. We're not in this fight to tear each other apart."

"Oh, spare me the lecture about brotherly love," Carter snapped, his fists clenched at his sides. "You think you can cozy up to her, and I'm just supposed to accept it? Do you even care about the family legacy?"

A familiar ache settled in my chest at the mention of legacy. It was a term that had haunted my own family, always dangling like a shadow over my every choice. "Carter, this isn't about choosing sides," I interjected, stepping between them. "It's about finding a way to unite—"

"Unite?" Carter interrupted, eyes flashing. "You mean use my brother as a pawn in some misguided attempt to change everything? You're naïve if you think it's that simple."

"Naïve?" I shot back, feeling the heat rise in my cheeks. "I'm not the one stumbling in here, half-drunk, throwing accusations. Maybe you need to take a step back and consider that this is bigger than you or me."

Jason placed a hand on my shoulder, grounding me, and I felt a surge of gratitude. "Let's all just take a breath, okay?" he said, his voice calm but firm. "What we're proposing is a way to bridge the gap between our families, to build something that can benefit all of us. You included, Carter."

Carter's gaze flickered, the edges of his anger wavering. "So, you want to hold hands and sing Kumbaya while our families' history weighs us down? You're dreaming, Jason."

"Maybe dreaming is all we have left," Jason said, his tone turning serious. "What's the alternative? Sticking to the same old grievances? Is that what you really want?"

Silence enveloped the room again, heavy and pregnant with unspoken truths. I could see the gears in Carter's mind turning, wrestling with the idea of collaboration versus the pressure of familial loyalty. The seconds stretched, and I held my breath, hoping he would see reason.

Finally, Carter sighed, tension melting from his shoulders. "I get it. I really do. But what makes you think this will work? What if our parents just laugh it off? They won't easily let go of decades of rivalry."

"Then we show them it's worth it," I replied, feeling a newfound confidence swelling within me. "We make it irresistible. If we can bring the community together, demonstrate the value of collaboration, they won't have a choice but to take notice."

"And what if they reject it?" Carter challenged, but there was less bite in his tone now.

"Then we keep pushing," Jason answered. "We owe it to ourselves and to the legacy of this distillery to try something different."

Carter's expression softened slightly, but doubt still lingered in his eyes. "Okay, let's say I'm on board. How do we even begin?"

As Jason and I exchanged glances, the thrill of possibility electrified the air around us. "We brainstorm," I said, my excitement bubbling over. "Let's list ideas for the festival—what it could look like, who we could invite, what kind of events we could hold. The sky's the limit!"

Carter's lips quirked up slightly. "You really think we can pull this off?"

"I know we can," I replied, and my heart raced at the thought of working alongside them. "It won't be easy, but nothing worth doing ever is."

With newfound determination, we dove into the planning, throwing ideas around like confetti—tasting stations featuring local artisans, workshops on whiskey blending, and even a competition for the best cocktail recipe. I couldn't help but smile as the tension began to dissipate, replaced by laughter and excitement.

For a brief moment, we were no longer representatives of rival families, but three individuals united by a common goal. I could feel the chemistry crackling between us, the walls that had once seemed insurmountable beginning to erode under the weight of our enthusiasm.

Just as we were reaching a crescendo of ideas, the lights flickered, and the mood shifted. I glanced toward the door, my heart sinking as I spotted a familiar figure. Olivia, Carter's girlfriend, strolled in, her expression a mix of confusion and concern.

"What's going on?" she asked, her gaze sweeping over the three of us, lingering on our animated discussion. "I heard shouting from outside."

"Just a family discussion," Carter said, his voice suddenly guarded, the warmth of the moment snuffed out like a candle in a draft.

Olivia's eyes narrowed as she took in the scene—the way Jason's hand rested on my shoulder, the lingering energy that crackled between us all. "It looks like more than that to me."

"We're planning a festival," Jason quickly interjected, his tone casual but edged with tension. "A way to bring our families together."

Her brow furrowed, skepticism painted across her features. "And you think this is going to work? You're still in the middle of a family feud, and now you want to invite everyone to play nice?"

I could feel the air grow thick with tension again. "It's about more than that," I said, stepping forward to face her. "We're trying to change the narrative, to shift the focus away from rivalry and towards collaboration."

Olivia folded her arms, unconvinced. "And you think a festival will magically erase decades of animosity?"

"Maybe not erase," Jason said, his voice steady. "But it's a step. We can't just keep fighting forever."

Her gaze shifted between us, and I could see the wheels turning in her mind. "What's the catch? You don't just decide to bury the hatchet without a reason."

I glanced at Jason, the tension rising again. "There's no catch. Just a hope that we can find common ground."

"And what if someone doesn't want that?" Olivia's eyes flashed with challenge, a dark glimmer that sent a chill down my spine.

As she spoke, the ground beneath us seemed to tremble, and I suddenly felt like we were standing on the edge of a cliff, the unknown looming below. I opened my mouth to respond, but before

I could formulate a coherent thought, a loud crash sounded from the back of the distillery. The commotion drew our attention, the moment of camaraderie shattered, leaving us standing in uncertainty.

"What was that?" Carter asked, his voice tense.

We exchanged worried glances, and as Olivia stepped forward, a look of alarm crossed her face. "I'll check it out," she said, turning on her heel and striding toward the source of the noise.

I wanted to call after her, to warn her to be careful, but the words caught in my throat as Jason and I remained rooted to the spot. My heart raced as I sensed an impending storm, the weight of secrets and lies threatening to drown us all.

And then, as if the universe conspired against our fragile plans, the lights flickered again, plunging us into darkness. A wave of panic washed over me, and in that moment, I realized: this was only the beginning.

Chapter 6: The Calm Before the Storm

The moon hung low that night, casting a silver glow over the old park, its familiar embrace wrapping around me like a worn quilt. Each step on the cracked pavement echoed memories of laughter and whispered secrets, fragments of childhood that seemed worlds away from the chaos of my life now. The chill in the air nipped at my cheeks, but I welcomed the bite; it was a distraction, a way to momentarily escape the turmoil roiling in my heart. I had fled my home, seeking refuge from the heated conversations and icy glares that followed my decision to become involved with the Blackwoods. It wasn't just about Jason; it was everything they represented—their privilege, their legacy, their dark, swirling rumors that clung to them like smoke.

And then, just as the shadows deepened, Jason appeared, cutting through the night with the force of a storm. He looked rugged and worn, his dark hair tousled as if he had been running against the wind. There was a tension in his posture, a defiance in his eyes that drew me in like a moth to flame. I felt a rush of emotions, the remnants of fear intermingling with the fierce longing that had been simmering beneath my skin ever since I met him. "We can't let our families dictate our lives," he said, the raw conviction in his voice sending a shiver through me that had nothing to do with the cold.

I leaned against the gnarled trunk of an ancient oak, feeling the rough bark against my back, grounding me as his words ignited something fierce within me—a rebellion, perhaps, or maybe just the hope that there was still a chance for us. "Easy for you to say," I shot back, trying to keep my voice steady, but it cracked, revealing the storm of emotions swirling just beneath the surface. "Your family practically owns this town, and mine wants to erase me from existence."

He stepped closer, and the scent of pine and something earthy enveloped me, anchoring my thoughts. "Then let's burn their plans to the ground," he replied, his smile a mix of mischief and determination. "You and me, against the world."

That moment shimmered with potential, a single point of light in an otherwise dark landscape. It was the kind of reckless adventure I had only ever dreamed about, the kind that would make even the most mundane life seem extraordinary. But the thrill was quickly overshadowed by the weight of reality. "And how do you propose we do that?" I asked, skeptical but intrigued, the fluttering in my stomach a mixture of anxiety and excitement. "We can't just wish away our families' expectations."

He ran a hand through his hair, frustration bubbling beneath the surface. "What if we didn't need to? What if we could create our own path?" His eyes sparked with a fierce light, and for a moment, I believed him. I wanted to believe him. "You don't understand," I said, my voice dropping to a whisper as I glanced around the empty park, as if the shadows could eavesdrop. "If we stand against them, it will tear us apart."

"Or bring us together," he countered, taking another step forward, the space between us narrowing. "What's life without a little risk? Aren't you tired of living in their shadows?"

Tired was an understatement. I had spent years navigating the treacherous waters of my family's expectations, tiptoeing around their ambitions while secretly dreaming of something more. "But what if it doesn't work?" I asked, a lump forming in my throat. "What if we fail?"

He paused, his gaze steady and unwavering. "Then we fail together. But at least we tried. At least we had something that was ours."

His words resonated deeply, echoing in the chambers of my heart. In that moment, the world around us faded, leaving only the two of us and the unspoken connection that crackled like electricity in the air. It was intoxicating, the promise of rebellion and freedom hanging just within reach.

"I don't want to lose you," I admitted, vulnerability bleeding into my voice, and for the first time, I saw a flicker of uncertainty in his eyes.

"Then don't," he replied, his voice low and firm. "We can forge our own destiny. Together."

As he spoke, the wind picked up, swirling leaves around us like a storm brewing on the horizon. The park, once a sanctuary, now felt like the edge of a precipice, the vast unknown stretching out before us. I could almost taste the adventure, sweet and terrifying all at once.

But the weight of our families loomed like a dark cloud, threatening to burst and drown us in their disapproval. Still, as I looked into Jason's eyes, I saw a reflection of my own desires—a world where we weren't bound by the chains of expectation, where love and dreams intertwined like the branches of the oak above us.

Just then, a sudden sound pierced the night—branches snapping underfoot. I froze, a surge of adrenaline coursing through me. Jason's eyes narrowed, his body tensing as he turned toward the noise, protective instincts ignited. "Stay behind me," he said, his voice a low rumble.

As I shifted slightly, a figure emerged from the shadows, shrouded in darkness but unmistakably familiar. My heart raced, and panic surged within me, threatening to swallow the moment whole. Would our fleeting taste of rebellion be snatched away just as it began?

The figure emerged from the shadows, and recognition struck me like a thunderclap. It was Lily, my younger sister, her wide eyes glinting with a mixture of confusion and worry. "What are you doing here?" I managed to ask, my heart still racing from the adrenaline.

She was supposed to be at home, tucked away under her cozy blanket, watching yet another teen drama where love triumphed against all odds. Instead, she stood before me, an unwitting intruder in a moment that felt so delicate, so poised on the brink of something profound.

"What are you doing here?" she countered, crossing her arms defiantly, mirroring the tone I often used on her. "I saw you slip out, and I—"

"Lily, this isn't the time." I glanced at Jason, who stood a few paces away, tension radiating off him like heat from a fire. He remained silent, observing the exchange, a half-smile on his lips that I couldn't quite decipher.

"Is this about Jason?" she asked, her voice rising incredulously. "Really? After everything that happened at the party? You're still—"

"Lily, stop! You don't understand!" I cut in, desperation leaking into my voice. The last thing I needed was for our already precarious situation to tip over the edge.

"I understand enough," she said, her stubbornness flaring like the vibrant leaves fluttering in the breeze. "You're putting everything on the line for someone who's practically a Blackwood."

The words hung heavy in the air, stinging like a slap. They echoed the fears I had buried deep inside. "And what if he's more than that?" I challenged, my voice steady despite the turmoil inside. "What if he's actually worth it?"

Lily hesitated, her resolve wavering. "You really think you can change things?" she asked softly, almost pleading. "You think running off into the night with him will solve anything? They won't let you go that easily."

I swallowed hard, my throat dry, knowing she was right but unwilling to admit it. "Maybe it's not about changing them. Maybe it's about finding what I want, what we want."

Jason stepped closer, his presence a steady force, grounding me against the whirlwind of emotions swirling around us. "She's right, you know. We can't change our families, but we can choose how we respond to them," he said, his voice low and calming. "If you want to stay, I understand, but if you want to fight—"

"Fight? What are we even fighting against?" Lily interrupted, her voice laced with concern. "This isn't some fairy tale where love conquers all. It's real life, and real life has consequences."

The tension crackled in the air, and I could feel Jason's energy mingling with my own, sparking an unholy mix of determination and doubt. "What do you want, Lily?" I asked, my voice softer now, coaxing. "Do you want me to be safe, or do you want me to be happy?"

She hesitated, her brow furrowing as she weighed the words. "I want you to be both," she finally admitted, her voice barely above a whisper. "But you're risking everything."

"It's my life," I said, a hint of defiance creeping in. "I can't just sit back and let our parents decide my future for me."

"Then why don't you just tell them that?" she asked, her frustration bubbling over. "Why hide out here instead of facing them?"

I opened my mouth to retort, but no words came. I had been running for so long, dodging their expectations like a bullet, yet here I stood, caught in a standoff between my sister and the life I yearned for. "Because it's easier this way," I admitted finally, the honesty burning on my tongue. "It's easier to pretend I can make a choice when I'm hiding in the dark."

Lily's expression softened, and in that moment, I saw a glimpse of the bond that had once been unbreakable between us. "You're stronger than this, you know. You always have been," she said, her voice earnest, and for a heartbeat, the chaos of our world receded.

"Thanks, sis," I replied, my heart swelling with affection for her, even amidst the turmoil. "But strength isn't always enough. Sometimes, it takes a little chaos."

"Speaking of chaos," Jason interjected, a sly grin breaking the tension, "should we make this a family affair? I mean, if we're going to defy the universe, we might as well do it together, right?"

Lily rolled her eyes, a smile tugging at her lips despite the seriousness of the moment. "I can't believe I'm standing here, listening to you both talk about rebellion as if we're not about to be grounded for life."

"Look at it this way," Jason continued, his tone playful, "if we do this right, your parents will have to be impressed. You know, 'Look at my sister, the revolutionary!'"

Lily burst out laughing, the sound like music against the heavy backdrop of our worries. "Okay, that's a solid point," she conceded. "But seriously, do you two have a plan? Or are we just winging it?"

Jason shot me a glance, his brow raised, as if inviting me to take the lead. My heart raced, a rush of adrenaline surging through my veins. "Winging it sounds about right," I admitted, feeling both exhilarated and terrified. "But maybe we can start by finding out what the Blackwoods really want and how we can turn that to our advantage."

"Now that's more like it," Jason said, a spark of mischief igniting in his eyes. "Let's dig deeper, find the truths they hide behind their polished smiles and shimmering facades. I'm in."

As the three of us stood there, the air thick with tension and possibility, I felt the stirrings of a plan forming. We were on the precipice of something monumental, a chance to take control of our futures, and as wild and unpredictable as it seemed, it was a risk I was willing to take. Together, we would navigate the storm that loomed on the horizon, armed with nothing but our resolve and a shared belief that love could conquer even the most daunting of challenges.

In that moment, beneath the starlit sky and the rustling leaves, I felt the weight of my choices, not as a burden but as an opportunity—a chance to carve out my own destiny and write a new story, one that was uniquely ours.

The plan, as it turned out, was a haphazard arrangement of impulsive decisions woven together by a thread of youthful defiance. With Lily's unexpected support and Jason's fiery resolve, we brainstormed over what felt like an eternal evening under the canopy of stars, where every glimmer was a challenge waiting to be claimed. "So, what's the first step in our glorious rebellion?" Jason asked, leaning back against the rough bark of the tree, arms crossed with an air of casual confidence that made my heart race.

"Operation: Unearth the Blackwood Secrets?" Lily suggested, her eyes sparkling with mischief, clearly warming up to the idea of rebellion herself.

Jason snorted a laugh, shaking his head in mock seriousness. "I like it. We'll just need capes and maybe some disguises. Perhaps a little flashlight for dramatic effect?"

"Maybe you should save the theatrics for the stage, Romeo," I shot back, half-joking, half-annoyed, but unable to keep the smile off my face. There was something invigorating about the way we were turning our anxiety into humor, spinning the chaos into something tangible.

"Fine, no capes," Jason conceded, rolling his eyes but grinning nonetheless. "But how do we get in? The Blackwoods don't exactly open their doors for casual visitors, and I'm pretty sure my name isn't on their guest list."

That was the heart of the matter. The Blackwood estate loomed in the distance, an ominous silhouette against the moonlit sky, where every window was a potential eye watching our every move. "We could sneak in through the back," I suggested, feeling the familiar thrill of adventure course through my veins. "The garden has those old hedges, right? We might be able to climb over."

"Are you suggesting we become garden gnomes?" Lily asked, her voice laced with sarcasm but the laughter bubbling just beneath. "Because I can totally see that working."

"Just think of us as horticultural spies," I replied, enjoying the playful banter. "We'll blend in with the scenery. No one will suspect a thing!"

With our laughter echoing through the stillness of the night, we mapped out a plan, each detail punctuated by the excitement of possibility. As we huddled together, ideas sparking like fireworks, I felt the tension from earlier dissolve into a shared thrill. For the first time in what felt like forever, I wasn't just running away from something; I was moving toward something extraordinary.

Once the plan was set, an electric buzz filled the air, mingling with the crisp autumn scent of fallen leaves. We agreed to meet at the park the following night, armed with flashlights, snacks, and a reckless desire to uncover the truth. As we made our way back to our homes, the promise of tomorrow hung like a dream just out of reach, tantalizing and delicious.

When morning broke, the sun cast a golden hue over everything, but the glow didn't last. The moment I stepped into the house, the weight of reality crashed down on me. My parents were gathered in the living room, voices low but urgent, and the tension was palpable, like a taut string ready to snap. I paused at the entrance, a deer caught in the headlights of impending doom.

"Did you hear about the Blackwoods?" my mother asked, her voice trembling with a mix of anxiety and anger. "They've been making waves, and you—" She turned abruptly, spotting me in the doorway. "You were at that party. With them."

"I didn't mean to—" I began, but my father cut me off, his voice booming with authority. "It's not about what you meant. It's about who you're associating with. You could ruin everything we've worked for."

The words sliced through me, raw and cold, leaving me speechless. "Ruin everything?" I echoed, feeling the sting of betrayal. "Maybe I'm trying to find my own path."

"Your path leads straight to disaster!" My mother's voice quaked with emotion. "Do you think they care about you? They only see you as a means to an end."

I recoiled at the accusation, my pulse racing. "You don't know that. Maybe they're not all bad."

"Oh, for heaven's sake, stop defending them!" My father's voice rose, echoing through the house like thunder. "It's not about them; it's about you and the choices you're making. We expect better from you."

"Expectations again," I muttered, unable to keep the bitterness from my tone. "When will it be about what I want? When will it be about me?"

"Enough!" my mother shouted, her voice shaking the very foundations of my resolve. "You need to listen, not only to us but to the people around you. This is serious. You have no idea what you're dealing with."

I felt the walls closing in, suffocating my spirit. "You don't understand anything," I whispered, the fight slowly draining from me. I turned and stormed out of the room, my heart pounding against my ribcage, the echo of their words bouncing off the walls of my mind.

I grabbed my jacket and fled the house, my breath coming in quick bursts as I raced to the park, each step a rebellion against the weight of their expectations. The air was still crisp, but the freedom I had felt just hours before had evaporated, replaced by a cloud of uncertainty. I was no closer to finding my way, and now I felt more lost than ever.

When I reached the park, I half-expected to see Jason waiting for me, but the shadows stretched long and empty. I sat on the swing, the rusted chains creaking softly, a reflection of my spiraling thoughts. I wrapped my arms around myself, trying to quell the shivering apprehension that gnawed at my insides.

Minutes dragged by, and just as I was about to give in to doubt, Jason appeared, his silhouette framed by the soft glow of the setting sun. Relief washed over me as he approached, but there was an intensity in his gaze that set my heart racing all over again.

"What happened?" he asked, concern etching his features as he settled next to me on the swing.

"They know about us. They know about you," I admitted, my voice trembling. "They think I'm making a mistake."

"And what do you think?" he asked softly, his gaze unwavering.

"I don't know," I confessed, my voice cracking. "I thought this was going to be about us—about finding out who we are. But now, I'm not so sure."

"Then we'll figure it out together," he replied, determination thickening his tone. "We're in this, remember? But you need to trust me."

As I looked into his eyes, I saw the flickering embers of our shared rebellion reigniting. It was intoxicating, the prospect of defiance, the thrill of facing the storm together.

Just then, the air shifted, and a noise broke the fragile moment—branches snapping and gravel crunching underfoot. My heart raced as a shadow emerged from the edge of the park, a figure looming with purpose, and as the fading light illuminated their features, I froze.

There, watching us with a smirk that made my skin crawl, stood none other than Ethan Blackwood, Jason's older brother. "Well, well," he drawled, his voice smooth and dripping with arrogance. "What do we have here?"

The chill that washed over me felt like the foreboding winds of a storm, and in that instant, everything changed. The air grew thick with tension, and I could almost hear the gears of fate shifting, the path ahead twisting into something I could never have anticipated.

Chapter 7: Fateful Decisions

The sun dipped low over the rolling hills, casting a warm, golden glow across the expansive fields that surrounded Willow Creek Distillery. Each evening, as the light began to wane, I found solace in the rhythmic hum of the distillation process, a comforting backdrop to my increasingly chaotic life. I had always thought of this place as a sanctuary, a retreat from the complexities of my world, but in the days following my decision to stand by Jason, it transformed into something else entirely—a battleground where hope and rivalry danced a precarious waltz.

Jason was as much a part of this place as the aged oak barrels that lined the walls, their darkened surfaces worn smooth by years of secrets and stories. We worked side by side, our hands dusty from grains and grains of crushed barley. Every laugh we shared over spilled mash, every playful jab about who could create the better blend, forged an invisible thread that pulled us closer. It was intoxicating, this connection, as heady as the scents wafting from the copper stills. But I couldn't ignore the undercurrents that lurked just beneath the surface. Our families were still at odds, their animosity simmering like a pot just waiting to boil over.

"Are you sure this is going to work?" I asked one day, brushing a stray lock of hair behind my ear as I eyed the concoction bubbling in front of us. The deep amber liquid shimmered under the flickering light of the distillery, a promise of what could be, if only we could navigate the storm that lay ahead.

Jason shrugged, the corner of his mouth quirking up in that infuriatingly charming way that made my heart race. "If it doesn't, we'll just blame it on the family feud. Nothing like a good rivalry to spice things up."

"Right, because nothing says 'let's end the generations of conflict' like creating a new signature drink that could blow up in our faces," I shot back, half-laughing, half-serious.

His laughter echoed in the cavernous space, a warm sound that soothed the edges of my anxiety. "At least we'll have a story to tell. 'The Great Harvest Brew: Born of Love and Chaos.'"

As we spent hours together, our playful banter turned into deeper conversations. I learned about his childhood dreams of becoming a master distiller, how he used to sneak into the distillery as a boy to watch the magic happen. He spoke with a passion that ignited something in me, a spark of inspiration that I hadn't felt in ages. The lines between us blurred further, until I was no longer just a Johnson, but a partner in his dreams, his laughter.

Yet, as we poured our hearts into our craft, shadows loomed in the distance. I could sense the disapproval from my parents, their skepticism wrapped tightly around my decision like an iron cage. My mother had spent years trying to protect me from the Palmer family, their reputation marred by generations of rivalry and bad blood. I had often heard whispered tales of the chaos that ensued when our families crossed paths—an almost mythical lore that painted Jason's family as the antagonists in our own personal epic.

"Are you prepared for the fallout?" My sister, Clara, asked one evening, her voice laced with concern. "You know how Mom is. This won't go over well."

I sighed, staring out the window at the swaying branches of the old oak tree, its leaves shimmering like coins in the fading light. "I'm tired of running from this, Clara. If I don't try, I'll always wonder what could have been."

Clara's brow furrowed. "And if it doesn't work out? What if this just makes everything worse?"

The truth of her words hung in the air, heavy and unyielding. My heart pounded, a discordant rhythm that mirrored the brewing conflict within me. "Then I guess I'll have to face the consequences, won't I?"

A week passed, the atmosphere thickening with anticipation as the Harvest Festival drew near. The townspeople buzzed with excitement, their chatter swirling around like the leaves caught in a playful breeze. But for me, the festival loomed like a storm cloud on the horizon, both exhilarating and terrifying.

Jason and I put the finishing touches on our special brew, a blend of sweet and spicy notes, reminiscent of the very essence of fall. We named it "Autumn's Embrace," a nod to the warmth we hoped to bring to our divided families. The day of the festival arrived with a crispness in the air, the scent of caramel apples and roasted chestnuts mingling with the unmistakable aroma of fresh whiskey.

As I set up our booth, my heart raced, not just from the thrill of the festival, but from the palpable tension that crackled in the air. I spotted my parents across the square, their faces a study in skepticism as they surveyed the scene. A knot formed in my stomach, twisting tighter as I caught sight of Jason's family on the opposite end, their body language a blend of arrogance and disdain.

"Ready to make history?" Jason asked, his eyes gleaming with excitement, oblivious to the chaos brewing just beyond our little world.

I forced a smile, but inside, my nerves twisted like vines around my heart. "I hope so. But history can be messy."

As the festival began, laughter and music filled the air, but the tension remained a taut string ready to snap. The moment we poured our first samples, the atmosphere shifted. It was intoxicating—our blend was a hit, drawing crowds eager for a taste of what we had created together. But as the sun set and the festival lights twinkled like stars, I felt the weight of the unspoken conflict looming larger than ever.

The first ripple of dissent came unexpectedly. A group of my family friends, their faces contorted in disbelief, approached our booth, their chatter filled with a mix of awe and shock.

"Are you serious?" one of them exclaimed, looking between Jason and me with a mix of disbelief and confusion. "You're actually working with the Palmers?"

My heart sank, a stone dropped into a still pond, sending waves of anxiety skimming across the surface. I could feel Jason stiffen beside me, the warmth of our shared triumph cooling in the face of this unwelcome reality.

"Yes, we are," I replied, forcing the words out with a confidence I didn't quite feel. "And it's about time our families found common ground."

But as their murmurs began to swell, I sensed the shadows closing in, the rivalry boiling just beneath the surface. The tension was palpable, a bitter undertow threatening to drag us under.

The murmurs around us swelled, a cacophony of disbelief that ricocheted off the wooden booths and colorful festival banners. I could feel my pulse quicken, an anxious drumbeat matching the rhythm of the lively folk band playing nearby. The initial thrill of our collaboration began to sour in the face of my family's disapproval. I glanced at Jason, who remained calm, his eyes fixed on the crowd, yet I could see the tension in the way his fingers tapped against the wooden table.

"Seems like we've stirred the pot," I quipped, forcing a lightness into my voice, though my heart felt like it was sinking into a pit. "Next time, we should just announce our love from the rooftops. That might create less drama."

He chuckled softly, his gaze unwavering. "I wouldn't put it past my family to throw a festival just for that. 'Welcome to the Love Showdown—witness the epic battle of the hearts!'"

The humor lingered briefly between us, a fragile barrier against the oncoming storm. As more people approached, curiosity and skepticism etched on their faces, I braced myself for the questions, the judgment.

"What were you thinking?" one of my childhood friends, Clara's friend Molly, exclaimed, her eyebrows shooting up as if I'd announced I was moving to Mars. "Do you really think this will fix everything?"

"It's not about fixing; it's about trying," I replied, my voice steady despite the storm brewing in my chest. "We have to start somewhere. And trust me, this is way better than another round of arguments at family dinners."

The crowd murmured, their skepticism palpable. Behind me, Jason was pouring samples into small cups, his movements smooth and practiced. The sweet and spicy aroma of Autumn's Embrace filled the air, weaving around us like a siren's song, but I couldn't ignore the weight of the eyes on us.

"Are you sure this isn't just another publicity stunt?" someone else chimed in, and the question hung in the air, heavy with implication.

"Publicity?" I echoed, a mix of incredulity and irritation sparking within me. "This is about creating something new, something that could actually bring us all together."

"Right, because nothing says unity like whiskey," someone muttered, a half-hearted laugh punctuating their words.

I took a deep breath, attempting to anchor myself amidst the rising tide of doubt. "Maybe not just whiskey, but a chance to celebrate. To have fun, together. Isn't that what festivals are about?"

Before anyone could respond, the sound of shattering glass shattered the moment, slicing through the festive air like a knife. My heart stopped as I turned, my eyes widening in disbelief. One of Jason's brothers, Tyler, stood at the edge of the crowd, his face twisted in anger. He glared at the fallen bottle of our brew, shards glimmering on the ground like shattered dreams.

"Of course, the Palmers would pull a stunt like this," Tyler spat, his voice loud enough for everyone to hear. "You think we'd just let you take over? This is our territory!"

The atmosphere shifted, tension crackling like electricity. I felt the weight of a hundred eyes, all turning towards us, the rift between our families threatening to explode in front of the entire town.

"Tyler, it's not a takeover," Jason said, his tone calm yet firm, stepping forward to defuse the situation. "We're trying to work together."

"Work together?" Tyler sneered, taking a step closer, his stance aggressive. "You're just another pawn in this ridiculous game. Everyone knows the Johnsons are the enemy."

A lump formed in my throat. "This isn't about enemies, Tyler. This is about finding a way forward. Can't you see that?"

Tyler's glare didn't waver. "Forward? You mean backward. You think playing nice will erase decades of hatred? You're delusional."

The crowd was growing restless, whispers racing through the group like wildfire. I looked around, seeking support, but my friends stood back, uncertainty clouding their faces. The warmth that had enveloped Jason and me moments ago felt like it had been extinguished, leaving only cold, hard reality.

Jason stepped between us, his jaw clenched but his eyes searching. "This is bigger than you and me. It's about our families, our legacy. We have a chance to change things."

"Change things?" Tyler laughed bitterly, the sound harsh against the cheerful strains of the festival music. "You're a fool if you think that's possible. The only thing that's going to change is the look on your face when our family wins again."

And just like that, the fragile peace we'd crafted shattered, splintering into a thousand pieces that mirrored the broken bottle on the ground. My heart raced as I turned to Jason, desperation clawing at my insides.

"We can't let this ruin everything," I whispered urgently. "We need to show them that we're serious, that we can make this work."

Jason nodded, determination hardening his features. "You're right. Let's give them a show they won't forget."

He raised his voice, drawing the crowd's attention back to us. "We're here not to fight but to share something beautiful. This brew isn't just a drink; it's a testament to what we can achieve together. We might be from different worlds, but that doesn't mean we can't meet in the middle."

I stepped beside him, feeling the heat of the moment wash over me like a wave. "Come taste it. You might be surprised. This isn't just about us; it's about everyone. Let's celebrate our differences instead of letting them divide us."

The crowd shifted, uncertainty mixing with curiosity. One by one, hesitant faces began to move closer, the earlier tension giving way to a flicker of interest. I could feel the weight of their gazes, the palpable need for something—anything—that might break the cycle of animosity.

Jason poured small samples of Autumn's Embrace into cups, handing them out with an inviting smile. "Trust me, you won't regret it. This is something special."

As I watched people tentatively take the cups, a spark of hope ignited within me. Each sip seemed to dissolve the invisible barriers that had kept our families apart for so long. Laughter slowly returned to the crowd, a gentle undercurrent that swirled around us, lifting the heaviness.

"Hey, this is actually really good!" someone called out, and the laughter spread like wildfire.

Emboldened, I found myself laughing too, the joy of the festival washing over me. For a moment, I forgot the looming storm. Jason caught my eye, a shared smile passing between us, and I knew that this battle was far from over, but perhaps, just perhaps, we were winning the first skirmish.

But even as the lightness surrounded us, I felt a pang of uncertainty settle deep within me. I knew the rivalry would not dissolve overnight; it was a deeply rooted vine that required more than a single sweet brew to untangle. Yet, standing there, watching the faces of friends and family light up as they tasted our creation, I felt a flicker of belief ignite within me. Maybe we were on the cusp of something transformative, a chance to rewrite the narratives that had haunted our families for generations.

The laughter and chatter swirled around me, a vibrant tapestry of sound woven into the very fabric of the festival. I watched as people leaned in to try our brew, their expressions shifting from skepticism to delight with every sip. For the first time in what felt like ages, the air crackled with an undercurrent of optimism, an almost tangible energy that ignited hope deep within me. But amid the warmth of camaraderie, I remained acutely aware of the shadows lurking at the edges, waiting for the perfect moment to pounce.

"Who knew mixing grains could create such a stir?" Jason's voice cut through the festive noise, and I turned to see him leaning against the booth, a grin spreading across his face. He looked effortlessly charming, the festival lights catching in his dark hair, making him seem almost ethereal.

"Careful now," I teased, nudging him playfully with my elbow. "If you keep smiling like that, you'll be the main attraction, and I'll be left here with the bottles."

"Never," he replied, his tone mock serious. "You're the star of this show. I'm just the supporting actor who happens to be good at pouring."

"Oh, please. You're the one with the charm," I shot back, savoring the moment of lightness, even as I felt the tension tightening around us like a noose.

But just as our banter settled into a comfortable rhythm, I spotted my mother across the crowd, her arms crossed and lips pressed into a thin line, watching with an intensity that could rival a hawk hunting for its next meal. I felt a familiar flutter of anxiety twist in my stomach.

"What's wrong?" Jason asked, his gaze following mine.

"Nothing that can't be handled," I said, plastering on a smile, though my heart raced in anticipation of the confrontation that lay ahead.

With a determined breath, I approached my mother, steeling myself for the impending storm. "Mom, can we talk?"

She looked at me, a mixture of disappointment and worry swirling in her eyes. "Talk? Or lecture?"

I held up my hands, a gesture of surrender. "Can't it be both? Just... give me a chance to explain?"

Her expression softened slightly, and she nodded, following me to a quieter corner of the festival, the sounds of laughter and music fading into the background.

"Do you realize what you're doing?" she began, her voice low but edged with urgency. "You're throwing away years of tradition, of family loyalty, for what? A fling with a Palmer?"

"It's not a fling," I argued, my voice rising despite my efforts to remain calm. "Jason and I are trying to create something new, something that can unite our families. You taught me that change is necessary. Why is this different?"

"Because it's reckless," she replied, her frustration bubbling just beneath the surface. "You don't know what you're getting into. They've always been trouble."

"Maybe it's time we stop seeing them as trouble," I retorted, my heart pounding in my chest. "Maybe it's time we start seeing them as people. People who want to change, just like we do."

Her eyes searched mine, and for a brief moment, I thought I saw a glimmer of understanding. "And what if they don't want to change? What if this backfires spectacularly?"

"Then we deal with it. Together," I said, my voice steady despite the uncertainty clawing at me. "But we have to try first."

As we stood there, the sounds of the festival enveloping us, I realized that this was more than just a conversation about Jason and me. It was about the weight of our families' history, the burdens we carried like stones in our pockets.

"I don't want to lose you, sweetheart," she finally admitted, her voice softening. "You mean everything to me."

"And I don't want to lose you either, Mom. But I can't keep living in the shadows of our past. I need to forge my own path."

She sighed, a deep, weary sound that echoed through the quiet space between us. "I just hope you know what you're doing."

Before I could respond, a sudden commotion erupted from the direction of the booth. I turned to see a group of men, faces flushed with anger, surging toward Jason, who stood helplessly behind the table. My heart dropped as I recognized Tyler leading the charge, flanked by a couple of his friends, their expressions hard and determined.

"This is ridiculous!" Tyler shouted, his voice cutting through the cheerful atmosphere. "You think we'll let you tarnish the family name with your little stunt?"

"Stunt?" Jason echoed, bewildered, yet he remained steadfast behind the booth, a protective barrier between the brewing storm and the festival-goers enjoying our creation.

"You're making a mockery of everything our families have built," Tyler continued, advancing closer, his fists clenched at his sides. "And you think it's going to end well?"

"Tyler, stop!" I shouted, stepping forward, but the crowd had begun to gather, eyes wide with excitement and fear.

"Stay out of this, Jane," Tyler warned, his gaze piercing. "This is between us."

"No, it's not!" I insisted, my voice rising above the murmur of the crowd. "This is about all of us. We can't keep fighting like this."

"Fighting? Oh, this is just the beginning," he spat, and I could see the anger boiling beneath his facade. "You really think a little festival can change years of hatred? You're dreaming if you think any of us will accept a Palmer."

Jason stepped forward, his voice steady but laced with defiance. "You're the one who's dreaming if you think this feud will continue. We can break the cycle. This is our chance."

Tyler laughed, a harsh, bitter sound that cut through the evening air. "Your chance? What a joke. This is just a game to you, isn't it? But we're not playing. You're messing with forces you don't understand."

Before I could respond, a piercing scream sliced through the crowd. A woman's voice, high and frantic. "Help! Someone help!"

Panic erupted as everyone turned toward the commotion. A few stalls away, a scene unfolded that sent shockwaves through the crowd. A little boy, no more than six, was clinging to a food stand, his face streaked with tears, while a burly man loomed nearby, his posture menacing and his intentions unclear.

"Someone's got to do something!" someone yelled, and the crowd buzzed with fear and uncertainty.

"Stay here!" I commanded Jason, not waiting for a reply as I dashed toward the chaos, adrenaline coursing through my veins. As I approached, the scene grew more intense. The boy looked terrified,

UNFINISHED PATHS

his small body trembling as he stared up at the man, who seemed oblivious to the concern surrounding him.

"Hey! Let him go!" I shouted, my heart racing. The man turned, surprise flashing across his face as he registered my presence, but the flicker of menace remained.

"Stay out of this, girl," he growled, his voice low and threatening.

But I wouldn't back down. Not now. "You're scaring him. Just walk away."

A few people from the crowd had started to gather behind me, their expressions a mix of concern and defiance. This was not just about Jason or our families anymore; this was about something bigger—about standing up when it mattered, about challenging fear and anger with courage.

The tension was thick enough to slice, but before I could take a step closer, I felt a heavy hand on my shoulder. Turning, I saw Jason standing behind me, determination etched on his face.

"Together," he said simply, the word hanging in the air like a promise.

In that moment, as we faced the looming threat together, I understood something profound. The road ahead would be fraught with challenges, but perhaps, just perhaps, we were beginning to find our way—out of the shadows, into the light, ready to confront whatever darkness awaited us.

And then, as the crowd held its breath, the ground beneath us seemed to shift, the air thick with unspoken tension. My heart raced as I braced for whatever might come next, not knowing that the true battle was only just beginning.

Chapter 8: Storm Clouds Gather

The air crackled with the sweetness of impending autumn as I stood beneath the sprawling oak tree at the edge of my family's property, its leaves whispering secrets to the cool breeze. The Harvest Festival loomed just days away, a celebration meant to unite our small town, but tension hung in the air, thick and electric like the weight of an approaching storm. The sky above wore a sullen gray, an ominous harbinger that felt too fitting against the backdrop of the brewing feud between our families.

Jason was waiting for me, his silhouette framed against the dusky horizon, the last remnants of sunlight glimmering off his tousled hair. He had a way of making the chaos around us seem less overwhelming, as if the world faded to a gentle hum when he smiled. I felt the flutter of excitement in my chest, a bright spark amid the gathering clouds, and I rushed to him, throwing my arms around him. The warmth of his body seeped into me, calming the storm of anxiety brewing within.

"What if we're caught?" he asked, pulling back slightly, his blue eyes dancing with mischief yet tinged with caution.

I laughed, a light sound that pierced the heavy air. "Caught? By who? My parents? Yours? They can barely stand to be in the same room, let alone figure out we're here together." The adrenaline of our secret rendezvous thrilled me, even as I felt the tightening grip of fear around my heart.

"I know. But you should be careful. The rumors..." He trailed off, casting a glance toward the distant lights of town. "People are talking. There's talk of sabotage, maybe even worse."

I waved a dismissive hand. "Let them talk. We're not doing anything wrong, right? Just working together."

His brow furrowed, the playful grin fading. "Together? Or is it something more?"

His question hung in the air, heavy with meaning. I wanted to say that it was more, that every moment we spent together felt like a thread pulling us closer, weaving a tapestry of dreams and hopes that I dared to envision. Instead, I turned my gaze to the ground, tracing the patterns in the dirt with my toe. "You know how my family feels about this... about us."

"It doesn't have to be like that forever." He reached for my hand, his fingers intertwining with mine, and I felt the rush of warmth. "We could find a way, make them see."

"Or make it worse," I countered, pulling my hand away, the thrill of our connection momentarily overshadowed by the reality of our situation. The thought of escalating tensions sent shivers down my spine, each whisper of wind through the trees sounding more like a warning than a serenade.

He took a step closer, his presence radiating a comforting heat. "So we just wait? Hide in the shadows forever?"

I took a deep breath, willing my heart to steady. "Maybe we don't hide. Maybe we fight. Together." The words tumbled from my lips before I could reel them back in, and Jason's expression shifted from uncertainty to something almost hopeful.

"Together," he echoed, his voice low and rich, like the deepening shades of twilight. "I like the sound of that."

We lingered under the vast expanse of stars, the air thick with unspoken promises and the weight of our choices. Just as I felt the tension ebb, a piercing shrill broke through the tranquility—the unmistakable sound of my phone ringing in my pocket. With a reluctant sigh, I reached for it, expecting yet another call from my mother reminding me of the endless to-do list that awaited me in preparation for the festival.

But it wasn't my mother. It was Jenna, my sister, her voice breathless and frenzied. "Sophie! You need to get to the distillery—now! There's been a fire!"

The words crashed over me like a wave, drowning out the warmth of the moment. "What? Is everyone okay?" My voice trembled, fear lacing through each syllable. I could already envision the flames consuming our family's legacy, the lifeblood of our community turning to ash.

"I don't know! Just hurry!" The line went dead, leaving a chilling silence that settled around me like a shroud.

Jason's hand was suddenly on my shoulder, grounding me. "What happened?"

"Fire at the distillery," I managed, my heart racing as the reality of the situation struck me. "I have to go. Now."

He nodded, the lighthearted banter of moments before evaporating into the cool night air. "I'll come with you."

"No, you can't," I protested, panic flaring within me. "It's too dangerous. If my family sees you there—"

"They need you. You need me." His voice was steady, a calm anchor in the tumult of my thoughts. "Let's go."

Together, we rushed towards the distillery, the world around us fading as my heart hammered in my chest. The shadows of the trees loomed large, the path lit only by the distant flicker of flames licking at the night sky. I could see the smoke rising, a sinister plume that twisted and curled, choking the stars above.

As we drew closer, the sharp scent of burning wood and sugar filled my lungs, panic twisting my insides. A crowd had gathered, their faces illuminated by the orange glow of the fire, and as I pushed through the throng, I felt the weight of their stares, judgmental and curious, settling heavily upon me. Jason was right beside me, his presence a silent reassurance, yet even that comfort felt fragile against the fear tightening my throat.

"Where is everyone?" I shouted over the crackle of flames, straining to spot my family among the chaos. My heart sank as I caught sight of Jenna, her eyes wide with fear, a trembling figure amidst the turmoil.

"There!" she called out, pointing towards the entrance, where my father and a few of our workers struggled against the fire, their faces set with grim determination.

I pushed forward, heart racing as I fought against the tide of onlookers. "Dad!" I screamed, the sound of my voice lost in the roar of the flames. The scene unfolded like a nightmare, the fire consuming everything in its path, and with each step closer, I could feel the heat seeping into my skin, a reminder of the urgency of the moment.

As I reached my father, the world around me blurred into chaos, yet my focus remained clear—on my family, on the distillery, on the unraveling threads of our lives. The storm that had gathered over the festival now raged within me, and as I stood there, I knew that the fight for everything I loved had just begun.

The crackle of the flames filled the air, a haunting symphony of destruction that drowned out everything else. I reached my father, sweat glistening on his forehead as he barked orders, the chaos swirling around him like a tempest. His usually warm brown eyes were now darkened with worry, etched deep with the lines of an unyielding burden. He glanced up as I approached, his face briefly softening before hardening again against the reality of the inferno.

"Sophie! Get back! It's too dangerous!" he shouted, his voice hoarse but commanding. I had never seen him like this, not even during the toughest harvest seasons when storms threatened our crops. There was a ferocity in his expression, a raw determination that both frightened and inspired me.

"I'm not leaving you!" I replied, my voice tinged with defiance as I pushed past the flames licking at the doorway. "What do you need? I can help!"

He hesitated for a moment, weighing the wisdom of my resolve against the flames that crackled and roared. "We need to get the tanks secured. If the fire spreads—"

"On it!" I dashed toward the rows of wooden barrels, their polished surfaces reflecting the flames, casting flickering shadows on the ground. Jason followed closely, his presence a steady anchor amidst the turmoil.

"Be careful!" he warned, his voice low and urgent. "If it's too much, just—"

"Just trust me," I snapped back, fueled by adrenaline and the instinct to protect what was ours. It was hard to think clearly with the heat rising around us, but the sight of the barrels, filled with our family's hard work and legacy, drove me forward. I could practically hear the whispers of my ancestors urging me on, guiding me through the chaos.

As I reached the first tank, the heat intensified, making it hard to breathe. I grasped the nearest barrel, feeling the rough wood against my palms, its weight both comforting and daunting. I could already see the flames creeping closer, eager to engulf our past in their ravenous hunger. Jason came alongside me, his brow furrowed, lips pressed into a thin line of determination.

"Together," he said, nodding toward the barrel.

"On three?" I replied, summoning a sense of teamwork that felt utterly vital in that moment.

"One, two, three!" Together, we pushed with all our strength, muscles straining against the weight, and I felt a surge of triumph as the barrel rolled away from the encroaching flames.

"Good!" My father's voice rang out, filled with a fierce pride that momentarily drowned out the fear. "Keep going!"

The sweat dripped down my back as we worked feverishly, shoving barrel after barrel, sweat mingling with soot as we made our frantic progress. Each victory felt monumental, a small act of rebellion against the destruction threatening to swallow us whole. With each roll, I could almost hear the stories of our family's history, their laughter and struggles, urging us to fight back.

But just as we were gaining momentum, a loud crack echoed through the chaos. My heart raced as I turned to see a part of the roof collapse, sending a shower of sparks cascading toward us. "Get back!" I yelled, panic lacing my words as I pulled Jason away from the flaming debris.

He stumbled back, eyes wide. "What about your dad?"

My father was still shouting orders, moving to secure another tank, oblivious to the danger above him. I felt a surge of fear for him, and it twisted my insides. "Dad! You need to get out!" I called, my voice breaking through the roar of the fire.

"I'm fine! Just keep moving the barrels!" he shouted back, his voice filled with resolve, but it was clear he was caught up in his own world, too focused on saving the distillery to see the flames inching ever closer.

"Not without you!" I shot back, heart pounding as I glanced at the growing inferno. "We're not leaving you behind!"

The heat was stifling, oppressive, but I could see the determination in my father's eyes as he turned toward me. "You are my priority, Sophie! You need to get out of here!"

Suddenly, the tension in the air shifted, a new sound blending with the crackle of flames—a siren, distant but growing closer. My heart leaped with hope, but it quickly dwindled as I realized that we had to hold the line until help arrived. "The fire department is on the way!" I yelled to Jason, trying to keep my fear at bay.

"Let's get these last barrels moved!" he shouted back, and together we launched into action once more, pushing against the weight of our legacy, against the flames that licked hungrily at the edges of our reality.

But as we moved the final barrel, I felt a sudden shift, a wave of heat that sent me stumbling backward. The ground beneath my feet shook, and before I could process what was happening, a large section of the roof collapsed, sending a cascade of sparks into the night sky. The flames erupted, roaring like a wild beast freed from its cage, illuminating the horror unfolding before us.

"Jason!" I cried, panic rising as I saw him caught in the shifting shadows, just outside the reach of the fire but dangerously close to the falling debris. Time seemed to stretch as I reached for him, desperate to pull him to safety, my heart racing with fear and urgency.

He met my eyes, and in that moment, I saw a flicker of something—fear mixed with determination. "Sophie, go! I can't leave you!"

"No!" I shouted, feeling my heart splinter at the thought of losing him. "You have to come with me! We can't fight this alone!"

With one final push, we reached for each other, fingers brushing as we fought against the chaos surrounding us. The sirens were now blaring, cutting through the thick haze of smoke, but the world had narrowed to just the two of us, a thread of connection woven tighter with every second we fought to hold on.

Suddenly, I heard a familiar voice behind me. "Sophie! Jason! Over here!" It was Jenna, her face streaked with soot, eyes wide with fear and determination. "The firefighters are here! We need to get out now!"

In that moment, the stakes crystallized. I glanced back at my father, still battling the flames. "We can't leave him!" I shouted, desperate, my heart torn between love and duty.

"They'll get him out! We have to go!" Jenna insisted, urgency driving her words.

With a final glance at Jason, I took a deep breath, summoning every ounce of courage. "Together," I said, squeezing his hand one last time before pulling him toward the exit.

"Together," he echoed, and we ran toward the safety of the outside world, our hearts racing, the sounds of the fire chasing us into the unknown. The flames roared behind us, but in that moment, I held onto the hope that we could fight back, that our story was not yet over.

The moment we burst through the doors, the cool night air hit us like a refreshing wave, but it did little to cool the turmoil in my chest. Sirens blared, a cacophony of chaos blending with the distant crackle of fire, while shadows danced on the ground, courtesy of the flickering flames still devouring the distillery behind us.

Jenna was already on the phone, her brow knitted in worry as she relayed frantic updates to someone on the other end. "Yeah, we're safe, but it's bad. I think Dad is still in there. No, I don't know how he's doing—just send everyone!" She hung up and turned to me, her face pale but determined. "They're on their way, but it's taking too long."

"Where is he?" I gasped, looking back at the inferno, my heart hammering in my chest. The thought of my father still inside sent a chill through my veins.

Jenna pointed towards a group of firefighters who had just arrived, their uniforms bright against the darkened sky, faces set with grim determination. "They're working to get him out. We have to trust them."

Jason moved closer to me, his presence a steady reassurance. "You should wait over there," he urged, nodding toward a safe distance away from the burning structure. "We can't do anything until they've got everything under control."

I nodded, the words hung heavy in my throat. Trust. It felt fragile, like a thin thread in the storm raging inside me. My instincts screamed for action, but fear held me still, tethered to the scene of destruction. As I glanced back at the building, flames erupted higher, casting a haunting glow over the landscape.

"C'mon, Sophie," Jason said, his voice steady as he took my hand, tugging me gently. "Let's get a better view. We'll stay close, just enough to see what's happening."

I squeezed his hand, grateful for his unwavering support. Together, we moved further away from the heat, still close enough to witness the firefighters battling the blaze. I could see their silhouettes darting in and out of the building, the rhythm of their movements choreographed like a dance against the backdrop of chaos.

A firefighter emerged, face smudged with soot, the look in his eyes one of urgency mixed with a heavy heart. He shouted commands, directing the others with sharp precision. "We need more water! Get the hoses!"

I felt a surge of anxiety as I caught snippets of their conversations. "We've got to contain it—if it reaches the main storage, we'll lose everything."

"Dad!" I screamed, the word tearing from my throat as if it could reach him through the chaos. I fought the urge to run back into the flames, the fear of losing him coiling tightly in my gut.

Jenna grabbed my arm, her grip firm. "We have to wait. They know what they're doing!"

"Easy for you to say!" I shot back, the fear morphing into frustration. "You're not the one who might lose everything!"

But even as I spoke, I could feel the tension in the air shifting. It wasn't just fear of loss; it was the desperate need for something good to come from this disaster. Jason's hand found mine again, grounding me. "Let's just breathe for a second. We'll get through this. We always do."

The firefighters moved with relentless determination, their voices overlapping, creating a cacophony that danced around us.

Suddenly, I spotted my father reemerging from the building, his face a mask of soot and worry. Relief flooded me, but it was quickly eclipsed by the sight of his expression. It was as if he had seen something that left a scar on his soul.

"Dad!" I called again, bursting forward, but Jenna held me back.

"Wait! He's talking to the firefighters!" she insisted, her eyes scanning the scene.

But the moment my father reached the perimeter, he was met with the urgency of the situation. One of the firefighters stepped forward, talking to him in hushed tones, gesturing back toward the building. My heart sank, dread curling around me like the smoke still rising from the embers.

"What's happening?" I whispered to Jason, my voice trembling.

"I don't know," he said, his brow furrowed as he leaned in closer, trying to catch snippets of the conversation. "But he looks serious."

As my father turned, his eyes met mine, and for a moment, it felt as if the world slowed. His gaze was filled with an emotion I couldn't quite decipher—a mix of fear, anger, and something darker that twisted my gut into knots.

"Sophie, stay back!" he yelled, his voice strained as he approached us. "It's not safe yet!"

"Dad, what did you see?" I pressed, fear for him igniting my courage.

"There's something more," he said, his voice low and urgent. "We have to leave—now!"

The intensity of his tone sent a chill down my spine, and Jenna gasped, exchanging worried glances with Jason. "What do you mean?" I asked, urgency creeping into my voice.

"There are things we didn't know... things I didn't want to believe," he said, his eyes darting back toward the building, the fire casting flickering shadows on his face. "I think it was sabotage."

"What?" Jenna exclaimed, disbelief flooding her features. "But who would do something like this?"

"I don't know, but we have to get out of here," he insisted, the weight of his words settling like lead in my stomach.

Before I could respond, the sound of shattering glass pierced the night. My heart raced as I turned to see one of the windows explode outward, sending shards flying into the air like deadly confetti. The fire blazed brighter, roaring hungrily, and I instinctively moved closer to Jason, feeling the heat radiate against my skin.

"Get back!" a firefighter shouted, urging everyone to move further away.

The chaos surged as people scrambled, fear igniting a primal instinct to flee. I clutched Jason's hand tighter, my heart pounding in time with the frenzy around us. "What are we going to do?" I asked, panic rising in my throat.

"We need to regroup," Jenna said, pulling us closer. "If there's sabotage, we need to figure out who's behind it."

"Right," I replied, my mind racing. "But how? We can't trust anyone right now."

Before Jenna could respond, another firefighter emerged from the building, his face pale, urgency radiating from his every move. "We need everyone to evacuate the area!" he shouted, voice booming over the chaos. "We've lost control of the situation!"

Panic shot through me like a bolt of lightning. "Dad!" I cried out, my voice drowned in the frenzy.

He turned, face grim. "We need to go—now! We're not safe here!"

But as we turned to run, a low rumble reverberated through the ground, and a menacing crack split the air. The building, already weakened by the fire, seemed to shift ominously. I looked back, dread seeping into my bones as I saw the roof sag under the weight of flames and debris.

"Run!" I yelled, pulling Jason and Jenna with me as we sprinted away from the chaos. The world blurred around us, a whirlwind of smoke and fear, but a voice in my head screamed that it was not over yet.

The last thing I saw before we reached safety was the fire flaring up, and a shadow moving in the flames—something darker than the smoke, something that didn't belong.

And then, without warning, a loud crash echoed behind us, and I felt the ground tremble beneath my feet. My heart raced as I turned back, but all I could see was the glowing silhouette of the building, a stark reminder of everything we had lost.

In that moment, the weight of dread settled over me, cold and relentless. Because as we stumbled to safety, I couldn't shake the feeling that the true danger was just beginning.

Chapter 9: A Race Against Time

Panic surged through me as I raced toward the distillery, my heart pounding in my chest. The sweet, earthy aroma of fermenting grains mixed oddly with the acrid smell of smoke, twisting my stomach into knots. Each footfall seemed to reverberate in my skull, drowning out the chaos around me. The sun had dipped low, casting a sinister glow on the flames that leapt from the building like angry serpents, devouring everything in their path. Firefighters, clad in heavy gear, shouted orders, their voices a frenzied symphony over the roar of the fire.

"Jason!" I shouted, desperation clawing at my throat. The sound echoed in the night, swallowed quickly by the inferno that engulfed the old brick structure, a family legacy smoldering within its charred bones. I barely registered the crowd gathered behind the police barricades, faces turned toward the flames, a mix of horror and curiosity etched on their features. Their eyes reflected my own panic, but I couldn't stop. I couldn't wait. I had to find him.

The heat washed over me in waves as I pushed past the barriers, ignoring the shouts of officers trying to restrain the curious onlookers. I could see Jason, silhouetted against the fiery glow, his figure flickering in and out of focus. My heart twisted in my chest at the thought of him, my rival, my childhood friend, and the man who had filled my dreams with what-ifs. "Jason!" My voice cracked, a sharp contrast to the crackling flames.

His gaze snapped toward me, and for a moment, I saw everything—the confusion, the fear, the fierce determination that had always characterized him. It made my heart clench, the memory of our shared laughter and our countless arguments flooding my mind. But there was no time for nostalgia. The flames danced hungrily, creeping closer to the entrance where he stood.

"Get out! It's not safe!" I shouted, a fresh wave of fear overtaking me as I watched him hesitate. The man I knew was strong and stubborn, but this time, he needed to listen. I could see the intensity in his eyes, the stubborn pride that had always driven him to protect his family's legacy at all costs. But what was a legacy without the living, breathing people who cherished it?

He shook his head, the determination only deepening the furrow in his brow. "I can't! My grandfather's journals are in there, and if I don't save them—"

"Forget the journals! We can't lose you too!" I shouted, my heart racing faster than my feet could carry me. My words hung in the air, heavy and raw, the weight of them pressing down on both of us. I saw the flicker of uncertainty in his eyes, a crack in his resolve that I clung to like a lifeline. He took a step back, his muscles taut, and in that moment, I knew I had to reach him before he made a choice that could endanger us both.

Without thinking, I lunged forward, fueled by a mix of adrenaline and fear. The heat intensified, the smoke swirling around me, stinging my eyes and coating my throat with a bitter taste. I could feel the heat of the flames behind me, a wild animal ready to pounce. "Jason!" I called again, pushing through the haze of smoke, each breath a battle against the rising panic.

He met me halfway, his eyes wide and unyielding. "You shouldn't be here! This is too dangerous!" he shouted, his voice barely rising above the crackle of the fire. I could see the way his jaw clenched, the way his hands trembled with the weight of his choice.

"I won't let you do this alone!" I took a breath, steadying myself against the heat that pressed in, wrapping around us like a sinister embrace. "We'll figure it out together, but you have to trust me."

His gaze flickered, uncertainty warring with the determination etched into his features. For a split second, the world faded around us—the chaos, the flames, the sirens wailing in the distance. It was just us, two lost souls amidst the raging storm, tethered together by something deeper than rivalry or pride. "I can't just walk away," he finally said, his voice thick with frustration.

"Then let's do this together!" I took a step closer, the flames licking at the edges of my resolve. "But we have to go now!" My heart raced, not just from fear but from the electrifying thrill of standing beside him again, of being united in this frantic moment. A flicker of hesitation crossed his face, but then, with a deep breath, he nodded, and we turned together, moving toward the door.

The air thickened with smoke, but I didn't let go of his hand, our fingers intertwining as we rushed toward the entrance. The heat was unbearable, but the weight of his presence beside me fueled my determination. With each step, I felt a flicker of hope mingling with the fear, igniting a fire within me that outshone the chaos around us. "Just a little further!" I urged, my voice steady even as the world threatened to crumble.

The moment we crossed the threshold, the heat intensified. I could feel the world narrowing, the flames closing in on us, but Jason's hand in mine anchored me. I glanced back to see the flames licking at the doorframe, an ominous reminder of what we were up against. "Keep moving!" I urged, my voice carrying the weight of my promise.

As we stumbled through the smoke and confusion, I couldn't shake the feeling that this was a turning point—not just for the distillery but for us. We were running not just from flames but toward a chance at redemption, a chance to redefine what we meant to each other. The stakes had never been higher, and in that moment, everything else faded away—the rivalry, the hurt, the past. All that mattered was saving him, and with that singular focus, I felt a sense of clarity amid the chaos.

"Hold on!" Jason shouted, and before I could process it, he pulled me to the side, ducking just as a beam crashed down where we had just been standing. The world seemed to tilt, the ground vibrating beneath us as we gasped for breath, the acrid smoke stinging our lungs. But he didn't let go, his grip unwavering as we navigated the chaos together.

In that moment, my heart pounded not just with fear but with a fierce determination to protect the man I had grown to love, flaws and all. We could rise from the ashes, stronger and more united, but first, we had to escape this fiery nightmare. And as we bolted toward the exit, the flames chasing us, I knew this was just the beginning of our fight—not just against the blaze, but against everything that had tried to keep us apart.

I barely noticed the firefighters scrambling around me, their shouts blending into a chaotic cacophony as I dashed into the fray. The heat radiated from the building like a living thing, a relentless beast that clawed at my skin and made every breath feel like a Herculean task. Jason's silhouette, framed against the inferno, filled my mind with a fierce urgency that surged through my veins like wildfire. How had it come to this? A night that should have been filled with celebration had transformed into a desperate race against time. The distillery had stood for generations, a sanctuary of memories, and now it was on the brink of destruction.

"Where is he?" I muttered to myself, my throat dry and my heart pounding like a drum. The doorway loomed ahead, an ominous portal into the inferno. I knew he wouldn't leave without a fight; the weight of family honor rested heavily on his shoulders. He had always been the one to shoulder the burden, to protect what mattered most, even when it put him in danger.

A rush of flames erupted from a window above, illuminating the night sky with an orange glow, and my resolve hardened. "I'm coming for you!" I shouted, more to rally my own courage than to call out to him. As I drew closer, the reality of the situation settled over me like a heavy shroud. The danger was palpable, yet the thought of him trapped inside ignited a fierce protective instinct within me.

I pushed through the smoky haze, dodging debris and shards of shattered wood that littered the ground like the aftermath of a battle. "Jason!" I called again, my voice straining against the roar of the flames. Suddenly, a figure stumbled out of the smoke, face streaked with soot, eyes wild and frantic. My heart leapt, but it wasn't Jason. It was one of the firefighters, and he looked worse for wear, his breathing labored.

"Get back!" he shouted, urgency rippling through his tone. "It's not safe!"

"Is Jason in there?" I pressed, unwilling to budge, my feet rooted in place. The fire seemed to swirl around us like a living thing, and I could feel the panic rising again.

He shook his head, frustration flaring in his eyes. "We're trying to get everyone out! You need to leave—now!"

"I can't!" My voice was sharper than I intended, fueled by an overwhelming mix of fear and determination. "He's in there!"

With a resigned sigh, the firefighter pointed toward the side entrance. "There's a chance he made it to the back. If you can get there before the fire spreads—"

"I will!" I didn't wait for him to finish. My instincts kicked in, propelling me toward the side of the building, my mind racing as I dodged more debris, the reality of my reckless behavior settling over me like a heavy blanket. Each step felt like a gamble, but there was no turning back. Jason needed me.

As I rounded the corner, the sound of the flames roared like a beast unleashed. I squinted against the heat, searching for any sign of him. The side of the distillery was marred by charred wood and melting metal, but as I took another step, I spotted a flicker of movement in the shadows. My heart soared, and I rushed forward, calling out his name.

"Jason!" I shouted, my voice cracking with urgency. But as I approached, my heart sank. It was him, but he was on the ground, coughing violently, his face pale and streaked with soot. Panic twisted in my chest as I dropped to his side. "Oh my God, Jason! Are you okay?"

He glanced up, and for a moment, the fierce pride in his eyes wavered. "I thought I could save—" he began, but the words choked in his throat as he broke into another fit of coughs.

"Don't talk," I urged, helping him to sit up, my hands trembling slightly as I brushed the dust and debris from his hair. "We need to get you out of here. Now."

He shook his head weakly, his brow furrowed. "But the distillery—my family—"

"Your family would rather have you alive," I insisted, my voice firm, cutting through the haze of smoke that hung in the air like an ominous cloud. "We can rebuild, but not if you're in there."

The intensity of the fire was a constant reminder that time was slipping away. I could feel the heat creeping closer, the urgency of the situation pressing down on us. "I'll carry you if I have to," I said, forcing a brave smile even as the weight of dread hung in the air.

He studied me, that familiar mix of vulnerability and strength in his gaze. Finally, with a resigned sigh, he nodded. "Okay. Just... help me up."

Together, we struggled to our feet, the heat bearing down on us like a relentless wave. I could feel the tremors in his body, the sheer exhaustion, but determination flared in his eyes, igniting a spark of hope within me. We could make it out of this, together.

As we staggered toward the entrance, the world around us morphed into chaos. The crackling flames roared hungrily, spitting embers that floated through the air like fireflies in a nightmarish dream. I pulled him closer, my heart pounding in sync with the thrum of adrenaline coursing through my veins. "Just a little further,"

I whispered, my voice steady even as my own panic threatened to bubble over.

Suddenly, an explosion rocked the ground beneath us, sending a shockwave of heat and debris flying in all directions. I threw myself over Jason, shielding him with my body, and the air erupted with a blinding light. The sound echoed in my ears, a deafening roar that drowned out the world.

When the smoke cleared, I raised my head, breathless, and pulled him up again. "We need to move!" I urged, panic setting in as I glanced back at the inferno now consuming the entrance, blocking our escape. My pulse raced. The exit was cut off, and the only way out was through the kitchen—the back door was our only chance.

"Follow me!" I shouted, my voice a sharp contrast to the chaos surrounding us. With renewed urgency, we staggered toward the kitchen door, the flames dancing ominously close behind us. The old distillery had a labyrinth of rooms, and I prayed we could find a way out in time.

The kitchen was filled with shadows and smoke, pots and pans scattered across the floor like forgotten memories. I spotted the back door and rushed toward it, pushing Jason ahead of me, but my heart sank when I saw the flames licking at the doorframe.

"It's too hot!" he gasped, panic flooding his eyes.

"There has to be another way," I muttered, scanning the room frantically. My mind raced as I recalled the layout of the distillery from countless visits over the years. The windows! If we could just get to the windows, maybe we could jump to safety.

"Over there!" I pointed, my heart racing as I led him through the haze, adrenaline fueling my every move. We pushed through the smoke, urgency propelling us forward, each breath a struggle as the heat threatened to swallow us whole.

The kitchen window was partially open, the screen torn away, and I could see the alleyway below, dark and inviting. "We can climb out here," I said, my heart racing. "It's our only chance!"

Jason grunted, taking a moment to catch his breath. "I'll go first. Just hold on—"

"No!" I grabbed his arm, my voice rising in urgency. "You need to follow me. I'm not leaving you behind."

His eyes softened, a flicker of gratitude mixed with disbelief. "You're insane."

"Maybe. But if we're going to die tonight, it won't be without trying," I replied, a wry smile on my lips despite the fear coiling in my stomach.

With a nod of determination, he stepped up beside me, our shoulders brushing against each other as we scrambled to the window. I lifted my leg, feeling the jagged edge of the frame dig into my thigh, and Jason followed, pushing against the heat of the flames that crackled behind us.

As we hoisted ourselves up, I felt a rush of exhilaration mixed with dread. The fire was relentless, a beast hungry for destruction, but together we would fight it. We had to. And as we prepared to leap into the unknown, I couldn't shake the feeling that this moment would forever change the course of our lives, no matter the outcome.

The moment I swung my leg over the jagged window frame, I felt an exhilarating rush of adrenaline coursing through me, a stark contrast to the oppressive heat licking at our heels. I glanced back at Jason, his expression a mix of determination and sheer disbelief, as if he couldn't quite wrap his mind around the fact that we were on the brink of escaping a raging inferno. "On three," I said, my voice steady despite the chaos swirling around us. "One... two... three!"

With a synchronized leap, we hurled ourselves through the open window, the world outside greeting us with a cool rush of night air that was both liberating and terrifying. I landed hard on the ground, the impact jarring my bones, but I rolled instinctively, turning to check on Jason. He followed closely behind, his feet barely hitting the ground before he stumbled, collapsing beside me, panting heavily as he struggled to catch his breath.

"Did we make it?" he gasped, glancing back at the now-collapsing structure. The flames illuminated his face in stark relief, casting shadows that danced across his features, but the sight of the distillery—once a symbol of family pride—now engulfed in fire and chaos filled me with an overwhelming dread.

"For now," I replied, my voice shaky as I surveyed the scene. Firefighters were working tirelessly, their figures moving like dark shadows against the blazing backdrop. But as I scanned the area, a cold wave of realization washed over me. The back alley was eerily quiet, the flames roaring behind us, but the world around us was strangely still, as if holding its breath.

"Is anyone else inside?" Jason's voice cut through my thoughts, a raw edge to it. I could see the flicker of concern in his eyes, and I felt the same knot of anxiety tightening in my chest.

"I don't know," I admitted, biting my lip as I thought of the others who might still be trapped inside. The distillery wasn't just a building; it was a home to many—workers, family friends, people who had poured their hearts into the legacy. "We should... we should tell someone," I stammered, the urgency palpable in the air.

But before we could move, a loud crack echoed through the night, a sound that sent a shiver down my spine. "Look!" Jason pointed, his face paling as a section of the roof collapsed inward, showering sparks into the air like a shower of angry fireflies. The reality hit me with brutal force: not everyone was safe. "We have to warn them!" he urged, scrambling to his feet.

"No! We can't go back!" I protested, grasping his arm as he took a step toward the inferno. "You just got out! You need to breathe, and we need to figure this out. There's nothing we can do from there!"

For a moment, we stood there, tension crackling between us like the flames licking at the building. I could feel the weight of his gaze, a mix of desperation and gratitude, and I knew he was battling his instinct to run back into the chaos. "What if someone else is trapped?" he countered, eyes wide with fear.

"Then we'll find a way to help them, but not like this," I said, determination infusing my voice as I took a deep breath. "Let the professionals do their job. We need to think clearly."

Jason clenched his jaw, torn between his instinct to save everyone and the harsh reality of our own narrow escape. "You're right," he conceded finally, though I could see the tension in his shoulders still taut, the weight of his family's legacy pressing down on him. "But I can't just stand here."

"Let's find someone—an officer, a firefighter," I suggested, scanning the area for help. My heart raced, both from the remnants of adrenaline coursing through my veins and the fear that clawed at my throat. Just then, a figure broke through the crowd, rushing toward us, and I felt a flicker of hope.

"Hey! You two!" It was a firefighter, his helmet reflecting the flames as he approached. "What are you doing out here? Are you hurt?"

"No, we just escaped from the back!" I explained quickly, gesturing toward the blaze behind us. "We think there might be others still inside."

He shook his head, his expression stern but concerned. "I'll relay the information. Stay put, alright?" He turned to leave, his radio crackling to life with frantic voices as he disappeared back into the chaos.

Jason's eyes were wide, still searching the darkened windows of the distillery as if hoping to see familiar faces. "What if they don't make it out?" he muttered, his voice barely above a whisper, filled with raw emotion.

"Then we'll keep fighting until they do," I replied firmly, putting a hand on his shoulder. "You're not alone in this. I won't let you go through this alone." The promise hung in the air, a fragile thread connecting us amid the turmoil.

Just then, a loud explosion shook the ground beneath us, and a cloud of smoke erupted from the building, sending debris flying. Jason instinctively stepped closer to me, wrapping an arm around my shoulder as we both staggered back, shielding ourselves from the sudden blast. My heart raced again, but this time, it wasn't just from fear; it was the thrill of knowing that I had someone to fight for, someone who was worth risking everything.

"What was that?" Jason yelled, his voice hoarse as he peered through the haze, his expression a mix of determination and dread.

"I don't know, but we need to get to safety!" I shouted back, my heart hammering in my chest as I grabbed his hand, pulling him away from the building. "Come on!"

We moved through the crowd, weaving past the onlookers who were captivated by the unfolding chaos, their faces a canvas of shock and disbelief. I could hear snippets of conversation—people speculating about what had happened, murmurs of lost memories and cherished moments, the air thick with a shared sense of loss.

Jason kept glancing back, anxiety etched on his face. "We can't just leave them!" he insisted, his grip tightening around my hand.

"Listen to me!" I stopped, turning to face him, my eyes locking onto his with an intensity that silenced the chaos around us. "You need to focus. If we want to help anyone inside, we have to stay safe ourselves first. We can't help them if we're caught in the fire, too."

He hesitated, the battle waging in his eyes. Then, with a defeated sigh, he nodded, his shoulders dropping slightly. "Alright, but we'll find a way back in," he promised, the fire in his eyes dimmed but not extinguished.

Just as we started to retreat, a piercing scream shattered the air, cutting through the noise like a knife. I froze, my heart plummeting as the sound of panic surged around us. Jason's face went pale. "What was that?" he asked, fear creeping into his voice.

I scanned the crowd, looking for the source of the distress, my heart racing. Then I saw her—a woman standing near the edge of the crowd, her face twisted in horror as she pointed back toward the building. "My daughter! She's still in there!"

Without thinking, Jason and I exchanged a glance that spoke volumes, a silent agreement passing between us. "We have to help her," he said, determination returning to his voice.

But before I could respond, the ground trembled again, another explosion shaking the air, and the sound of shattering glass echoed through the night. My stomach dropped as a bright flash of fire erupted from one of the windows, lighting up the night like a beacon of despair. The fire had taken a new turn, and the stakes had risen once more.

"Get back!" the firefighter shouted, waving people away as the flames spread dangerously. But Jason was already moving, breaking into a sprint toward the woman.

"Jason, wait!" I yelled, my heart pounding in my chest. "We can't—"

But he was already gone, racing back toward the inferno, his silhouette swallowed by the smoke. "I'm coming!" he shouted back at me, his voice echoing with urgency.

A wave of panic crashed over me. "No! Jason!" I screamed, but my words were lost in the chaos, my heart racing as I watched him disappear into the darkness. I could feel my own fear clawing at my throat, and the moment stretched endlessly as I stood there, torn between the desire to chase after him and the instinct to pull back, to stay safe.

The fire roared around us, consuming everything in its path, and I knew I had to act. With my heart pounding like a war drum, I took a deep breath and dashed forward, unwilling to let him face this alone. The flames flickered dangerously close, and as I approached the doorway, I could feel the heat wrapping around me, like the arms of a beast ready to devour.

"Jason!" I shouted again, desperation coloring my voice. "Where are you?"

As I stepped into the smoke-filled void, a deafening crash sounded behind me, and the building seemed to groan under the weight of its own destruction. I had to find him—before it was too late.

Chapter 10: Ashes and Rebirth

As I charged into the burning distillery, smoke enveloped me like a thick shroud, obscuring my vision and stinging my lungs. The chaos was overwhelming—firefighters shouted orders, and the crackling of flames drowned out everything else. I could barely see, but I knew Jason was somewhere inside, risking everything to save what remained of his family's legacy. A sudden explosion sent debris crashing to the ground, and I instinctively ducked. "Jason!" I screamed again, my voice hoarse and desperate. Each passing moment felt like an eternity, my heart racing as I fought against the flames, driven by a single thought: I wouldn't leave without him.

I stumbled through the doorway, the heat radiating against my skin like a furious sun. The air was thick, clinging to me like a wet blanket, and the acrid scent of burning wood and charred metal clawed at my throat. I pressed forward, squinting through the haze, every instinct screaming for me to turn back, but the image of Jason, his dark hair tousled and his blue eyes fierce with determination, anchored me to my purpose. I could see the outline of the massive copper stills, their once-shining surfaces now dulled and blackened, a monument to the devastation that surrounded me.

"Jason!" I shouted again, the word slipping from my lips like a prayer. The roar of the fire swallowed my voice, leaving me feeling small and insignificant against the inferno. I forced my way deeper into the building, each step a battle against the rising heat. A beam above me creaked ominously, and I cursed under my breath, casting quick glances upward. I had always admired Jason's bravery, but now, it bordered on reckless. He wouldn't leave the distillery without trying to save something, and that something could very well be his life.

Suddenly, a silhouette emerged from the billowing smoke, and I felt my heart leap. "Jason!" I called, rushing toward the figure, but the smoke thickened, blurring my vision again. As I got closer, my stomach twisted in a knot. The person was too tall, too broad to be him. Panic shot through me, and I nearly stumbled backward when I realized it was a firefighter. He raised a hand to stop me, his face masked in soot and panic, his eyes wide with urgency.

"Get back!" he barked, his voice booming above the chaos. "This place is going to collapse!"

"No!" I pushed past him, shaking my head in disbelief. "I'm looking for Jason! He's in here!" The firefighter hesitated, glancing back toward the flames before fixing his gaze on me. I could see the conflict in his eyes; he knew I was putting myself at risk, but I didn't care. Jason was in here, and I had to find him.

With a quick nod, the firefighter gestured toward a narrow corridor on the left. "He might have gone that way! Just—" His warning was swallowed by a deafening roar as another explosion rocked the building, sending a shockwave through the air. I grabbed the wall for support, feeling the tremors echo through my bones.

Ignoring the instincts that screamed for me to turn back, I sprinted down the corridor, the flames licking at my heels. The heat intensified, and I felt it clawing at my clothes, a searing reminder of the danger that lurked just behind me. "Jason!" I called again, desperation fueling my voice. "Please, where are you?"

As I rounded a corner, I was met with an eerie silence, the fire suddenly muffled, as if it had receded for a moment, allowing me a breath of relief. I stepped cautiously into the room, my eyes scanning the darkness. A glimmer of light caught my attention, and I rushed toward it. The sight that met my eyes was both a relief and a new wave of terror.

Jason lay on the ground, surrounded by debris, his face smeared with ash and blood. "Jason!" I cried, kneeling beside him, my heart racing with fear. He groaned, struggling to sit up, and I rushed to support him, feeling the heat radiating from his body.

"Gwen," he murmured, his voice weak but filled with a familiar warmth that sent a wave of hope coursing through me. "What are you doing here? It's not safe."

"Neither is it for you," I shot back, my voice cracking as I took in the sight of him—his shirt torn, and the skin on his arm raw and blistered. "You need to get out! We need to get out!" I felt a surge of anger at his stubbornness, the kind that often drove me crazy but also made me love him more than I thought possible.

"I can't leave," he said, his voice hoarse, but there was a fire in his eyes. "I have to save the barrels—the whiskey... it's all we have left." His determination was admirable, but I could feel my heart sinking. This wasn't just about whiskey; it was about his family, his legacy, and the weight of that burden was too much for anyone to bear alone.

"Forget the whiskey, Jason! Your life is worth more than this place!" I pleaded, my hands gripping his shoulders. I could see the gears turning in his mind, the conflict of duty and survival playing out in the depths of his gaze.

"I can't," he whispered, and for a moment, I saw the flicker of defeat behind his bravado. "I won't let it all go up in flames without a fight."

A crashing sound echoed from outside, followed by shouts and the frantic blaring of sirens. Time was running out. I scanned the room, desperate for a way to help him see that this was not a battle he had to fight alone. I reached for his hand, intertwining my fingers with his, grounding us both in that moment. "We can figure this out together. But first, we have to get out of here."

He hesitated, looking around the room as if trying to weigh the value of the barrels against our lives. I could see the wheels turning in his mind, the tug-of-war between responsibility and survival, and I knew this was the moment. The moment that would define not just our fate but also the kind of man he would choose to be.

"Together," he finally agreed, his voice gaining strength. I could see him pushing past the fear, the weight of the flames closing in. With a determined nod, we hoisted him up, his arm slung around my shoulder as I steadied him. The fire roared behind us, but ahead lay a chance at rebirth—a chance to rise from the ashes, to emerge stronger together.

The world outside the distillery was a swirling mass of chaos, but in that moment, it all faded into the background. The crackling heat of the flames was a beast behind us, chasing us with every footstep. Jason's weight leaned heavily against me, but I pushed onward, dragging him toward the exit, where the cool night air beckoned like a siren. I could feel his breath against my cheek, labored and uneven, a stark reminder of the toll this was taking on him.

"I should've grabbed more barrels," he gasped, his voice strained but laced with that stubborn determination I had come to know so well. "The distillery needs those—"

"No," I interrupted, my tone sharper than intended. "It needs you alive first. You can't save the whiskey if you're a charred memory!" My heart raced as I propelled us forward, dodging falling debris and smoldering remnants of the distillery's once-thriving spirit.

A flash of light surged behind us as a window shattered, sending shards of glass scattering like tiny diamonds across the darkened floor. I yanked Jason closer, my pulse racing with every crunching step. The heat was relentless, a suffocating blanket that wrapped around us, and the smoke, thick and black, clung to my skin, soaking into my clothes like a desperate lover. I felt like I was drowning, yet the urgency of our escape fueled me, igniting a fire of its own within.

"Gwen," Jason rasped, and I felt him falter beside me. I turned, meeting his gaze, which flickered with that fierce blue fire I adored. "We need to—"

"No we don't!" I retorted, my voice firmer than I felt. "We need to get out. Now!" I wrapped my arm around his waist, urging him forward once more. There was a determination in his eyes that I couldn't ignore, the kind that hinted at the depths of his loyalty to his family. "You can rebuild, Jason. That legacy can still live on. But not if you're a pile of ashes."

He swallowed hard, and I could see the gears in his mind shifting, the tug-of-war between duty and survival playing out in his expression. I was grateful for the moments of silence that filled the space between us, the tension palpable as we made our way to safety, but I could feel him resisting. "What if we could save just one barrel? One—"

"We can save a million barrels later," I insisted, almost shouting over the growing roar of the flames. "If we get out of here first. Right now, that's all that matters."

With every step, I felt the fire behind us clawing its way forward, greedy and unrelenting. I finally spotted a glimmer of light ahead—a beacon of hope flickering through the haze. "Look! The exit!" I pushed Jason toward the sliver of freedom, my heart swelling at the prospect of escape.

As we stumbled into the open air, a rush of cool night breezes met us, cutting through the heat and smoke like a knife. I felt alive again, each breath of fresh air igniting my senses. I glanced over my shoulder, half expecting to see the distillery erupt in flames, a fiery phoenix rising from its own ashes. But my gaze quickly shifted back to Jason, who leaned heavily against me, his eyes closed, but his spirit still flickering like the embers behind us.

"Are you okay?" I asked, worry threading through my voice. He nodded, though it was a small, weak motion. I reached up, brushing a stray piece of hair from his forehead, feeling the heat radiate from his skin.

"I will be, just...give me a second." He took a deep breath, drawing in the fresh air like a lifeline. I could see his muscles twitching with adrenaline, and for a moment, the chaos melted away, leaving just the two of us beneath the canopy of stars, glowing brightly against the night sky.

"Come on, we need to get you checked out," I urged, glancing around to locate any emergency personnel. A few yards away, firefighters were organizing hoses, their voices mingling with the distant wail of sirens.

Before we could take a step, a figure rushed toward us, drenched in the glow of flashing lights. It was one of the firefighters, his uniform sooty but his demeanor all business. "You two! You need to get away from the building!" he barked, eyes scanning us for injuries.

"He needs help," I said, urgency spilling from my lips. "He inhaled smoke, and I think he's burned."

The firefighter nodded sharply, signaling for a medic as he moved closer to assess Jason. "Let's get you checked out, buddy. Can you stand?"

Jason pushed himself upright, though I could see the effort it took him. "Yeah, I—" He grimaced, swaying slightly. "I just need a moment."

I shot him a look, one that combined equal parts concern and annoyance. "You've had enough moments for a lifetime, Jason. Let them help."

He managed a weak grin, that signature charm of his lighting up the darkness. "I didn't think you cared so much."

"Oh, I care. Trust me." I crossed my arms, adopting a faux-serious expression that didn't quite mask the worry lurking in my chest. "You know how I get when my whiskey-making boyfriend acts like a hero without telling me?"

A muffled chuckle escaped him, easing the tension just a little. "You mean, like a recklessly stubborn hero?"

"Exactly," I replied, exasperated yet relieved to see a hint of his spirit returning. "If you weren't already mine, I'd have to wrestle someone for you."

"Yeah? Who would that be?" His voice was stronger now, teasing even as the medic arrived, ready to evaluate him.

"I dunno. Someone who makes bad choices," I said, casting a glance at the distillery, now a raging inferno. "Or someone who runs into burning buildings without thinking twice."

The medic interrupted, her voice soothing yet authoritative. "Okay, let's take a look at you, Jason. Can you walk to the ambulance?"

With a bit of a push, he straightened up, a bit of his bravado returning. "I guess I'll have to since my superhero partner won't let me stay here and risk more explosions."

"Exactly," I said, matching his tone. "Now go on. Your army awaits."

As he started to move, I felt a swell of pride mingling with fear, watching him as he leaned on the medic for support. This was just one battle won, but I knew the war ahead would be even more challenging. A sense of purpose filled the air around us, and despite the ashes falling like dark snow from the sky, I felt a strange sense of hope emerge from the wreckage. Together, we would rebuild—not just the distillery, but everything that had been forged in its flames.

I watched as Jason leaned on the medic, his face pale but determined, the shadows of the burning distillery dancing behind him like angry ghosts. The air was thick with smoke and the bitter scent of charred wood, but all I could focus on was the way his lips curved into a small, defiant smile despite the chaos surrounding us.

"Who knew my biggest obstacle today would be my girlfriend, the self-appointed fire marshal?" he teased, his voice still hoarse but gaining strength.

"Consider it my special talent," I shot back, half-heartedly rolling my eyes. "Maybe we should add it to my résumé."

"Firefighter slash superhero?" He grinned, but his eyes flickered toward the inferno behind us, a veil of worry crossing his features. "Just wait until I get better, then I'll show you how a real hero operates."

Before I could retort, the medic, a sharp-eyed woman with an air of authority, began examining his burns. "We need to get you checked out, Jason," she said, her tone leaving no room for argument. "You inhaled too much smoke, and those burns need treatment."

As they moved toward the waiting ambulance, I lingered for a moment, the weight of the distillery pressing down on me. The flames had begun to consume more than just wood and metal; they were eating away at memories, erasing the legacy that Jason had fought so hard to protect. I felt an unsettling knot tighten in my stomach, a blend of fear for his well-being and dread for what we were losing.

"Gwen, come on!" Jason called, his voice cutting through my thoughts. I turned to see him half-turned in the medic's grip, the smile on his face a bright contrast to the disaster looming behind him. I joined them, my heart pounding, the weight of my own fears momentarily forgotten in the warmth of his spirit.

Once inside the ambulance, the medic wasted no time. She turned to me, her eyes sharp and assessing. "You should have someone check you too, miss. Smoke inhalation can be sneaky."

"I'm fine," I insisted, though the smoky taste still lingered in my mouth and the heat of the flames was imprinted in my memory. My focus was on Jason, who sat on the edge of the gurney, watching the medic work on his arm with a mix of irritation and humor.

"Not everything is about you, you know," I added, attempting a light tone to mask the worry creeping back in.

"Of course, it's not," he replied, mock-serious. "Some of it's about my newfound fame as a distillery disaster survivor."

"You're lucky your sense of humor survived too," I shot back, unable to suppress a smile. But inside, I felt a storm brewing. His burns were serious, and the reality of what had just happened was beginning to settle over me like a weight.

The medic wrapped Jason's arm, her hands efficient and practiced. "You'll need to keep this bandaged and avoid any strenuous activities for a while," she instructed. "And for the love of all things holy, don't try to save any more barrels, okay?"

Jason winced slightly but nodded. "No more barrels. I promise."

Just then, a commotion outside the ambulance caught my attention. Voices rose, and I could hear the urgency in them. I glanced toward the open doors, and my heart sank as I saw firefighters rushing toward the remains of the distillery.

"What's happening?" I asked, my voice barely above a whisper.

The medic, catching the shift in the atmosphere, paused and turned to follow my gaze. "There's been a collapse," she said, concern knitting her brow. "They're trying to rescue anyone still inside."

Panic gripped my chest like a vice. "Jason!" I turned to him, my heart racing. "What if someone else is still in there? What if they need help?"

"I don't know, Gwen," he said, his expression shifting to one of dread as he realized the gravity of the situation. "But we can't go back in there. It's too dangerous."

My instincts screamed at me to act, to do something, but a sense of helplessness washed over me. I glanced around the ambulance, spotting the medical supplies and the frantic activity outside. "We can't just sit here," I said, my voice rising in desperation. "We need to help them!"

Before Jason could respond, the medic's voice broke through, firm yet compassionate. "Your job right now is to heal, both of you. Let the professionals handle the rescue."

But I couldn't shake the feeling that something was wrong. There was a flicker in my mind, a voice whispering that perhaps someone I knew was still inside that burning shell. Someone who had been in that very building, laughing and pouring whiskey just hours before the fire consumed it.

"I need to know," I said suddenly, urgency tightening my throat. "I can't just sit here knowing that someone might be trapped."

Jason's gaze softened, but I could see the frustration brewing beneath. "Gwen, you're not thinking straight. You just ran into a burning building! You need to take care of yourself."

"I can't," I insisted, shaking my head vehemently. "Not when there might be someone in there!"

The medic exchanged a glance with Jason, her expression unreadable. "Fine. But we'll need to get you both evaluated afterward."

"Deal," I said, already swinging my legs over the edge of the gurney. I felt a surge of adrenaline, the need to act propelling me forward.

As I jumped down, the cold night air hit me, and I turned toward the chaotic scene unfolding before us. Firefighters were darting around, their silhouettes illuminated by the dancing flames. My heart pounded as I scanned the area, searching for familiar faces.

"Gwen, wait!" Jason called, but I was already moving. I dodged past the medics and emergency personnel, my focus narrowed on the smoldering wreckage that had once held laughter, warmth, and a piece of Jason's heart.

I could hear the muffled calls of the firefighters and the distant sounds of machinery whirring as they worked to stabilize the structure. But in the midst of that chaos, one voice stood out—urgent and desperate.

"Help! Is anyone there?"

My heart dropped, and I sprinted toward the sound, each step heavy with determination and fear. I could see shadows moving amid the smoke, figures huddled against the debris. "I'm here!" I shouted, my voice rising above the din. "I'm coming!"

"Stay back!" a firefighter yelled, but I pushed forward, fear transforming into resolve. "I can help!"

As I reached the perimeter of the wreckage, I spotted a familiar face among the smoke—Maggie, Jason's childhood friend and one of the distillery's best bartenders, crouched near a fallen beam. She was struggling to pull herself free, her eyes wide with panic.

"Maggie!" I called, rushing toward her. "Hold on! I'll get you out!"

"Gwen, no!" Jason's voice was a sharp edge behind me, but I couldn't stop. I knelt beside Maggie, assessing the situation.

"Stay still, okay?" I instructed, trying to keep my voice steady despite the chaos swirling around us. "We'll figure this out."

But as I reached to help her, a low rumble echoed through the ground, a warning that sent a jolt of dread through me. My heart raced as I glanced back at the distillery, where flames licked the sky, painting the darkness with fiery hues.

Then, without warning, the structure creaked ominously, and I froze. "Maggie, we need to move—"

Before I could finish my sentence, the ground shook violently, and I looked up just in time to see the roof of the distillery begin to cave in. Time slowed, my breath catching in my throat as debris rained down, and everything inside me screamed to run.

"Maggie!" I shouted, reaching out as the world fell apart around us.

But the last thing I saw before darkness consumed us was the look of fear in her eyes and the flames closing in, determined to take everything from us.

Chapter 11: A Fragile Alliance

The distillery stood like a wounded beast, its once vibrant façade now marred by ash and despair. Wooden beams sagged under the weight of charred memories, and the air was thick with the smell of smoke that lingered like an unwanted guest. As I stepped inside, the ghosts of laughter and clinking glasses haunted the rafters, mingling with the acrid scent of burnt wood. I could almost hear the echo of Jason's laughter, bright and unyielding, even now. My heart squeezed at the thought of him, the boy whose courage had become a beacon in this tempest of chaos, yet whose vulnerability was laid bare for all to see.

"Is it too late to call the fire department?" I muttered, forcing a weak smile as I nudged the front door open, still coated in soot from the rescue. The door creaked like a rusty hinge, protesting the intrusion as I stepped into the shattered world we once knew. "Or maybe a miracle worker?"

Jason was there, surveying the wreckage with a mix of determination and resignation. His dark hair, usually tousled with an effortless charm, lay flat against his forehead, damp from the sweat of exertion. He looked up, his blue eyes sparkling with a blend of resolve and vulnerability that made my breath hitch.

"At least we know the distillery can withstand a little fire," he quipped, a lopsided grin breaking through the grime. "This place is tougher than it looks."

"Sure, if only we could say the same about the barrels," I shot back, my voice tinged with playful sarcasm. "You'd think the whiskey would've protected itself a bit better."

He laughed, a sound that felt like sunlight breaking through the clouds. It was a reminder of why I had thrown myself into the flames to save him—because even in the face of despair, Jason had a way of pulling joy from the ashes. But that joy felt complicated now, knotted in the tension between our families.

"We need to get to work," he said, sobering quickly as he rubbed the back of his neck, a nervous habit I had come to recognize. "We can set up a fundraiser, something that brings the community together. We can turn this disaster into something hopeful."

I nodded, suddenly feeling the weight of responsibility settle upon my shoulders. It wasn't just the distillery we had to mend; it was the rift between our families that had festered for too long. My father's disapproving gaze lingered in the back of my mind, a constant reminder of the expectations I felt suffocating me.

"Right," I replied, my voice steadier than I felt. "How do you want to start?"

Jason's expression shifted, the intensity of his focus pinning me in place. "Let's brainstorm ideas. We could host a barbecue, something simple but fun. People love food, and whiskey. They'll come."

"A whiskey-tasting barbecue?" I raised an eyebrow, a grin creeping onto my face. "Now that sounds like a recipe for disaster."

"Or a recipe for a fantastic night," he countered, his smile infectious. "Imagine the stories that will come out of it. A few laughs, some good food, and we can help get this place back on its feet."

"Okay, I'm in. But you have to handle the grilling. I don't want to be responsible for anyone's stomach problems."

"You wound me," he feigned offense, clutching his heart dramatically. "I'll have you know I make a mean rib."

We settled into a rhythm, the conversation flowing effortlessly as we tossed around ideas like confetti. But beneath the camaraderie lay an undercurrent of tension, the unspoken truths lingering between us. Every time our hands brushed together as we flipped through pamphlets or reached for pens, a spark ignited, making it hard to concentrate on anything other than the heat pooling in my cheeks.

The afternoon wore on, and with it came the weight of the work ahead. The sun hung low in the sky, casting a warm, golden glow over the ruins of the distillery, transforming the brokenness into something beautiful, if only for a moment. I watched as Jason moved about, directing the few community volunteers who had shown up to help. His presence was magnetic, and the way he engaged with everyone—a quip here, a laugh there—made me marvel at his effortless ability to connect.

"Hey," I said, stepping up beside him as he surveyed the scene. "You have a gift for bringing people together."

He shrugged, a humble gesture that contradicted the spark in his eyes. "I just believe that everyone has a part to play. We all need to help each other out."

"Even when it's tough?"

"Especially then." His gaze locked onto mine, and in that moment, the weight of our families' animosity faded, replaced by a fragile alliance forged in the fires of shared purpose.

Just then, a voice broke through the tension like a storm cloud. "What are you two whispering about over here?" My brother, Adam, strolled into the distillery, hands tucked into his pockets, his brow furrowed with suspicion.

"Just planning how to save the world, one barbecue at a time," I replied, a wry smile dancing on my lips.

Adam shot Jason a wary glance, and I felt a pang of frustration. I was tired of the way our families hovered over us like shadows, always ready to pounce at the slightest hint of connection.

"Well, good luck with that," Adam said, his tone flat as he turned to survey the damage. "You know Dad's not going to like this, right?"

"Can't keep the world from turning just because our parents don't see eye to eye," I shot back, feeling the weight of my convictions rise to the surface.

Jason placed a hand on my arm, a gentle reminder that we were in this together. "We can prove them wrong," he said quietly, his voice laced with determination.

Adam's gaze flickered between us, suspicion still hanging in the air. "Just be careful," he warned, his expression softening slightly. "This could blow up in your faces."

"Or it could bring everyone together," Jason countered, the fire in his eyes reigniting.

As Adam walked away, I couldn't shake the feeling that the fragile alliance we were trying to build was hanging by a thread. The tension between our families was a tempest waiting to unleash itself, but standing beside Jason, I felt a flicker of hope. Together, we could transform the destruction into something beautiful—a chance to heal not just the distillery but the wounds that had festered for too long. The night stretched out before us, filled with possibility, and I could almost taste the sweetness of a new beginning.

The day of the fundraiser dawned with a promise of warmth, the kind that whispered of summer yet lingered on the cusp of fall. I stood at the edge of the distillery's yard, my heart fluttering like a hummingbird trapped in a glass jar. Long tables draped in white cloth stretched across the grass, adorned with flickering lanterns that swayed gently in the breeze. The smell of smoked meats wafted from the grill, mingling with the sweet aroma of baking pies—a feast that would have made any heart swell with joy, yet anxiety knotted my stomach.

As the sun climbed higher, casting a golden hue over the event, the first wave of guests arrived. I felt like a reluctant actress in a play where the lines had been hastily scribbled. There were familiar faces—friends from high school, neighbors who had stopped by to offer their support, and even a few townsfolk I hadn't seen in years. But my gaze kept drifting toward Jason, who was busy chatting with a group of volunteers, his laughter carrying across the yard like music.

"Look at him," I whispered to my brother Adam, who stood beside me, arms crossed, surveying the crowd with his usual skepticism. "He's practically glowing."

"Or is that just the smoke from the grill?" Adam replied, smirking, his tone teasing yet protective. "You sure you want to get mixed up with him? I mean, have you seen how fast he runs toward danger?"

"Only to save me," I shot back, the heat rising in my cheeks. "It's not like I'm the only one putting my heart on the line here."

"Yeah, well, remember what Dad said. That boy's got a reputation. And not the good kind."

I rolled my eyes, watching as Jason tossed a piece of meat onto the grill, the sizzle echoing like laughter through the air. "Maybe it's time we let him be more than just a 'boy from the wrong side of the tracks,'" I retorted, wishing I could shake off the weight of my family's judgment like dust from an old book.

Adam raised an eyebrow but didn't reply, instead taking a deep breath and finally uncrossing his arms. The tension between us eased just a bit, and I felt a flicker of hope that perhaps he could come around.

As more guests arrived, the atmosphere shifted into something electric, laughter bubbling up like the fizzy drinks we had set out. I floated through the crowd, greeting familiar faces and giving my best effort to keep the mood light. Yet, beneath the surface, a current of apprehension pulsed—an awareness that our families were watching, judging, waiting for something to go wrong.

"Sarah! Over here!" Jason called, and I turned to see him waving me over. The way he said my name sent a thrill through me, as though it were a secret shared just between us.

I approached, finding him surrounded by a small group who were already pouring whiskey samples into small cups. "You have to try this," he said, his eyes sparkling with mischief. "It's our special reserve. I think it could put some hair on your chest."

"Funny," I quipped, rolling my eyes. "I've got enough hair, thanks."

"Not yet," he replied, smirking, a glint of challenge in his expression. "But after this? You might."

I accepted a cup, swirling the amber liquid before taking a cautious sip. The warmth spread through me, igniting a fire of courage I hadn't known I needed. I glanced around, watching as others joined in, laughing and chatting, a few even dancing to the music drifting from the makeshift speakers.

"This is amazing," I said, nodding toward the crowd. "I can't believe how many people showed up."

"Of course they did. This place means something to everyone," Jason replied, his voice growing serious. "And with everything that happened, it's like they needed a reason to come together again. To heal."

His gaze held mine for a moment longer than necessary, and I felt a connection building, woven from shared moments and unspoken understanding. But as quickly as it came, the spell was broken when my father appeared, his expression grim as he surveyed the scene like a hawk scanning for prey.

"Sarah," he said, his voice low and firm, "we need to talk."

I excused myself from Jason's side, my heart sinking. "Sure, Dad. What's up?"

He led me a few steps away, his posture rigid, arms crossed tightly over his chest. "You need to be careful with that boy. I don't want you getting too involved. He's trouble."

"Trouble?" I echoed, my voice rising in disbelief. "He just saved the distillery. He's trying to bring our community together."

"Or he's trying to play you," my father countered, the edge of concern cutting through his tone. "You know how these things go.

He'll charm you, and before you know it, you'll be caught in something you can't escape."

"Or maybe you're the one who needs to let go of the past," I shot back, anger flaring. "You see a kid who made mistakes, but I see someone who's willing to fight for what matters."

He shook his head, frustration etched on his features. "You think you know him? You barely know him. This isn't just about you, Sarah. It's about our family."

I took a deep breath, feeling the weight of his words pressing down on me. "And what about my happiness? Does that not matter?"

"Of course it does," he replied, softening slightly, yet still guarded. "But you have to think about the consequences. This could affect everything."

"Or it could be the best thing that ever happened to us," I retorted, the passion behind my words surprising even me.

As we stood there, a silence fell between us, thick and suffocating, the sounds of the fundraiser fading into the background. The laughter and chatter felt like a world away, and I realized that the tension was not just between my father and me—it was woven into the very fabric of our families, threatening to unravel the delicate strands of trust we were trying to forge.

Just then, Jason's laughter broke through the silence, a buoyant note that pulled my attention back to the crowd. I could see him, animated and full of life, the very embodiment of hope. In that moment, I made a choice—a decision that sent a rush of adrenaline coursing through me. I would fight for what I believed in, for the connections that mattered, no matter how fragile they were.

I turned back to my father, my heart steady. "I'm going to help him. I believe in this, Dad. In him. Whether you see it or not."

His expression softened slightly, but the concern remained. "Just be careful. I don't want to see you hurt."

"I'll be fine," I promised, the conviction in my voice echoing through the air. As I stepped away, leaving behind the weight of his gaze, I felt lighter, almost unburdened. The crowd called to me, their laughter wrapping around me like a warm embrace, inviting me back into the fray.

Jason caught my eye as I approached, his smile breaking through the haze of tension. "Everything okay?" he asked, the genuine concern etched into his features.

"Yeah," I said, my heart racing as I stood beside him, the distance between us charged with something unspoken yet palpable. "Just family drama. You know how it is."

"Family can be complicated," he said, raising his cup in a mock toast. "To families and their quirks, then."

"To families and their quirks," I echoed, clinking my cup against his. As I took a sip, the warmth of the whiskey surged through me, igniting a fire of hope. It was time to embrace the chaos, to lean into the unexpected, and to forge this fragile alliance that felt so right in the depths of my heart.

The sun dipped low in the sky, casting an amber glow that danced across the yard, illuminating the faces of friends and neighbors gathered for the fundraiser. The mood was buoyant, laughter spilling into the air like the bubbles from the drinks we served. As the smell of grilled meats mingled with the sweet aroma of pies, I found solace in the moment, even if the echoes of my father's warning still lingered in my mind.

"Are you ready for this?" Jason asked, a playful glint in his eyes as he adjusted the collar of his shirt, a rare departure from his usual laid-back attire. "Because I'm about to unleash my secret weapon."

"Your secret weapon? Please tell me it's not your dance moves," I teased, elbowing him lightly. "I've heard they're a hazard to the innocent."

He feigned shock, his expression a perfect blend of offense and amusement. "You wound me, Sarah. I'll have you know my moves are legendary. They've been known to cause spontaneous bouts of joy."

"Or a quick exit from the dance floor," I retorted, laughing at the image of him attempting to twirl an unsuspecting guest. But the laughter faded as I caught sight of my father across the yard, his arms crossed, his brow furrowed in disapproval. I could feel his gaze boring into me, like a spotlight highlighting every decision I made.

"Just remember, if this goes south, I'll be the one doing the footwork to cover your retreat," Jason said, his tone shifting slightly, a hint of seriousness creeping in.

I appreciated his attempt at levity, yet I couldn't shake the feeling that I was standing on a tightrope, balancing precariously between family loyalty and the pull of something deeper with him. "You know, I'm not one for running away. I'd rather face whatever comes head-on, preferably while dodging my father's critiques."

"Now that's the spirit!" he exclaimed, grinning. "Just remember: if I'm the one being chased, I'll expect you to throw a few well-placed distractions my way."

"I'll have a pie ready as my weapon of choice," I said with a wink.

The evening unfolded beautifully, with more people than I had anticipated showing up, united by a common goal and a shared love for the distillery. Jason and I worked side by side, pouring drinks and chatting with guests, laughter flowing like the whiskey itself. The sense of community wrapped around us like a warm blanket, making it easy to forget the tension that had shadowed our families.

As night settled in, string lights twinkled overhead, casting a magical glow that turned the yard into an enchanting space. The atmosphere was electric, charged with excitement and possibility. I was in the zone, mingling with friends when Jason pulled me aside, his expression serious yet playful.

"Alright, it's time for my secret weapon," he declared, his eyes sparkling with mischief. "I've arranged for a little entertainment. Brace yourself."

"What do you mean by entertainment?" I asked, feigning a gasp as I followed him to the center of the yard.

Before I could fully grasp what was happening, a local band set up on the makeshift stage, strumming familiar tunes that made people sway and sing along. Jason leaned closer, his voice low and conspiratorial. "They're going to lead us in a dance-off. Think you can handle it?"

"Me? Dance-off? I thought we were here to raise money, not turn this into a talent show."

"Trust me," he said, determination gleaming in his eyes. "This is exactly what we need. We'll draw people in, get them laughing, and before you know it, they'll be throwing money at us to join the fun."

I hesitated, the thought of performing in front of everyone sending a jolt of anxiety through me. "What if I trip and fall flat on my face?"

"Then we'll both fall flat on our faces together. Just remember—nothing brings people together like a good laugh. Besides, it's not about perfection; it's about having fun."

His enthusiasm was infectious, and despite my reservations, I felt my heart race with a mix of dread and exhilaration. Maybe this was the distraction I needed, a way to shake off the weight of my father's expectations and the pressures of my family.

"Fine," I relented, a grin creeping onto my face. "But if I end up on the ground, you're taking full responsibility for the rescue."

Jason's laughter rang out, bright and carefree, as he took my hand and pulled me into the crowd. The band kicked off their first song, and the energy soared as people started to dance, letting loose beneath the stars.

We joined in, moving together in a carefree rhythm, the weight of the world fading away with every step. I found myself laughing, the sound echoing in the warm night air, and for a moment, I forgot about everything else—the rift between our families, my father's concerns, the uncertainty of what lay ahead.

As the song reached its crescendo, Jason pulled me close, the world around us blurring into a haze of twinkling lights and laughter. "See? This is what I meant about joy," he said, breathless from the dancing. "It's all around us."

"I'll admit, you might be onto something," I replied, feeling the heat of his body against mine. In that moment, everything felt perfectly aligned, as if the universe conspired to draw us together.

But just as the last notes faded and applause erupted from the crowd, a sudden commotion rippled through the guests. I turned to see my father standing at the edge of the gathering, his expression a mix of anger and disbelief, pointedly glaring at Jason.

"Sarah!" he shouted, his voice cutting through the festive atmosphere. "We need to talk. Now."

My heart sank, dread pooling in my stomach as I met Jason's gaze, the spark between us dimming under the weight of reality. "I'll be right back," I said, my voice barely above a whisper.

As I walked toward my father, every step felt heavy, the thrill of the evening replaced by a sense of impending confrontation. "What's wrong?" I asked, trying to keep my tone steady.

He stepped closer, lowering his voice, but his intensity remained. "You think this is a game? You think you can just waltz around with that boy? You have no idea what you're getting into."

"It's not like that!" I countered, frustration bubbling to the surface. "We're working together for the distillery. This is about rebuilding, not about—"

"About him? Because that's all I see," my father interrupted, his voice rising. "You're risking everything for someone who doesn't belong in our world."

"Maybe it's time we redefine what that world looks like," I shot back, my heart racing. "This isn't just about you or me; it's about the whole community. And if you can't see that, then maybe you're the one who needs to rethink things."

Before he could respond, I felt a hand on my arm—Jason, stepping up beside me, a reassuring presence. "Is everything alright?" he asked, concern etched into his features.

"Everything's fine," my father spat, his gaze shifting to Jason, the hostility palpable. "This isn't your concern. Stay out of it."

"Actually, it is my concern," Jason replied, his voice steady. "If Sarah's involved, then I'm involved. We're in this together."

The tension in the air crackled, the energy of the fundraiser replaced by a charged silence. I felt the world narrow down to this moment, the stakes rising as our families collided. I couldn't help but glance at the gathering crowd, their eyes flicking between us, uncertainty rippling through the air like an approaching storm.

"Sarah," my father said, his voice lowering to a threatening whisper. "You need to choose. It's either him or us."

The weight of his ultimatum settled over me like a heavy shroud, and I could feel my heart pounding in my chest. The laughter and joy of the evening felt like a distant memory, overshadowed by the impossible decision looming before me. Would I stand by Jason, risking everything I knew for the sake of our fragile alliance, or would I retreat back into the safety of my family, choosing the familiar over the uncertain?

As the silence stretched, tension tightening around us like a noose, I realized I had only moments to respond. What I chose now would change everything.

Chapter 12: Unraveling Secrets

The flickering light of the desk lamp cast long shadows across the room, dancing with the laughter and chatter of the small crowd outside. I could hear the clinking of glasses and the soft strumming of a guitar filtering through the windows, blending harmoniously with the sweet scent of aged whiskey wafting in from the distillery. The fundraiser was mere days away, but my focus was consumed by the disheveled pile of photographs sprawled across the table.

Jason leaned in closer, his shoulder brushing against mine as he reached for an old album. His warm presence brought a sense of calm amid the whirlwind of organizing. I turned my head, catching a glimpse of his tousled hair and the way his eyes sparkled with mischief, a reminder of the friendship we had forged through countless hours of brainstorming and planning. "What do you think? Can we make this event a success?" he asked, his tone light, but I could sense the underlying weight of expectation behind it.

"Only if you stop eating all the hors d'oeuvres before we even get to the event," I shot back, playfully nudging him with my elbow. He chuckled, the sound rich and infectious, and I couldn't help but smile, appreciating the ease with which he navigated our budding camaraderie.

Our laughter echoed in the small office, a stark contrast to the solemnity of the task at hand. As Jason flipped through the pages of the album, I leaned in closer, curious to see what memories lay hidden within its yellowed pages. The first few photographs were mundane—family gatherings, picnics, the awkward smiles of relatives I barely recognized. But then, beneath a stack of faded images, something caught my eye. A letter, folded neatly, sat between the pages as if waiting for us to discover it.

"Hey, what's this?" I asked, my heart racing slightly at the thought of uncovering some old family tale. Jason pulled it out and began to unfold it, the paper crackling softly under the strain.

I watched, breath held, as he read the words aloud. Each line felt heavier than the last, drawing us into a web of family ties and secrets. The letter revealed a connection between our families, a friendship long forgotten, marred by misunderstandings and the passage of time. My mind raced as I processed the implications. The distillery wasn't just a shared passion; it was the very ground where our histories intertwined.

"Can you believe this?" Jason murmured, his brow furrowed in thought. "I mean, our grandparents were best friends. It's like... like fate or something."

I took a moment to absorb the magnitude of the revelation. It felt surreal, almost like a plot twist in one of those sappy romances we'd both laughed about. "Maybe it is fate," I replied, a smile creeping onto my face as I felt an unexpected warmth in my chest. "Or a very elaborate setup for a family feud."

We shared a laugh, but beneath the surface, I could sense an urgency growing within me. If our families had been intertwined so closely before, perhaps we could find a way to mend the rift that had separated us. "We have to show this at the fundraiser. This could be the bridge we need to bring everyone together," I proposed, my mind racing with ideas.

Jason nodded slowly, a pensive look crossing his features. "But what if they don't react well? What if they don't want to acknowledge the past?"

"Then we make them. They need to see how ridiculous this all is," I insisted, my voice firm but light. "Imagine the look on their faces when they realize the people they've held grudges against were once like family."

As the idea took root, excitement coursed through me. This was more than just a fundraiser now; it was a chance to rewrite history, to reclaim the narrative that had long been twisted and buried under layers of resentment. "We can put together a presentation," I suggested, adrenaline surging. "We'll share stories, show the photos, and end with the letter. It'll be the centerpiece of the event!"

Jason's expression shifted, a mixture of awe and doubt clouding his features. "You really think that'll work?"

"Why not? People love a good story, especially when it involves redemption. It'll be like the plot of a great movie!" I grinned, buoyed by my enthusiasm. "And besides, if it doesn't go well, we can always blame it on the whiskey."

He laughed, the tension easing between us. "True. But you're the one in charge of the drinks."

We spent the next few hours brainstorming, our laughter punctuated by bursts of inspiration as we plotted out the evening's program. It felt invigorating, the kind of synergy that sparked new ideas and drove away the shadows of doubt. But beneath the surface excitement, the reality of the task loomed large, heavy with the weight of history and expectation.

As we finalized the details, a thought crept into my mind. What if our families weren't ready to confront their past? What if we were opening wounds that had barely begun to heal? I brushed the worry aside, determined to believe in the power of our revelation.

Later, as I tucked the letter back into its album, a sense of purpose enveloped me. The distillery wasn't merely a business venture; it was a shared legacy, a testament to the love and friendship that had once existed between our families. If Jason and I were to save it, we needed to confront those buried truths head-on.

That night, as the laughter from the fundraiser swelled outside, I felt a resolve settle within me. We were on the brink of something significant—something that could change everything. Jason glanced over, catching the determination in my eyes. "You ready for this?" he asked, his voice steady yet tinged with excitement.

I nodded, a smile dancing on my lips. "More than ever. Let's do this."

The day of the fundraiser dawned with a crispness in the air that hinted at the arrival of autumn. The leaves on the trees surrounding the distillery blazed with fiery hues of red and orange, a natural celebration of change that felt almost fitting for the occasion. I stood in the main hall, surveying the transformed space, a blend of rustic charm and modern flair. Twinkling fairy lights draped across the wooden beams, illuminating the handmade banners that Jason and I had spent countless hours crafting. Every detail, from the carefully arranged tables to the strategically placed barrels, echoed the warmth and history of the distillery.

"Okay, let's be honest," Jason said, strolling up beside me, an exaggerated frown on his face as he surveyed the setup. "If the distillery doesn't make it through tonight, I think I might start selling decorative bottles on Etsy."

I turned to him, unable to suppress a laugh. "Only if you model for them. I can already see the title: 'Whiskey Chic—The Bold Look of Distilled Dreams.'"

He rolled his eyes, but the corners of his mouth twitched, betraying his amusement. "Just promise me you'll at least consider my Etsy venture. I could use the extra income from my questionable fashion sense."

"Let's save that for our fallback plan," I replied, my gaze drifting to the crowd of attendees beginning to filter in. "Right now, we have an actual fundraiser to pull off."

The room buzzed with laughter and conversation, and I felt a swell of pride. Each familiar face mingled with newcomers, all of them drawn to the promise of whiskey tastings and good company. As the minutes passed, the energy intensified, and I could see the old family rivalries simmering just below the surface, a tension that both excited and terrified me.

Jason and I shared a quick glance, an unspoken agreement passing between us. This was more than just an event; it was a chance to bridge the divide that had long separated our families.

When the moment arrived to reveal the letter, my heart pounded like a bass drum in my chest. I stood before the assembled crowd, feeling both exhilarated and petrified. "Thank you all for coming tonight. It means a lot to us and the distillery," I began, my voice steady, yet laced with a nervous excitement. "But tonight isn't just about saving this place. It's about acknowledging the bonds that have been lost along the way."

Jason stepped up beside me, a reassuring presence. "And it's about making new memories," he added, his tone lightening the mood. "Like all those times my cousin tried to convince me that drinking whiskey makes you more attractive. Spoiler alert: it doesn't."

Laughter rippled through the crowd, easing the tension. I took a breath and continued, "We found something while preparing for tonight—a letter that reveals a long-buried connection between our families." I unfolded the document, its edges worn, and began to read the words that had changed everything for Jason and me.

The silence hung thick in the air, each word drawing the audience deeper into the narrative. As I finished, the room felt charged, a mixture of curiosity and disbelief dancing among the attendees. I scanned the faces, searching for signs of understanding, for moments of realization that perhaps our families' pasts were intertwined in ways they hadn't imagined.

"Wow," a voice called out from the back, breaking the quiet. It was Grandma Betty, known for her sharp tongue and sharper wit. "So you're telling me all these years we've been hating each other over a misunderstanding?"

"More like a comedy of errors," Jason chimed in, nudging me with his elbow. "Think of it as an epic family drama that got out of hand."

The crowd erupted into laughter again, and I could feel the barriers beginning to crumble. It was a small victory, but a victory nonetheless. Conversations sparked and began to flow, people sharing their own stories of familial strife and misunderstandings. For the first time in what felt like eons, I glimpsed the possibility of reconciliation.

However, amidst the laughter and camaraderie, I noticed the shadow of discomfort creeping into the corners of the room. Not everyone was ready to embrace the past. I caught sight of Uncle Harold, arms crossed tightly over his chest, his expression dark and brooding. He had been the most vocal opponent of the fundraiser, convinced it was a foolish endeavor.

"Some things should stay buried," he muttered loudly enough for those nearby to hear, his tone dripping with disdain. The laughter in the room dulled, a thick silence settling as everyone turned to watch him.

Before I could think, I stepped forward, adrenaline rushing through my veins. "But isn't it time we stopped letting the past control our futures?" I countered, my voice unwavering despite the tremor in my heart. "If we don't confront our history, we'll never move forward."

Harold's brow furrowed, and I could see the internal battle raging within him. The air felt heavy, anticipation swirling like the smoke from a well-aged whiskey.

Jason joined me, standing shoulder to shoulder, creating a united front. "We're not here to erase the past. We're here to acknowledge it—to celebrate it," he said, his voice steady and sincere. "If we can come together, maybe we can create something beautiful. Isn't that worth a shot?"

A murmur of agreement rippled through the crowd, and I sensed a shift in the atmosphere. One by one, faces softened, and hesitance began to melt away.

Finally, Grandma Betty raised her glass. "To family, then! Whether we like it or not, we're stuck with each other!" The laughter that erupted from her comment shattered the tension, and glasses clinked as people raised their drinks in solidarity.

As the evening wore on, conversations bloomed like wildflowers. Stories filled the air, laughter echoed, and for the first time, the walls between our families began to dissolve. The whiskey flowed freely, and I watched as old grudges were put aside, replaced by a sense of unity I hadn't thought possible.

But as I glanced over at Jason, whose laughter rang out with a warmth that made my heart flutter, I couldn't shake the feeling that our journey was only just beginning. The path to healing was fraught with challenges, but for the first time, I felt hopeful. And I knew that no matter what lay ahead, Jason and I would navigate it together, side by side, as allies in this unpredictable journey.

As the evening progressed, the atmosphere in the distillery transformed into something almost electric. Laughter and clinking glasses filled the air, weaving a tapestry of shared stories and unexpected connections. I felt a lightness in my chest, as though the very walls of the distillery were exhaling, relieved to finally shed the weight of old grudges. It was surreal, watching familiar faces smile and share anecdotes that had once been hidden under layers of animosity.

I caught sight of Aunt Clara, her cheeks flushed from the whiskey and her laughter infectious, regaling a group of attendees with tales from her youth. "You see, it all started when Harold tried to prove he could outdrink me. Spoiler alert: he couldn't," she announced, throwing a cheeky grin in my uncle's direction. Harold, who had retreated to a corner, merely rolled his eyes, unable to resist the laughter that rippled through the crowd.

The energy in the room surged as old rivalries melted into camaraderie. But as I glanced at Jason across the room, the warmth of the moment contrasted sharply with the knot of tension still nestled in my stomach. His gaze caught mine, and I felt an unspoken understanding pass between us. We had more work to do; the secrets of our families were only just beginning to unravel.

"Shall we toast to our families' newfound friendship?" Jason suggested, moving closer. He poured two glasses of whiskey, the amber liquid catching the light as it swirled. "Here's to understanding, forgiveness, and all the drama we've managed to avoid until now."

I raised my glass, but before I could respond, Grandma Betty interjected. "Just make sure that drama doesn't involve me! I've had my fill of family feuds!" Her voice boomed with playful authority, and everyone erupted into laughter again, lightening the mood further.

As we drank, a burst of applause suddenly echoed through the distillery, drawing everyone's attention to the makeshift stage at the front of the room. A local band had set up earlier, and with the evening in full swing, they had taken the opportunity to entertain us. I felt my heart lift with the music, a rhythmic pulse that matched the heartbeat of the crowd.

"Come on, let's dance!" Jason urged, grabbing my hand and pulling me toward the small dance floor that had formed at the front. The guitar twanged a lively melody, and soon, I found myself swept into the movement of the crowd, laughter spilling from my lips as we twirled and stepped to the music.

Jason moved with a lightness that belied his height, and as I danced beside him, it felt as though we were coconspirators in this unexpected adventure. "You're a surprisingly good dancer," I teased, weaving through the throng of bodies.

"Surprising? I'll have you know I'm a seasoned expert in two-stepping and dodging awkward family conversations," he shot back, a playful glint in his eyes.

Just as I was about to reply, I noticed Harold stepping away from the gathering. A frown marred his features, and he moved toward the back of the distillery, where the old storage room lay. Something about his expression sent a shiver down my spine. I excused myself from the dance floor, slipping through the crowd with purpose.

"Where are you off to?" Jason called after me, his brow furrowed with concern.

"Just a moment!" I called back, keeping my eyes fixed on Harold as he disappeared through the heavy door leading to the storeroom. Curiosity and trepidation bubbled within me as I followed him, the din of the party fading behind me.

The storeroom was dimly lit, filled with the scent of aged wood and whiskey barrels. I paused at the doorway, watching as Harold rifled through a stack of dusty boxes. My heart raced as I considered whether I should confront him or retreat back to the lively festivities.

"Harold," I said cautiously, stepping inside. "What are you doing back here?"

He turned sharply, eyes narrowed. "Nothing that concerns you, child," he replied, his tone curt and defensive.

"Come on, I know it's not nothing. It's the fundraiser of the year! Everyone is in high spirits; why would you want to ruin that?" I pressed, my voice steady even as I felt a flutter of apprehension.

He sighed, running a hand through his thinning hair. "You don't understand," he said, his voice softer but still tinged with frustration. "There are things—secrets—that are better left buried. This whole event... it's stirring up memories that should stay hidden."

"Memories can be painful, but they can also lead to healing," I countered, trying to reach him. "Isn't that what we're doing here? Trying to fix what's been broken?"

He hesitated, his expression momentarily softening before hardening again. "You think you can just fix everything with a few drinks and some heartfelt speeches? You're playing with fire."

I took a step closer, my curiosity piqued. "What do you mean? What's really going on here?"

His gaze flickered to the floor, and for a moment, I saw a flicker of vulnerability in his eyes. "I just don't want you to find out things that could tear your family apart even further," he murmured, almost to himself.

Before I could press further, a loud crash echoed from behind me. My heart dropped as I spun around to see a stack of boxes tumbling to the floor, a cascade of papers and dusty bottles scattering across the ground. Panic surged through me as I reached for Harold. "What was that?"

"Stay back!" he barked, his demeanor shifting again, cold and defensive. But it was too late; I had already spotted something half-buried beneath the mess of papers—a leather-bound journal, its cover worn and aged, the clasp still intact.

With a sense of urgency, I bent down and reached for it, the cool leather sending a shiver down my spine. As I lifted it, the weight of its contents seemed to resonate with all the secrets it might hold. "What is this?" I whispered, glancing up at Harold. His expression had shifted, a mix of anger and fear darkening his features.

"You shouldn't have touched that," he warned, his voice low and dangerous.

Ignoring him, I flicked open the journal, the pages crackling softly as I turned them. What lay within could change everything—the past woven into its lines, the threads of our families' histories intertwining in ways I had never imagined.

But just as I began to read, a shout rang out from the main hall, sharp and frantic. "Everyone, get out! There's a fire!"

Panic erupted, the joyous celebration spiraling into chaos. Adrenaline surged through my veins as I felt the weight of the journal in my hands. Harold's eyes widened, and in that moment, as the reality of the situation set in, I realized we were no longer merely facing our families' pasts. Now, we were fighting for our future.

"Come on!" I shouted, grabbing Harold's arm and pulling him toward the door. But just as we stepped out, a loud crack echoed from above, and I turned in time to see the first flames licking hungrily at the wooden beams.

"Run!" I screamed, the world around me fading into a blur of smoke and heat as I raced toward the chaos that awaited outside, the journal clutched tightly in my hands—a secret that could change everything.

Chapter 13: Shadows of Doubt

The autumn air crackled with an uneasy tension as I stood in the center of our community hall, surrounded by hastily arranged tables decked with cheerful centerpieces of orange and gold. The vibrant colors, meant to evoke warmth and camaraderie, only amplified the chill that had settled deep within my bones. A pumpkin spice candle flickered hesitantly, its sweet scent twisting in the air, and despite the inviting aroma, it felt like the calm before an unexpected storm. My heart raced with a restless energy, fluttering like a moth drawn to the flame of uncertainty.

I had always prided myself on being the heart of our little town, the one who organized everything from bake sales to charity runs. But this year's fundraiser was different—bigger, bolder, and more crucial than ever. It wasn't just about the money; it was about the lives we could change. Yet, whispers of sabotage loomed over me like a dark cloud, casting shadows that stretched longer with each passing day.

Jason leaned against the doorway, arms crossed, his presence a steady anchor in the swirling chaos of my thoughts. He wore that leather jacket of his, the one that made him look effortlessly rugged, and somehow it added to the sense of danger that surrounded us. "You're not eating enough," he said, his voice cutting through the fog of my worry. I shot him a glare, though it lacked any real heat. He knew me too well; I was too busy preparing for the event to care about dinner.

"I'm fine," I replied, my tone clipped. "There's just too much to do. We need to finalize the guest list, confirm the catering, and—"

"Look at me." He stepped closer, his intense gaze boring into mine. "If there's a threat, we can't afford to overlook anything. You need to be at your best. Not to mention, we're doing this together, remember?"

The corners of my mouth quirked up at his persistence. "And what if I faint from hunger right in front of the mayor?"

"Then I'll catch you." A smirk danced across his lips, lightening the moment just enough to remind me that humor was still allowed in the midst of our looming dread.

I couldn't help but smile back, the warmth of his reassurance momentarily dispelling the gnawing anxiety. But beneath the surface, the weight of the unknown settled heavily upon my shoulders. An anonymous tip had arrived two days prior, its contents chilling me to the bone. "Someone's planning to ruin the fundraiser," it had read, the paper yellowed and creased, as if it had been passed through too many hands. "Trust no one."

The words echoed in my mind, a mantra of paranoia that twisted and turned, taunting me with every glance. I had shared the tip with Jason, of course, but his calm demeanor had only deepened my unease. "We need to be cautious," he had said, and I had nodded, but the truth was, I didn't know how to proceed.

As the day wore on, we plunged deeper into preparations. The hall buzzed with the chatter of volunteers and the soft hum of music, but my heart was a wild drum in my chest, thrumming with uncertainty. Each time I turned a corner or stepped out into the hallway, I felt a prickle at the back of my neck, as if someone were watching, waiting for the opportune moment to strike.

"What if we set up a security detail?" Jason suggested as we finalized the seating arrangements. "We can ask a few of the local police to keep an eye out during the event."

I tilted my head, considering. "That might raise more questions than answers." The last thing I wanted was to alarm everyone and set off a wave of panic. But the image of sabotage played in my mind like a twisted film reel, a horror movie where the protagonist was blissfully unaware of the villain lurking just out of sight.

Just then, a sharp laugh cut through my thoughts. It was Vanessa, the town's self-appointed socialite, striding through the entrance with an exaggerated air of importance. Her glossy curls bounced as she glided toward us, a pink phone glued to her ear, the sound of her laughter grating against my already frayed nerves.

"Darlings, the décor is utterly charming," she chirped, oblivious to the heaviness in the air. "But do you really think you'll get that caterer on such short notice?"

I braced myself, knowing all too well that Vanessa had a flair for the dramatic, especially when it came to pointing out flaws. "We're on top of it," I replied, forcing my tone to remain cordial.

"Oh, I do hope so," she continued, her voice dripping with faux concern. "We wouldn't want any mishaps, would we?" She shot a sidelong glance at Jason, her painted lips curling into a sly smile. "Especially not with such important people attending."

The tension in the room thickened, and I could feel Jason stiffening beside me. "Let's keep the focus on the event, shall we?" he said, his voice cool and steady, but there was a hint of an edge that danced just below the surface.

Vanessa, momentarily taken aback by his tone, glanced between us, and I could practically see the gears turning in her head, attempting to dissect our dynamic. "Of course, darling. I'm sure you two have it all under control."

As she walked away, her heels clicking like a countdown, I let out a breath I hadn't realized I was holding. "She's a piece of work," Jason muttered, shaking his head. "We can't let people like her derail us."

I nodded, grateful for his support, but my thoughts were still racing. Who else could be behind the threat? Could it be someone from within our own ranks, or had an outsider slipped into our tight-knit community? The possibilities spiraled out like an intricate web, each thread leading to darker conclusions.

As the evening approached, the hall transformed under the glow of twinkling lights, the scent of rich food mingling with the sweet perfume of flowers. Laughter and chatter filled the air, creating a tapestry of joy that should have been comforting. But the shadows lingered, reminding me that amidst the laughter, danger lurked just beneath the surface.

The moment the first guests arrived, my heart sank. I scanned the crowd, searching for any flicker of suspicion, any shadow that moved just a bit too quickly. And in that moment, surrounded by smiling faces and laughter, I realized that no matter how festive the atmosphere, trust was a fragile thing, easily shattered. And as I stepped further into the fray, determined to uphold the spirit of the evening, I couldn't shake the feeling that the real challenge was just beginning.

The evening unfolded like a carefully choreographed dance, each movement calculated yet infused with an underlying tension that made my skin prickle. Guests milled about the hall, laughter bubbling like champagne, while the warmth of community enveloped us in a cocoon of hope. Yet, I felt like an intruder in my own celebration, each smile a potential mask hiding secrets I couldn't afford to ignore. I slipped through the crowd, accepting greetings and compliments with a practiced grace that masked my turmoil.

"Have you tried the bruschetta?" Vanessa's voice cut through the haze, a sliver of irritation making my stomach turn. "It's divine. But I'm sure you've been too busy to taste anything."

Her sharp eyes glinted with mischief as she leaned closer, her perfume an intoxicating blend of floral and something far more dangerous. "You know, you really should let me help more. I have a way of getting things done."

I held her gaze, steeling myself against the urge to roll my eyes. "And here I thought my superpower was surviving on coffee and panic."

"Only a matter of time before it catches up with you," she said, tossing her hair back with a dramatic flair, "but I guess that's your style, isn't it? A little chaos makes life interesting."

"Interesting is one way to put it," I replied, forcing a smile. "But I think I prefer my life without the chaos, thank you very much."

Her laughter chimed like a bell, both light and mocking, and I felt a flicker of resentment. She was entertaining, yes, but her glib demeanor belied an uncanny knack for stirring the pot. I stepped back, shaking off the weight of her presence, moving instead toward the bar. A glass of merlot might calm my nerves, and I hoped it would drown out the unease nesting in my gut.

As I sipped the wine, the deep red liquid swirling in the glass caught my attention. The way it glistened in the soft light reminded me of the crimson thread of danger I could feel lurking beneath the surface of our gathering. I spotted Jason across the room, engaged in a conversation with a few local business owners. His expression was earnest, his gestures animated, yet I noticed the slight tightening of his jaw every time Vanessa's name floated through the air.

I approached him, weaving through the clusters of well-wishers. "Everything okay?" I asked, concern etching lines on my forehead.

He met my gaze, and the warmth in his eyes felt like a shield against the chaos. "Just wrapping up a conversation about donations. We're on track, but..." His voice dropped to a conspiratorial whisper. "Did you notice how she keeps trying to insert herself into the planning?"

"Like a mosquito at a barbecue," I muttered, glancing over my shoulder to make sure Vanessa was out of earshot. "But what are we supposed to do? Just ignore her?"

"We need to keep an eye on her. The last thing we want is for her to feel empowered to interfere." He sighed, running a hand through his hair. "And that tip... it's unsettling."

I shivered, the weight of our shared anxiety pulling at my heart. "What if it's not just a prank? What if someone really does have it out for us?"

"Then we'll face it together," he said, the determination in his voice making me feel a bit more grounded. "Just remember, if it gets too crazy, I'm your wingman. We'll tackle whatever comes our way."

With a renewed sense of purpose, I straightened up and offered him a smile, grateful for his presence. "Okay, then. Let's put on our brave faces. Who knows? Maybe we'll find out who our real friends are tonight."

As the night progressed, the laughter flowed like the wine, and people began to let down their guards. I moved among them, sharing stories and connecting over shared experiences, but my mind kept returning to the idea of the anonymous tip. Who had sent it? Why now? Each question hung in the air, a specter haunting our joyful gathering.

The evening's program unfolded smoothly, speeches filled with heartfelt gratitude and hopes for the future. The auction items were displayed, glittering under the soft lights, each a promise of the good we could do together. Yet, I couldn't shake the feeling that, even among friends, secrets loomed in the shadows, their whispers swirling around us like leaves in a tempest.

Just as I was getting lost in the sea of camaraderie, a commotion erupted near the buffet table. A sharp scream cut through the laughter, and the room fell into a stunned silence. I pushed through the crowd, my heart racing as I spotted a small group huddled around Vanessa, who stood with a tray of appetizers spilled at her feet.

"I swear, it was right here! It just—" she stammered, eyes wide with feigned horror. "One moment I was reaching for the truffle oil, and the next, everything went flying!"

I knelt to help her gather the scattered food, trying to gauge her expression. Was it shock, or was it something else? The anxious energy in the room felt palpable, a collective breath held in suspense.

"Are you okay?" I asked, concern genuine despite my earlier irritation. "Did you trip?"

"Oh, I'm fine, dear," she replied, tossing her hair back with an exaggerated sigh, her voice dripping with drama. "But this is simply unacceptable! I was planning to take the first bite of that bruschetta!"

Jason appeared beside me, his brow furrowed. "It looks like it was an accident. Do you need help?"

"Help?" Vanessa's tone shifted, laced with indignation. "What I need is a new assistant who knows how to keep things in order!"

I caught Jason's eye, a silent understanding passing between us. While her antics were tiresome, the underlying current of chaos felt more significant than her drama. "Let's focus on getting the food back in order. We can't let one small mishap derail the evening," I said, trying to take control.

A chorus of murmurs rippled through the crowd, but as we worked to clean up the mess, I felt a prickling sensation of eyes on me. Every glance, every whisper turned into a potential threat, twisting into a tight knot of anxiety deep within.

"Are you sure you're okay?" Jason asked quietly as we gathered the last remnants of the fallen appetizers.

"I will be," I replied, forcing my tone to remain upbeat. "But something feels off tonight. The atmosphere is electric, and not in a good way."

As we finished tidying up, I stole a glance at Vanessa, who had moved to the bar, a conspiratorial whisper curling around her lips as she spoke to a newcomer. Was she merely playing the part of the dramatic diva, or was there a deeper game at play?

The evening stretched on, and the auction began, bids rising like the tension in the air. Laughter broke out again, but it felt strained, as if everyone was pretending to be unaffected by the lingering shadows. I cast a quick glance around the room, searching for anything unusual, any sign of the danger I feared was lurking just out of sight.

As the first item—a beautiful handmade quilt—was auctioned off, I felt a wave of anxiety wash over me. What if the sabotage wasn't just an act of mischief? What if it was a calculated plan to ruin everything we had worked so hard for? I needed to stay alert, to decipher the truth hidden beneath the surface of our seemingly joyful gathering.

And just when I thought the night might hold some semblance of normalcy, a loud crash reverberated through the hall, punctuating the air with a jolt of dread that coursed through my veins. All eyes turned toward the commotion, and I felt my heart race, bracing for the revelation of the night's true threat.

The crash echoed like thunder, a cacophony that jolted everyone from their conversations. Glass shattered, the sharp sound slicing through the air, and for a heartbeat, the room fell silent. I felt my pulse quicken, a primal instinct urging me to move, to find the source of the chaos.

The crowd parted, and I caught sight of Vanessa standing amidst a sea of broken glass and scattered auction items, her expression a mix of shock and something almost gleeful. "Oh my God! Can you believe this?" she shrieked, hands flailing as she pointed at a fallen display that had tipped over. An elaborate cake, intended as the evening's crowning dessert, lay in ruin, its frosting splattered like graffiti across the polished floor.

"What happened?" I called out, urgency threading through my words as I made my way toward her, Jason close at my heels.

"Someone knocked it over!" Vanessa wailed, dramatically placing a hand to her chest as if the very sight of the mess had wounded her. "This is a disaster! A complete disaster!"

Jason's jaw tightened, and I could see his frustration boiling just beneath the surface. "Was it an accident or something more deliberate?" he asked, his voice low and steady, eyes scanning the crowd for any hint of mischief.

"I don't know!" Vanessa replied, her tone laced with mock innocence, though I detected a flicker of satisfaction in her eyes. "Maybe it was just too beautiful to last?"

"Right, because it's obviously so difficult to keep your hands to yourself," I muttered under my breath, feeling a surge of irritation. I knelt down, my fingers brushing over the remnants of what had been an impressive creation. The scent of vanilla and chocolate wafted up, mixing with the lingering aroma of the previous courses, and for a moment, I let myself focus on the sweet smell, trying to ground myself amid the chaos.

"Maybe we should call for security," Jason suggested, his brow furrowing in thought. "If this was intentional, we need to take it seriously."

"Security?" Vanessa scoffed, eyeing Jason with disdain. "Really? Isn't that a bit over the top for a cake? I mean, it's not like someone got hurt."

"No one was hurt, but this isn't just about the cake. It's about the event. And I'd like to keep it that way," he replied, his patience wearing thin.

I stood up, brushing crumbs from my hands as I surveyed the scene. "Let's just clean this up for now and keep the mood light. If we can manage to keep the night rolling, maybe no one will notice." I glanced at Jason, who nodded in agreement.

"Fine," Vanessa huffed, crossing her arms. "But I won't be responsible for the inevitable fallout. This could ruin our reputation!"

As we began picking up the shards of glass, the mood in the room shifted. Laughter, which had flowed freely just moments before, turned into whispers, and the tension escalated. A group of guests edged closer, eyes darting from the cake catastrophe to the concerned faces of Jason and me. I felt their curiosity morph into suspicion, and I swallowed hard, aware that my leadership was under scrutiny.

With the wreckage finally cleared away and the remaining desserts being served, I tried to redirect the energy in the room. I launched into a light-hearted speech, making jokes about my own clumsiness, throwing in self-deprecating humor to diffuse the tension. The crowd chuckled, a few smiles appearing, but I could still feel the atmosphere crackling with uncertainty.

Just as I felt the evening start to regain its footing, a newcomer arrived, cutting through the crowd like a knife. Tall and striking, with a confident stride and an enigmatic smile, she made her way toward us. Her dark hair framed her face, and her eyes sparkled with mischief, but there was something in her demeanor that felt sharp—like she was slicing through the polite pretense that had held the room together.

"Am I late to the party?" she asked, her voice smooth and captivating. "I heard there was quite a commotion. What's a little disaster without a dash of drama, right?"

"Who are you?" I asked, crossing my arms as a wave of wariness washed over me.

"Just a friend of Vanessa," she replied, unfazed by my scrutiny. "The name's Clara. I've come to lend a hand—or perhaps stir things up a bit."

Vanessa's eyes lit up with recognition. "Oh, Clara! You've got to help us! We're in the middle of an absolute catastrophe."

I exchanged a quick glance with Jason, and I could see his concern mirrored in my own expression. Something about Clara's arrival felt like a plot twist, like she was a character who had stepped straight out of a thriller novel, and I had no idea if she was a hero or a villain.

"Help? Or perhaps you're here to make things more interesting?" I countered, my tone wary but playful. "Because we've had enough excitement for one evening."

Clara chuckled, her laughter melodious yet laced with an undercurrent that sent a shiver down my spine. "Oh, don't worry. I'm just here for the show—at least for now. I wouldn't dream of ruining your little fundraiser...yet."

"Yet?" Jason echoed, his eyes narrowing slightly.

"Relax, darling. I'm all about supporting the community. But it's so much more fun when there's a little tension, don't you think?"

With her enigmatic charm, Clara was like a match thrown into a barrel of dry hay. The air around us grew heavier, charged with the sudden awareness that the stakes were higher than I had anticipated. Was she genuinely here to support the cause, or did she have her own agenda?

"Let's focus on the event, shall we?" I suggested, forcing a smile despite the wariness blooming in my chest. "We're raising funds for a good cause, and every dollar counts. There's plenty of room for all kinds of fun, as long as it's the right kind."

As I spoke, I felt the tension coiling around us like a snake ready to strike. Guests were watching with bated breath, and I sensed their growing unease.

Just as I turned to gather my thoughts, a loud commotion erupted from the other side of the room. Chairs scraped against the floor, voices rose in confusion, and my stomach dropped as I recognized the shrill sound of shouting. I pushed past the gathering crowd, Jason at my side, my heart racing as we approached the scene.

When we arrived, a group had formed around a man who stood frozen, his face pale as he clutched a broken wine bottle. "I didn't mean to! It just slipped!" he exclaimed, panic threading his words. But what caught my attention was the figure slumped against the wall behind him, clutching their arm, blood seeping through their fingers.

My breath hitched, and as I glanced at Jason, I knew we were standing on the precipice of something far more dangerous than we had anticipated. The tension that had brewed all night had erupted into chaos, and as I scanned the room, I felt the shadows of doubt closing in, wrapping around me like a noose, leaving me to wonder who would strike next.

Chapter 14: Sparks in the Darkness

The day of the fundraiser unfolded with a surreal blend of exhilaration and anxiety, a crisp reminder that life could turn on a dime. As the sun broke over Evergreen Hollow, its rays filtered through the leaves of the towering oaks, painting the ground in dappled gold. I stood at the entrance of the distillery, where vibrant banners fluttered like flags of celebration. The air was rich with the tantalizing aroma of smoked meats mingling with freshly baked bread, a feast for the senses that promised an unforgettable evening.

Inside, laughter echoed off the wooden beams of the distillery, a hearty symphony of joy and anticipation. The space had transformed from a simple gathering place into a banquet hall, adorned with twinkling fairy lights that wrapped around the barrels like ethereal vines. Tables were draped in white linens, each set with glistening glasses that caught the light and flung it around the room like fireflies on a summer night. The band, a local favorite, strummed a lively tune, sending ripples of movement through the crowd. My heart swelled at the sight of familiar faces, friends and neighbors mingling in a swirl of color and conversation, all united for a cause that stirred deep within me.

But beneath the festive facade, a tension simmered like the distillery's finest whiskey, potent and unsettling. My eyes darted to the front of the room where the mayor stood, his charismatic smile barely concealing the weight of his office. As he spoke about the importance of community and the need for support, I could see a flicker of uncertainty in his eyes, a hint that the success of the evening rested on the precipice of unspoken worries. I felt the knot tightening in my stomach, a visceral reminder of the stakes involved. This was not just a night of celebration; it was a lifeline for so many.

"Are you ready for this?" Jason's voice broke through my thoughts, pulling me back to the present. He leaned against the doorway, the light casting a halo around him that momentarily stole my breath away. His dark hair was slightly tousled, and the playful glint in his eyes hinted at mischief. "Because if I'm going to embarrass myself tonight, I'd like a little support from my partner-in-crime."

I laughed, the sound bubbling up unexpectedly. "You're going to do great. Just remember, the key is to look confident. Even if you're not sure what you're doing."

He grinned, and the warmth of his expression sent a flicker of something electric through the air between us. "Confidence is my middle name. Well, that and 'Desperate,'" he replied, his tone teasing yet sincere.

We shared a moment of unspoken understanding, a bond forged in the fires of past challenges and victories. I relished the way he could lift the weight off my shoulders with just a word or a look. As I watched him, I couldn't help but wonder where we stood in the grand scheme of things. We were friends, partners in this wild adventure of fundraising, but was there something more lurking in the shadows? The gentle brush of his fingers against mine sent shivers down my spine, igniting a spark I was desperate to explore.

"Let's get back in there before they think we've run away," I suggested, reluctant to break the spell. As we reentered the distillery, the energy enveloped us like a warm embrace, but I felt the tendrils of anxiety creeping back in.

The night unfolded like a well-choreographed dance, filled with laughter and tears, but always underpinned by a sense of urgency. I moved from table to table, sharing stories and dreams, laughter and hopes, but always mindful of the underlying tension that flickered like the candle flames dancing on the tables. Jason was by my side, his presence a steady anchor amidst the chaos. Together, we navigated the sea of well-wishers, a united front against the backdrop of uncertainty.

As the evening progressed, I found myself drawn into conversations that turned serious as the hour grew late. One couple spoke of their dreams for their children, the sacrifices they made just to give them a chance at a brighter future. Another friend poured out their heart about the struggles of running a small business in a town where every penny counted. With every story, the reality of our cause became clearer, the importance of this night pulsating through the air like a heartbeat.

Jason caught my eye from across the room, a silent question in his gaze. I nodded, and we approached the podium where the mayor stood, ready to deliver the evening's most significant moment. The room fell silent, all eyes turning toward the front, anticipation hanging thick in the air. As the mayor outlined the financial goals we needed to hit, my heart raced. Every second felt like an eternity, each number a stark reminder of the weight we were carrying.

I could feel Jason's hand inching closer to mine, the warmth radiating from him calming my racing heart. Just as I thought I might burst from the pressure, the unexpected happened. A loud crash echoed through the room, followed by gasps as the crowd turned in unison. A table had tipped, sending glasses shattering to the ground, their contents pooling on the polished floor like spilled secrets. I caught a glimpse of a small child, wide-eyed and shocked, standing beside the wreckage. In that instant, I saw the fragile balance we were all trying to maintain, a delicate dance between hope and despair.

With a shared glance, Jason and I sprang into action. We were no longer just fundraisers; we were a team, united by a common purpose. As we moved to help the little one, I felt the tension of the evening transform into something more profound—a connection, a shared resolve. We were here to lift each other up, to weather the storms together, and maybe, just maybe, to forge something beautiful amidst the chaos.

The aftermath of the toppled table rippled through the crowd, a mixture of shock and laughter that broke the tension like a wave crashing against the shore. As Jason and I rushed to help the little boy, I felt the weight of the room shift. It wasn't just about the fundraiser anymore; it was about community, about coming together in the face of chaos. The child, a whirlwind of tousled hair and wide eyes, looked up at us with a mix of fear and embarrassment, his bottom lip quivering like a tightly strung bow.

"Don't worry, buddy. We've all had our moments," I said, crouching down to his level. The reassuring smile I offered was genuine, fueled by the empathy swirling within me. "This just means you're destined for greatness—greatness that requires a little dramatic flair."

Jason chuckled, clearly enchanted by my attempt to lighten the mood. "And we all know that greatness needs a dramatic entrance. Just look at how you've stormed in tonight, creating quite the show."

With a playful nudge, I encouraged the boy to help us gather the shattered pieces, the sound of laughter returning as other guests rushed over to assist. Jason's presence beside me was a grounding force. He moved with the ease of someone who had been in this position before, kneeling to comfort the child and coaxing him into a giggle that bubbled over like soda fizz.

"What's your name, superstar?" Jason asked, ruffling the boy's hair as he brushed away the last remnants of shattered glass.

"Finn," he replied, his voice barely above a whisper.

"Well, Finn, let me tell you something," I said, giving him my best conspiratorial grin. "You're going to have the best story to tell after tonight. Everyone will remember you as the boy who brought down the house."

The tension that had held us all captive melted into a sense of camaraderie. People returned to their conversations, laughter intermingling with the music, transforming the moment into an unexpected highlight of the evening. Finn's laughter rang out as he joined his parents, a wide grin plastered across his face, leaving us with the remnants of joy and relief.

As the night wore on, the fundraiser took on a life of its own, moving beyond a mere collection of donations. Each speech from local leaders was met with enthusiasm, the crowd's energy building like the crescendo of a beloved song. Jason and I circulated, collecting donations, and sharing stories, our shared mission deepening the bond between us.

At one point, we found ourselves at a table laden with handmade crafts, the centerpiece crafted by an elderly woman whose eyes twinkled like stars. She was a local legend, known for her knitting and storytelling. Her name was Miss Edith, and she had an uncanny ability to weave magic into every stitch and word.

"You two are quite the pair," she said, her voice warm and crackling like the fireplace on a chilly night. "I can't help but notice the sparks between you. Is there a story there, or is it all just the whiskey talking?"

I felt a blush creep up my cheeks, not entirely sure how to respond without revealing the whirlpool of emotions that had formed between Jason and me. But Jason, ever the charmer, leaned in and said with a smirk, "Just a few sparks, Miss Edith. We haven't quite ignited a wildfire yet."

"Ah, but wildfires start with a single spark," she winked, her knowing smile lingering as she handed us a small knitted heart. "Take this. It's a reminder that warmth can grow from the tiniest of embers."

I couldn't help but admire her wisdom, her years of life echoing in her words. Holding the heart felt symbolic, almost like a charm bestowed upon us by a benevolent fairy godmother. It nestled in my palm, warm and comforting, grounding me in the moment.

The rest of the evening passed in a blur of laughter and cheers. The auction items drew enthusiastic bids, some playful banter flying back and forth, transforming the event into an impromptu comedy show. A local man, known for his outrageous antics, threw in quips that left the audience in stitches, while Jason and I exchanged glances, barely able to suppress our laughter.

At one point, I leaned close to him, our shoulders brushing, a fleeting spark igniting anew. "If we survive this fundraiser without tripping over our own feet, I'd call that a success," I whispered, my breath warm against his ear.

Jason turned to face me, his expression teasing yet sincere. "It's all part of the plan. I mean, if we can tackle this chaos together, imagine what we could conquer in a quieter setting. Like a movie marathon. With popcorn."

The way he said it made me chuckle, a sound that felt light and free. "What makes you think I'd be interested in a movie marathon with you? There's a lot of competition out there for my attention."

His brows shot up playfully, and he leaned in just a fraction closer, making my heart race. "Oh really? What's more captivating than me? I'll wait."

I pretended to ponder his question seriously, tapping my chin. "Well, I hear the couch is exceptionally good company. Also, popcorn doesn't talk back."

"Touché," he conceded, his grin widening. "But let's not forget about the fun of a little banter."

As the evening progressed, the music shifted to softer melodies, drawing couples to the dance floor. I felt a tug at my heart, the desire to be swept into a world where worries faded into the background, and all that existed was the rhythm of life shared with someone special. The air thickened with promise and unspoken words, my pulse quickening at the thought of dancing with Jason.

With a quick glance around, I caught sight of Finn still lingering at the edge of the dance floor, his tiny feet tapping along to the beat, longing for a moment of his own. "Shall we?" I asked, nodding toward him.

Jason smiled, and without a word, he took my hand, guiding me to the little boy. "Would you like to join us for a dance, Finn?" he asked, kneeling down to meet the child's gaze.

Finn's eyes lit up, and he nodded vigorously. "Yeah!"

As we danced together—Jason, Finn, and I—laughter erupted around us. I spun Finn around, and he let out a squeal of delight, his little hands grasping mine tightly. The connection felt electric, each moment an unbroken chain of joy that wrapped around us like a warm blanket. In that instant, surrounded by laughter and the flickering lights, the uncertainties of the evening faded, leaving only the sweet promise of something more—something that, like the finest whiskey, would only grow richer with time.

The music swelled around us as Jason, Finn, and I spun in a whirl of laughter and innocence, our feet moving to a rhythm that felt timeless. The dance floor transformed into a makeshift stage, where every clumsy step became a part of our performance, and I was struck by the simple joy radiating from Finn. He beamed like a small sun, his happiness contagious. For a fleeting moment, I forgot the weight of the fundraiser, the stakes involved, and let myself be swept away in the dance, reveling in the warmth of connection.

As the song reached its crescendo, I caught a glimpse of the crowd. Their smiles and laughter lit the dimly lit space, filling it with a glow that rivaled the fairy lights strung overhead. I noticed the mayor, his serious demeanor momentarily softened as he clapped along, and Miss Edith's knowing smile shone like a beacon among the attendees. But my heart thumped not just from the rhythm of the music; it raced for another reason entirely. Jason's eyes, bright with amusement and something deeper, were locked onto mine.

"See? I told you I could pull off the awkward dance moves!" he teased, pulling Finn into a spin that sent the boy into a fit of giggles. "A true artist in his element!"

I couldn't help but roll my eyes, though I was laughing too. "You're more of a comedic relief than an artist, my friend. But it works."

"Oh, I'm versatile," he replied, feigning grandeur as he struck a pose, his hand dramatically placed on his forehead as if he were a tragic hero. "I can do both!"

As the song came to an end, the room erupted in applause, and Finn bowed like a seasoned performer, making the audience erupt into cheers. I felt a rush of affection for the little boy; his unabashed joy was a reminder of why we were here. This fundraiser wasn't merely about raising money; it was about creating memories, fostering connections, and igniting hope within the community.

But just as the exhilaration reached its peak, the lights flickered ominously, causing a hush to fall over the room. Unease settled in the pit of my stomach, and I exchanged a worried glance with Jason. The dim lighting cast long shadows across the faces around us, morphing the cheerful atmosphere into something unsettling.

"Did you see that?" I asked, my voice a whisper, heavy with the weight of unspoken fears.

"Yeah. Probably just a power outage. They did say the storm was coming," he replied, though I noticed the crease forming between his brows, mirroring my own concern.

Before I could respond, the lights flickered again, this time plunging us into darkness. Gasps rippled through the crowd, and a nervous laughter echoed in the gloom. Finn squealed, "It's like a ghost party!" and despite my unease, I couldn't help but chuckle at his innocent view of the chaos.

The band's music halted, leaving only the sound of murmuring voices and the faint rustle of clothing as people shifted nervously.

I gripped Jason's arm instinctively, feeling his warmth seep into me, grounding me amidst the growing tension. "What's going on? Shouldn't someone check the generator?"

"I'll find out," he said, his tone steady but his expression betraying a flicker of worry. He squeezed my hand before breaking away, leaving me in a swirling mix of unease and anticipation.

In the dimness, I strained my ears for any sign of clarity amidst the rising chatter. The darkness wrapped around me like a thick fog, blurring the edges of my world. Shadows danced ominously against the walls, a disorienting play that made the familiar feel foreign.

Then came a sharp crack, a sound so loud it echoed off the distillery's walls, followed by a series of frantic whispers that spiraled into a clamor. A moment later, the lights blinked back on, casting everything in harsh illumination. People squinted, their eyes adjusting, and as clarity returned, confusion morphed into something darker.

A figure stood at the far end of the room, just beyond the crowd, shrouded in shadows but unmistakably tense. The atmosphere shifted again, becoming heavy with a sense of foreboding. I could feel the electricity in the air, a prickling awareness that something was very wrong.

The mayor stepped forward, his voice ringing out above the rising murmur, "Everyone, please remain calm! We just had a small technical issue. We're back on track!"

But as he spoke, my gaze remained fixed on the figure. Something about their stance—the way they hovered at the edge of the crowd, eyes darting with intensity—sent a shiver down my spine. It felt as though they were waiting, lurking, biding their time for something more.

"Lena, are you okay?" Jason's voice broke through my thoughts as he returned to my side, concern etched across his features.

"I don't know," I replied, my voice low, the words barely escaping my lips. "Did you see that person?"

"Which person?" he asked, scanning the room as I gestured subtly toward the figure.

"Over there, at the edge. Something's not right."

He turned, eyes narrowing as he tried to locate the shadowy figure. But in a heartbeat, it vanished into the throng, absorbed into the pulsating crowd. The unsettling sensation of being watched pressed against my chest, the feeling amplifying with each passing second.

"Stay close," Jason instructed, his grip tightening around my arm. The urgency in his voice felt like a jolt, igniting my instincts.

As the mayor continued to reassure the guests, Jason and I edged toward the direction where I'd last seen the figure. The crowd swelled around us, a mass of laughter and conversation, yet it felt like an island of chaos in a sea of uncertainty.

Suddenly, a commotion erupted from the other side of the room, shouts and cries melding into a cacophony of alarm. I grabbed Jason's hand tightly, heart racing as we wove through the crowd, adrenaline surging through me.

As we approached the source of the commotion, a group had gathered, their faces contorted with shock and concern.

"What's going on?" I asked, breathless.

"Someone's been hurt!" a woman cried, her voice breaking through the chaos. "We need help!"

Panic gripped my heart as Jason and I pushed through the throng, the knot in my stomach tightening. The figure—had they been involved? The question hung in the air, weighty and ominous.

Jason's grip on my hand tightened as we made our way closer, the atmosphere growing heavier with every step.

"Please, let it not be serious," I murmured, dread pooling in my gut.

As we broke through the crowd, I was confronted with a scene that sent my heart plummeting. There, at the center, surrounded by a circle of concerned faces, lay a familiar figure on the ground, their eyes closed, motionless. My breath caught in my throat, and the world tilted beneath me, the vibrant colors of the evening fading into a dull gray.

"Is it...?" I whispered, unable to finish the sentence, dread hanging heavily in the air.

And just as Jason opened his mouth to speak, the figure stirred, and a chilling whisper slipped into the air, "Help me."

Chapter 15: Sabotage Unveiled

The evening had begun with such promise, the air heavy with the sweet, earthy scent of aged whiskey and the warmth of laughter bubbling from every corner of the distillery. Strings of golden lights twinkled overhead, reflecting in the polished surfaces of barrels lined with meticulous care, each a testament to the hard work and dedication that had gone into reviving this hidden gem. As guests milled about, glasses clinking, I felt a surge of pride watching Jason effortlessly charm our attendees, his dark curls bouncing as he gestured animatedly, the enthusiasm practically spilling from him like the fine whiskey we poured.

I lingered near the entrance, taking in the vibrant scene—a kaleidoscope of colors dancing under the warm glow. My heart swelled with a sense of belonging; after months of late nights and countless spreadsheets, this was our moment. But just as I was about to lose myself in the sheer joy of the occasion, a deafening crash echoed through the distillery, slicing through the laughter and the music like a jagged knife.

Gasps erupted, and I darted inside, my stomach dropping as I beheld the chaos unfurling before me. One of the displays, showcasing vintage bottles and memorabilia that told our story, lay shattered on the floor, shards of glass glistening ominously among the whiskey-soaked wood. The sight sent a jolt of disbelief through me, followed swiftly by a pang of anger. How could this happen? A murmur of disbelief swept through the crowd, the atmosphere shifting from festive to frantic in an instant.

"Who did this?" Jason's voice broke through the din, thick with confusion and anger. I turned to find him standing at the forefront of the gathering, his face a portrait of disappointment, the light in his eyes dimmed by shadows of uncertainty. "This was supposed to be our night."

I could almost hear the thoughts racing through his mind—was it sabotage? An accident? My heart sank at the prospect, the implications curling like smoke in the back of my mind. The crowd's whispers transformed into accusations, suspicions flying from lips that were once full of laughter. I stepped closer to Jason, determination hardening my resolve. We had poured our souls into this place, and I refused to let it be tarnished by fear or chaos.

"Stay calm," I urged, my voice steady despite the turmoil brewing inside me. "We need to find out what happened. This isn't over yet." I reached for his hand, giving it a reassuring squeeze, grounding both of us in the present.

He met my gaze, the fire returning to his eyes. "You're right. We can't let this ruin everything." His jaw set, determination igniting a spark that fueled my own. Together, we would unravel the mystery behind this calamity, and I felt the energy crackle between us like a live wire.

As we surveyed the damage, I noticed a few guests whispering among themselves, eyes darting suspiciously. I could feel the tension thicken, each moment stretching into eternity as I weighed the potential suspects in my mind. The rich tapestry of our community had woven together many personalities—some vibrant and welcoming, others more enigmatic and shadowy.

Then, I spotted her—Madeline, the town's self-proclaimed historian, her sharp eyes glinting with intrigue. She hovered near the edge of the crowd, her fingers tapping her chin thoughtfully as she surveyed the wreckage, an amused smile playing on her lips. My instincts flared. Madeline thrived on chaos, often reveling in the drama she could stir among our neighbors. Could she be behind this?

"Let's talk to her," I suggested to Jason, my voice low but insistent. "She might know more than she's letting on."

He nodded, the weight of the situation settling heavily on his shoulders. "All right. But we need to approach her carefully. She can be... unpredictable."

We made our way through the crowd, weaving between guests who were still buzzing with the shock of the crash. Madeline's laughter cut through the tension, an odd mix of amusement and schadenfreude that only deepened my suspicion. I couldn't shake the feeling that she was enjoying this moment far too much.

"Madeline," I called, forcing a smile to mask my unease. "Do you have a moment? We could use your insight on this disaster."

Her gaze flickered to me, then to the wreckage. "Oh, dear," she said, a hint of feigned sympathy lacing her tone. "What a shame. Such a beautiful display, now so tragically ruined. It's almost poetic, isn't it?"

"Poetic?" Jason echoed incredulously, his disbelief plain. "This isn't some artistic statement. It's vandalism!"

Her laugh rang out, light and mocking. "Vandalism? Perhaps. But accidents do happen, don't they? Maybe someone was a little too enthusiastic while enjoying the whiskey." She leaned closer, lowering her voice conspiratorially. "Or maybe it was a message. It's a tough world for entrepreneurs, after all."

The hairs on the back of my neck prickled as I sensed the undertone of her words. I exchanged a glance with Jason, silently agreeing to probe deeper. "Do you know if anyone seemed... overly interested in the display before it fell?" I asked, keeping my voice casual while my heart raced.

Madeline shrugged, a practiced nonchalance that did nothing to quell my suspicion. "Just the usual suspects, I suppose. You know how it goes in a small town—everyone has an opinion, and everyone loves a good story."

But there was something else in her eyes, something that flickered with a hint of mischief. I felt a growing certainty that she held the key to the truth, buried beneath layers of veiled sarcasm and her typical antics.

"Thanks for your... insights," I said, trying to keep my tone neutral as I gestured for Jason to move away. "Let's regroup and brainstorm how to handle this."

As we stepped back into the fray of the party, Jason's frustration was palpable. "I can't believe she would insinuate it's our fault. What kind of person enjoys stirring up trouble like this?"

"It's not just trouble; it's a distraction. We need to stay focused," I replied, my mind racing with possibilities. "If this is sabotage, we have to find out who's behind it. We can't let them win."

Jason's eyes darkened with determination. "We'll get to the bottom of this. I won't let anyone tear down what we've built."

With each passing moment, I could feel the weight of the night bearing down on us, the joyful ambiance around us now suffocating in the face of uncertainty. But deep within, I felt the stirring of resolve, a fierce determination to uncover the truth and protect our dream. Together, we would expose the saboteur lurking in our midst, and in doing so, we would reclaim our night, our hard work, and our future.

The clamor of the crowd surged and receded like waves against a rocky shore, their murmurs blending into a cacophony of confusion and disbelief. Jason and I exchanged glances filled with unspoken words, our connection grounding us in the storm of uncertainty. I felt the pulsing beat of the distillery, the heart of our efforts, throbbing beneath the surface, desperate to reclaim its rhythm.

As the guests fanned out, searching for explanations and trying to make sense of the chaos, Jason and I retreated to a corner, hidden from the prying eyes of those still grappling with the incident. "We need a plan," he said, running a hand through his tousled hair, frustration etched across his handsome features. "This is our night, and I refuse to let some coward ruin it for us."

His determination sparked something deep within me, a quiet strength urging me to rise above the chaos. "Agreed. But first, we should gather some intel. Let's split up. You talk to the guests—find out if anyone saw anything suspicious. I'll see what I can get from the staff. Maybe someone in the back saw something."

He nodded, his brow still furrowed, but I could see the fire returning to his eyes. "You're right. Let's do this. We'll make it right." With that, we parted ways, each stepping into our respective roles as detectives in this unexpected drama.

I made my way toward the staff area, where the kitchen hummed with activity. The air was thick with the aroma of fresh herbs and spices, a stark contrast to the tension permeating the main hall. I spotted Clara, one of the kitchen staff, her hands deftly slicing vegetables for a dish that would likely never be served. She looked up, her eyes wide, clearly shaken by the earlier commotion.

"Clara!" I called, moving closer. "Did you see anything happen? Any strange behavior from the guests?"

She paused, her knife hovering mid-air as her brow knitted in thought. "I didn't see much, but I heard the crash. It was loud. I thought maybe someone tripped over something. But then, a few minutes before, I saw that guy—" she leaned in, her voice a conspiratorial whisper—"the one with the mustache and the terrible Hawaiian shirt. He was hanging around the display, acting all shifty, like he was looking for something."

The mention of the man made my stomach churn with unease. I had noticed him earlier, hovering near the vintage bottles with a drink in hand, a flicker of mischief dancing in his eyes. "Do you think he could have done this on purpose?"

Clara shrugged, but there was a flicker of concern in her gaze. "I wouldn't put it past him. He seemed a bit too interested in things that weren't his."

The seed of suspicion burrowed deeper in my mind as I thanked Clara and moved back toward the main room. I needed to share what I had learned with Jason, but first, I took a moment to observe the guests. The laughter that had once filled the air was replaced by nervous chatter, with small knots of people huddled together, whispering. I could see fear in their eyes, and the thrill of the evening had dissipated like mist under the morning sun.

As I maneuvered through the crowd, I caught sight of Jason speaking animatedly to a couple near the bar. His hands animatedly traced the outline of our project, a passionate glow illuminating his face even in the aftermath of chaos. I couldn't help but admire his resolve. It was that spark of hope I needed, a reminder that we had built something beautiful here.

"Jason!" I called, making my way over. He turned, his expression shifting from concern to relief. "I think I have a lead. Clara mentioned seeing a guy in a Hawaiian shirt acting suspiciously near the display before it fell."

He raised an eyebrow, his interest piqued. "The guy with the mustache? I thought he seemed odd. I'll bet he's the one spreading the rumors of sabotage to make us look bad. We need to find out what he knows."

"Exactly," I said, my heart racing with the thrill of the chase. "Let's confront him. If he's behind this, we need to catch him red-handed."

Together, we wove through the crowd, searching for our elusive suspect. As we scanned the room, I spotted him leaning against a barrel, casually sipping from his glass as he chatted up an older woman with a bemused smile. I gestured to Jason, who nodded in agreement, a determined look crossing his face.

"Stay close," he whispered, an air of seriousness enveloping him. "We can't let him slip away."

With calculated steps, we approached the duo. The man's laughter echoed, a hollow sound that set my teeth on edge. "Excuse me," Jason interrupted, his tone firm yet composed. "Mind if we have a word?"

The man turned, his expression shifting from joviality to irritation in an instant. "Can't you see I'm busy?" he snapped, his voice dripping with disdain.

"It'll only take a moment," I added, keeping my tone steady, trying to defuse the tension. "We heard you were near the display when it fell. We'd like to know if you saw anything unusual."

His eyes narrowed, the jovial facade slipping to reveal something more sinister lurking beneath. "I didn't see anything. Just some old junk that doesn't matter anyway."

A flare of anger ignited within me. "It matters to us. That 'old junk' is part of our story, our hard work. You wouldn't want to be associated with causing chaos, would you?"

He scoffed, and I noticed a flicker of something in his expression, an almost imperceptible hesitation. "I don't have time for your little theatrics," he said, shoving past us, but I caught a glimpse of his fingers twitching, as if he were hiding something.

"Wait!" Jason called, stepping in front of him. "You can't just walk away. Not after everything that's happened."

For a brief moment, the man's eyes flared with something akin to panic before he regained his composure. "You think you can pin this on me? Good luck with that." He glanced back toward the crowd, his body language shifting from confrontational to evasive. "I'm outta here."

"Something's off," I whispered to Jason, my heart racing as I watched the man slip into the throng of guests. "We need to follow him."

As we maneuvered through the crowd, a sense of urgency gripped me. Each step felt like a heartbeat, quickening with the rhythm of the impending confrontation. The air buzzed with tension, whispers following us like a trail of smoke, igniting my instincts. Whatever this man was hiding, I was determined to unveil it before the night was entirely engulfed in shadows. The stakes had never been higher, and in the midst of all this turmoil, one thing became crystal clear: we weren't just protecting a celebration; we were fighting for our future.

I moved through the sea of faces, the buzzing crowd blurring into a kaleidoscope of worry and intrigue. The Hawaiian shirt man had melted into the throng, but my instincts screamed that he wasn't done yet. Jason followed close behind, his expression a mix of determination and concern, a handsome shadow flickering in the dim light of the distillery. I could feel the electric tension crackling between us, pushing me forward, each heartbeat resonating with purpose.

"Did you see where he went?" I asked, scanning the crowd. "He couldn't have vanished that quickly."

"Maybe he ducked into the restroom," Jason suggested, scanning the nearby areas. "Or he could be trying to slip out the back."

As if on cue, the sound of hurried footsteps echoed from the rear entrance. My pulse quickened as I caught sight of his gaudy shirt disappearing through the door. "There!" I shouted, grabbing Jason's arm and bolting toward the exit.

Outside, the air was cooler, tinged with the faint scent of freshly mown grass, but it was charged with an urgency that set my nerves alight. I pushed through the door and spotted him slipping away along a gravel path that wound behind the distillery. "Hey!" I yelled, my voice piercing through the night.

He turned, a look of surprise flashing across his face before he broke into a sprint. "Not today!" Jason shouted, and we took off after him, our footsteps crunching over the gravel, each sound amplified by adrenaline.

"Why are you running?" I called out, my breath coming in sharp bursts. "You're not getting away that easily!"

The man glanced back, his eyes wide with panic. "You wouldn't understand!" he shouted back, his voice laced with a mix of fear and defiance.

"Oh, I think we do!" Jason replied, pushing himself harder, his long legs gaining ground. "You're hiding something, and we intend to find out what!"

The chase wound around the back of the building, where the shadows loomed like silent witnesses, and the night sky above twinkled with indifferent stars. The man stumbled, his foot catching on a loose stone, and for a split second, I thought we had him. But he recovered quickly, darting around the corner of the distillery like a cornered animal, desperate and wild.

"We need to cut him off!" I shouted, gesturing toward a side entrance that led to a storage area, an idea forming in my mind. Jason nodded, and we veered left, taking a shortcut through a narrow path lined with wooden crates.

The air was thick with anticipation as we rounded the corner. I could hear the man's ragged breathing mingling with the sound of our own footsteps, a relentless symphony of pursuit. Just as we reached the entrance to the storage area, a loud clang echoed from inside, followed by a shuffling sound. My heart raced with urgency as I pushed open the door, the wooden frame creaking in protest.

Inside, the dim light flickered from a single overhead bulb, illuminating dusty shelves and forgotten barrels stacked high like sentinels guarding long-lost secrets. The sight sent a thrill of apprehension coursing through me. We stepped cautiously into the space, every sense heightened, ready for confrontation.

"Where are you?" Jason called, his voice steady but laced with tension. "You can't hide forever!"

A shuffle sounded from the back corner, and we both turned, our eyes narrowing. "Why don't you just come out?" I urged, trying to keep my voice even. "We're not here to hurt you. We just want to talk."

"Talk?" he sneered from the shadows, his silhouette barely visible against the backdrop of old barrels. "You think I'm just going to waltz out and tell you my plans? You're out of your league, sweetheart."

The use of that word sent a jolt of indignation through me, the casual dismissal riling me up more than I expected. "You don't know who you're dealing with," I shot back, stepping forward, unafraid. "We've built something real here, and I won't let you tear it down."

He stepped into the light, revealing his face twisted in anger, and a glint of something sharp caught my eye—a small blade tucked into his belt. My heart raced as I assessed the situation. This was no mere prankster; this was someone who meant business.

"Why are you doing this?" Jason asked, his tone softening as he stepped beside me, ready to shield me from whatever this man might do. "What do you gain from ruining our night?"

The man's expression shifted, a flicker of vulnerability peeking through his bravado. "You don't understand," he spat, his voice trembling slightly. "This place was supposed to be mine. I put in the work, but you—" he jabbed a finger toward us—"you took it all away."

The bitterness in his words hung heavy in the air, a tale of ambition turned to resentment. "This was your plan?" I asked incredulously. "To sabotage us? Do you really think that will get you anywhere?"

"It's not sabotage; it's reclaiming what's mine," he hissed, eyes narrowing with fervor. "You have no idea what I sacrificed to make this place what it is."

Jason took a step closer, hands raised in a placating gesture. "Let's talk this out. We can find a way to work together. There's enough room for everyone in this town."

But the man's gaze hardened, and the knife glinted ominously. "You think I'd let you two ruin everything? This is my shot. My last chance."

In that instant, I realized the depth of his desperation. Fear and ambition had twisted him into something unrecognizable. "You're wrong. This isn't about one person; it's about a community," I said, my voice firm. "You don't have to do this."

The tension in the air crackled, electric and suffocating. For a heartbeat, time stood still, each of us caught in a web of choices and consequences. "Step back," he warned, his voice low and dangerous, shifting on his feet, the blade now fully visible.

I felt Jason's presence beside me, an anchor amidst the storm, but I could sense the air growing thick with uncertainty. "We can help you, but you need to put down the knife," I pleaded, my heart pounding against my ribs. "This isn't the way."

A flicker of uncertainty crossed his features, but it was gone in an instant, replaced by a mask of resolve. "I won't let you take this from me."

Before I could respond, a loud crash erupted from outside, rattling the walls of the storage area. Instinct kicked in, adrenaline surging through my veins. "What was that?" I asked, my voice rising in urgency.

He glanced toward the door, a split-second decision playing out in his eyes, and then, with a swift movement, he lunged toward me, the knife aimed in my direction. The world narrowed to a single moment, the cacophony of the night fading away, leaving only the two of us suspended in a dance of fear and desperation.

But just as he reached for me, Jason surged forward, shoving me out of the way. "No!" I screamed, my heart lurching as I saw the blade glint ominously in the light, a sharp flash of impending danger.

And then the door swung open, revealing a figure silhouetted against the bright exterior light, a dark presence emerging from the chaos outside. "Stop right there!" the newcomer commanded, voice steady and authoritative.

In that instant, time froze, the outcome teetering on a precipice, and I could only hold my breath as the climax of our tense confrontation hung in the air, the weight of the moment pressing down like the heaviest storm cloud, ready to burst.

Chapter 16: Fractured Loyalties

Every moment spent in the sprawling Blackwood estate felt like stepping into a tempest, the air thick with unspoken tensions and the lingering scent of aged wood and polished marble. I stood at the edge of the grand foyer, my fingers lightly brushing against the intricate bannister that spiraled upwards into shadows. Outside, the autumn wind whipped the leaves into a frenzied dance, mirroring the chaos that had erupted within our lives since the sabotage. My family, with their well-meaning yet suffocating concern, seemed to forget that love was as much about choosing your battles as it was about nurturing peace.

Jason emerged from the darkened hallway, his silhouette a beacon of familiarity amidst the uncertainty. His dark hair fell over his forehead, and those deep-set eyes, filled with an intensity that could both mesmerize and terrify, locked onto mine. I could almost hear the crackle of electricity in the air between us, a reminder that despite everything, our connection had not been severed. "You shouldn't be here," he said, his voice low, laced with a gravelly warmth that sent a shiver down my spine.

"And yet, here I am," I replied, a hint of defiance slipping through my lips. I couldn't let fear dictate my choices. Not now. Not when every heartbeat echoed with the unspoken promise of solidarity. I stepped closer, the plush carpet absorbing the weight of our shared secrets. "We need to talk about what happened."

He ran a hand through his hair, a gesture of frustration I had come to recognize. "Talk? About what? About how my family is falling apart? About how they think I'm to blame for everything?" His voice trembled slightly, a betrayal of his steely exterior. "They've always wanted me to be the perfect son, but look at what being perfect has cost me."

I reached out, my fingertips brushing against the rough fabric of his shirt, grounding him as much as myself. "Jason, you're not responsible for their choices. We're tangled in something bigger than us, and we have to face it together. You can't shut me out."

The pain flickering in his gaze deepened, turning those midnight eyes into stormy pools. "I can't let you get hurt because of me. My family isn't just a burden; they're a threat." He paused, his breathing uneven as he leaned closer, his forehead nearly touching mine. "You don't understand what they're capable of."

"But I understand you," I said, my voice steady despite the turmoil swirling within. "You're not them. We can break free from this legacy if we choose to."

His lips curled into a wry smile, a fleeting glimpse of the boy who once found joy in the simplest things. "You really believe that, don't you? That love can conquer chaos? That we can outrun our shadows?"

"I believe we can at least try," I challenged, feeling a rush of adrenaline course through me. "Staying apart only feeds into their narrative. We need to be bold enough to challenge them."

The faint sound of footsteps echoed from the hallway, breaking our moment. Jason stepped back, his expression shifting from vulnerability to a hardened resolve. "You should go. It's too dangerous for you to stay here."

"No," I insisted, feeling the walls close in as panic surged. "If you push me away, you're giving them what they want. I'm not going to let fear dictate our choices."

He looked torn, and in that moment, I saw the weight of his lineage hanging heavy on his shoulders. "They won't stop until they've ruined everything," he murmured, his voice thick with emotion. "You have no idea how far they'll go."

"But I do know how far I'm willing to go," I countered, my heart racing. "I won't run. Not from you, not from them. We'll find a way to fight back."

The tension between us crackled with unspoken words, a fragile thread tethering our fates together. But as the door swung open, revealing a figure that sent a chill through the room, I realized that the battle lines had been drawn.

A tall, imposing man stepped into the foyer, his presence radiating authority. It was Victor Blackwood, Jason's father, whose reputation for ruthlessness preceded him. His sharp features glinted in the low light, and his gaze swept across us with a mixture of disdain and curiosity. "What's this?" he asked, his voice smooth like silk over a blade. "A clandestine meeting? How... romantic."

Jason stiffened beside me, the air thickening with dread. "Dad, I—"

"Don't," Victor interrupted, his tone as cold as the marble beneath our feet. "I won't have you dragging this girl into our family's mess." He turned his eyes towards me, sizing me up as if I were an unwanted guest at a gathering. "You have no idea what you're stepping into, young lady. This isn't a fairy tale. You're playing with fire."

"I know exactly what I'm stepping into," I retorted, the defiance in my voice surprising even myself. "But I'm not afraid of the heat. Jason deserves a choice, and so do I."

Victor's smile was thin and menacing, his amusement unmasked. "How noble of you. But let me make one thing clear: loyalty is a fragile thing, easily fractured, and often costly. If you think you can stand by him and emerge unscathed, you're in for a rude awakening."

The silence that followed was palpable, tension coiling tighter in the air. Jason's hand found mine, squeezing it with a ferocity that both terrified and exhilarated me. Together, we faced Victor, the embodiment of the chaos we were determined to challenge.

"Let's see just how far your loyalty stretches, shall we?" he said, his voice dropping to a low whisper, full of promises of danger and intrigue. "Because I assure you, the game has only just begun."

In that moment, I realized that we were not just caught in the crossfire of familial feuds; we were destined to be players in a game far greater than ourselves, and the stakes were higher than I could have ever imagined.

"Maybe it's time you learned what loyalty really means," Victor's voice echoed through the grand foyer, a low rumble that sent a shiver down my spine. His gaze flicked between Jason and me, a predator savoring its prey. The air thickened, the tension almost palpable, and I felt the urge to step closer to Jason, to draw strength from his presence. But the barrier between us, constructed from family loyalty and impending threats, felt insurmountable.

"Loyalty?" I said, my voice steady despite the storm swirling around us. "You mean blind allegiance to your whims? That's not how this works." My words hung in the air, defiant and bold. I hadn't planned to confront him, but fear had ignited a fire within me, a desire to stand up for what was right—even if it meant facing the patriarch of the Blackwood family head-on.

Victor's brows arched, a flicker of surprise crossing his features. "You are either remarkably brave or hopelessly naïve." His gaze sharpened. "What's your name again?"

"Claire," I replied, refusing to back down. "And I might not know everything about the Blackwoods, but I know enough to understand that family shouldn't come at the cost of integrity."

Jason's grip on my hand tightened, grounding me even as uncertainty swirled in his expression. "Claire, you don't have to—"

"I do," I interrupted, casting a quick glance at him. "I can't just stand by and let him dictate our choices."

Victor smirked, the kind of smile that dripped with arrogance and mischief. "Ah, young love. So many believe it can conquer all.

But let me remind you, Claire, in this world, love often gets sacrificed on the altar of loyalty." He stepped closer, invading my space, and I fought the instinct to recoil. "You'd do well to remember that."

The words lingered in the air, heavy and foreboding, but I refused to let fear sway my resolve. "You think I'm scared of your family? I'm not afraid of chaos; I thrive in it."

"Oh, Claire," he said, a mocking tone slipping into his voice, "you're quite the firecracker. But even fire can be extinguished." He turned his gaze back to Jason, and I could feel the tension crackle like static electricity between them. "You're playing with fire too, son. You should consider who you choose to align yourself with. Her naivety might just be your downfall."

Jason's eyes darkened with a mix of anger and determination. "I'm not afraid of my family's shadow anymore, Dad. I'm tired of living in fear of what you and your reputation dictate. I choose my own path."

Victor laughed, a chilling sound that reverberated through the grand space. "And what path would that be? A path of rebellion? Think carefully about your choices. The Blackwoods are not to be trifled with, and neither am I."

"Neither are we," I declared, the conviction in my voice ringing true as I stepped beside Jason, our hands still intertwined. "We will fight for what's right, together. Your threats don't intimidate us."

The flicker of admiration in Jason's eyes bolstered my confidence, but Victor's smile remained, filled with menace. "This isn't a game you want to play, Claire. You may find yourself in far deeper waters than you anticipate."

And with that, he turned sharply on his heel, the echo of his footsteps fading down the corridor like a fading storm. The weight of his words settled heavily in the air, a haunting reminder of the stakes we were facing.

As the door closed behind him, a suffocating silence enveloped us. I turned to Jason, my heart racing, the gravity of the moment crashing over me. "Are we really doing this?"

He searched my eyes, his expression a mix of awe and concern. "I'm not sure what we're walking into, but I know that I can't let him dictate my life any longer. If it means standing by you, then I'll do it. But it won't be easy, Claire."

"I didn't expect it to be," I replied, the rush of adrenaline still coursing through me. "But we'll figure it out together."

His lips twitched into a smile, and I felt a flicker of warmth amidst the chaos. "You're incredibly brave. Or perhaps you're just a little insane."

"Maybe both," I shot back, a playful grin breaking through the tension. "But at least we'll be in this mess together."

The corners of his mouth lifted in response, the weight of the moment lightening slightly. "Just promise me you won't back down, even when it gets rough."

"I promise," I said, the sincerity in my voice wrapping around us like a shield. "But we need to prepare for what's coming. We have to gather information, find allies. Victor's not going to let this go."

Jason nodded, his expression shifting to one of determination. "We need to talk to my sister, Eliza. She's been digging around, trying to uncover some of the family secrets. She might know something that could help us."

"Good idea," I replied, feeling a surge of hope. "We should meet her somewhere discreet. Somewhere we won't be under watchful eyes."

The thought of bringing in more people felt daunting yet exhilarating. This was no longer just our battle; it was becoming something larger, a coalition against the shadows that had loomed over us for too long.

Jason hesitated, a shadow crossing his features. "What if she doesn't want to get involved? She's always been the peacemaker."

"Then we'll convince her," I said, my resolve hardening. "She deserves to know what's happening, and if she truly cares about you, she'll want to help."

"Okay," he agreed, his voice firming. "Let's go find her. But we need to be careful. The last thing we need is to walk into another trap."

"Agreed," I replied, my heart racing with the thrill of the unknown. As we stepped out into the crisp evening air, the setting sun painted the sky in hues of orange and purple, and I felt a sense of urgency wash over me. We were on the brink of something monumental, and the weight of our choices loomed large.

Together, we walked into the fray, determined to confront the chaos that awaited us. The shadows of our past may have threatened to consume us, but we were ready to stand firm against them, our loyalty forged not in fear but in love and conviction. And perhaps, just perhaps, we would find a way to carve our own destiny amidst the fractured loyalties that surrounded us.

As we made our way through the winding corridors of the Blackwood estate, the shadows seemed to stretch and thrum with life, whispering secrets of the past that clung to the ornate walls. I followed closely behind Jason, the weight of our impending confrontation with his sister pressing heavily on my shoulders. The air was thick with tension, almost suffocating, and I couldn't shake the feeling that we were being watched.

Jason paused at a grand door, glancing back at me with an intensity that made my heart race. "This is it. Are you ready?"

"Ready as I'll ever be," I replied, trying to infuse my voice with confidence, though my insides twisted with uncertainty. The door swung open to reveal a dimly lit room adorned with plush furnishings and heavy drapery, the atmosphere heavy with unspoken words. Eliza sat at a large mahogany desk, her brow furrowed in concentration, a cascade of papers strewn about as if she had been grappling with the weight of their family's legacy for days.

"Eliza," Jason called softly, and she looked up, her expression shifting from surprise to concern in an instant.

"Jason! You're here!" she exclaimed, rising to her feet. But then her gaze landed on me, and the warmth in her demeanor evaporated, replaced by a cautious distance. "What's going on?"

"Can we talk? It's urgent," Jason said, stepping further into the room. I followed, determined to stand by him, even as Eliza's eyes darted between us, suspicion brewing beneath her surface.

"Talk about what? And why are you dragging her into this?" she demanded, crossing her arms.

"Because we're in it together now," I interjected, feeling the need to assert my place in this chaos. "Your family is involved in something dangerous, and we need your help to unravel it."

Eliza's eyes narrowed, skepticism etched across her features. "Dangerous? You don't know what you're talking about."

"Actually, I do," I countered, my voice steady as I pulled a chair closer to the desk. "We know about the sabotage, about the forces at play within the Blackwood family. We can't just sit back and pretend it isn't happening."

The tension in the room crackled, and Eliza's expression shifted as realization dawned. "You're serious," she said slowly, processing the implications of our words. "The sabotage... That was a warning. You shouldn't be here, either of you."

"No one gets to decide that for us," Jason asserted, his voice firm. "We're not letting fear dictate our actions any longer. We need to uncover the truth, Eliza."

The room felt smaller, as if the walls were closing in on us, and I could see the struggle within her—caught between family loyalty and the potential for change. "You really think we can confront this head-on? The Blackwoods don't just let things go."

"We have to try," I urged, desperation creeping into my tone. "We can't live in the shadows any longer. It's time to expose the chaos for what it is."

Eliza's shoulders sagged, and she glanced around as if the room itself might betray us. "Fine," she said finally, her voice barely above a whisper. "But if we're doing this, we need a plan. I've been piecing together information, but it's risky. We'll need to be careful."

"Risky is my middle name," I replied with a small grin, trying to lighten the mood. But the corners of Eliza's mouth barely twitched, a reminder of the gravity of our situation.

"Then let's get started," Jason said, determination lining his features. "What do you have?"

Eliza leaned over her desk, gathering the scattered papers into a semblance of order. "There have been rumors," she began, her voice low, "whispers of a faction within the family that's been undermining our business dealings. They're the ones who might have orchestrated the sabotage. If we can identify them, we can bring everything to light."

"Who are they?" I asked, the tension coiling tightly in my chest.

"Names have been floating around—some of them are close to home," she said, her eyes darting to the door, as if expecting someone to burst in at any moment. "But the biggest name is my uncle, Henry. He's been known to play both sides, and he has connections to unsavory characters."

"Henry Blackwood," Jason muttered, his jaw tightening. "I've heard the stories. He's ruthless."

"Exactly," Eliza affirmed, her voice filled with conviction. "And if he's involved, then we have to tread carefully. He won't hesitate to eliminate anyone who threatens his plans."

The weight of her words settled heavily in the air, and a chill ran down my spine. "What if he finds out we're investigating? We need to act quickly, but we also need to be smart about it."

"I can gather more information," Eliza offered, a flicker of hope igniting in her eyes. "I have a contact at one of the family functions coming up. If I can get close to Henry without raising suspicion, it might provide us with the intel we need."

"Good plan," Jason said, admiration threading through his voice. "But we'll need to protect you. If he senses anything off, it could blow back on all of us."

Eliza waved her hand dismissively. "I can handle myself, Jason. I'm not a child anymore."

"Right, because it went so well last time you confronted him," Jason shot back, his tone teasing yet serious. "But seriously, we need to be careful. We're all at risk here."

As the three of us laid out a plan, a sense of camaraderie began to form, knitting our fates together in ways I hadn't anticipated. I felt a swell of determination, ready to take on the world with these two formidable allies by my side.

Just as we began discussing our next steps, a sudden commotion outside the door caught our attention. Raised voices echoed through the halls, the unmistakable sound of a confrontation brewing.

"What was that?" Eliza asked, her brow furrowing as she moved toward the door, curiosity piquing her interest.

"Stay back," Jason warned, positioning himself protectively in front of me. "It could be a trap."

But curiosity overpowered caution as Eliza swung the door open. I peered around Jason, my heart racing at the sight before us. A group of men, sharply dressed yet menacing, stood facing Victor. The tension was palpable, their posture rigid, as they exchanged harsh words laden with threats.

Victor's voice rose above the others, his tone steely and authoritative. "I told you to stay out of this. The Blackwoods don't take kindly to intrusions."

"We're here for the information, Victor," one of the men replied, his voice low and dangerous. "Hand it over, or we'll make this personal."

In that instant, I felt the world tilt on its axis, the weight of the chaos pressing in on us like a vice. I glanced at Jason and Eliza, their expressions mirroring my own shock. This was the storm we had been warned about, the very chaos we had sought to confront.

"Now," Jason whispered urgently, "we need to get out of here. Fast."

But before we could react, a loud crash echoed through the hall, followed by the unmistakable sound of splintering wood. My heart raced as the door swung open wider, revealing a frantic Eliza's wide eyes. "We're out of time! We need to move, now!"

Just as we turned to escape, a figure barreled into the room, blocking our path. I froze, my breath hitching as I recognized the man before us. It was Henry Blackwood, his expression a mask of cold calculation, and in that moment, I realized we were cornered—caught between two worlds spiraling into chaos.

"Going somewhere?" he sneered, his eyes glinting with malice as the door slammed shut behind him, sealing our fate in the ever-tightening grip of the Blackwood legacy.

Chapter 17: The Search for Answers

The early evening sky draped itself in a soft indigo hue, casting a cool glow over the quiet streets of Maplewood. It was the kind of evening that invited secrets to unfold, the kind that felt pregnant with possibility. Jason and I leaned against the weathered wooden rail of the town's old gazebo, the creaking wood beneath us whispering stories of a simpler time. The air was thick with the mingled scents of blooming lilacs and the faintest trace of fried food from the nearby fair, a perfect disguise for the undercurrent of tension that crackled between us.

"Do you really think it was someone from the fundraiser?" Jason asked, his brow furrowed, eyes scanning the shadows as if expecting someone to leap out and confess. He had that determined look, the one that made his jaw tighten and his brow furrow, like a man on a mission—and I loved that about him.

"Someone had to know about the proposal before it was made public," I replied, absently twisting the silver bracelet on my wrist. It was a gift from my grandmother, and in moments like this, I could almost hear her voice reminding me to trust my instincts. "And if they did, they had a reason to stop it."

He sighed, frustration lacing his tone. "And we have no idea how deep this rabbit hole goes."

We turned our focus to the town hall, where the light flickered from the second-floor office. It had become our unofficial headquarters. I had spent countless hours there as a child, draping myself over the desks and pretending to be a city council member. The thought brought a smile to my lips, but now, it felt tainted. I shoved the nostalgia away; this was serious.

We had decided to start with the people who had attended the fundraiser—the ones who might have overheard something they weren't meant to. Jason grabbed his notebook, flipping through the pages until he found the meticulously scrawled list we had compiled. I marveled at how focused he could be, yet how easily he found himself distracted by the smallest detail, like the way he brushed his fingers through his hair every time he was deep in thought.

"I think we should start with Mrs. Henderson," he suggested, a glimmer of mischief in his eyes. "She always has her nose in everyone's business, and she knows how to keep secrets."

"Right, the unofficial town gossip," I replied, suppressing a laugh. "She's practically a one-woman newspaper."

Jason chuckled, but then his face turned serious. "But she might know something. It's worth a shot."

As we strolled down the streets, I couldn't shake the feeling that the night was shifting, like the atmosphere before a storm. Mrs. Henderson's house was a quaint little cottage with vibrant pink shutters and a garden overflowing with wildflowers. Her home was as inviting as her personality, yet I knew her sharp tongue could cut deeper than any blade if she felt it necessary.

"Do you think she'll be home?" I asked, half-hoping she wouldn't be. Part of me dreaded what she might reveal.

"Only one way to find out." Jason reached for the doorbell, his fingers hovering just above the button, hesitating for a heartbeat before pressing it.

The chime echoed through the house, followed by the sound of hurried footsteps. The door swung open, revealing Mrs. Henderson, her eyes twinkling with mischief and curiosity. "Well, well, if it isn't my favorite duo! What brings you to my humble abode?"

"Hi, Mrs. Henderson," I said, forcing a smile despite the churn of nerves in my stomach. "We're looking into some things that happened at the fundraiser. Do you have a moment?"

Her expression shifted subtly, a flicker of recognition passing over her features. "Ah, the sabotage. I heard all about it. Come in, come in!"

The interior was a kaleidoscope of colors—walls adorned with family photographs, and the aroma of freshly baked cookies wafted through the air, beckoning me closer. I felt my tension ease slightly, knowing this was a place of warmth, yet I remained on edge, fully aware of the gravity of our inquiry.

As we settled into her cozy living room, Mrs. Henderson poured us glasses of sweet tea, her hands steady, a testament to years of practice. "Now, what exactly are you two looking for? I must say, it's quite brave of you to delve into this mess."

Jason leaned forward, his tone earnest. "We believe someone at the fundraiser had prior knowledge of the proposal and may have tried to sabotage it. We want to know if you heard anything unusual."

She took a moment, her gaze drifting as if she were sifting through memories, her fingers tracing the rim of her glass. "You know, my late husband had a saying: 'In every storm, there's a hidden treasure.' Perhaps you're looking for something that isn't meant to be found."

"What do you mean?" I pressed, intrigued and apprehensive all at once.

"There are stories woven into this town's fabric—stories of love, betrayal, and secrets. You might want to look beyond the obvious."

Her cryptic words hung in the air like the last note of a symphony, heavy with meaning. I exchanged a glance with Jason, the unspoken questions lingering between us. Just then, the door creaked open again, and a gust of wind swept through the room, carrying with it the scent of impending rain.

"Did you feel that?" Jason asked, his voice barely a whisper, the chill in the air raising goosebumps on my skin.

Mrs. Henderson smiled knowingly. "Ah, the wind always knows more than we do. It carries secrets from one corner of the world to another. Pay attention to it, dear. It might just guide you to your answers."

In that moment, as the storm brewed outside, I felt an electric charge in the air, a promise that we were about to plunge deeper into a tangled web of secrets. The tension pulsed, and the stakes had never felt higher. Little did we know, the answers we sought were just the beginning of an adventure that would change everything we thought we knew about our families—and about ourselves.

The wind howled outside, rattling the windows as if it were eager to spill secrets of its own. I could almost feel the storm echoing Mrs. Henderson's enigmatic words as we left her cozy cottage. Jason and I stood for a moment on the porch, the fresh scent of rain mingling with the sweetness of the cookies we'd just eaten. I glanced at him, catching the flickering light of determination in his eyes, igniting a fire in my own chest.

"Okay, so where to next?" I asked, feeling the adrenaline surge through me.

"Let's head to the library. If there's any dirt to dig up, it'll be there." His confidence felt like a warm blanket in the chill of the approaching storm.

The town library had always been my haven—a place filled with the scent of aged paper and the promise of knowledge waiting to be unearthed. The stone building loomed ahead, its facade heavy with history. Inside, the soft glow of lamps bathed the rows of books in a golden hue, creating cozy nooks that invited whispered conversations.

As we made our way past the reading tables, I couldn't help but feel a twinge of nostalgia. I remembered countless afternoons spent here, nestled in a corner, losing myself in stories while the world outside faded away. But today, the atmosphere buzzed with urgency, each step bringing us closer to unearthing the truth.

"Do you think anyone's here at this hour?" I asked, my voice barely a whisper.

Jason smirked. "In a place like this? Probably the ghost of some ancient librarian scolding us for making noise."

I chuckled softly, glancing around to see if the specter of a shushing figure would materialize. We approached the main desk, where Mr. Thompson, the librarian, sat hunched over a stack of books. His round glasses slid down the bridge of his nose as he peered at us over them, a mixture of surprise and delight lighting up his features.

"Ah, the intrepid duo! What brings you to my domain after hours?" he asked, adjusting his glasses.

"We're on a bit of a quest for information," I replied, feeling a spark of excitement. "Do you have any records of the town's history? Maybe something about family feuds or scandals?"

Mr. Thompson's eyebrows shot up, a grin creeping onto his face. "Scandals? Now that's the sort of inquiry I can sink my teeth into! You know, there's always been talk of some old grudges buried deep within these walls. Follow me."

As he led us through the labyrinth of shelves, I caught snippets of conversations from the past, echoing through the dusty air. The history of Maplewood felt alive, swirling around us like the dust motes that danced in the beams of light. Mr. Thompson guided us to a back room where old records were kept, the musty scent of paper and time wrapping around us like a familiar embrace.

"We might find something in the archives," he said, pulling out a large, leather-bound tome. The spine cracked as he opened it, revealing yellowed pages filled with faded ink. "This chronicles the founding families of Maplewood. Rumor has it that some of them weren't always on friendly terms."

I leaned in, scanning the pages filled with names that made my heart race. There it was: the Kincaid family, our family, intertwined with the Hawthornes, the very family at the center of our investigation. The animosity was palpable, each entry revealing layers of tension that had festered over generations. "This is it!" I exclaimed, my finger tracing over the names like a touchstone to a forgotten past.

Jason leaned closer, his shoulder brushing mine. "What does it say?"

"There was a property dispute back in the day," I read aloud, my voice tinged with disbelief. "It escalated to accusations of theft and betrayal. The Kincaids and the Hawthornes nearly came to blows in the town square. It ended with a bitter separation and promises of revenge."

"Revenge? That sounds dramatic enough for a soap opera," Jason remarked, his eyes sparkling with intrigue. "What else?"

I flipped through more pages, the weight of the stories thickening the air around us. The further I dug, the more unsettling the revelations became. The Kincaids had not only been embroiled in property disputes; there were whispers of secret romances and affairs that crossed family lines, scandalous enough to shatter reputations.

"Listen to this," I said, my voice dropping to a conspiratorial whisper. "It mentions a secret meeting between a Kincaid and a Hawthorne under the old oak tree in the center of town. They had planned to unite the families."

"Until someone found out and made it a tragedy instead," Jason finished, a shadow crossing his face.

I felt a chill run down my spine as the pieces began to fit together. "What if the current sabotage is just the latest act in a long line of betrayals? This isn't just about the fundraiser—it's about something much deeper."

"Great," Jason said, his sarcasm evident. "Nothing like a little family drama to spice up our lives. Let's hope we don't end up in the middle of a modern-day feud."

We spent hours pouring over records, the shadows lengthening around us as the storm outside intensified. Each new finding felt like unearthing buried treasure, yet it brought more questions than answers. The library, once a sanctuary, transformed into a haunting place where echoes of the past lingered like the scent of old books.

Just as I was about to turn to another dusty volume, a figure appeared at the door, silhouetted against the harsh fluorescent lights of the hallway. My heart raced as the figure stepped into the room, revealing a familiar face—Lydia Hawthorne, her expression unreadable, a storm brewing behind her eyes.

"Fancy meeting you here," she said, her tone dripping with sarcasm. "Digging up dirt on my family, are we?"

Jason's posture stiffened beside me. "Lydia, we—"

"Oh, don't bother. I know all about your little investigation." Her voice was sharp, cutting through the air. "And trust me, you'll want to stop digging before you unearth something you can't handle."

The air thickened with tension, the flickering fluorescent lights above casting ominous shadows. I exchanged a glance with Jason, the unspoken understanding flickering between us. Lydia wasn't just a player in this game; she was a potential wild card, and I could feel the stakes rising as we stared each other down, ready for the next move in this twisted game of secrets and lies.

With a fresh resolve, Jason and I spent long days and even longer nights trying to piece together the puzzle that threatened not only our families but also the burgeoning relationship we were desperately trying to nurture. The weight of old grievances felt heavier with each conversation, and the air crackled with a sense of impending revelation. Each name we uncovered was tied to another, creating a tapestry of betrayal that threatened to ensnare us both.

Our first visit was to Ms. Wilkins, the elderly town librarian, who had more than just dusty tomes lining her shelves; she had a memory sharper than a tack and a penchant for eavesdropping that rivaled a seasoned detective. Her small, cluttered office smelled of paper and time, and as we approached, she looked up from her crossword with a raised eyebrow. "Ah, the dynamic duo returns. What dark secrets are you unearthing this time?"

"We're not sure, but we think it might involve the fundraisers," I replied, feeling a strange mix of excitement and dread swirl in my stomach.

"Fundraisers, you say? Oh, those have always been a hotbed for scandal. My dear, you wouldn't believe the stories I could tell," she mused, a glint of mischief in her eye.

Jason leaned forward, intrigue evident in his expression. "What kind of stories, Ms. Wilkins?"

"Only the juiciest, of course. But you know what they say: if you dig too deep, you might just find what you didn't want to know." She chuckled lightly, a sound that hinted at years of holding onto secrets, and gestured for us to sit. "I've been cataloging the past fundraisers. They're filled with not just names but a tapestry of alliances, rivalries, and yes, betrayals. You might want to look through the records. Start with the last one and work your way back."

We spent hours sifting through the town's history, feeling like archaeologists unearthing artifacts that had long been buried under layers of silence. As we flipped through yellowed papers and brittle photographs, I could almost hear the whispers of our ancestors echoing through the hall. With each name, the tension grew thicker, wrapping around us like a warm blanket, yet fraught with unease.

At one point, I stumbled across a name that sent chills down my spine: the Hawthorn family. I glanced at Jason, who was engrossed in a faded newspaper clipping. "Hey, you might want to see this," I said, my voice barely above a whisper.

"What did you find?" he asked, his eyes lighting up with a flicker of hope.

"A fundraiser from five years ago. Look who was prominently featured," I pointed, heart racing. "Your father and my mother. Together. Again."

His brow furrowed as he scanned the article, and the silence stretched between us like an unspoken acknowledgment of a truth we weren't ready to confront. "They never mentioned that they were involved together like this. Not once. It's as if they've wiped the slate clean for us."

"Maybe that's the point," I suggested, my mind racing. "What if this is all connected? What if they're trying to keep us from digging into the past?"

The atmosphere shifted, thick with realization. The darkness of family secrets loomed over us like storm clouds, and a palpable fear settled into my bones. "Do you think they'd go so far as to sabotage the fundraiser to protect their own interests?"

"I don't know, but it seems like they have more to lose than we thought," he murmured, a hint of anger lacing his tone.

That evening, under the dim light of a flickering bulb in my living room, we pored over our findings, marking connections between families that felt both familiar and foreign. The more we uncovered, the more tangled the threads became. It was as if we were unwittingly digging a grave for truths that had long been buried. The air was thick with the scent of betrayal, and each revelation echoed through the silence, making our hearts race with an anxiety we couldn't ignore.

The next day, we decided to confront Jason's father. His demeanor was calm, almost too composed, as he listened to our findings. "You kids have quite the imagination," he said, dismissing our concerns with a wave of his hand. "Family history isn't something you should meddle in."

Jason clenched his fists, a storm brewing behind his eyes. "You mean the family history that includes our parents trying to keep us apart? This isn't just some fairy tale, Dad! People's lives are at stake!"

His father's expression darkened, a shadow passing over his features. "You need to stay out of it. Trust me; some secrets are best left buried."

"But we deserve to know the truth," I interjected, my heart racing. "We're not afraid of the past."

With that, he turned away, dismissing us like we were a couple of misbehaving children. We left the meeting feeling like a small boat lost at sea, tossed around by waves of uncertainty and confusion.

The weight of what we had learned pressed down on us as we made our way home. Just as I thought I could catch my breath, my phone buzzed ominously in my pocket. It was a message from Jason: "Meet me at the old church. Now."

My stomach dropped. The old church had been abandoned for years, and I couldn't shake the feeling that whatever awaited us there would change everything.

As I arrived, the door creaked open, revealing a dimly lit interior. Dust motes danced in the air, illuminated by the slanted beams of sunlight filtering through broken windows. Jason stood at the front, tension radiating from him like heat from a fire.

"Have you ever thought about what we might find here?" he asked, his voice steady yet urgent.

"What do you mean?" I stepped closer, anxiety pooling in my gut.

"This place has always been a meeting point for our families. It's where they made decisions, struck deals, and hid secrets. I think we might find something that links our parents to the sabotage," he said, determination etched into his features.

As he led me deeper into the shadows of the church, the air became charged with anticipation. The creaking floorboards seemed to echo our racing hearts. Suddenly, a loud crash echoed from the back of the church, freezing us in place.

"Did you hear that?" I whispered, my pulse quickening.

Jason nodded, his gaze locking on the source of the sound. "We need to check it out."

Just as we started to move, a figure stepped out from the shadows, their face obscured. "You shouldn't have come here," they said, voice low and menacing.

And just like that, the veil of secrecy began to unravel, revealing a danger neither of us had anticipated. In that moment, all I could think was that whatever truths lay ahead would demand a steep price—one I wasn't sure we were ready to pay.

Chapter 18: The Confrontation

The barn was an anachronism, its wooden beams splintered and faded like old memories, clutching at the past with every creak. Sunlight streamed through the gaps in the weathered planks, casting long shadows across the dirt floor, illuminating motes of dust that danced like restless spirits. The air was thick with the scent of hay and something more bitter—tension, electric and suffocating, a warning hanging heavy in the silence. I felt the warmth of Jason's presence beside me, a steadfast anchor in a world turned upside down.

As we waited, I caught a glimpse of him, his dark hair tousled by the wind, his jaw set in grim determination. It was odd how that fierce resolve was both comforting and disconcerting. Our breaths synchronized, a quiet rhythm that seemed to underscore the uncertainty stretching before us. I wished I could reach out, squeeze his hand, offer him the solace of shared strength, but the weight of the moment held me firmly in place.

Then, the creaking of the barn door shattered the stillness, each groan echoing our dread. He walked in—Lucas, the last person I had ever expected to see in this intimate, sacred space that held our shared childhood, filled with laughter and the promise of adventure. I felt as if the ground had been ripped from beneath my feet, the familiar comfort of this place morphing into a stage for a dark drama unfolding before us.

"Surprised to see me?" Lucas's voice dripped with a honeyed sarcasm that made my skin crawl. He had always possessed that charm, an effortless charisma that masked a cunning edge. Today, that charm felt like a thin veneer, easily shattered by the weight of betrayal hanging in the air.

"What are you doing here, Lucas?" Jason's voice cut through the tension like a knife, sharp and demanding. He stepped forward, his body taut with anger, the muscles in his arms flexing with barely contained rage. I admired his courage, but I could also sense the fear rippling beneath the surface.

"Isn't it obvious?" Lucas leaned against the wall, a disconcertingly casual posture that belied the chaos he had wrought. "I came to clear the air. After all, it seems we've all been led astray."

"Led astray? You orchestrated this entire mess!" My voice emerged louder than I intended, echoing in the vastness of the barn, fueled by a mix of disbelief and fury. "You've manipulated everything, turned us against each other for your own gain."

Lucas's smile faltered for a fleeting moment, but then it returned, a predatory grin that made my stomach churn. "Manipulated? That's a rather dramatic word, don't you think? I simply nudged things in a certain direction. You two made it so easy."

Jason took a step forward, closing the distance, and I felt a surge of pride for him. "You're a coward, hiding behind smiles and pretty words while you play games with our lives. Why, Lucas? What do you gain from this?"

"Isn't it obvious?" Lucas straightened, his expression shifting from playful to serious, the mask slipping away to reveal a chilling determination. "I want what you two have. The connection, the support. Your families have always had power and influence, and I—well, I've always felt like the forgotten child. The shadow."

My heart sank at his confession, recognizing the echoes of a loneliness I could understand, but his twisted sense of justice was far from just. "You think destroying our lives would bring you happiness?" I interjected, my voice trembling with a mix of empathy and outrage.

"Not just happiness," he countered, his tone almost wistful. "I wanted recognition. To finally be someone, not just the afterthought. But I see now that maybe I've overplayed my hand."

UNFINISHED PATHS

Jason's eyes blazed with anger. "You think you can fix this? You think we'll just forgive you because you were hurt? This isn't some childhood game, Lucas. We're not children anymore."

"Then why are we still playing?" Lucas shot back, a sardonic lilt to his voice that belied the seriousness of our predicament. "You think your lives are so perfect? Look around you. You're standing here, barely holding it together, and it's all because of me. I made you confront your own weaknesses."

In that moment, I felt a surge of clarity amid the chaos. Lucas was right about one thing: our lives had been spiraling out of control, but not because of him. It was because we had allowed our fears, our insecurities, to fester unchecked. My heart raced as I turned to Jason, the fire in my chest igniting a deeper resolve.

"This isn't just about you, Lucas," I said, my voice firm, despite the tremor of anxiety lurking beneath. "It's about all of us. We've all been lost in our own ways, but this? This isn't the answer."

Lucas's eyes flickered, uncertainty flashing across his face, and for a brief moment, the masks slipped away. "What do you suggest, then? A group hug and a chat over coffee?" His laughter was bitter, but I saw the flicker of vulnerability beneath his bravado.

"Maybe," I replied, daring to take a step closer, "but it has to start with honesty. You can't keep tearing us down to build yourself up. It doesn't work that way."

The three of us stood there, the air thick with unsaid words, the weight of our shared history binding us in ways that felt both comforting and suffocating. I wanted to reach out to Lucas, to bridge the gap that had widened between us, but I also felt the need to protect what Jason and I had fought to maintain.

The silence stretched on, each second echoing with potential. The confrontation loomed like a storm cloud above us, threatening to unleash chaos or deliver clarity. I felt the tremors of a change beneath the surface, a shift that might either shatter everything we had known or forge something unexpected and new.

The silence stretched out, thick and oppressive, wrapping around us like a shroud. Lucas leaned against the barn wall, the confident facade he had worn slipping ever so slightly. His fingers drummed against the wood, a nervous habit I had never noticed before, and I couldn't help but wonder if perhaps he wasn't as in control as he wanted us to believe.

"You think you can just show up here and make all this right?" Jason's voice cut through the tension, sharper than the edge of a broken glass. "You've turned our lives into a soap opera. People are hurting, and for what? Your petty insecurities?"

Lucas straightened, but his bravado faltered, revealing the boy behind the mask. "I didn't intend for it to go this far," he said, his voice softer now, almost pleading. "I just wanted to feel like I belonged somewhere, like I mattered."

"By trying to destroy us?" My voice was steady, but beneath it lay the tremor of hurt that pulsed with every word. "You could have come to us, Lucas. You could have been honest."

"Honesty doesn't get you anywhere when you're drowning in the shadows," he shot back, the bitterness seeping into his tone. "I had to make you see me. Make you feel the pain I've carried."

Jason shook his head, disbelief written across his features. "By dragging us into your mess? You think we'd just roll over and give you the life you think you deserve?"

"I didn't want your lives, Jason," Lucas said, his voice rising, crackling with unspent energy. "I wanted our lives—together. I thought if I could shake things up, maybe you'd finally notice I existed."

The words hung in the air, an unexpected confession that twisted my heart. Lucas, in all his charisma, had been aching for connection while shrouded in envy and resentment. I glanced at Jason, the confusion on his face reflecting my own. Could it be that this whole ordeal had spiraled from a desperate need for acceptance?

"You should've trusted us, Lucas," I said gently, the anger ebbing away to reveal the sadness beneath. "You didn't have to go to such extremes."

Lucas's eyes darted away, the weight of shame suddenly palpable. "Trust doesn't come easily to someone who's been left in the dust his whole life. You think I haven't watched you both shine while I've been in the background? The quiet one, the nobody?" He shoved his hands into his pockets, shoulders hunched like a shield against our scrutiny.

It was the first time I had seen him vulnerable, a glimpse of the boy I had known years ago before the darkness crept in. The realization hit me hard. We had been so focused on the sabotage that we had overlooked the root of the issue—the loneliness and alienation that had twisted him into this version of himself.

"Lucas," I said softly, stepping closer, "we're not your enemies. We never were. But you can't keep hurting others to make yourself feel better. That's not how it works."

He looked up at me, eyes searching, and for a brief moment, I caught a flicker of hope. Maybe, just maybe, there was still a chance for redemption here, but the weight of the past loomed heavily over us.

"Trust is a fragile thing," Jason said quietly, his anger cooling as he processed Lucas's confession. "It can be rebuilt, but it takes time, and you've done a lot of damage. Are you ready to face the consequences?"

"What consequences?" Lucas shot back, a defiance flaring in his eyes. "You think I care about being the villain in your story? The way I see it, I'm the hero of my own."

"Heroes don't tear others down to build themselves up," I interjected, my heart racing with the urgency of the moment. "You have to take responsibility for what you've done."

The silence that followed was deafening, a tense standoff where the past clashed violently with the possibility of the future. Lucas's posture softened, and I could see the realization dawning on him, like the first rays of sunlight breaking through a dark storm.

"What do you want from me?" he asked, the bravado fading, leaving a young man who felt utterly lost.

"I want you to be better," Jason replied, his voice steady and sincere. "We all have our battles. It's how we fight them that defines us. You can still choose to turn this around."

There it was—the glimmer of hope in an unexpected place. But would Lucas embrace it? The air crackled with anticipation as he stood there, torn between the person he had become and the potential he still held.

As Lucas's gaze shifted from Jason to me, the weight of our shared history hung between us like a fragile thread, ready to snap. "I don't know how," he admitted, vulnerability laying bare his heart. "I've made so many mistakes."

"That's the first step," I said, my voice steady. "Admitting you're lost is the bravest thing you can do. We all stumble. It's what happens next that matters."

He swallowed hard, glancing at the ground as if seeking answers in the dirt beneath his feet. "I thought I'd have to destroy you both to matter. I never wanted this."

"Then don't keep doing it," I urged, moving closer until I could almost feel the heat radiating from him, a testament to the turmoil inside. "Let's work through this together. Start fresh. You don't have to carry this burden alone."

The air between us shifted, a palpable tension transforming into something else—possibility. Lucas straightened, his eyes shimmering with the weight of unspoken emotions. "Together, huh?"

"Yeah," Jason said, a hint of a smile breaking through his serious demeanor. "If you're willing to drop the facade and be honest, we can figure this out."

Lucas nodded, slowly at first, then with growing conviction. "Okay. I'll try."

The words felt like a fragile promise, the first step on a long and winding road to redemption. In that moment, we stood together in the barn, the sunlight filtering through the wooden beams, illuminating our path forward. It wouldn't be easy, and there would be scars left behind, but maybe, just maybe, we could forge a new beginning from the ashes of our past. The echoes of laughter, the warmth of connection—it was all still there, waiting to be rediscovered if we dared to take the leap.

The sun dipped lower in the sky, casting an orange glow through the barn's weathered slats, illuminating the dust motes swirling in the air like tiny stars caught in a twilight dance. I could feel the weight of the moment pressing down on us, a tangible force that was almost suffocating. The flickering light transformed Lucas's face, revealing the boyish charm that had always drawn us in, now twisted with uncertainty and regret.

"Let's just say I'm a work in progress," Lucas replied, his tone lightening slightly, though the underlying tension remained taut like a bowstring. "But if we're being honest, I've always had a knack for turning things upside down."

Jason crossed his arms, the motion a protective barrier. "That's one way to put it," he muttered, skepticism coloring his words. "More like a knack for destruction."

"I guess I've always believed chaos breeds creativity," Lucas shot back, a flash of his old arrogance creeping into his demeanor. But beneath the bravado, I sensed a flicker of vulnerability, a boy still clinging to the hope that he could be more than just the sum of his mistakes.

"Creativity? Is that what you call ruining lives?" I asked, my heart racing as I struggled to balance my emotions. The urge to reach out and reassure him warred with the desire to hold him accountable. "You could have brought us in. We could have helped you find your place without the theatrics."

Lucas's gaze dropped, and he kicked at a clump of dirt on the barn floor, frustration mixing with something deeper—longing, perhaps. "I didn't think you'd understand. You both had everything I ever wanted. Friends, support, love. I was just... there."

"Being 'just there' is a choice too," Jason said, his voice softer now, as if the anger had finally given way to empathy. "But you don't have to be invisible anymore. You're standing here, aren't you? Make it count."

I took a step forward, closing the distance between us, my heart pounding in my chest. "Lucas, we've all felt lost at some point. But what you did—using us as pawns in your game—wasn't the answer. You don't have to go through this alone anymore. We can help you find your way."

He looked up at me, the flicker of hope rekindling in his eyes. "You really mean that?"

"Absolutely," I affirmed, sincerity flooding my voice. "It's never too late to start over. But it requires honesty, real honesty, and you have to want it."

"I want it," he whispered, a tremor of desperation lacing his words. "I just don't know how to begin."

"Start by being truthful," Jason advised, his expression softening. "No more games. Just tell us what you want and need."

Lucas swallowed hard, his shoulders trembling as he took a deep breath. "Okay. I want to stop feeling like a shadow. I want to be part of something real. But I'm scared of screwing it up again."

"Scared is good," I replied, hoping to reassure him. "It means you care. You're not the same kid who thought destruction was the way to make a mark. You're here, trying to find a better path. That's progress."

"Maybe I'm just a mess," Lucas said, his voice cracking, and I could see the boy I once knew peeking through the cracks in the façade. "Maybe I'm not meant for this."

"Don't say that," Jason interjected fiercely. "Everyone's a mess in some way, but you don't get to decide your worth based on your past mistakes. It's how you move forward that counts."

Lucas ran a hand through his hair, the gesture both anxious and defiant. "You think I can really change? That you'd want me around after everything?"

"Of course, we want you around," I insisted, feeling a surge of emotion. "We can't just erase the past, but we can learn from it together. That's what friends do."

A flicker of hope danced across Lucas's face, and for a brief moment, I dared to believe we could pull him back from the brink. But before I could voice the thought, a shadow fell across the entrance of the barn, shrouding us in sudden darkness.

"Look who decided to join the party," a voice sneered from the threshold, dripping with disdain. I turned, my heart plummeting as I recognized the figure standing there—Jordan, Lucas's older brother, with a smug grin plastered across his face. He leaned casually against the doorframe, arms crossed, the very picture of menace.

"What's this? A little heart-to-heart? How sweet," Jordan mocked, stepping forward, his presence enveloping the barn like a storm cloud. The air grew thick with tension as he assessed the scene, his eyes flickering with amusement. "I didn't realize we were having a pity party."

"Jordan," Lucas said, his voice barely above a whisper, fear replacing the hope that had just begun to bloom.

"Don't 'Jordan' me, little brother. I heard you were making friends," he sneered, the words laced with venom. "How pathetic. Still trying to find your place? It's adorable, really."

Jason took a protective step forward, shielding me from the threat. "You should leave, Jordan. This doesn't concern you."

"Doesn't concern me?" Jordan laughed, a hollow sound that echoed against the barn's walls. "Oh, but it does. You've all become a joke, floundering in your own little world. Did you think you could just forget what I've done? That I wouldn't come back to reclaim what's mine?"

"Stop," Lucas said, a tremor of defiance lacing his voice. "I'm done letting you control me. You don't get to dictate my life anymore."

Jordan's smile faltered, and for a moment, I saw something raw beneath the surface—rage, resentment, but also a desperate need for validation. "You think you can just walk away? You're nothing without me, Lucas. You'll always be my little shadow."

With a swift motion, he lunged forward, the atmosphere shifting as if the barn itself held its breath. My heart raced, instincts screaming at me to intervene, but before I could react, Jason stepped in front of me, the protective instinct radiating off him like a shield.

"Touch him, and you'll regret it," Jason warned, his voice low and steady, every word saturated with authority.

The moment hung between us like a tightly drawn bowstring, the tension palpable. I held my breath, my heart racing, a whirlwind of emotions swirling within me. Would this confrontation end in chaos, or could we somehow pull Lucas back from the edge?

In that instant, as the air crackled with impending conflict, Lucas turned to us, his expression a mix of fear and determination. "I'm done hiding. I'm done being afraid."

Jordan's laughter rang out, mocking and cold, a sharp blade cutting through the fragile resolve building around us. "You think you can stand against me? You've always been weak, Lucas. You'll never change."

But as Lucas faced his brother, something flickered in his eyes—a spark of defiance that had been absent moments before. "I'm not weak. I'm done being your pawn."

The ground felt unsteady beneath me, a precarious balance on the edge of something monumental. With every heartbeat, the stakes rose higher, and I realized this confrontation was far from over. Would Lucas embrace the strength he had discovered, or would he slip back into the shadows that had haunted him for so long?

And just as I prepared to step forward, to fight for him, a sharp noise shattered the tension—a sound so jarring that time seemed to freeze around us. The barn door slammed shut, echoing ominously as darkness enveloped us, leaving us suspended in uncertainty, caught in a moment that promised to change everything.

Chapter 19: A Heart Divided

The kitchen was the heart of the house, or at least it was supposed to be. Today, however, it pulsed with an uncomfortable tension that hummed beneath the surface, a discordant note that threatened to shatter the porcelain calm of the morning. The sun streamed in through the window, casting golden rays onto the worn wooden table, illuminating the half-finished cup of coffee that I had abandoned moments earlier. I watched the steam swirl upward, vanishing into the air, much like my hope for a peaceful breakfast.

My mother stood at the counter, her back to me, meticulously chopping vegetables for a salad. The rhythmic sound of the knife striking the cutting board echoed through the silence, punctuating the thick air with each calculated slice. I could sense her tension—a tightness in her shoulders that spoke volumes, a clear reflection of the storm brewing in her heart. I had thought we would weather this storm together, but now I could feel the chasm widening between us.

"Isn't it too early for a dinner salad?" I ventured, my voice soft, almost tentative. "We could just grab something quick instead." The words hung between us, heavy with unsaid things.

"I don't want to hear about Jason," she replied sharply, her voice clipped, the knife pausing mid-cut. The air crackled with the electricity of our unspoken arguments, the weight of familial loyalty at odds with my yearning for love. Jason. The name lingered in the air like a forbidden fruit. Just saying it felt like treason.

My mind drifted back to our last encounter, where emotions ran high and the truth, once buried beneath layers of affection and laughter, exploded into a painful revelation. Jason had opened a door I thought would remain closed forever, a door to the past that exposed the festering wounds between our families. I had never intended for the truth to emerge like this, tearing through our lives like a whirlwind, yet here we were, each of us grappling with our fractured histories.

"It's not just about him," I pressed, leaning against the counter beside her. "It's about us, about what we're going through."

"Your loyalty should be to your family," she said, her voice strained but firm. I could almost hear the unyielding script of her convictions. "Jason is part of a history that has hurt us, and you're willing to throw everything away for a relationship that might not even survive this?"

"Mom, you don't understand!" My frustration flared, an ember kindling into flame. "I'm not throwing anything away. I love him. We can't be defined by the mistakes of the past."

Her knife clattered onto the board, the sound sharp and accusing. "Love doesn't change the past. Love doesn't erase the hurt. He's just a reminder of everything that went wrong."

The truth of her words hung heavy in the air, a dark cloud that loomed over us, but I refused to let it envelop me. The sharp pang of resentment bit into my resolve. "Maybe it's time we stop letting our past dictate our present. I want to build a future, one where love can heal."

I knew I sounded naive, a dreamer clutching at straws, but wasn't that what love demanded? Wasn't it worth fighting for? Just then, the doorbell rang, echoing through the silence. The sound seemed to slice through the tension like a knife, and my heart leaped. Could it be Jason? The thought filled me with both hope and dread.

"I'll get it," I said, urgency threading through my voice as I rushed to the door. I opened it to find Jason standing there, his expression a mixture of determination and apprehension. The sight of him sent a rush of warmth through me, a balm against the cool reality that awaited us inside.

"Can we talk?" he asked, his voice low, eyes searching mine. The gravity of the situation loomed between us like an invisible wall, but I could feel the connection that had always pulled us together.

"Now isn't a good time," I said, glancing back toward the kitchen, where my mother was likely still fuming, armed with her indignation and unyielding opinions.

"Please," he pressed, stepping closer, his gaze steady and earnest. "I can't let this go. We need to figure this out."

I felt the familiar tug of my heartstrings, the way he always knew just how to draw me in, but the chaos of our families lingered in the background like a storm waiting to break. "Okay," I relented, taking a deep breath, "but it needs to be quick."

We moved to the porch, where the morning sun enveloped us in warmth, yet an unsettling chill snaked down my spine. "I'm sorry for what happened," Jason began, his tone low and sincere. "I never wanted to hurt you or your family."

His words struck a chord deep within me, awakening the pain of that day, the hurt we both bore. "It's not just about the past, Jason. My mom is... she's struggling to understand us. To understand you."

"I can't change who I am," he said, frustration threading through his voice. "But I can change how I handle this. I want to fight for us, for something real."

With every word, I felt the weight of my own resolve wavering. Could I stand firm against my family's expectations, against the tide of their anger? I wanted to believe in our love, but the distance between loyalty and desire felt like a chasm, and I was terrified of losing everything I held dear.

As we stood there, the world faded away. The sun warmed our faces, but the chill in my heart only grew. Would my loyalty to my family extinguish the flames of our love, or could we find a way to bridge the gap?

The afternoon sun filtered through the trees, casting playful shadows on the wooden deck where Jason and I stood, our earlier conversation hanging in the air like the sweet scent of blooming jasmine. The peaceful ambiance seemed to mock the turmoil brewing within me. I shifted on my feet, searching for the right words, but the weight of uncertainty crushed any coherent thought.

"I didn't come here to complicate your life further," Jason said, running a hand through his tousled hair, an action that made my heart flutter against the backdrop of anxiety. "But I refuse to let fear dictate our relationship." His eyes, dark and earnest, searched mine for understanding.

"I wish it were that simple," I replied, my voice barely above a whisper, as if speaking louder would break the fragile truce between us. "Every time I try to envision a future with you, I see my family's anger flaring up like a wildfire. It terrifies me."

He stepped closer, his presence radiating warmth, yet my heart was a battleground, a chaotic mix of longing and dread. "You can't let their opinions define your happiness, Claire. I thought we were in this together."

"Together?" I scoffed lightly, frustration bubbling to the surface. "We're like oil and water right now. Our families don't even want to acknowledge each other, let alone our relationship. I feel like I'm stuck in a twisted version of a soap opera."

Jason's expression softened, his brow furrowing in thought. "What if we turned that soap opera into our own story? One where we're the protagonists fighting for what matters? We could show them that we're not just defined by our families."

His determination sparked something within me, a flicker of hope against the crushing weight of familial loyalty. "I want that, I really do," I said, the words tumbling out, "but what if they never see it that way? What if they only see the past?"

"Then we'll have to show them a different future," he said, taking my hands in his, a gesture that sent warmth flooding through me. "Let's start small. We'll confront them, talk it out. Maybe the truth isn't as ugly as we fear."

My heart raced at the thought of confronting our families. "Are you crazy? Have you met my mother? She'd rather host a tea party for a pack of rabid raccoons than have a heart-to-heart with you."

"Challenge accepted," Jason grinned, a spark of mischief dancing in his eyes, chasing away the shadows of doubt. "I'll bring the tea. You bring the raccoons."

I laughed despite myself, the sound freeing, like a bird unshackled from its cage. "You're impossible. But maybe you're right. We do need to face this, if only to make our peace with it."

Just as I was beginning to feel hopeful, a sharp voice cut through the air like a blade, making both of us jump. "What on earth is going on here?" My mother stood at the door, arms crossed, her expression a blend of disbelief and disapproval.

"Mom!" I exclaimed, guilt flooding my veins like ice water. "It's not what it looks like."

"Then what is it, exactly?" she snapped, her eyes darting between Jason and me as if trying to catch us in a lie. "I hope you're not planning some romantic escape while our family is falling apart."

Jason straightened, a brave front masking the apprehension that crept into his posture. "Ma'am, I think it's time we all had a talk. Claire and I want to address everything that's happened."

My heart sank at the trepidation in his voice. He was walking into a minefield with a smile, and I was terrified he might be blown away. "You really don't have to do this, Jason," I whispered, my voice trembling.

"No," he insisted, determination lacing his tone. "This is our chance. We need to be honest."

With a resigned sigh, I gestured toward the kitchen, where tension still crackled like static electricity. "Fine, let's do this."

As we stepped inside, the atmosphere was thick with the smell of vinegar and the fading aroma of roasted vegetables, a stark contrast to the turmoil brewing in our hearts. My father leaned against the counter, arms folded, his expression a fortress of skepticism.

"Claire, I hope you're not thinking of bringing him back into this house," he said, his voice steady, betraying none of the emotions roiling beneath.

"We need to talk," I stated firmly, trying to channel every ounce of courage I had. "About everything."

"What's there to talk about?" he shot back, the disdain in his voice like cold steel. "He's the enemy, Claire. He always has been."

"He's not the enemy!" I protested, my voice rising in desperation. "He didn't create this mess. We can't keep hiding from the past."

"Your mother and I made mistakes," he said, shooting a glance at her. "But we didn't let them dictate our future. Why should you?"

I felt Jason's hand slide into mine, a steadying force amid the tempest. "Because we're trying to create our own future," he interjected, his voice calm and steady. "We deserve a chance to build something together, away from the shadows of our families."

"Together?" My mother's tone dripped with skepticism. "You're talking about a fantasy. This isn't some fairy tale where everyone rides off into the sunset."

"Maybe it could be," I shot back, emboldened by Jason's presence. "But only if we're willing to let go of the past and make room for something new."

Silence enveloped the room, thick and suffocating. I could see the gears turning in my parents' minds, caught between their protective instincts and the reality of my stubbornness.

Jason's fingers tightened around mine, and I felt a surge of determination wash over me. This was it—the moment when we could either sink or swim, cling to our love, or let it drift away in the current of family loyalty.

"I'm not asking you to forget," I continued, my voice steadying. "But I am asking you to try and understand. We want to move forward, and we need your support."

My father exchanged a glance with my mother, the tension in the air palpable as they weighed their options, caught between their fierce love for me and their own biases.

After a moment that felt like an eternity, my father sighed, his shoulders dropping slightly. "Fine. But this isn't going to be easy. We need to talk things through—like adults."

Jason met my gaze, the flicker of hope in his eyes mirrored my own. It was a small victory, but in that moment, it felt monumental. Maybe we were on the cusp of something greater, a future built on understanding instead of fear.

The conversation unfolded like an intricate dance, each word a careful step toward reconciliation. My father leaned against the counter, his arms crossed tightly over his chest, as if to shield his heart from the reality that was slowly being presented before him. Jason stood resolute beside me, our fingers interlocked, a silent pact of solidarity. The kitchen felt smaller, the walls closing in, heavy with unspoken histories and unresolved tensions.

"Let's make one thing clear," my father began, his voice low but firm. "We don't want any more drama in our lives. We've had enough of that to last a lifetime."

Jason nodded, his jaw set with determination. "I understand, sir. But if you're willing to hear us out, I believe we can find a way forward together."

"Finding a way forward?" my mother echoed, skepticism lacing her tone. "That's quite the aspiration. What makes you think you two can manage that when your families can't?"

The air crackled with tension, the question hanging between us like an uninvited guest. I took a deep breath, summoning my courage. "Because we believe in what we have," I said, my voice steadier than I felt. "We're willing to fight for it. But we need your support, not your resistance."

My mother's brow furrowed, her gaze flickering between Jason and me. "Support for what, exactly? For a relationship born from chaos?"

Jason stepped forward, the sincerity in his eyes piercing through the layers of animosity. "I know my family has caused pain. I can't change the past, but I can change how I approach the future. Claire means everything to me, and I'm willing to put in the work if you are."

The silence that followed felt like a fragile thread, stretched taut and trembling, ready to snap at the slightest provocation. "You expect us to just accept this?" my father challenged, his voice edged with incredulity. "Your families have a history of conflict."

"We can't ignore that history," I interjected, my heart racing. "But we can rewrite the narrative. It's not just about the past; it's about what we choose to do now."

"Life isn't just a series of choices," my father countered, his brows knitting together in thought. "It's about consequences, too. Are you prepared for those?"

"I've never been more ready for anything in my life," Jason replied, confidence radiating from him like the sun breaking through the clouds.

There was a flicker of something in my mother's eyes, a hint of consideration that melted the frost in her demeanor. "So what are you proposing? That we all sit around and sing Kumbaya?"

"Actually," I said, trying to infuse some levity into the charged atmosphere, "I was thinking more along the lines of a family dinner.

You know, to hash everything out. Perhaps a neutral territory where we can all get our grievances out in the open."

My father raised an eyebrow. "A dinner? And you think that's going to fix this?"

"It's a start," I replied, my heart thumping with a mixture of hope and fear. "An opportunity to clear the air. If we can't do that, how can we move forward?"

"Dinner it is," my mother said slowly, her voice thoughtful. "But you must understand this isn't a guarantee of acceptance. You'll have to face the consequences of your choices, and we'll have to confront our own."

Jason squeezed my hand tighter, grounding me as I faced the uncertainty ahead. "We're prepared for that," he said, the certainty in his voice giving me strength.

"Then let's get this over with," my father grumbled, his face a mask of resignation, though I sensed a glimmer of reluctant acceptance in his eyes.

As we discussed potential dates, a flicker of excitement built inside me. Maybe, just maybe, we were beginning to forge a new path. But even as I felt the warmth of hope blooming, a shadow flitted across my thoughts. This was only the beginning; a single dinner wouldn't erase the complexities woven into our families' histories.

With tentative plans set, Jason and I decided to take a short walk to clear our minds. The evening air was thick with the scent of blooming roses, and I reveled in the vibrant colors of the setting sun. As we strolled side by side, my heart surged with a mixture of exhilaration and fear. "Do you really think this will work?" I asked, my voice tinged with uncertainty.

"I don't know," Jason admitted, his expression serious yet hopeful. "But I'm willing to try. You're worth it, Claire."

A smile crept onto my lips, brightening the worry lines that had settled there. "You always know how to say the right thing. Maybe this will be the start of something better."

Just as the last rays of sunlight dipped below the horizon, casting the world in soft twilight, my phone buzzed in my pocket, jolting me from my reverie. I pulled it out, glancing at the screen. It was a message from my brother, Sam.

We need to talk. It's about Jason.

My stomach dropped, a cold dread pooling in my gut. "What is it?" Jason asked, sensing my sudden shift in mood.

"It's my brother," I said, frowning at the screen. "He says we need to talk. I don't like the sound of that."

"Can it wait?" he asked, concern creasing his brow. "We just made some progress. I don't want anything to jeopardize that."

"I don't know," I said, my thoughts spiraling. "What if he's heard something? What if he wants to... I don't know, confront you?"

"Then we'll confront it together," Jason replied, his voice steady. "I'm not going to let anyone tear us apart, especially not your brother."

My heart fluttered at his words, a rush of gratitude coursing through me. But before I could respond, my phone buzzed again, this time vibrating violently in my palm. I glanced down, and my heart sank.

You need to come home. Now.

"Claire?" Jason's voice broke through my thoughts, concern etched into his features.

"I need to go," I said, urgency clawing at my insides. "Sam's in trouble. Something's wrong."

As I turned to rush home, Jason grasped my hand, anchoring me for just a moment longer. "We'll figure this out. Together."

The promise hung between us, but as I sprinted toward home, a deep-seated fear gnawed at me. Whatever was waiting on the other side of that door, I could feel it looming—an unseen storm ready to unleash its fury. And just like that, I knew I was standing on the precipice of a new chapter, where love and loyalty would be put to the ultimate test.

Chapter 20: The Calm Before the Storm

The old oak tree stood like a sentinel by the shimmering lake, its gnarled branches twisting toward the sky, casting a mosaic of shadows on the ground. Sunlight filtered through the leaves, dappling the ground with light as warm and golden as memories. Each step I took toward the bench felt laden with anticipation, my heart pounding a rhythm that echoed my unease. The familiar sight of the lake, its surface undisturbed except for the occasional ripple, seemed almost surreal, a serene painting juxtaposed against the turmoil swirling within me.

As I approached, I spotted Jason leaning against the thick trunk, his silhouette framed by the sprawling branches. He looked contemplative, his brow furrowed slightly as he stared out at the water. The breeze tousled his dark hair, creating a disheveled charm that made my breath catch. For a moment, he seemed lost in thought, and I wondered what troubled him as much as the confrontation had troubled me.

"Hey," I called out, attempting to infuse some lightness into the air thick with tension. He turned, his expression shifting from pensive to relieved, and I saw a glimmer of hope in his eyes.

"Hey," he replied, pushing himself off the tree. "I wasn't sure you'd come."

I shrugged, my heart fluttering like a trapped bird. "Where else would I go? It's either here or back to the chaos."

"Good point." His smile was small but genuine, like sunlight breaking through clouds. "I thought we could use a moment away from it all."

I settled onto the bench, its surface warm from the sun, and he sat beside me, the distance between us both comforting and unnerving. The world around us faded as we fell into an easy rhythm of conversation, laughter punctuating our words like birdsong in the quiet of the afternoon. We reminisced about our childhood adventures, the innocent laughter that once rang out beneath this very oak, blissfully unaware of the storms that adulthood would bring.

"Remember that time we tried to build a raft?" Jason asked, laughter bubbling in his voice. "We thought we could sail across the lake like explorers."

"Right! And it sank within minutes," I chuckled, shaking my head at the absurdity of it all. "We just ended up splashing around, soaked and shivering."

"Yeah, but we still claimed we conquered the great unknown." He leaned back, a playful glint in his eye. "At least we were brave. Not like now, when we're dodging real storms."

The laughter faded, replaced by the weight of our shared silence. The truth hung between us, heavy and unyielding, each unspoken word a reminder of the confrontation we were still grappling with. The situation loomed like a thunderhead, dark and foreboding. I could almost feel the crackling tension in the air, a precursor to what lay ahead.

"Have you thought about what we discussed?" Jason broke the silence, his voice softening. "About confronting them?"

I hesitated, my heart racing as I contemplated the potential fallout. The idea of facing our adversaries, the very people who had plunged our lives into chaos, made my stomach churn. "I have. But I'm not sure I'm ready. It feels... overwhelming."

"Together," he said, his gaze steady and reassuring. "We'll do it together. You don't have to face them alone."

His words wrapped around me like a comforting blanket, and I felt the warmth seep into my bones. Jason had always been my anchor, the one constant in a world filled with uncertainty. "What if they don't listen? What if they come at us even harder?"

"We'll be prepared," he insisted, determination lacing his voice. "We've weathered storms before, remember? We can do this."

I wanted to believe him. I wanted to take his hand and charge into the fray, confronting our adversaries head-on. But beneath my resolve lay a trembling doubt, a whisper of fear that gnawed at the edges of my courage. "And if we fail?" I whispered, the question slipping from my lips like a secret confession.

He turned to me, his eyes blazing with a fierce intensity that sent a shiver down my spine. "Failure isn't an option. Not for us. We've fought too hard to let them win."

The air crackled with unspoken promises, a silent agreement forging an invisible bond between us. The sun dipped lower in the sky, casting long shadows over the lake as we exchanged determined glances, a silent understanding passing between us. The world around us faded further, the sounds of nature fading into a muted backdrop against our heartbeat.

Just then, a gust of wind rustled the leaves above, stirring up the dust and leaves on the ground. It felt like a sign, an omen of the storm that awaited us. As if sensing the shift, Jason leaned closer, his voice dropping to a conspiratorial whisper. "If we're going to do this, we need a plan. We need to be smart, strategic."

"Right. So, what's our strategy?" I asked, leaning in, the excitement threading through my veins. The tension melted away, replaced by a spark of adrenaline.

"We gather intel," he said, his eyes narrowing with purpose. "We find out everything we can about their next move. Then we strike when they least expect it."

"Sounds like a plan," I said, a grin breaking across my face despite the weight of the situation. "We'll be like secret agents, plotting our grand revenge."

Jason chuckled, his laughter rich and warm, dispelling the last remnants of tension. "And who says we can't have a little fun while we're at it? We'll show them they can't push us around."

In that moment, I felt invincible, ready to face whatever storm awaited us. With Jason by my side, I believed we could conquer anything, even the chaos that loomed just beyond the horizon. Together, we would find a way to turn the tide, reclaiming our peace and proving that we were stronger than any storm that dared to challenge us.

The next few days were a delicate dance of anticipation and dread. Each morning, I awoke to the sound of birds singing outside my window, their melodies bright and hopeful, yet it felt like a cruel joke against the backdrop of my inner turmoil. With every flutter of wings, I could almost hear the whispers of impending conflict echoing in the corners of my mind. I kept replaying the events of the confrontation, each moment etched into my memory like a tattoo I couldn't erase. The fear of the unknown clung to me like a damp fog, refusing to dissipate, but amidst that haze, the thought of meeting Jason again ignited a flicker of hope.

When I arrived at the oak tree, the late afternoon sun was a warm embrace against the cool air. I spotted him already there, pacing like a restless tiger, his hands shoved deep into his pockets. There was something about his demeanor—an energy that crackled just below the surface, simmering with an intensity that was hard to ignore.

"You're late," he said, though a teasing smile broke through his faux sternness. "I was about to send a search party."

"Late? Please. You're lucky I even showed up," I quipped, my own smile slipping onto my face despite the nerves swirling in my stomach. "The squirrels were having a conference about the acorns and I couldn't very well leave them hanging."

"Ah, of course! Priorities," he chuckled, shaking his head. "I should have known."

We settled onto the bench again, the familiarity of the spot grounding us in a way that felt comforting yet fraught with tension. "So," I began, folding my hands tightly in my lap, "what's the plan, oh fearless leader?"

His expression shifted, seriousness washing over him. "First, we need to know what we're up against. I've heard some rumors floating around town. There's talk that they might be planning something big."

"Big as in 'let's throw a block party' or big as in 'let's ruin lives'?" I asked, trying to keep the mood light despite the gravity of the situation.

"More like the latter," he replied, his voice low. "People are worried. They've been dropping hints about new tactics—sneaky stuff that could catch us off guard."

The knot in my stomach tightened. "Sneaky? Like what? You're not talking about sabotage, are you?"

"Not yet, but it could escalate." He ran a hand through his hair, a gesture I recognized as his way of dealing with frustration. "I've been thinking we should gather more intel. Find out who's been spreading these rumors and where they're coming from."

"Sounds like we're heading into enemy territory, then," I said, a mix of excitement and anxiety surging through me. "I'm in. But how do we do this without getting caught?"

Jason's eyes gleamed with mischief. "We go undercover. Become our own little spy duo. Blend in with the crowd, charm them, and find out what they know."

"Undercover? I like the sound of that," I said, my adrenaline pumping. "What's our cover story? I could be a clueless tourist who just stumbled into town looking for a good cup of coffee."

"And I'll be your overly enthusiastic tour guide who can't stop talking about the local legends," he suggested, a grin spreading across his face. "We can throw in some historical trivia to make it believable."

"Perfect! But what if they don't buy it? I mean, you do have that whole 'I've faced down bullies' look about you, which might intimidate them," I teased.

"Intimidation is an art form," he shot back, his eyes sparkling with humor. "But seriously, if we play it cool, they won't suspect a thing."

As we hatched our plans, the tension in the air began to shift. There was something invigorating about taking control, about turning the tables on those who had instilled fear in us. For the first time in days, the weight on my shoulders felt lighter, the storm looming ahead less daunting. We were allies now, united against a common enemy.

"We can meet tomorrow at that little café on Maple Street," Jason suggested. "It's always bustling. Perfect for blending in."

"Good thinking. And I'll bring my best fake tourist outfit," I replied, nudging him playfully. "Nothing says 'I'm just here for the coffee' like a fanny pack."

"Please tell me you're joking," he laughed, shaking his head. "But if you actually show up wearing one, I might have to reconsider our partnership."

"Deal! No fanny pack, but I'm still wearing the sun hat," I teased, imagining how ridiculous I might look.

"Only if I get to wear sunglasses, and we both pretend we're on a glamorous vacation," he countered, laughter in his eyes.

"Sounds like a plan. We'll be the most fabulous tourists this town has ever seen."

As the sun dipped below the horizon, painting the sky in hues of orange and pink, a sense of resolve washed over me. Here we were, two unlikely heroes plotting our next move beneath the old oak tree that had witnessed our childhood innocence. With each shared laugh and playful jab, the camaraderie between us deepened, transforming the weight of our reality into something bearable, even exciting.

But beneath the surface of our playful banter lay the unspoken understanding of the challenges ahead. The reality was that we were stepping into a world fraught with uncertainty. I couldn't shake the feeling that the storm was not just external but brewing within me, a tempest of emotions that swirled as fiercely as the wind gusting through the branches overhead.

Yet, with Jason by my side, the uncertainty felt a little less daunting. As we wrapped up our conversation and prepared to leave, the shadows lengthened around us, and I realized that maybe this was not just a battle against our adversaries. Perhaps it was also about confronting our fears, our insecurities, and emerging stronger on the other side. Together, we would face whatever storm came our way, fortified by laughter and a shared determination to reclaim our peace.

The next day arrived with a sense of urgency that thrummed beneath the surface of the mundane. I awoke to the sun filtering through my curtains, casting stripes of golden light across my room, yet my heart felt heavy, weighed down by the promise of what lay ahead. Jason and I had planned to meet at the café on Maple Street, our ruse of being oblivious tourists an ambitious cover for the gravity of our mission. I dressed carefully, opting for a cheerful sundress that felt like armor against the storm brewing in my mind. The fabric swayed gently around me, a small comfort as I prepared to step into the unknown.

At the café, the air was rich with the scent of freshly brewed coffee and warm pastries, a sweet chaos of laughter and conversation filling the space. I spotted Jason seated at a small table by the window, his dark curls tousled and an eager glint in his eye. He was already in character, sporting aviator sunglasses that made him look more like a spy than a tourist.

"Nice disguise," I teased, sliding into the seat across from him. "I didn't know we were going for a secret agent vibe."

"Would you prefer I wear a Hawaiian shirt?" he shot back, grinning. "Because I can totally pull that off, too."

"Let's save that for when we're actually on vacation," I replied, scanning the café. "So, any intel yet?"

"Just a few whispers here and there," he said, lowering his voice. "But the locals seem on edge. I overheard a couple of them talking about unusual meetings happening in the old warehouse down by the docks."

I leaned in, intrigued. "Meetings? What kind of meetings?"

"Something about a shipment coming in. They were being unusually cryptic. It felt like they were talking in code."

I raised an eyebrow, the thrill of the chase lighting a fire in my belly. "You think it's related to the confrontation?"

"It's possible. If they're making moves behind the scenes, we need to find out what they're planning. If we can get close enough to listen in, it could give us the upper hand."

The coffee shop buzzed around us, but our focus was sharp, narrowed to the task at hand. "Okay, what's our next move? Do we need disguises for that, too? Maybe I could bring a wig."

"Let's not overcomplicate things just yet," he replied, his tone half-serious, half-amused. "We'll keep it simple. We can head down to the docks and see if we can spot anything out of the ordinary. If nothing else, we'll at least look like we're just out for a leisurely stroll."

"Sounds like a plan," I said, suddenly eager for action. "Let's do it."

We finished our drinks quickly, the warmth of the coffee fueling our determination. The streets were bustling as we walked toward the docks, our conversations peppered with half-joking banter that masked the rising tension in my gut. Each step felt like crossing a threshold into a world where danger lurked just beyond the horizon.

The docks stretched before us, a maze of crates and containers stacked haphazardly against the backdrop of the setting sun. The air was tinged with the salty scent of the sea, but beneath it was something more sinister—an electric charge that whispered of secrets and hidden intentions. I glanced at Jason, who appeared calm on the outside, but I could sense his heart racing just as fast as mine.

"Where do we start?" I asked, peering into the shadows where the evening light struggled to reach.

"We'll keep it low-key. Just walk around, act natural. If we see anything suspicious, we'll investigate," he said, his tone measured, but I could see the flicker of anxiety in his eyes.

We meandered through the docks, keeping our voices light as we pretended to admire the boats and the occasional fisherman pulling in his catch. I couldn't shake the feeling that we were being watched, an unsettling awareness prickling at the back of my neck. As we rounded a corner, I caught sight of a group of men gathered around a stack of crates, their hushed voices urgent, their expressions shrouded in shadows.

"Do you see them?" I whispered, nodding toward the group. "They look... serious."

"Yeah, they definitely fit the profile," Jason muttered, squinting to get a better look. "We need to get closer."

As we inched forward, I felt the weight of the moment bear down on us, the thrill of the unknown mingling with a gnawing apprehension. I could hear snippets of their conversation, words like "shipment" and "tonight" tumbling into my ears like shards of glass.

Suddenly, one of the men turned his head, eyes locking onto us, and I felt a jolt of panic. "Jason, we need to—"

Before I could finish, the man called out, his voice cutting through the evening air like a knife. "Hey! You two! What are you doing here?"

In an instant, Jason grabbed my hand, pulling me back into the shadows of a nearby shipping container. "Run!" he hissed, and my heart leapt into my throat as we darted behind the crate, adrenaline flooding my veins.

We ducked low, breaths coming in sharp gasps as we peered around the corner. The men were now looking in our direction, confusion etched on their faces as they tried to figure out what we were up to.

"We can't stay here," I whispered urgently, my mind racing. "They'll see us!"

Jason nodded, determination flooding his features. "We'll circle around. If we can get to the other side of the dock, we can blend in with the crowd."

As we crept away from the men, every sound felt amplified—the distant call of a seagull, the slosh of water against the hulls of the boats. My pulse raced, the fear of discovery a tangible force at my back. Just as we reached the edge of the dock, I glanced back to see if they were following us.

That's when I saw him—a figure stepping out from behind a stack of crates, a familiar face that sent ice through my veins.

It was someone I never expected to see here, a person from my past, someone I had thought was long gone. A smile danced on his lips, but it held none of the warmth I remembered. Instead, it was cold and calculating, a shadowy grin that made the hairs on my neck stand on end.

"Going somewhere?" he called out, his voice dripping with mockery, as though he had been waiting for this moment all along.

My heart sank, panic clawing at my throat. In that instant, the world around me faded, the sound of the waves becoming a distant roar. All I could think was that the storm we had braced ourselves for had finally arrived, and it had a face I recognized all too well.

Chapter 21: Unraveling the Past

The oak tree loomed overhead, its gnarled branches reaching out like the arms of a long-lost friend. Sunlight filtered through the thick foliage, casting playful shadows on the ground that danced around us. I breathed in the earthy scent of damp soil mingled with the sweetness of wildflowers, a fragrant reminder of the beauty in a place so steeped in conflict. Jason sat beside me, his silhouette framed by the dappled light, a figure caught between resolve and doubt.

"We can't let this define us," he declared, his voice steady yet laced with an undercurrent of emotion that tugged at my heartstrings. It was as if the weight of our families' feuding histories had settled between us, an unwelcome guest at our reunion beneath this ancient sentinel. I could see the tension in his jaw, the way his fingers fidgeted with the frayed edge of his jeans, revealing the cracks in his stoic facade.

I nodded, feeling the coolness of the grass beneath my fingertips. "You know, I never really understood why our families hated each other so much," I admitted, my voice barely above a whisper. The air between us shimmered with unspoken truths, secrets hidden in the whispers of the past. "It always felt like this shadow hanging over everything, a legacy we didn't choose."

Jason turned to me, his brow furrowing in thought. "It's like a puzzle, right? Pieces scattered everywhere, and we're stuck trying to make sense of it all." His eyes sparkled with a hint of mischief, a flash of warmth that momentarily dispelled the gravity of our conversation. "Only, it's more like one of those brain-bending puzzles no one wants to solve."

A laugh bubbled up in my throat, surprising me. "Right? Who even likes puzzles? They're just an exercise in frustration." I leaned back against the sturdy trunk of the tree, feeling its ancient strength seeping into my bones. "But this one feels different. It's not just about the past; it's about us."

"Exactly," Jason said, leaning closer, his expression shifting from playful to serious. "If we can understand the roots of this rivalry, maybe we can find a way to uproot it. We can't let our families' choices dictate our lives anymore." His determination ignited a spark within me, and I felt my resolve harden like the tree we rested against, unyielding and steadfast.

As we delved deeper into the histories that entwined our families, I felt a rush of warmth and connection. Memories surfaced like bubbles in a glass of champagne, each one effervescent with significance. I recalled stories my grandmother used to tell—tales of fierce battles fought not with swords, but with words, sharp as daggers. I shared them with Jason, my voice growing stronger with each revelation.

"They were kids when it all started, just like us. Two families in a small town, neighbors turned enemies over something so trivial it hardly seems real now." I paused, lost in the whirlwind of emotions that accompanied each story. "But here we are, generations later, still tangled in their mess."

Jason's brow furrowed as he processed my words. "What if we could be the ones to change that? What if we started our own story, one that doesn't end in bitterness?" His eyes sparkled with an intensity that sent shivers down my spine, igniting something deep within me—an urge to fight, to reclaim what had been lost.

"Yeah," I said, the word tumbling out with unexpected fervor. "What if we broke the cycle? What if we confronted them, told them we won't be part of this feud anymore?" A thrill of defiance surged through me, racing in time with the pulse of the earth beneath us.

"But how do we do that?" Jason leaned back, his eyes never leaving mine. "They won't listen to us, not after all these years of animosity."

"Maybe they need to see that we're not the same," I suggested, the idea blossoming in my mind like a wildflower. "If we can show them that we refuse to carry their burdens, maybe they'll realize how absurd this all is."

He nodded slowly, a smile creeping across his face, a rare sight that made my heart flutter. "I like that. But what about our friends? Do they even want to hear this?" There was a hint of worry in his voice, a vulnerability that made him even more relatable.

I laughed again, a more vibrant sound this time. "Who cares what they think? They're just kids caught in the crossfire of a family feud. If they can see us doing something different, maybe it'll inspire them, too." The vision of it all warmed me, a blazing sun piercing through the shadows of doubt that had once clouded my mind.

"Okay," he said, his determination solidifying. "Let's do it. Let's talk to our families, face them head-on." His enthusiasm was infectious, a surge of adrenaline that thrummed through my veins, invigorating and terrifying all at once.

We spent the rest of the afternoon unraveling the stories, mapping out our plan like cartographers of our own destinies. The air crackled with possibility, each laugh echoing like a promise that whispered through the leaves. And as the sun dipped lower in the sky, casting long shadows that danced around us, I felt an unshakeable belief blossom within me—a certainty that our connection would guide us through the labyrinth of our families' pasts, one story at a time.

As the sun sank lower in the sky, its golden rays slipping away like whispers of a forgotten dream, Jason and I finalized our plan with a sense of urgency that made my heart race. The air felt electric, charged with the promise of confrontation and the uncharted territory ahead of us. With each passing moment, I felt less like a child trapped in the weight of family expectations and more like a warrior ready to carve my own path through the underbrush of history.

"Okay, so we meet them tomorrow," I said, determination lacing my words as I traced circles in the dirt with my finger. "But how do we even start?" The question hung between us, heavier than the impending dusk, a storm cloud of anxiety and anticipation.

Jason rubbed the back of his neck, his brow furrowing. "I don't know. Maybe we just... say it? Lay it all out on the table?" His words rolled off his tongue with the casualness of someone tossing a pebble into a pond, yet the ripple effect felt monumental.

"Yeah, but what if they flip out? What if they start hurling insults like we're in a medieval jousting match?" I grinned, hoping to lighten the tension, but the seriousness of the situation loomed too large. "I mean, my family specializes in dramatic flair. Last Christmas, Aunt Mildred practically staged a one-woman show about why she hated your family."

He chuckled, a rich sound that echoed through the branches, dispelling some of the heaviness. "True. I've never seen someone throw a fruitcake like that. If only the Olympics had a category for it."

"Right? We'd be medal contenders." I leaned back against the oak, feeling its rough bark against my skin, grounding me in the moment. "But seriously, we need a strategy. What if we approach them separately first? Like, ease them into it?"

Jason's eyes brightened, as if a light bulb had flickered to life in the dimming light. "I like that. It's like a covert operation. We could meet with them one-on-one, gauge their reactions. If they seem open to it, we bring it up together."

"Operation: Family Feud," I proclaimed, striking a pose as if I were directing an imaginary play. Jason laughed again, the tension between us easing just a bit. "Starring us, two reluctant heroes on a quest for peace."

"Epic," he agreed, a sparkle of mischief dancing in his gaze. "And I'm sure there will be plenty of obstacles, like my father's stubbornness or your mother's tears. They could make for some gripping scenes."

"Don't forget Aunt Mildred's fruitcake," I added with a wink. "That's definitely a hazard."

As laughter floated around us, I realized how easy it was to fall into this rhythm with Jason. The casual banter, the shared humor—it all felt like a lifeline. It was a reminder that amidst the chaos of family expectations, I had this moment with him, filled with lightness and hope.

We made a pact to meet at the tree the next day, both of us brimming with a blend of optimism and apprehension. I felt the weight of my decision settle like a cloak around my shoulders, both heavy and empowering. The world around us seemed to dim, the shadows lengthening, but I welcomed the darkness as a protective shroud for the burgeoning hope within me.

The following morning dawned with an unusual brightness, the sun spilling over the horizon like an artist brushing vibrant strokes across a blank canvas. I woke with a flutter of nervous energy, anticipation thrumming in my veins. The air was thick with the promise of change, and I could almost taste the tang of it on my tongue.

With a few calming breaths, I dressed with purpose, choosing a bright blue dress that felt like armor against the weight of the day. My reflection in the mirror offered a glimpse of determination—a girl ready to fight for her own narrative. I grabbed my bag, making sure to tuck away a small notebook filled with thoughts and sketches of what I hoped to say.

When I arrived at the oak tree, the sun warmed my back, and I spotted Jason pacing nervously beneath the branches, his hair tousled by the gentle breeze. He stopped, eyes widening as he saw me approach. "You look ready to take on the world," he declared, a hint of awe in his voice.

I grinned, adjusting my dress. "And you look like you've just emerged from a battle with a windstorm."

"Thanks, I think? Maybe I should have gone for a more put-together look." He gestured to his casual jeans and T-shirt, the sleeves rolled up, revealing toned forearms.

I stepped closer, letting the energy of the tree wrap around us. "No need for that. It's about authenticity, remember? We're not here to impress; we're here to reclaim our stories."

"Right," he said, taking a deep breath as if readying himself for a plunge into the unknown. "So, who do you want to talk to first? Your mom or my dad?"

"Let's go with your dad. Mine has a flair for the dramatic. I'd like to ease into this."

We exchanged nods, a silent agreement solidifying our resolve. With each step toward Jason's house, the ground felt more real beneath my feet, a tangible reminder of the momentous journey we were about to undertake.

The old wooden door creaked open, and there was his father, a tall figure with a graying beard and a weathered face, like an ancient map charting stories of battles fought long ago. He looked at us, curiosity flickering in his eyes.

"Hey, Dad. We need to talk," Jason said, his voice steadier than I felt.

"About what?" His father's tone held the weight of skepticism, and I could feel Jason's muscles tense beside me.

"About... us. Our families."

As we stepped into the swirling depths of the conversation, the tension thickened, but it felt like a necessary storm—one that would cleanse and renew, opening pathways to a brighter future.

The atmosphere in Jason's living room crackled with tension, as if even the air itself understood the gravity of our conversation. His father leaned against the kitchen counter, arms crossed tightly over his chest, his brow furrowed in a way that suggested he was bracing for impact. Jason and I exchanged a quick glance, silently reaffirming our resolve. This was it; there was no turning back now.

"We've been talking," Jason started, his voice steady yet tinged with the slightest quiver of uncertainty. "And we think it's time to address the feud between our families."

His father's eyes narrowed, suspicion creeping into his expression. "What feud? That's just how it is, son. It's tradition. Families have disagreements; it's not the end of the world."

Jason pushed forward, determination flooding his voice. "But that's just it. We're tired of living in the shadow of something that happened years ago. We want to move forward."

"Forward?" His father's tone dripped with skepticism. "And how do you propose to do that? You think you can just sit down and have a chat with the Kesslers, like it's some kind of tea party?"

"I don't know," I interjected, my heart pounding in my chest. "But we think it's worth a shot. We can't keep letting this divide us. It's ridiculous."

His father's expression darkened, a storm brewing in his eyes. "Ridiculous? You think it's ridiculous? You don't know the half of it. This isn't just some petty squabble over a fence or a parking space. It's about pride, history, and loyalty to family."

"Loyalty? Is that what you call it?" I challenged, my cheeks warming with a mix of indignation and fear. "You're willing to let your loyalty destroy any chance we have of a future?"

Jason stepped closer, his body radiating an energy I could only describe as protective. "Dad, we're not asking you to abandon your family's legacy. We're asking you to recognize that times have changed. We're different."

His father remained silent for a moment, the room thick with uncertainty. I could see him grappling with the shifting tides of tradition and change, his brow furrowed as if searching for words that wouldn't betray the weight of his family's past. Finally, he shook his head slowly, disbelief evident in his gaze.

"You both think you can just waltz in here and rewrite history? It doesn't work that way."

"Why not?" I shot back, my frustration boiling over. "Why can't we break this cycle? Why can't we stop the pain?"

"Because the past has a way of catching up with you," he replied, his voice low and rough, like gravel grinding underfoot. "And you might not like what it finds."

I exchanged a look with Jason, an unspoken understanding passing between us. This wasn't just a conversation; it was a battleground, and we were fighting for more than just our futures. We were battling against the weight of history, the burdens that our families had placed on our shoulders.

"Dad," Jason said, his voice softer now, almost pleading. "Just think about it. We're willing to put ourselves out there, to risk everything. Don't you want that for us?"

For a moment, it looked as though his father might relent, his expression softening just a fraction. But then, a shadow crossed his face, hardening his features. "You don't understand the consequences of what you're asking. There are repercussions to crossing lines drawn long ago."

My heart sank as I realized the depth of the chasm we were trying to bridge. It was more than just a disagreement; it was a legacy steeped in bitterness, and we were the ones expected to endure it. I felt my resolve slipping, fear creeping in like an unwanted guest.

Before I could gather my thoughts, the door swung open, and a gust of wind rushed through the room, carrying with it a sense of urgency. Standing in the doorway was Jason's younger sister, Lily, her face pale and eyes wide, as though she had just stumbled upon a ghost.

"Jason! You need to see this," she exclaimed, her breath coming in quick bursts. The atmosphere shifted instantly, and the gravity of our conversation momentarily faded in the face of her panic.

"What is it?" Jason asked, stepping away from his father, concern etched across his features.

Lily hesitated, glancing nervously between us, before taking a deep breath. "It's about the Kesslers... they're at our house."

"What do you mean they're at our house?" Jason's voice rose in disbelief. "Why would they come here?"

"Mom and Dad are arguing with them right now. They said something about wanting to talk." Her words tumbled out in a rush, urgency spilling over as she continued. "I think they want to confront you two."

I felt the blood drain from my face, the implications of her words crashing over me like a tidal wave. "This isn't good," I muttered, panic clawing at my throat.

Jason's father looked as if he had just been struck by lightning, his face paling. "They have no right to come here. I'll handle it."

But as he moved toward the door, Jason grabbed his arm. "No. We need to handle this. Together."

And just like that, the battlefield shifted. The lines were drawn not just between families, but between generations, and the weight of our decisions pressed heavily against us. As we rushed toward the door, I felt a mix of fear and adrenaline pumping through my veins.

What awaited us on the other side? Would it be a confrontation or an opportunity? With each step toward the unknown, I could feel the tension mounting, as if the very air was alive with possibilities. And as I crossed the threshold into the sunlight, I knew that nothing would ever be the same again. The future was about to unravel, and I was right in the middle of it, teetering on the edge of everything I had ever known.

Chapter 22: The Breaking Point

The sun poured through the tall, dusty windows of the distillery, casting slanted beams of light that danced across the rustic wooden beams overhead. The air was thick with the sweet, slightly sour scent of aging whiskey, and as I inhaled deeply, I could feel my heart racing. This was it—the moment when we would lay everything on the table. Jason stood beside me, his presence a solid anchor against the storm brewing in the hall. His hands were clenched into fists, his usual calm demeanor masked by a tightness around his jaw.

When our families began to trickle in, the atmosphere turned electric. My mother was the first to arrive, her expression a whirlwind of concern and determination. She always had a way of making the world seem like a fragile glass vase—beautiful but precariously balanced. I could see the flicker of worry in her eyes as she scanned the room, searching for answers that had eluded her for years.

"Is this really necessary?" she whispered, her voice low but filled with urgency, as if I might crumble under the weight of her expectations.

Jason's father followed closely, his sharp gaze landing on me like a hawk sizing up its prey. I had long since learned to ignore the way he looked at me, as if I were the very embodiment of every mistake he had ever made. The tension between us crackled like static in the air, a silent acknowledgment of the unspoken feud that had simmered just beneath the surface for too long.

"Let's just get this over with," Jason murmured, a trace of defiance lacing his words. I nodded, our silent pact reinforcing our resolve. We were in this together, no matter how daunting the odds seemed.

Once everyone had gathered, I took a deep breath and stepped forward, the room falling into a thick silence. "Thank you all for coming. We wanted to talk about... everything." My voice trembled slightly, but I pressed on. "We've been doing some digging, and there are truths that have been hidden, things we need to face as a family."

A murmur rippled through the group, eyes darting from me to Jason, who stood beside me with a quiet intensity. His unwavering gaze met mine, urging me on. "We've discovered that the animosity between our families is rooted in misunderstandings and old grudges. There's more that connects us than divides us."

The weight of my words hung in the air, and for a moment, I dared to hope. My mother's eyes softened, and Jason's father shifted uncomfortably in his seat. But just as the atmosphere began to thaw, like ice melting in the warmth of spring, a voice sliced through the room—a jagged edge of bitterness that caught us all off guard.

"Why should we believe anything you say?" Carter spat, leaning against the wall, arms crossed defiantly. His eyes burned with resentment, each word dripping with disdain. "You think a little truth-telling is going to fix everything? It's naïve."

My heart sank. Carter was Jason's older brother, and the embodiment of all the animosity that had festered between our families. The scars of the past wrapped tightly around him like barbed wire, and his skepticism ignited a spark of tension that threatened to engulf us all.

"Carter, please—" Jason began, but his brother cut him off, his voice rising, drowning out the tentative hope that had begun to bloom.

"You think you can just play the hero now? You're the one who dragged us into this mess," Carter continued, his gaze flicking between Jason and me like a tennis match, his anger palpable and visceral. "You think you can rewrite history with a few heartfelt speeches?"

"I'm not trying to rewrite anything," I said, my voice steady despite the adrenaline coursing through me. "I just want us to understand what really happened. We can't move forward without knowing the truth."

Carter scoffed, a harsh laugh escaping his lips. "And what's that truth? That you both have been living in a fantasy world? This isn't some fairy tale where love conquers all. This is real life. People get hurt. Families tear apart."

His words struck like arrows, sharp and precise. The air turned heavy, and I felt the room closing in around us. I could see the tension etched in my mother's features, her eyes darting toward Carter with a mix of disappointment and disbelief.

"Carter, enough!" Jason's voice cut through the rising tide of emotions, shaking with a mix of anger and desperation. "This isn't just about us. It's about our families. Can't you see that? You're holding onto this bitterness like it's some kind of shield, but it's only hurting you."

For a brief moment, silence reigned. The crackling tension began to wane, and I could feel the fragile thread of understanding weaving its way through the air, binding us together in a common struggle.

"You think you can change everything with some heartfelt speeches?" Carter's voice was softer now, a hint of uncertainty creeping into his tone. "You think your parents will forgive everything? Just like that?"

"No," I said, my voice quiet but resolute. "But we can start by understanding each other. We can begin to heal."

Jason's hand brushed against mine, a comforting warmth amidst the coldness that had seeped into the room. The bond between us felt stronger, forged in the crucible of shared pain and unspoken dreams. If we could only break through the barriers built on past mistakes, perhaps we could find a way to forge a new path.

In that moment, as I looked around the room at the faces of our families—confused, angry, hopeful—I knew we were standing at a precipice. It was a crossroads where forgiveness and understanding could lead to something profound, or where bitterness could consume us all. The choice was ours to make.

Jason's eyes darted toward Carter, a tempest brewing behind his calm facade. The tension in the room thickened like molasses, each breath feeling heavier than the last. "Carter, you can't keep hiding behind that wall of anger," he urged, frustration creeping into his voice. "We're all hurting here."

Carter shook his head, laughter tinged with disbelief bubbling up. "Hiding? Oh, please. It's not hiding when the world is throwing punches and I'm just dodging them. What's next? A group hug? A heartfelt round of 'Kumbaya'? I didn't come here for your feel-good resolution."

I felt a prickle of irritation as Carter's sarcasm sliced through the sincerity of the moment. "We're not asking for a magic fix," I interjected, my patience wavering. "We're just trying to talk, to understand. Maybe even—God forbid—connect."

His gaze narrowed, a flash of vulnerability crossing his face before he masked it with bravado. "Connect? You think we're going to be one big happy family just because you found some dusty old truths? That's rich."

The crack in his armor was subtle, but I didn't miss it. Beneath the anger lay something deeper, a pain he couldn't quite articulate. "No one is expecting that, Carter. But you need to acknowledge that you're carrying the weight of this past all by yourself. You're not alone in this," I insisted, my voice softer, hoping to reach whatever flicker of warmth might still exist within him.

A brief silence followed, punctuated only by the distant ticking of a clock, each tick marking the time we spent navigating this emotional minefield. Finally, Carter's arms dropped to his sides, and his expression shifted from confrontation to confusion. "It's not that easy, you know. My life isn't just some after-school special where everyone hugs it out and goes home happy."

"True," Jason chimed in, his tone earnest. "But it doesn't mean we can't try. You've been holding onto this resentment for so long that it's consuming you. Can't you see that?"

"Why do you care?" Carter shot back, eyes blazing. "You've always been the golden boy, the one who can do no wrong. You've got your perfect life, your perfect girlfriend—what do you want from me?"

"I want you to let go," Jason said, the intensity in his voice rising. "It's suffocating you, Carter. It's okay to be angry, but it's not okay to let it ruin your life. You've got to make a choice. Are you going to keep being this person, or do you want to figure it out together?"

I watched as a flicker of doubt danced across Carter's face. The walls he'd built around himself were crumbling, piece by piece. "Together?" he echoed, a slight tremor in his voice.

"Together," I affirmed, matching his gaze, my heart racing. "But it means confronting the past. You have to let us in."

For a moment, I thought he might relent. Then the flicker vanished, and his stubbornness returned like an unwelcome guest. "Let you in? Do you even know what you're asking?" His voice was thick with disdain. "It's not just about us. There's a history here—a mess that runs deeper than either of you could possibly understand."

The words hung in the air like a dark cloud, threatening to swallow us whole. I glanced at Jason, his brow furrowed in thought, and I knew we had to shift tactics. "Then let's talk about that history. What are you so afraid of?"

Carter stepped closer, his posture tense, eyes narrowing. "Afraid? Oh, sweetheart, I'm not afraid of anything. I'm just aware of the reality of our situation. Some wounds don't heal, and some truths don't set you free; they just keep you locked in a cage, scared to move."

"Then let's break that cage," I challenged, my resolve hardening. "If we don't face these truths, we'll never find a way forward."

A heavy silence followed my words, the weight of our history pressing down on us like the oppressive heat of summer. Finally, Jason spoke, his voice steady. "You don't have to carry this alone, Carter. We're here for you."

Carter hesitated, glancing at the faces of our families, his defenses wavering like a flame in the wind. "You think it's that simple? You think I haven't tried? I've spent years trying to keep my family from falling apart, and all I got was a front-row seat to the destruction."

"Then let's rebuild together," I urged, pushing through the discomfort that threatened to overwhelm us. "You've spent so long trying to protect everyone that you've forgotten how to let anyone in."

The challenge hung in the air, and for a heartbeat, I thought I saw a crack in Carter's armor, a flicker of something that resembled hope. But just as quickly, it vanished, replaced by a hardened resolve. "You don't get it. I'm the one who has to fix this. I'm the one who's supposed to carry the weight."

"Carter, that's not fair to you or to us," Jason shot back, his voice rising again. "You can't fix everything on your own. We're a family. We should face this together, not apart."

But Carter's expression turned cold, and a sharp edge sliced through the air. "Family? This family is a mess! We're not some Hallmark movie waiting for a happy ending. We're just people trying not to drown in our own pain."

The tension in the room flared, my heart pounding in my chest as the reality of our situation settled in. We were at an impasse, the divide between us like a chasm that seemed impossible to bridge. Yet, despite Carter's harsh words, I sensed something beneath the surface, a desire for connection battling against the weight of expectations.

"Then let's find a way to swim," I suggested, my voice firm but gentle. "Let's pull each other up instead of pushing each other down."

His gaze flicked toward Jason, the battle waging in his mind almost visible. The vulnerability he kept buried beneath layers of bravado was surfacing, and I could almost hear the internal struggle echoing within him.

"I can't keep pretending it doesn't hurt," Carter finally admitted, his voice barely above a whisper, as if saying it aloud might break some unspoken pact of silence that had held our families captive for too long.

"Then don't," Jason urged softly. "Let it hurt, but let us be here with you while it does. We're stronger together."

With those words hanging in the air, I felt a shift, the tide turning ever so slightly. As Carter looked between us, the walls he had built around himself wavered, and for the first time, the possibility of healing felt tangible. It was raw and unrefined, a painful beauty that hinted at the potential for something more. In that moment, I realized we were on the edge of something profound, a new beginning waiting to unfold in the aftermath of our tumultuous past.

Carter's words hung in the air like a thundercloud, threatening to unleash a storm. Jason stood firm, his jaw clenched as if bracing for a blow. I could feel the tension in the room shift, a palpable force that pressed down on us all. "This isn't just about you, Carter," Jason said, his voice cutting through the weight of silence. "We're all affected by this mess. Can't you see that?"

Carter scoffed, shaking his head with a bitter smile. "Oh, please. Spare me the theatrics. What do you think this is? A family therapy session? This is real life. People get hurt. We can't just slap on a bandage and pretend everything is fine."

"Then what do you suggest?" I asked, stepping closer, wanting to close the distance between our hurt and his stubbornness. "Keep festering in this anger? It's not doing any of us any good."

His gaze flickered with uncertainty, and for a moment, I thought I'd reached him. But just as quickly, he recoiled, the hard shell around his heart encasing him once more. "You don't understand," he shot back. "You haven't walked in my shoes. You don't know what it's like to carry the weight of our family's failures."

"Maybe not," I admitted, my voice steady. "But I know what it's like to want to break free from the past. To want to be more than just a name on a family tree."

A moment of silence stretched between us, a tenuous thread connecting our different worlds. Jason's father shifted uncomfortably, his disapproving gaze now slightly less hostile, as if he were wrestling with the idea that maybe, just maybe, we could bridge this chasm together.

"Carter, we're all flawed. We've all made mistakes," Jason said, desperation creeping into his tone. "But we can't let those mistakes define us. We have to confront them, face them, and find a way to move forward."

For a brief instant, Carter's façade cracked. I saw a flicker of something—doubt, vulnerability, a glimmer of the brother I knew lurked beneath all that bravado. But just as quickly, he slammed the door shut, masking it with anger. "You think I'm going to just forget everything that's happened? Pretend like it's all sunshine and rainbows?"

"No, I don't," I replied, my heart racing. "But I believe we can work through it. Together. If we don't at least try, we're just going to keep repeating the same cycle of pain."

A heavy silence enveloped us again, broken only by the distant sound of barrels creaking and the faint whisper of the wind outside. The distillery felt alive, a witness to our struggle, echoing the weight of the past and the promise of the future.

"Fine," Carter said, the challenge lingering in the air. "Let's say I'm willing to entertain this idea of moving forward. What's next? We all hold hands and sing 'Kumbaya'?"

"Something like that," Jason replied with a wry grin that brought a flicker of amusement to the tension. "But maybe we could skip the singing part."

A reluctant chuckle escaped from the corner of the room where my mother stood, arms crossed, a mixture of skepticism and curiosity dancing in her eyes. "Maybe it's time we all put our cards on the table," she suggested, her tone softening. "No more hiding behind the walls we've built."

Carter glanced around, gauging the faces of our families. "And what if those cards reveal things we don't want to see? Things we can't take back?"

"Then we face them," I answered, my heart pounding. "The only way out of this mess is through it."

Carter's gaze locked onto mine, searching for signs of sincerity. For a fleeting moment, the room felt charged with possibilities, the air thick with the potential for something greater than all of us. Then, with a huff of resignation, Carter dropped his arms to his sides, a sign that perhaps he was finally willing to engage.

"Alright," he said, his voice low. "Let's do this. But don't expect me to play nice."

The words hung in the air, a promise and a threat wrapped in one. The undercurrent of tension shifted again, crackling like static electricity. I could feel my heart race, but beneath it lay a flicker of hope. Maybe we were on the brink of breaking through the barriers that had kept us apart for so long.

As we began to share our stories, our fears, and our hopes, the initial hesitance began to dissolve. I listened as Jason recounted moments from our childhood, laughter mixing with tears as he painted vivid images of summers spent exploring the woods, stealing kisses under the stars, and dreaming of futures untainted by our families' legacies. I shared my own memories, of the love that had first brought Jason and me together, the dreams we had built, and the reality that had tried to tear us apart.

But just as the atmosphere began to warm, Carter's voice sliced through the air, laden with venom. "And what about the night of the accident? The night everything changed? You think we can just gloss over that?"

The room fell silent, the air thickening with the weight of his words. The accident—an unspeakable tragedy that had cast a shadow over our families for years. I could see the flicker of pain in Jason's eyes, a flash of memories that I knew haunted him. "We're not glossing over anything," Jason said, his voice steady yet strained. "But we can't stay stuck in that moment either."

Carter's jaw tightened, anger simmering just below the surface. "You say that like it's easy. You say that like we can just forget the chaos it brought. Our families shattered that night, and you think a few heartfelt conversations are going to fix it?"

"It's not about forgetting," I interjected, the urgency in my voice rising. "It's about acknowledging the pain and choosing to heal from it. We have to face it to let it go."

Carter stepped back, his expression a storm of emotions. "And what if healing means uncovering truths we're not ready to face? What if it means tearing open old wounds?"

"Then we do it together," Jason replied, his voice firm, the determination shining in his eyes. "We can't keep running from the truth. It's a part of us, whether we like it or not."

The room grew heavier, shadows creeping in as we hovered on the precipice of something monumental. And then, as if the universe were conspiring against us, the sound of shattering glass echoed from the back of the room—a cacophony that sliced through our fragile resolve like a knife.

All heads turned, the moment suspended in time. I could feel the air shift, a new tension taking hold, and the uneasy silence morphed into a cacophony of gasps and hurried whispers. "What was that?" my mother asked, her voice trembling.

Carter's eyes flared with confusion and anger, his previous bravado flickering like a candle about to extinguish. "What now?" he demanded, a mixture of anxiety and anticipation coursing through him.

The atmosphere was electric, charged with a potent mix of fear and uncertainty as all eyes turned to the back of the distillery. A figure stepped out of the shadows, silhouetted against the dim light, holding something in their hands—a glimmering shard of glass catching the light just so, reflecting a thousand different possibilities.

"Surprise!" the figure called, their voice dripping with sarcasm and mischief, and in that instant, the reality of our fragile truce hung in the balance, teetering on the edge of chaos, leaving us all wondering just what had come crashing into our carefully crafted moment of reconciliation.

Chapter 23: Unforeseen Consequences

The tension hung heavy in the air, thick as smoke from a fire that threatened to consume everything in its path. Carter's voice was the spark that ignited the powder keg of emotions swirling around the room. I could feel the heat of his fury radiating toward me, and it sent a shiver down my spine. The faces of my family twisted in shock and anger, their loyalty to the truth overshadowed by years of unspoken grudges and whispered accusations. I never expected this confrontation would escalate so quickly, but there we were, caught in a web of history that felt impossibly tangled.

"You think you can just rewrite history?" he spat, the disdain dripping from his words like venom. I could see the anger boiling in his veins, the way his hands clenched into fists, every inch of him radiating the same fierce pride that had long characterized the animosity between our families. It was a battle cry, the kind that signaled a long-dormant feud was being resurrected from the ashes of our collective memories.

I glanced at Jason, who stood beside me, his brow furrowed in disbelief. Our earlier resolve, the plans we'd meticulously crafted to bring our families together, began to slip through my fingers like sand. What had we done? The truth we had fought so hard to uncover felt fragile, vulnerable in the face of this chaos. The hope we had nurtured was fading, suffocated by the intensity of their accusations.

"Stop!" I shouted, my voice piercing through the cacophony. Silence fell, heavy and expectant, as every head turned toward me. I could feel the weight of their gazes, questioning, judging, all waiting for me to bring order to this maelstrom. My heart pounded, a frantic rhythm matching the anxiety swirling in my stomach.

"Listen to yourselves," I implored, my voice steadier than I felt. "We're fighting over something we barely understand. We need to talk this out, not tear each other apart."

Carter scoffed, his posture still taut with rage. "Talk? You mean like how your family has been lying to mine for decades? How many more secrets are you going to sweep under the rug?"

"Secrets?" I echoed, the word tasting bitter on my tongue. "We've all been living in a house of mirrors, Carter. Each reflection distorting the truth. Don't you see? This isn't just about our families anymore; it's about breaking the cycle. We can't move forward unless we confront the past."

Jason placed a comforting hand on my back, grounding me amidst the turmoil. His presence was a balm to my frayed nerves, reminding me that we were in this together. "Carter, we've all been hurt," he added, his voice calm but firm. "But fighting won't heal those wounds. We need to understand each other, not destroy each other."

The tension in the room shifted slightly, the angry flames dimming as hesitant glances passed between family members. It was a flicker of hope, a crack in the armor of resentment. But Carter remained unmoved, his jaw set in stubborn defiance.

"Understanding? You think we can just sit around a campfire and sing Kumbaya after everything that's happened?" His voice dripped with skepticism, and I could see the hurt behind his bravado.

"Why not?" I countered, my heart racing with the thrill of pushing against the walls he'd built around himself. "What do you want from this? What do you think it'll take to finally put this feud to rest?"

A tense silence followed, the air thick with unresolved emotions. I could see Carter's facade cracking, a brief flash of uncertainty crossing his face. But just as quickly, he masked it with anger, as if it were easier to cling to the fury than to confront the vulnerability lurking beneath.

"What do you want?" he shot back, his voice a challenge, but it trembled just a touch.

I took a deep breath, gathering my thoughts like shards of glass that could either cut or create something beautiful. "I want to know why this fight matters to you, to us. I want to understand what our families have lost and how we can rebuild. But it starts with honesty."

"Honesty?" Carter's expression was incredulous, but there was a flicker of interest in his eyes, a glimmer of curiosity that offered a fragile lifeline amidst the chaos.

"Yes, honesty," I replied, my voice steadier now, the words flowing with a confidence I didn't quite feel. "We can't change the past, but we can acknowledge it. We can share our stories, our hurt, and find a way to move forward."

The room remained silent, the charged atmosphere shifting like the wind before a storm. I could feel the weight of unspoken words, buried emotions begging to be unearthed. Slowly, as if testing the waters, I began to speak of my own family's history—the heartbreak and loss, the secrets we had carried like burdens.

As I shared my truth, I watched as Carter's expression softened, the lines of anger around his mouth easing. He was still guarded, but there was a flicker of something else—vulnerability. "You really think sharing our stories will change anything?"

I nodded, my heart pounding with the urgency of this moment. "It's a start, isn't it? It's how we turn the page. You can't rewrite history, but you can write a new chapter."

A slow exhale escaped him, the fight draining from his posture. "Fine. But I'll share my side, and you have to promise to listen—truly listen."

"Deal," I said, a cautious smile creeping onto my face.

As he began to speak, the chaos of our families faded into the background, the fragile threads of understanding weaving through the tension. The world outside seemed to vanish, leaving just the two of us and the weight of our stories—the chance to reshape our fates in the wake of unforeseen consequences.

The air was thick with tension, punctuated by the sharpness of voices clashing like swords in a duel. I stood at the center of this whirlwind, a reluctant referee in a battle that felt both familiar and foreign. Carter's furious gaze was relentless, boring into me as if I held the keys to the secrets we were all desperate to unravel. With every accusation, the walls of this room seemed to close in, shadows flickering across faces filled with disbelief and fury.

"Maybe we need to look at what really happened," I suggested, desperation leaking into my tone. "Perhaps we've been so busy hurling blame that we haven't even tried to understand the story behind our pain."

Carter scoffed, his disbelief like a slap across my cheek. "You think we can just pretend like everything is okay now? Like we haven't been at each other's throats for years?"

"Pretending is the last thing I want to do," I shot back, the fire igniting within me. "But we can't fix what we don't acknowledge. If we're going to get anywhere, we need to be honest about our pasts and our families' roles in all of this."

The room quieted, curiosity momentarily eclipsing the anger that had taken root. I could see uncertainty flicker in the eyes of our relatives, and I clung to it like a lifeline. Perhaps this was the moment I needed to forge a connection amid the wreckage.

Jason stepped closer, his presence a reassuring anchor. "Why don't we all take a moment?" he proposed, his voice low and steady. "Let's gather our thoughts and then share what's been buried."

Carter, however, remained unmoved. "You really think I'm just going to sit here and spill my family's secrets to the very people who've kept me in the dark? It's ridiculous!"

"No one is asking you to do that," Jason interjected. "But if you want to keep shouting over each other, fine. Just know that we're not going to get anywhere."

His words hung in the air, a challenge that seemed to resonate even with those who had previously been consumed by anger. I could see heads nodding in reluctant agreement, a silent acknowledgment that maybe, just maybe, this was a chance to break free from the cycle of animosity that had defined our lives.

"I'll start," I said, feeling a wave of courage surge through me. "My grandmother always told me stories about our family's history, how pride and jealousy had driven a wedge between us and the other family. But she never told me the full truth. It was like she was protecting me from the bitterness that still hung like fog over our gatherings."

The silence was thick as I continued, drawing on the memories that had shaped my childhood. "She used to say that love is stronger than hate, but it's hard to believe that when all you see is resentment. My family has carried this weight for so long, I almost forgot what it feels like to have lightness in my heart."

Carter shifted, the muscles in his jaw working as he considered my words. "So, you're saying it's not just about what happened but how we let it affect us?"

"Yes! Exactly!" I exclaimed, feeling the momentum build. "We have a choice. We can either keep feeding this fire or douse it with understanding. What do you want to do, Carter?"

His expression softened for just a moment, and I seized the opportunity. "We could start with something small. Maybe share one story, just one thing that shaped how you see this whole mess?"

As if drawn into a whirlpool, the family members exchanged glances, uncertain but intrigued. The atmosphere shifted, the tension loosening like a long-held breath finally released. Carter hesitated, a flicker of vulnerability crossing his face, and then he inhaled deeply, as if preparing for a dive into unknown waters.

"My father always told me that the Kincaid family had it out for us," he began, his voice quieter now, yet laced with an intensity that made everyone lean in. "I grew up believing that they were the reason for every misfortune we faced. He painted them as villains in a story where we were the heroes, and I bought into it completely."

A murmur rippled through the crowd, as people shifted, clearly invested. I nodded, encouraging him to continue, my heart racing with the realization that perhaps he was starting to let down his guard.

"But as I got older, I began to wonder if maybe he was wrong. I started digging into the past, uncovering stories that didn't fit the narrative I had been told. And every time I learned something new, it felt like I was peeling back layers of lies." He paused, frustration flickering across his features. "I just wish I could understand why my family has always kept me in the dark."

The honesty in his words struck a chord deep within me. "Carter, it's not just you. We've all been living in the dark, locked in our own perceptions. Our families have kept us apart, blinded us to the truth, all while we let pride dictate our actions. Maybe it's time we shed that darkness."

As I spoke, I noticed a ripple of agreement flowing through the room. With each story shared, the boundaries between our families seemed to dissolve a little more. Tension ebbed like a tide, and I could sense that we were finally moving toward something greater.

Jason took a step forward, his voice steady as he continued the conversation. "My family wasn't perfect either. We had our fair share of skeletons in the closet. But at the end of the day, I think we can all agree that this is about more than just our families. It's about creating a future that's not shackled by the past."

The words hung in the air, reverberating with an undeniable truth. As we shared, the dialogue began to shift, each story weaving a tapestry of understanding that slowly bridged the gap between us. Laughter broke through the tension like sunlight piercing clouds, unexpected and refreshing. I could see the walls crumbling, brick by brick, as we connected through our shared humanity.

Carter finally allowed a reluctant smile to creep onto his face. "Well, if we're going to do this, I suppose I should at least mention that my mother is an excellent cook. We could always start there, right?"

The laughter that erupted was infectious, lightening the atmosphere. The journey ahead remained uncertain, but in that moment, amid shared stories and newfound connection, it felt like a new chapter had begun—one where we could write our own destinies, free from the shadows of our past.

The laughter echoed like a fleeting promise, and for the first time, the weight of generations began to feel a little lighter. Carter's reluctant smile seemed to illuminate the room, and I caught a glimpse of the boy he once was, hidden beneath the layers of anger and resentment. Yet, even as we shared stories and laughter, a part of me remained alert, aware that the shadows of our past were not so easily banished.

"Okay, so let's have a cooking contest," Carter suggested, mischief glinting in his eyes. "My mom's secret chili recipe against your grandmother's famous lasagna. Winner takes bragging rights."

"Oh, please," I retorted, crossing my arms playfully. "Your mom's chili is a weapon of mass destruction. The last time I had it, I thought I might need a fire extinguisher!"

Carter chuckled, the sound warm and genuine, igniting a spark of camaraderie between us. "That's just because you couldn't handle the heat."

"Heat? More like a full-blown inferno!" I shot back, the tension dissipating as laughter filled the space.

"Let's not forget the fact that you're the one who set off the smoke alarms during last Thanksgiving's attempt at cooking," Jason chimed in, winking at me. "I don't think you're in any position to critique anyone's culinary skills."

I rolled my eyes, a grin creeping onto my face. "Touché. But we all know that was a one-time event. I'm basically a gourmet chef now."

Carter raised an eyebrow, clearly amused. "Gourmet chef? Last I checked, a gourmet chef doesn't use instant ramen as a base for their culinary experiments."

"Hey! Ramen is an art form," I defended, throwing my hands up in mock indignation. "It's versatile. Just ask the internet."

As the banter continued, I marveled at the way the atmosphere shifted, lightening with each shared story and playful jab. For years, we had allowed bitterness to define our interactions, but here we were, finding common ground amid the chaos of our families' histories.

Yet, as I watched Carter and Jason exchange playful jabs, an unsettling thought began to gnaw at me. This fragile peace felt too good to be true, like a mirage in the desert. I could sense the potential for more tension lurking beneath the surface, just waiting for the right moment to rear its ugly head.

"Let's not get too comfortable, people," I said, the playful tone slipping from my voice. "As much as I love our culinary competitions, we still have a mountain of family baggage to unpack."

"True," Jason agreed, sobering. "But maybe we've already started climbing that mountain. Today felt like a step in the right direction."

Carter nodded, but there was a flicker of doubt in his eyes. "It's a start, I guess. But let's be honest, this isn't just about us. Our parents won't simply roll over because we had a little bonding session."

"Then let's do something about it," I proposed, my voice rising with conviction. "Let's confront them together. If we really want to break this cycle, we need to face the source of our problems."

Carter's brows furrowed, a shadow falling over his features. "You think that's going to work? You really think they'll listen?"

"Why not?" I shot back, determination surging through me. "If we can find common ground here, surely they can do the same. It's about time they see that the world doesn't revolve around their grudges."

Jason leaned in, his gaze earnest. "We can't let fear dictate our actions anymore. We have to show them that we're willing to bridge the divide, even if it scares them."

The room fell silent as we contemplated the enormity of the task ahead. Would our parents, steeped in pride and past grievances, really be willing to listen? I glanced around the room, gauging the reactions of our families. The intensity of their expressions revealed a kaleidoscope of emotions—curiosity, skepticism, and an undeniable spark of hope.

"Fine," Carter said slowly, a hint of resolve creeping into his voice. "But if we're doing this, we have to be prepared for a battle. Our parents won't go down without a fight."

"Bring it on," I replied, adrenaline coursing through my veins. "This is our moment to change the narrative."

As we began to brainstorm how to approach our families, laughter mingled with ideas, building a newfound sense of unity that felt electrifying. But just as I was starting to feel a sense of possibility, the door swung open with a jarring creak.

My mother stormed in, her expression a tempest of fury. "What on earth is going on in here?" she demanded, her gaze sweeping over the gathered families like a hawk assessing its territory. The energy in the room shifted immediately, the lightness evaporating as quickly as it had appeared.

"Mom, we were just—" I began, but she cut me off with a wave of her hand.

"Just what? Laughing it up while our families are at each other's throats? You think this is a game?" Her voice dripped with disappointment, each word striking like a sharp blade.

Carter straightened, his earlier humor vanishing. "We were trying to work things out. It's not what you think."

"Oh really?" my mother shot back, her eyes narrowing. "Because it looks to me like you're just perpetuating the very drama we've been trying to escape."

"Mom, please, just listen," I pleaded, my heart racing as the air grew thick with tension again. "We're trying to bring everyone together—"

"Together? Is that what you call this farce? You're all just going to make things worse!"

Before I could respond, the door slammed shut behind her, and the room fell into a suffocating silence. My heart raced, caught between the tension that had suddenly escalated and the unexpected reality of our confrontation.

Jason shifted uncomfortably, and I could sense the storm brewing within him. "What now?" he whispered, uncertainty lacing his words.

"I guess we show them we're serious," I replied, my voice steady despite the uncertainty churning inside me. "But if we're going to do this, we need to be ready for whatever comes next."

As the weight of my words settled, I realized the stakes were higher than I had anticipated. Our families were standing on the precipice of a significant change, but would they leap into the unknown with us? Or would they cling to their anger and resentment, dragging us all back into the depths of the past?

The clock ticked on, and I felt the urge to rush ahead, but a lingering doubt clawed at the edges of my resolve. In that moment, uncertainty hung like a thick fog, and I knew that the real battle was just beginning. And I couldn't shake the feeling that we were standing on the brink of something monumental—a reckoning that would change everything, but at what cost?

And just as the air crackled with anticipation, a loud knock reverberated through the silence, each rap echoing like a war drum, signaling that someone—something—was about to break into our fragile truce.

The sunlight filtered through the trees, casting dappled shadows on the path as I made my way to our secret spot, the familiar route tugging at my heartstrings. Each step felt heavier than the last, a silent testament to the tumult within me. I could hear the gentle lapping of the lake against the shore, a soothing sound that had always brought me peace, but today it felt like a mockery of my inner chaos. As I reached the edge, the water shimmered under the sun, alive with the promise of a summer day, yet it reflected none of the tumultuous emotions swirling in my chest.

Jason had been my rock through countless storms, but now, I wondered if our foundations could withstand the weight of this latest upheaval. The confrontation with my family had felt like standing on the edge of a cliff, the winds of expectation and tradition howling around me, daring me to jump. They wanted one thing for me, a path paved with security and familiarity, while my heart craved the thrill of the unknown, the magnetic pull of Jason's laughter and the warmth of his hand in mine. I had tried to explain my feelings, but words seemed to slip through my fingers like sand, impossible to grasp when I needed them most.

Reaching our meeting spot, a secluded cove adorned with wildflowers that danced in the gentle breeze, I took a deep breath, filling my lungs with the scent of pine and fresh earth. It was here that Jason had first kissed me, a moment frozen in time, when the world faded away and all that existed was the two of us. I closed my eyes, willing that feeling to return, hoping it would blanket the fear gnawing at me.

"Hey," his voice cut through my thoughts, rich and warm like the late afternoon sun. I turned to see him standing a few paces away, hands tucked in his pockets, his expression a mix of concern and eagerness. There was something about the way he stood, slightly tense, that made my heart flutter. It mirrored my own inner turmoil, and I suddenly felt the urge to reach out and bridge the gap that had formed between us.

"Hey," I replied, my voice barely above a whisper. The moment hung between us, charged with unspoken words. I could see the questions swimming in his eyes, each one a ripple in the stillness, and I knew we both felt it—the uncertainty that had woven itself into the fabric of our relationship.

"Did you... did you mean what you said the other night?" he asked, taking a tentative step closer. "About needing space?" There was a vulnerability in his voice that pierced through my defenses, and my heart twisted at the thought of having hurt him.

"I did," I admitted, my throat tightening. "But it's not what you think. I just—" I hesitated, searching for the right words, the ones that would convey my turmoil without tearing us apart. "I just feel like I'm being pulled in two different directions. My family... they want what's best for me, but what if what's best for me is you?"

His expression softened, a flicker of hope igniting in his eyes. "I want to be what's best for you. I want to be with you, no matter what." The sincerity in his words wrapped around me like a comforting blanket, and I couldn't help but take a step closer, closing the distance between us.

"Then how do we make this work?" I asked, the desperation creeping into my voice. "How do we fight against everything that seems determined to tear us apart?"

Jason reached for my hands, his touch grounding me in the chaos. "We start by being honest. With each other, and with ourselves." His thumb brushed over my knuckles, a tender gesture that sent shivers down my spine. "What do you really want, Marissa? What does your heart say?"

I opened my mouth to answer, but the words tangled in my throat, caught between fear and desire. My heart ached with the weight of my answer, and I hesitated, the moment stretching between us like a taut string ready to snap. The lake shimmered behind us, an idyllic backdrop that contrasted sharply with the storm brewing in my soul.

"I want you," I finally whispered, my voice trembling with the truth. "But I don't know if I can face my family if I choose you." The vulnerability in my admission hung in the air, palpable and raw.

Jason's eyes searched mine, his grip on my hands firm yet gentle. "You're not alone in this. We can face them together. You're not just choosing me; you're choosing your happiness, and that matters more than anything else." His words were like a lifeline, pulling me from the depths of my doubt.

"But what if they can't accept it? What if it tears us apart?" The fear was real, gnawing at the edges of my resolve.

"Then we fight," he said with an intensity that ignited a spark within me. "We fight for us. For what we have. Love isn't just about the good moments; it's about standing together when the world tries to tear you apart."

As the sunlight danced across the lake, I felt a flicker of hope mingling with my fear. The uncertainty was still there, lurking like a shadow, but in that moment, surrounded by Jason's unwavering gaze, I began to believe that love might just be worth the risk.

In the stillness, as the world around us faded away, I realized this was a turning point. The air felt charged, heavy with the weight of unspoken promises and newfound determination. We were standing on the edge of something beautiful and terrifying, and for the first time, I felt ready to leap.

"Together?" I asked, my heart racing.

"Always," he replied, his smile breaking like dawn over the horizon, brightening the shadows that had clung to us for far too long.

The sun hung low in the sky, casting a golden glow over the lake as I and Jason stood shoulder to shoulder, the world around us fading into the background. My heart thrummed in time with the gentle lapping of the water against the shore. I could feel the weight of his hand still holding mine, the warmth seeping into my skin like sunlight through leaves, anchoring me in a moment that felt both infinite and fragile.

"Are you sure about this?" he asked, his voice low and steady, as if he feared that any sudden movement could shatter the fragile peace we'd created. The sincerity in his gaze cut through the doubts swirling in my mind. This was it—my chance to finally lay everything on the table.

"I'm sure I want to try," I replied, my voice firming as I spoke. "But it won't be easy. My family—"

"They don't get a say in our happiness," Jason interrupted, his brow furrowed with determination. "You deserve to be happy, Marissa, not just content. If they can't see that, then maybe they don't understand you as well as you think they do." His words sent a ripple of reassurance through me, but the fear lingered like a specter in the background.

"I know you mean that," I said, squeezing his hand. "But it's not just about me. They've invested so much in the plans they have for me. They want to see me settled, safe." I hesitated, the memories of family dinners and carefully laid plans rushing back, a torrent of guilt and obligation. "And then there's the reputation..."

"Forget the reputation," he said with a hint of frustration. "Your happiness is what matters. People will talk no matter what. You can either give them something to gossip about or make a life for yourself that you actually want." He looked deep into my eyes, and for a moment, the world around us blurred away, leaving just the two of us suspended in a bubble of hope and possibility.

"I want us, Jason. But how do we deal with the fallout? What if they turn their backs on me?" The words slipped from my lips before I could stop them, heavy with the fear of rejection.

"I won't let that happen," he promised, his voice steady, but a shadow of uncertainty passed over his features. "We'll face it together, remember?"

The promise hung in the air like a fine mist, thick and tangible. I wanted to believe him, to trust that we could weather whatever storm was brewing just beyond the horizon. But as the sun dipped lower, casting an orange hue over the lake, I felt the weight of the world on my shoulders.

"What about your family?" I asked, the thought nagging at me. "How will they react if things escalate?"

Jason sighed, his grip tightening momentarily before relaxing. "They'll have their opinions, but they've always supported me in pursuing what makes me happy. If that means standing by you, then I can't imagine they'll be anything but proud." His confidence was infectious, and for a moment, the shadows of doubt retreated.

Just then, a rustling in the nearby bushes startled me. My heart raced, and I instinctively stepped closer to Jason, who frowned and glanced toward the sound. "What was that?" I whispered, my pulse quickening.

"Probably just a deer," he reassured, but I could sense his unease. We both held our breath, the moment stretched thin like the fabric of a long-forgotten promise.

"Should we check?" I asked, my curiosity piqued and my sense of adventure ignited.

"Let's not," he replied, though there was a slight smile playing on his lips. "I'd rather not meet a deer that might take offense to our love story."

"Fair enough," I laughed, the tension breaking like a wave crashing against the shore. But the moment of levity quickly faded, and we returned to the heavy silence that enveloped us.

The sun dipped lower still, its final rays casting long shadows over the water, and the atmosphere shifted, filled with the scent of impending change. "Okay, let's do it," I finally said, straightening my shoulders. "Let's tell them."

He nodded, a blend of pride and anxiety flickering in his eyes. "Together?"

"Together."

As the words left my lips, I felt a surge of determination. It was time to confront my family, to stand tall and unapologetic for my choices. But before we could gather ourselves for that daunting confrontation, the sound of hurried footsteps broke through the stillness, followed by a familiar voice calling my name.

"Marissa! Jason!"

I turned to see my younger brother, Alex, barreling down the path, his expression a mix of panic and excitement. "You have to come quick! Mom and Dad are looking for you!"

"What's wrong?" I asked, my heart sinking as I exchanged glances with Jason.

"I don't know, but it seems serious. They've been asking about you, and I think they're... they're not happy."

Panic surged in my chest, turning the air thick with dread. "What do you mean?"

"I overheard them talking. They were arguing about you... and Jason." His words landed like stones in my stomach.

I looked at Jason, whose face had paled slightly, a mix of concern and dread washing over him. "We need to go," he said, urgency lacing his voice.

As we rushed back along the path, each step felt heavier than the last, my heart racing with every word Alex had shared. The sunlight faded behind the trees, shadows stretching ominously as we approached the clearing where my family had gathered.

"Marissa! Jason! There you are!" My mother's voice sliced through the air, sharp and edged with tension. The look on her face told me everything I needed to know. "We need to talk."

My stomach twisted, a knot of anxiety settling deep within me. Jason's hand found mine again, our fingers interlocking like a lifeline as we stepped into the circle of my family. I could feel the weight of expectations pressing down on us, the air thick with unspoken accusations and fears.

"What's going on?" I asked, forcing my voice to remain steady despite the turmoil inside.

My father took a step forward, his jaw clenched, and I braced myself for the storm I knew was coming. "We need to discuss your future. There are some things you need to understand."

In that moment, I felt the world tilt beneath me, the weight of choices and love colliding in a deafening silence, ready to break.

Chapter 25: Decisions of the Heart

The sun dipped low on the horizon, casting a warm golden hue across the lake's surface, where tiny ripples danced in harmony with the evening breeze. I could hear the faint lapping of the water against the wooden dock, a soothing soundtrack that usually eased my racing thoughts. Yet today, it did little to quell the storm brewing within me. The air was thick with anticipation, charged with the weight of unspoken words as Jason approached, his silhouette framed by the soft glow of twilight.

"Hey," he greeted me, his voice a whisper against the whispering trees. The worry etched on his face deepened the lines around his eyes, making him look older than the twenty-five years we'd shared. I wanted to reach out, to smooth away the furrow of his brow, but I held back, unsure if my touch would bring comfort or ignite a fire of unresolved tension.

The quiet of the lake wrapped around us like a familiar blanket, yet it felt frayed at the edges, as if it were straining under the weight of our shared silence. Jason settled beside me on the dock, our shoulders brushing against one another, a tentative connection that spoke volumes in this moment of uncertainty. I turned my gaze to the horizon, where the sun's final rays bled into the water, creating a canvas of swirling oranges and purples that felt painfully beautiful—a stark contrast to the turmoil stirring in my heart.

"We can't keep living like this," I finally admitted, my voice a fragile tremor that echoed across the water. "I need to know where we stand."

He inhaled deeply, the air hitching in his chest, and for a moment, I feared he might drift away into the depths of his thoughts, leaving me alone in this moment of clarity. But his eyes found mine, and I saw the storm of emotions swirling within him—fear, frustration, and an undeniable affection that pulled at my heartstrings. "I can't lose you," he replied softly, his honesty wrapping around me like a comforting embrace.

Yet, the weight of his words settled heavily on my shoulders. "But I also can't ignore my family," he continued, his gaze dropping to the wooden planks beneath us. It was an unspoken truth between us, a fragile line that divided our worlds. The love we shared had become a shimmering thread, delicate yet unyielding, but it was also entwined with the expectations and obligations of the lives we led outside this peaceful sanctuary.

Each word we exchanged felt like a delicate dance, weaving in and out of the complexities that had brought us to this moment. I wanted to reach out and pull him closer, to erase the distance that our circumstances had created, but I knew I had to navigate this carefully. "Jason," I started, the name heavy with implications. "What if your family never accepts us?"

He met my gaze, his expression resolute yet tinged with sadness. "Then I have a choice to make," he said, his voice steady, though I could see the flicker of doubt lurking in the depths of his eyes. "Do I choose my family's approval, or do I choose you?" The question hung in the air like a bitter fruit, ripe with potential yet laden with consequences.

A light breeze rustled the leaves above us, the sound whispering secrets of nature that felt so far removed from the decisions we faced. "That's not a fair choice," I said, my heart racing at the thought of being a reason for his rift with his family. "You shouldn't have to choose. Family is everything."

Jason shook his head, his jaw tight. "Is it everything if it means losing the person I love?" His words struck a chord deep within me, a visceral understanding of the tug-of-war waged in the depths of his heart. The twilight deepened around us, shadows stretching like fingers eager to grasp at our fears, leaving me torn between my desire to protect him and the ache of my own longing.

"We both know love isn't always enough," I said, a quiver in my voice as I struggled to articulate the tangled emotions swelling inside me. "It's a beautiful thing, but it doesn't erase the real-world consequences." I took a deep breath, feeling the coolness of the evening air fill my lungs, grounding me as I dared to lay my heart bare. "I can't be your secret anymore, Jason. I refuse to be hidden away like some forbidden dream."

His gaze pierced mine, intense and unwavering. "I don't want you to be a secret," he said, urgency coloring his tone. "I want the world to know how much you mean to me. But I'm scared. Scared of what my family will think, scared of what it means for us if they reject you."

His vulnerability resonated within me, but I couldn't help but feel the sting of inadequacy creeping in. "What if they never accept me?" I whispered, the words tasting like salt on my tongue.

"Then we find a way," he insisted, determination igniting the air between us. "Love is supposed to challenge us, isn't it? It's supposed to push us to grow, to fight for what we believe in."

I watched him, this man I had fallen for under a canopy of stars, in the stillness of shared laughter and stolen kisses. My heart fluttered with the weight of his conviction, but it also trembled with doubt. "What if we lose everything?"

Jason's hand found mine, his fingers intertwining with mine, grounding me in the moment. "We won't lose everything. We'll create something new together." His grip tightened, and I felt a surge of hope mingling with fear. Perhaps love was about risk, about forging a path against the currents that threatened to sweep us away.

As the last slivers of sunlight faded into darkness, the world around us transformed, leaving only the soft glow of stars above—a reminder that even in the vast unknown, we weren't truly alone. And perhaps, just perhaps, in the heart of uncertainty, we might discover a way to navigate this delicate dance between love and duty, guided by the strength of our commitment to each other.

The silence stretched between us like a taut wire, humming with the unsaid. The sun dipped below the treetops, pulling shadows into the spaces where our words should have filled. "You know," I said, breaking the tension with a half-hearted attempt at humor, "if the world ends tonight, I'd rather be here with you than anywhere else—preferably with a bottle of wine in hand, maybe some popcorn for good measure."

Jason chuckled softly, a sound that momentarily eased the tightness in my chest. "I like how you think. But I'd still want the popcorn, too. You know, for proper world-ending etiquette." His eyes sparkled with that familiar light, the one that always made my heart race, even in moments like these when we stood on the precipice of uncertainty.

"But seriously," I said, letting my laughter fade into the stillness of the evening, "what happens if the world doesn't end and we're just left with this? A never-ending loop of what-ifs and could-have-beens?" I leaned back on the dock, letting the rough wood dig into my palms as I stared at the stars beginning to wink into existence, as if mocking our very real dilemma.

Jason shifted closer, the warmth radiating from him like a beacon in the gathering dark. "I think we'd have to take a leap of faith. Trust that love, in all its messy glory, can find a way to navigate through this chaos." His voice dropped to a conspiratorial whisper. "But I'm not much of a faith guy, you know? I prefer evidence—like a convincing PowerPoint presentation that lays everything out neatly."

"Maybe we can make one together," I suggested, half-teasing, half-serious. "Point one: family drama. Point two: romance on the rocks. Point three: potential solutions."

He laughed, shaking his head. "As if any slide could possibly encompass the magnitude of our issues."

"Touché," I admitted, biting back a smile. The playful banter was a welcome distraction from the reality of our situation, but as I watched the last glow of the sunset slip beneath the horizon, the weight of our conversation crept back in, curling around my heart like the night air.

"What do you want?" I asked suddenly, the question hanging between us, heavy and fragile, like the first tender notes of a haunting melody.

He paused, his brow furrowing in thought. "Honestly? I want you to be happy. But if I'm being selfish, I want you to be happy with me."

I swallowed hard, the lump in my throat threatening to choke me. "And what if that happiness means standing up to your family?"

He didn't answer right away, the hesitation in his silence cutting deeper than I expected. "That's the hard part," he finally said, his voice barely above a whisper. "I don't want to hurt them. But I can't keep pretending I don't love you. It feels like I'm living a lie, and the longer we do this dance, the more it eats away at me."

A part of me ached to reach out and reassure him, to tell him that we'd figure it out together. But as the stars twinkled into existence, I felt the enormity of our situation loom larger. "What if they can't accept us?" I ventured, my voice trembling as I met his gaze.

"Then we fight for it," he said, a fire igniting in his eyes. "Love isn't easy, and it never has been. But I'm willing to face whatever comes our way if it means we get to explore what this—" he gestured between us, "—really is."

I wanted to believe him. I wanted to dive into this chaos, arms wide open, ready to embrace whatever came next. But the fear of losing him—of losing everything—held me back. "What if your family tries to tear us apart?"

"Let them try," he said with a fierce resolve, and I marveled at the depth of his conviction. "I'm not afraid of them if it means I have you by my side. We'll be like those brave little ducks you see crossing the road, waddling through traffic while everyone honks and yells. We can do this."

I couldn't help but laugh at the image he painted, even as my heart fluttered at his words. "So, we're the ducks, huh? That's a pretty glamorous comparison."

"Well, someone has to be brave enough to cross the road," he said with a smirk, and in that moment, a flicker of hope ignited within me.

The conversation flowed easily from there, easing the tension as we swapped silly anecdotes and shared more laughter. The weight of our earlier discussion hung in the air but was interwoven with threads of lightness, reminding me that there was still joy to be found even in uncertain times.

As darkness enveloped us, the lake mirrored the night sky, a shimmering tapestry of stars reflecting our shared aspirations and fears. I breathed in the cool air, filled with the scent of pine and earth, a grounding reminder of where we were. "What if we started by introducing you to my parents?" I suggested, surprising myself with the boldness of my words. "They may not be perfect, but at least you'd have a taste of what you're getting into."

He raised an eyebrow, clearly intrigued. "Are you trying to scare me away?"

"Not at all! Just thought you might want a warm-up before facing the real deal."

"Fine, then," he chuckled, "I'll consider it a practice round. But you better prepare them for my duck-like qualities."

"Only if you promise not to waddle too much," I replied, a grin spreading across my face.

The night continued to stretch on, our laughter mingling with the sounds of nature. We fell into a rhythm, trading stories that spiraled from our childhoods to dreams of the future, our fears and hopes entwined. In those moments, the world felt vast and inviting, a canvas where we could sketch our destinies however we wished.

But beneath the laughter, I sensed an undercurrent of tension, a gnawing doubt that lingered like an unwelcome guest. As the stars twinkled above, I couldn't shake the feeling that our decisions were just the beginning of a much larger journey, one that would test the strength of our love and the depths of our courage.

Yet, as Jason leaned closer, his warmth radiating through the chill of the night, I knew that whatever came next, we would face it together, a united front against the chaos of the world beyond the lake's tranquil shores.

The air shimmered around us, a tangible mix of anticipation and uncertainty. I leaned against the dock, drawing in a deep breath infused with the crisp scent of pine and damp earth. "So, ducks it is," I mused, breaking the spell of seriousness that had settled like mist. "We'll waddle our way through this together, quacking all the while."

Jason laughed, the sound slicing through the tension like a ray of sunlight breaking through clouds. "As long as you promise to be my quacking partner. I'm not doing this alone."

"Great," I replied, smirking at the image of us navigating family dinners like a pair of bumbling waterfowl. "But what if your family turns out to be a flock of angry geese?"

"Then we're toast," he quipped back, his eyes dancing with mischief. "But I've always been fond of toast."

We laughed together, but beneath the humor, my heart raced with the gravity of what we were contemplating. Jason's playful banter felt like a lifeline, yet I couldn't ignore the reality that loomed ahead. The distance between his family's expectations and our reality was vast, and navigating it would require a deft touch, perhaps a small miracle.

The night deepened, wrapping us in its velvety embrace. Stars twinkled overhead, punctuating the darkness with their indifferent light, as if to remind us of the world beyond our little sanctuary. I found myself wishing for a clearer path, a sign that we were doing the right thing. "Do you think they'll even give us a chance?" I asked, the question slipping out before I could censor it.

"Your parents? Sure, they love you. They'll want you to be happy," he said, although I detected a note of uncertainty in his voice.

"What about yours?" The question hung in the air, heavier than I'd anticipated.

Jason's expression shifted, the playful glimmer replaced by something darker. "I hope so. But they've always been about appearances, about keeping up with the Joneses, you know? Being with you could shatter that image."

"And how do you feel about that?"

"I feel like I'd rather be with you, even if it means my family thinks I'm a disappointment," he admitted, his voice resolute.

I bit my lip, the gravity of his words sinking in. "I'm not asking you to choose between us and them. But the way you say it makes it sound like that's exactly what's on the table."

He sighed, running a hand through his hair in frustration. "You're right. I want it all—my family and you. But it's not that simple."

The tension coiled tighter, wrapping around us like a thick fog. "No, it's not," I replied softly, the realization that we were stepping into a storm together dawning on me. "But maybe it's not impossible either. People change. Families adapt. Sometimes love can pave the way."

"You really think so?"

"I have to believe that," I said, summoning every ounce of hope I could muster. "Because otherwise, what's the point of all this? If we don't fight for what we want, we'll just end up as two people who never took the chance."

His gaze locked onto mine, a spark igniting between us. "You're right. We have to take that leap."

With newfound determination, we set aside our fears, focusing instead on the tangible possibilities of tomorrow. The conversation shifted as we exchanged plans—how I'd introduce him to my parents first, a softer landing before he faced the tempest of his own family's scrutiny. Our dreams wove together, threads of ambition and hope intertwining with the uncertainty of the future.

As the conversation flowed, I felt a surge of exhilaration. Each shared dream ignited the air around us, and I allowed myself to envision a future where love conquered all obstacles, where we could build a life together free from the shackles of others' expectations. But beneath that excitement lurked a nagging doubt, a shadow I couldn't shake off.

"Let's make a pact," I said suddenly, my heart pounding as the words spilled out. "No matter what happens, we promise to be honest with each other. No secrets, no half-truths. We owe it to ourselves to be real."

Jason nodded, his expression serious. "Agreed. No matter how hard it gets, we face it together."

"Together," I echoed, a sense of warmth blooming within me.

Yet, even as we clung to our promises, an unsettling thought nagged at the edges of my mind. How would his family respond? Would they welcome me with open arms, or would they see me as a threat to their carefully crafted world? The question loomed larger than ever, whispering doubts that echoed in the back of my mind.

The first hint of dawn peeked over the horizon, painting the sky in soft shades of pink and orange, signaling the start of a new day. Jason leaned closer, his breath warm against my cheek. "We've got this," he murmured, and for a fleeting moment, everything felt perfect.

But just then, the tranquility shattered. A sharp sound echoed across the lake, startling us both into alertness. I glanced toward the shore, where a dark figure emerged from the trees, silhouetted against the rising sun. The hairs on the back of my neck prickled with unease as recognition hit me like a thunderclap. It was Jason's brother, Tom, his expression set in a tight line that hinted at confrontation.

"Jason!" Tom shouted, striding toward us with a purpose that made my heart race. "We need to talk. Now."

The warmth of our moment evaporated, replaced by a rush of cold dread. I glanced at Jason, whose eyes mirrored my own shock and fear. The world around us blurred into insignificance as I processed the reality of what was unfolding.

"Tom, wait!" Jason called, his voice a mixture of frustration and concern.

But Tom didn't pause, the tension radiating off him like an electric current. He was a storm on the horizon, and I couldn't shake the feeling that whatever he had to say would change everything. My heart pounded as I braced myself for the storm that was about to break.

Chapter 26: Allies and Enemies

The smell of freshly brewed coffee mingled with the scent of warm pastries, wrapping around me like a cozy blanket as I slid into the worn leather seat across from Madeline. The café, with its mismatched furniture and eclectic wall art, felt like a haven from the storm of family drama swirling outside. Sunlight streamed through the tall windows, casting a warm glow that made everything look softer, more inviting. I sipped my latte, the rich foam clinging to my upper lip like a playful reminder to stay present, and glanced at Jason, who was fidgeting with the edges of a napkin.

"Okay, let's get to it," I said, trying to inject some energy into the atmosphere. "Madeline, you know the history between our families. We can't let it drag on any longer. We need to come together, not just for us but for everyone in this town."

Madeline, with her soft curls bouncing slightly as she nodded, leaned forward. Her emerald green eyes sparked with a mix of hope and skepticism. "I believe in what you two are trying to do," she said, her voice steady yet warm. "But you'll need more than just my support. We need a real plan."

"What do you mean?" Jason chimed in, his voice laced with urgency. He always had this way of getting a little too passionate too quickly, like a match struck in the dark.

"I mean we need to gather allies," she replied, her tone crisp and clear. "It's not enough to just want peace; we need to demonstrate why it's essential. There are folks in town who are tired of the rivalry too, but we need to make them believe it's worth their while to stand with us."

A flicker of anxiety danced in my chest. The thought of rallying more people was daunting. "But how do we get them to listen?" I asked, my fingers tapping nervously against the table.

Madeline leaned back, her mind visibly churning. "We host a town meeting," she suggested, her enthusiasm building. "Invite everyone, create a space for discussion. You two can present your vision, and I can help spread the word."

Jason's eyes lit up, the tension in his shoulders easing. "That could work! If we can show people that coming together is more beneficial than fighting, maybe we can turn the tide."

I nodded slowly, trying to shake off the lingering doubt. "Okay, but what if the others don't want to listen? What if they want to keep the feud going?"

Madeline met my gaze with unwavering confidence. "Then we show them that unity has power. We highlight the benefits—businesses flourishing, families thriving. It's time to put a spotlight on what we can achieve together, rather than being mired in past grievances."

Jason chuckled, his excitement infectious. "And if they don't bite, we can always bring cookies. Everyone loves cookies."

Madeline laughed, the tension breaking like a fragile bubble. "Cookies, yes! But we need more than baked goods. We need real reasons for them to care."

As the conversation flowed, ideas blossomed like wildflowers in spring, vibrant and unpredictable. We discussed everything from banners to speeches, the energy in the air crackling with possibility. But just as I began to feel the weight of hope settle in my chest, the bell above the café door chimed, and in walked a figure cloaked in familiar arrogance.

"Madeline, darling! I didn't think you'd be mingling with these two misfits." The voice was like gravel, unmistakably belonging to Ben, my brother's childhood best friend. He sauntered over with a cocky grin plastered on his face, as if he owned the world—and especially this café.

"Ben," I said, my tone flat, trying to keep my irritation at bay. "What do you want?"

"Just came in for a coffee," he replied, waving a hand dismissively. "But now I see I've stumbled into an... interesting conversation." His eyes flicked from Madeline to Jason and back to me, the gleam of mischief dancing in his gaze. "Planning a little rebellion, are we?"

Madeline stiffened slightly beside me, but I refused to let his presence throw me off. "We're actually trying to do something constructive," I shot back, unable to mask the sharpness in my voice.

"Constructive?" Ben leaned against the table, feigning deep thought. "And what could possibly be constructive about trying to unite the families that have been at each other's throats for decades? Sounds like a recipe for disaster to me."

Jason's jaw clenched, but I reached out, placing a hand on his arm. "We're tired of the feud, Ben. We want to find common ground."

"Common ground?" he scoffed, shaking his head in mock disbelief. "You really think they'll just roll over and agree to that? It's a fairy tale, sweetie. Nice idea, but this isn't a Disney movie."

I took a breath, my resolve hardening. "Maybe not. But if we don't try, we'll never know. Besides, isn't it better to try and fail than to keep living in this toxic rivalry?"

Ben shrugged, his smirk faltering for just a moment before returning. "Suit yourself. Just don't come crying to me when it all blows up in your faces." He turned to leave, but not before glancing back, a flicker of something—was it concern?—crossing his features. "Good luck, you'll need it."

As the door swung shut behind him, I felt the tension in the air shift, the laughter and excitement we'd shared moments before now tinged with uncertainty. "That guy really knows how to dampen the mood," Jason muttered, frustration evident in his voice.

Madeline sighed, her eyes still on the door. "He's not wrong about one thing: it won't be easy. But we can't let him or anyone else discourage us. We have to believe in this."

Her conviction washed over me, and I realized that despite the jarring encounter, a flicker of hope ignited within. "You're right," I said, determination creeping into my voice. "Let's gather our allies, start planning that meeting, and show everyone that unity is stronger than rivalry. If Ben wants to doubt us, that's on him. We've got work to do."

With a renewed sense of purpose, we began to outline our next steps, fueled by the thrill of a challenge and the warmth of friendship, as the world outside continued its tumultuous dance.

The sun hung low in the sky, casting a golden glow that danced across the café's wooden floorboards as we strategized. Our table, once just a piece of furniture, had transformed into a battleground of ideas and aspirations. With Madeline on our side, the atmosphere buzzed with a sense of possibility, each sip of coffee heightening our resolve.

"Alright," Madeline said, her voice slicing through the chatter of the café. "Let's make a list of potential allies. We need a solid mix of voices, people who can influence others." She pulled a notepad from her bag, her pen poised like a sword ready for battle.

Jason leaned in, a glimmer of mischief in his eye. "I can think of a few folks. What about the Reynolds? They're well-liked around town and have always been pro-peace."

Madeline nodded, jotting down names. "Good. What about the school board? If we can convince them that unity will benefit our kids, they might jump on board."

"Especially since they've been stuck in the middle of our families' feud," I chimed in, feeling the tide of our plan swell. "They'd love to see us settle this."

As we rattled off names and ideas, the tension of the previous encounter with Ben began to dissipate. The café hummed with life around us—laughter spilled from the tables of friends catching up, the barista bantered with customers, and the aroma of pastries filled the air like a warm hug. It felt like a secret haven where dreams and plans could take flight.

But as the sun dipped further into the horizon, painting the sky in hues of pink and orange, the weight of the task ahead loomed large. "It's not just about gathering allies," I mused, my fingers absentmindedly tracing the rim of my cup. "We need to convince them that this isn't just our fight but a community issue."

Madeline looked up, her eyes sparkling with inspiration. "What if we frame it around a community event? Something fun that can bring people together—like a fair or a potluck. Everyone loves good food and games."

"Count me in for the food part," Jason said, grinning widely. "I'll whip up my famous chili. It's been known to unite even the most stubborn of souls."

I laughed, picturing the usual chili showdown at the annual town fair. "And I can bake—chocolate chip cookies that are definitely better than anything Ben could throw together."

Madeline raised an eyebrow playfully. "What a bold claim. Are you ready to back that up?"

I smiled, an idea bubbling to the surface. "How about we challenge him? If we can get enough people to come, I'll bake a dozen cookies for everyone who attends. If he wants to try and pit his against mine, let's see who wins the 'Cookie of the Year' award."

The thought of Ben being forced to compete in a baking showdown made me laugh, the kind of laugh that chased away lingering doubts. "That's it!" Madeline exclaimed, clapping her hands. "A friendly competition could really draw in the crowds. Everyone loves a little drama."

With the plan taking shape, we moved into the logistics of making it happen. Madeline had a talent for organization, her energy infectious as she rattled off ideas. "Let's set a date two weeks from now. We'll need a location—maybe the town square? It's central, and we can decorate it to draw in the locals."

"Good thinking," Jason said, his eyes narrowing with determination. "We'll need to design some flyers, too, to spread the word. If we create enough buzz, people will have to show up."

"I can handle the flyer design," I offered, my fingers itching to start drafting something eye-catching. "I know a thing or two about graphic design. We could include a fun tagline—something catchy that pulls people in."

Just then, the café door swung open, and a gust of cool evening air swept through, bringing with it the unmistakable sound of boots striking the wooden floor. I turned to see Sarah, one of my closest friends, walk in. Her expression was a delightful mix of curiosity and mischief. "What are you scheming about over here? I can practically feel the conspiratorial vibes from across the room."

"Join us!" I beckoned, gesturing for her to take a seat. "We're plotting to unite the families and rally support for a community event."

"Count me in! I've always wanted to throw a fair," she said enthusiastically, her dark curls bouncing as she settled into the seat beside me. "What can I do?"

Madeline glanced at her, an idea sparking. "Actually, we need someone who can work the crowd, get people excited. You have that natural charisma."

"Charisma? Oh, please," Sarah laughed, waving a dismissive hand. "I just know how to talk to people. But you're right; I could do that. I can get the word out and stir up some excitement."

As we huddled together, weaving our plans like a tapestry, the atmosphere shifted. It was no longer just a gathering of friends but a coalition, our mission taking root in the shared energy of hope and determination.

"Okay, let's recap," I said, pulling out my phone to take notes. "We need to finalize the date, book the town square, design flyers, and brainstorm activities. We also need to be sure to include Ben. This will drive him crazy."

Jason raised an eyebrow. "You really want to invite him?"

"Of course! He'll either have to participate or watch from the sidelines. Either way, it'll be entertaining." I grinned, imagining the look on his face as he watched our plan unfold.

Sarah leaned back, her eyes twinkling with excitement. "And when we win over the townsfolk, Ben will be left sulking in his corner, alone with his stale cookies."

"Exactly," I said, the vision of our success painting a vivid picture in my mind. "Let's give him a reason to change his tune or at least keep him too busy to stir up trouble."

With laughter and enthusiasm filling the air, we began to sketch out the details, the night unfolding like a well-loved story. But as we immersed ourselves in our plans, a nagging feeling in the pit of my stomach reminded me that the path ahead wouldn't be smooth. The storm of rivalry still loomed over us, a reminder that while we could gather allies, the enemies we faced were not just the ones outside but also the doubts that brewed within.

Just as we settled into a rhythm, the café door swung open again, revealing an unexpected figure: my brother, Alex. He stepped in with his usual swagger, looking far too pleased with himself. "Well, well, what do we have here? A secret club I wasn't invited to?"

My heart sank momentarily. Alex had a way of throwing himself into the middle of our plans like a bull in a china shop, often leaving chaos in his wake. But this time, I was determined to keep our mission intact. "It's not a secret, just a strategy session for uniting our families," I said, my tone light but firm.

He sauntered over, crossing his arms. "Oh, is that all? I'd be careful with that—last time I checked, family meetings usually end in shouting matches."

Madeline shot me a knowing glance, but I kept my smile steady. "That's why we're taking a different approach this time. We want to make it fun, to show everyone that we can be more than rivals."

"Fun? Really?" Alex scoffed, but there was an amused glint in his eye. "You think you can charm everyone into peace with cookies and games?"

"Why not?" I challenged, my resolve solidifying. "It's time to break the cycle, Alex. Don't you want to see our families get along?"

He paused, clearly weighing his options. "Alright, I'm in. But if this backfires, don't come crying to me."

"Deal," I said, feeling a rush of triumph. With each ally we gained, I felt the weight of the past lift ever so slightly. Maybe, just maybe, we could turn this rivalry into something more vibrant than old grievances.

As our group huddled together, laughter echoing off the café walls, I realized that while the road ahead would be fraught with challenges, the warmth of camaraderie was worth every effort. With our allies at our side, we were ready to embark on this uncharted adventure, determined to rewrite the narrative of our families' legacy.

The following days slipped by in a whirlwind of planning and excitement, the town square transforming into a canvas for our dreams. Banners swayed gently in the breeze, each one a colorful promise of unity, while the scent of blooming flowers danced in the air like a hopeful whisper. We assembled a ragtag team of volunteers, each bringing their unique flair to our community event. Jason was in charge of the chili competition, his enthusiasm as fiery as the dish he vowed to serve. Madeline dove into organizing games and activities, her meticulous nature ensuring that everything would go off without a hitch. And Sarah? Well, she transformed into our social media maestro, whipping up a frenzy of anticipation online.

As the date approached, the buzz around town grew palpable, and I found myself caught up in a mix of excitement and nerves. I had spent hours designing flyers, pouring over the perfect wording to evoke both humor and intrigue. "Join us for a day of fun, food, and friendly competition!" they proclaimed, flanked by colorful graphics of dancing chili peppers and cheerful cookies. The visuals made my heart swell with pride. This was more than just an event; it was a chance to reshape the narrative of our families.

But as much as I tried to focus on the positive, the shadows of doubt loomed over me like storm clouds. Every time I closed my eyes, I could see Ben's smug smile, hear his dismissive laughter. It felt like he was always lurking just out of sight, ready to sabotage our efforts. That gnawing worry clung to me, whispering doubts that perhaps our efforts were futile.

"Okay, time to put those doubts to rest," I muttered to myself one evening while tidying up the kitchen, running my fingers over the cookie jars that lined the counter. A sudden knock at the door jolted me from my thoughts. I opened it to find Sarah standing there, her eyes wide with urgency.

"C'mon! You won't believe what I just saw!" She burst in, her energy infectious.

"What is it?" I asked, curiosity piqued as I followed her into the living room.

"I just passed by Ben's house, and he was pacing back and forth in front of his front porch, looking frantic. I swear I heard him talking to someone—like he was plotting something."

My heart raced, adrenaline flooding through me. "Plotting? What do you mean?"

"I don't know, but it didn't look good. He was waving his hands around, and there was definitely someone with him. I couldn't get close enough to see who it was, but it felt… conspiratorial."

I felt a chill run down my spine. "This can't be a coincidence. He knows we're trying to bring everyone together. What if he's rallying people against us?"

"Or worse," Sarah said, her voice low. "What if he's trying to sabotage the event? We need to figure out what he's planning before it's too late."

"Okay," I replied, determination surging through me. "We can't let him ruin everything we've worked for."

The night air had cooled as we left my house, stepping into the familiar streets that felt charged with unspoken tension. It was quiet, too quiet, the kind of silence that enveloped a neighborhood just before a storm. We crept toward Ben's house, our hearts pounding in sync as we approached the front porch. I peered through the curtains, my breath hitching as I spotted Ben standing with another figure—someone tall, clad in dark clothing, their features obscured by the night.

"Do you recognize them?" Sarah whispered, leaning closer.

I shook my head, trying to squint through the dim light. "No, but I don't like this. We have to hear what they're saying."

We inched closer, crouching down low. The shadows concealed us, but I felt my heart racing louder with every word that drifted toward us.

"…they think they can pull this off," Ben's voice carried through the evening air, thick with contempt. "But if we disrupt their little fair, it'll show everyone that they can't just erase years of rivalry with cookies and games."

The stranger chuckled, a sound devoid of warmth. "And how do you propose we do that? We can't just storm in and ruin it. We need something that will leave a mark."

"I have a plan," Ben replied, his voice dropping to a conspiratorial whisper. "If we can create a scene—something explosive enough to embarrass them in front of everyone—we'll crush their little coalition before it even starts. And then, when the families see how ridiculous they are trying to play nice, they'll come back to us."

A chill washed over me, realization striking like lightning. "He's going to ruin everything," I whispered to Sarah, my voice barely above a breath.

"We can't let this happen," she said fiercely, her eyes glinting with determination. "We have to warn Madeline and Jason. They need to know what's coming."

Just as we turned to leave, a sharp sound echoed behind us. I whipped around to see a figure emerging from the shadows—a tall silhouette that moved with predatory grace. My breath caught in my throat as recognition hit me like a freight train.

"Looks like we've got some eavesdroppers," Ben's voice dripped with amusement, the earlier urgency replaced by a smug confidence.

"Run!" I shouted, grabbing Sarah's arm as we darted down the street, adrenaline surging through me. The sound of footsteps thundered behind us, a mix of laughter and taunts, sending us racing toward safety.

As we rounded the corner, I could feel the weight of what was at stake crashing down around us. They were onto us, and the clock was ticking. We had to regroup, to strategize against this new threat before the fair turned into chaos.

Breathless and shaken, we skidded to a halt in front of Madeline's house, our hearts pounding like war drums. I could see lights flickering inside, a sign of life in the midst of the gathering storm.

"Madeline!" I yelled, hammering on the door. "We need you! It's urgent!"

Moments later, she appeared, her brow furrowed with concern as she opened the door. "What's wrong?"

"Ben and someone else are plotting to ruin the event. We need to act fast!"

Madeline's expression hardened, and I could see the gears turning in her mind. "Okay, let's gather everyone—Jason, Sarah, and anyone else we can trust. We need to strategize now, before it's too late."

Just as we moved inside, a loud crash echoed from the direction of the fairgrounds, the sound of chaos ripping through the night like thunder.

"Did you hear that?" Sarah gasped, eyes wide with fear.

Madeline's expression hardened, determination lighting up her features. "We have to get to the fairground. Whatever they're doing, we can't let them succeed. It's time to stand our ground."

As we rushed toward the door, I felt a surge of resolve. We were no longer just fighting for our families; we were standing up for our community. The stakes had never been higher, and the outcome of our efforts hung precariously in the balance.

But as we stepped outside, ready to face whatever awaited us, a figure emerged from the shadows, blocking our path—a familiar face, one I hadn't expected to see, casting doubt on everything we had fought for.

"Going somewhere?" he smirked, and the world around us tilted, the weight of his words crashing down like a tidal wave.

Chapter 27: Rebuilding Bridges

The sun dipped below the horizon, casting a golden glow over the distillery that danced through the air like a well-rehearsed ballet. As I stepped onto the wooden porch, the scent of rich oak and sweet malt wafted around me, mingling with the floral notes from the blooming wildflowers that lined the path. Each step echoed a rhythmic anticipation in my heart, a pulse that matched the hum of excitement growing within the crowd.

Families from both sides of our fractured community began to filter in, their faces a tapestry of curiosity and wariness. I tucked a loose strand of hair behind my ear, the warm breeze lifting the strands like playful whispers urging me forward. As I scanned the gathering, I spotted a group of children darting between adults, laughter spilling from their lips like sparkling water, a stark contrast to the tension that had hung in the air like an unwelcome fog for too long. They were the reminder I needed—innocence unharmed by the battles of their parents.

"Are you ready for this?" Jason's voice broke through my reverie. He stood beside me, his presence a comforting anchor in the sea of uncertainty. His eyes, a deep shade of blue that reminded me of the summer sky, held a warmth that washed over my nerves like a soothing balm.

"As ready as I'll ever be," I replied, trying to muster a smile that would conceal the storm of anxiety brewing within. "Just don't let me say anything too ridiculous up there."

"You? Ridiculous? Never," he teased, a playful smirk dancing on his lips. "Just remember to breathe. This is about bringing people together, not winning a debate."

"Easy for you to say. You thrive on public speaking. I'm just trying not to trip over my own words."

"Consider this your stage. Just look at the crowd; they're here because they want to be. That's already a win." His confidence wrapped around me like a cozy blanket, and I took a deep breath, feeling the energy in the air shift as more familiar faces arrived.

Madeline, our indefatigable supporter, floated through the crowd like a vibrant butterfly, her laughter infectious. She approached, her cheeks flushed with excitement, clutching a clipboard in one hand and a glass of the distillery's finest apple cider in the other. "The food trucks are set up, the games are ready, and the musicians are warming up. This place is alive with possibility!"

"Did you manage to talk to the Johnsons?" I asked, my voice barely a whisper as I scanned the crowd for the couple known for their fierce loyalty to their side of the divide.

"Of course! And I think I convinced them to at least try the nachos from that new food truck. Baby steps, right?" Her eyes sparkled with mischief. "They might just start smiling if the cheese is gooey enough."

Laughter bubbled within me, a sound that felt foreign but welcome. "Here's hoping," I replied, glancing back at the crowd.

As the event kicked off, I took my place at the makeshift podium, Jason by my side. The strumming of guitars mingled with the chatter, and I could feel the hesitant energy shift as I prepared to speak. I looked out at the sea of faces—some familiar, some foreign. Each pair of eyes held a story, a history entwined with the fabric of our community.

"Thank you all for coming tonight," I began, my voice steady but soft, cutting through the noise. "This evening is a celebration of our shared humanity, a chance for us to reconnect, to remember what binds us instead of what tears us apart."

A murmur rippled through the crowd, and I could see heads nodding, the glimmer of hope flickering like candlelight in the shadows. Encouraged, I continued, "We've faced challenges that have left scars, but tonight, let's focus on healing. Let's share stories, laughter, and maybe a few good meals."

The crowd chuckled, the tension dissipating like morning mist under the sun's warm gaze.

Just as I was finding my stride, a commotion erupted from the far end of the distillery. I turned to see a small group gathered, voices raised in agitation. My heart sank; had we come this far only to witness a fight?

"Stay here," Jason said, his grip on my hand tightening. "I'll check it out."

I nodded, my stomach tightening as he made his way through the crowd. The warm ambiance transformed into something more chaotic, the laughter turning to sharp whispers. I strained to hear snippets of conversation, my pulse quickening.

"...can't believe they're here..."

"...it's not safe..."

I stepped down from the podium, weaving through the people, determination propelling me forward. When I reached the cluster of onlookers, I pushed my way through to find Jason standing with his arms crossed, a frown etched deep across his brow.

A familiar face caught my eye, and I felt the color drain from my cheeks. It was Sarah, a fiery spirit I'd grown up with, her loyalty unwavering. But tonight, her anger was palpable, aimed directly at the Johnsons.

"This is exactly why we can't trust them!" she shouted, her voice rising above the din. "They think they can waltz in and take over!"

"Sarah, please," Jason implored, stepping closer. "Tonight isn't about division; it's about coming together."

"No! They don't get to dictate our narrative. We've fought too hard to let them in!" Her words pierced through the night, sharp and unforgiving.

I could feel the atmosphere shift, the hopeful energy of the evening waning like a candle snuffed out too soon. I knew I had to intervene, to restore the fragile sense of unity we had just begun to cultivate.

"Sarah!" I called out, my voice steady despite the storm raging within me. She turned, her expression a mix of disbelief and anger. "Let's talk, just the two of us."

"Talk? What's there to talk about?"

"Everything," I replied, my heart pounding. "We owe it to ourselves and to everyone here to at least try."

For a moment, silence enveloped us, the crowd's attention shifting back to the scene unfolding. I could see the glimmer of uncertainty in Sarah's eyes, the walls she had built around her slowly beginning to waver.

"Fine," she huffed, crossing her arms defiantly. "But I'm not making any promises."

"Neither am I," I countered, a small smile breaking through the tension. "But I think we owe it to our community to at least try."

As we stepped aside, the murmurs of the crowd faded into the background, replaced by the quiet resolve that lingered in the air. In that moment, surrounded by the echoes of laughter and music, I felt the first spark of hope ignite within me. We might just be on the precipice of something extraordinary.

The warmth of the evening air swirled around me, alive with the sweet notes of the distillery's brewing and the tantalizing aroma of food wafting from the nearby trucks. Children darted between adults, their laughter twinkling like fireflies in the dusk. I watched as families began to mingle, the initial tension slowly melting away like ice on a summer sidewalk. Yet beneath the surface, I sensed an undercurrent of apprehension—a collective holding of breaths as everyone cautiously navigated this tentative reunion.

As I stood with Jason, his hand in mine a grounding force against the potential chaos, I couldn't help but marvel at the way the distillery had transformed for the night. String lights hung overhead, casting a warm glow that illuminated the wooden barrels and scattered hay bales we had arranged for seating. Madeline's meticulous planning had paid off; we had created a space that felt inviting, festive, and—dare I say it—hopeful.

Just as I started to feel the excitement brewing within me, a commotion erupted near the food truck serving tacos. I squinted through the gathering twilight to see Sarah, her arms animatedly gesturing, her voice a high pitch that sliced through the chatter. I could feel the tension coiling in my stomach again. "Oh no, not again," I muttered under my breath.

"Let's go," Jason said, moving towards the commotion with purpose. I followed closely, my heart racing. I knew Sarah was fiery, but tonight felt different; she was a match poised to ignite the kindling of discontent.

As we approached, I caught snippets of her conversation with Mr. Johnson, whose grizzled features were set in a frown, his arms crossed defiantly. "You can't just assume we'll stand by while they—"

"Mr. Johnson, this isn't a competition! We're all here for the same reason," Sarah interjected, her voice rising like the crescendo of an opera.

"Then why do they get to claim this space?" he shot back, gesturing to a group of families who were animatedly chatting near the taco truck.

I stepped closer, desperate to diffuse the situation. "Sarah, Mr. Johnson, let's take a breath. This evening is about more than our differences. It's about finding common ground."

"Easy for you to say, Ashley," Sarah huffed, spinning on her heel. "You didn't have your family torn apart by these people."

"True, but we can either continue the cycle of blame or choose to be better. Isn't that worth trying?" I challenged, my heart pounding. The air thickened with anticipation, and I could feel Jason's steady presence behind me, a silent reassurance.

"Look, I'm not saying we should all become best friends," I added, striving for a lighter tone. "But what if we approached this evening like a buffet? We can each pick what we like and leave behind what we don't. There's plenty to go around."

The corner of Mr. Johnson's mouth twitched, and for a moment, I thought I saw a flicker of amusement in his eyes. "A buffet, huh? You think just because you dress it up, it changes what's being served?"

"Sometimes the presentation matters," I replied, allowing a smile to break through the seriousness of the moment. "You might even find a new favorite dish."

There was a beat of silence before the corners of Sarah's lips twitched up slightly. "Fine. But if they start serving pineapple on pizza, I'm out."

"Who even does that?" Jason interjected, stepping into the conversation with a playful grin. "You're safe tonight, I promise. No fruit on your pizza."

The tension began to dissolve, and laughter bubbled up from the surrounding crowd, easing the tightness in my chest. The night was still young, and perhaps the seeds of connection were taking root beneath the surface of discomfort.

Once the taco dispute was settled, I returned to my position near the makeshift stage, adrenaline still humming through me. The live band had started to play, the soft strumming of a guitar providing a soothing backdrop. I turned to Jason, my heart swelling with gratitude. "Thank you for backing me up."

"Always," he replied, his gaze steady and reassuring. "And you handled that like a pro. I'm proud of you."

With the music swirling around us, I scanned the crowd, seeing groups forming, laughter echoing through the night. But my gaze fell upon a couple standing a few feet away, their body language unmistakably tense. As I watched, I realized it was Margaret and her husband, Fred, both known for their vocal opinions during community meetings.

"Here we go again," I murmured to Jason, my voice laced with a hint of dread.

"Want me to jump in?" he asked, a playful glint in his eye.

"No," I chuckled. "Let's see if we can't keep this one civil without intervention."

As I approached, I took a deep breath, summoning every ounce of charm I could muster. "Margaret, Fred! How wonderful to see you both here."

"Would be nicer if we didn't have to share the space," Margaret replied, her voice flat, but the way her fingers twitched suggested a bubbling frustration.

"Maybe tonight we can find common ground," I offered, trying to keep my tone light. "What if we each share one thing we love about the distillery? It could be fun!"

"Fun?" Fred scoffed. "What's fun about pretending everything is fine?"

I tilted my head, feeling the urge to challenge him. "What if you share a memory instead? Something that made you smile about this place."

He paused, the challenge evident in his eyes, but after a beat, he relented. "Fine. I suppose the first time we had a family reunion here wasn't so bad."

"See? We're making progress," I encouraged, my heart warming at the shift in his demeanor.

"Great," Margaret muttered, crossing her arms. "I can think of better places to be."

"But can you think of a better way to spend tonight?" I countered. "All of us, right here, together. We owe it to ourselves and this community."

Margaret shifted on her feet, her expression softening ever so slightly. "Maybe if the music wasn't so loud, we could actually hear ourselves think."

"Maybe that's the point," I quipped. "To drown out the noise of our disagreements for a while and just... enjoy."

Jason, watching from a distance, winked at me, and I felt a surge of hope. Perhaps we weren't just rebuilding bridges; we were building something new entirely—a community that might just learn to laugh together again.

In that moment, the music shifted to a familiar tune, and laughter bubbled up from a nearby group, drawing me in. I felt a pull toward the dance floor, an irresistible invitation. "Come on, let's show them how it's done," I said to Jason, my spirit lifting. "If we're going to break down walls, we might as well do it with style."

He laughed, taking my hand and leading me toward the crowd, where the night was still young, and the music was a heartbeat away from possibility.

As Jason and I made our way to the dance floor, the upbeat rhythm of the band swept us up like a wave. The warm light created a magical glow around the scene, highlighting the laughter that punctuated the air. I could feel the tension begin to melt away with every beat of the music, and the mingling scents of grilled corn and sweet cider wrapped around me like a comforting embrace. I caught sight of Madeline, her laughter ringing like chimes in the wind as she danced with a group of kids, their faces flushed with joy.

"Now, this is the spirit we need!" I exclaimed, nudging Jason with my elbow as we joined the throng of dancers. He grinned, his movements effortlessly in sync with the music, his energy infectious.

I tried to keep up, but his natural rhythm made me feel like a clumsy marionette.

"Come on, Ash! You've got this!" he cheered, his eyes sparkling with delight as he twirled me around. I laughed, letting the music take over, my worries slipping away. For a few glorious minutes, the world outside this moment faded into nothingness.

Just as I started to lose myself in the music, a commotion at the edge of the dance floor pulled my attention. A few heads turned, and I could see a small crowd gathering again, their expressions a mix of confusion and concern. My heart sank, memories of the earlier confrontation bubbling up like a tide threatening to overtake the beach.

"Let's check it out," Jason said, his tone shifting to serious. We weaved through the crowd, our earlier joy evaporating like dew in the morning sun. As we approached, I saw that Sarah was at the center of it again, this time facing off against an older gentleman I recognized as Mr. Thompson, a longtime resident known for his stubbornness.

"Why are we even listening to them?" Mr. Thompson's voice boomed, his face flushed. "They've done nothing but bring trouble!"

"Mr. Thompson, we're trying to build a community here, not relive old grudges," Sarah shot back, her fists clenched at her sides, a storm brewing in her eyes.

"We can't just forget what they've done," he replied, his words heavy with years of resentment. "They don't care about us!"

"Stop!" I interjected, stepping forward with a deep breath, my heart racing. "This is exactly what we're trying to avoid tonight. We're all here to enjoy ourselves, not to reignite past arguments."

"Easier said than done," he retorted, a glare in his eyes. "You're young and idealistic. You think this will all just magically fix itself?"

"Maybe not magically," I said, fighting to keep my voice steady. "But if we don't at least try, we'll never know. We owe it to ourselves to give it a shot, don't you think?"

For a moment, silence enveloped us, the crowd shifting uneasily as they waited for someone to take the lead. I could feel the weight of every gaze on me, like a thousand invisible hands pressing down. But then, as if pulled by an unseen force, a woman stepped forward—Mrs. Dunne, a soft-spoken neighbor known for her kindness.

"I remember when my family first moved here," she said, her voice barely above a whisper. "We were scared, just like you all are now. But we found a way to come together and build something beautiful. It wasn't easy, but we did it because we believed in each other."

Her words hung in the air, wrapping around us like a warm blanket. The tension eased just a fraction, but I could see the uncertainty still lurking in the shadows. "What do you think, Mr. Thompson?" I asked gently. "Wouldn't it be better to share a moment of happiness than to stand here fighting?"

He hesitated, looking around at the faces in the crowd. "I suppose... but I still don't trust them."

"I get that," Jason chimed in, his tone calm and steady. "But trust isn't built overnight. Maybe tonight is a step in the right direction."

At that moment, I felt a surge of hope, a flicker of possibility igniting within me. "Let's take that step together. Come dance with us! Show them how we celebrate. You can be the first to step onto the dance floor!"

The crowd buzzed, a mix of apprehension and curiosity. Mrs. Dunne smiled, and I could see the spark of camaraderie starting to ignite. "I'll join you," she said, her tone brightening.

With that, she stepped forward, her feet moving hesitantly but determinedly toward the center of the gathering. "Come on, everyone! We can dance like we used to!"

As the band played on, people began to join her, laughter breaking through the tension like the first rays of dawn. I felt a rush of relief as others began to move, encouraged by her courage. Even Mr. Thompson was slowly swaying, albeit grudgingly.

With a knowing look exchanged between Jason and me, we stepped into the fray, twirling, laughing, letting the music sweep us up again. I could see families beginning to loosen their grips on their reservations, sharing tentative smiles and hesitant dance steps. It was exhilarating and heartwarming, a balm for all the wounds that had festered for too long.

Just as I thought we had turned a corner, the unexpected happened. A loud crash echoed from the back of the distillery, and the music screeched to a halt. A gasp swept through the crowd as everyone turned to see what had caused the disturbance. A couple of barrels had toppled over, sending glass bottles rolling across the wooden floor like errant marbles.

"What the hell just happened?" Sarah shouted, her eyes wide as she darted away from the dance floor to assess the situation.

I rushed forward, heart pounding, as I caught sight of someone scrambling to their feet, brushing dirt off their pants. "Are you okay?" I called, recognizing one of the older kids from the neighborhood, Jamie, who had been trying to help with the setup earlier.

"I'm fine! I just tripped," Jamie said, looking embarrassed but relieved. "But I think we might have a bigger problem..."

My stomach dropped as he pointed to the far end of the distillery. Shadows were moving, and I realized too late that something was off. A figure cloaked in darkness lingered by the doorway, watching us intently. The atmosphere shifted again, an electric tension replacing the warmth we had just built.

"Who's that?" Jason murmured, his expression serious as he strained to see. The crowd fell silent, eyes wide and alert, all focus now drawn to the unexpected stranger.

In that moment, with the celebration hanging by a thread, I felt a chill run down my spine. Who had crashed our party, and why did it feel like the night was teetering on the edge of something far more dangerous? The revelry had given way to uncertainty, and I knew we were about to face whatever shadows lurked just out of sight.

Chapter 28: The Night of Reckoning

The event unfolded beautifully—laughter and music echoed through the distillery, filling the cavernous space with warmth and joy. Twinkling fairy lights draped from the exposed beams above, casting a golden glow that shimmered against the polished oak barrels lining the walls. The air was rich with the scent of aged whiskey, mingling with the aroma of delicious hors d'oeuvres circulating on trays carried by attentive staff. I could feel the electric hum of anticipation as old grudges were being set aside, if only for a night. This was supposed to be a celebration, a chance to mend the rifts that had splintered our families for years, but the moment was tinged with a foreboding shadow.

As I navigated the crowd, I spotted familiar faces—friends and family, all dressed in their finest, their smiles bright against the backdrop of the rustic venue. The chatter was lively, punctuated by bursts of laughter, and for a moment, it felt as if the universe had conspired in our favor. My heart swelled with hope, each new connection forged like a promise whispered into the night. I exchanged pleasantries, my fingers brushing against a glass of whiskey, and I savored the warmth that spread through me. It was intoxicating, not just the drink, but the possibility of what could be.

But then, like a dark cloud rolling in, I noticed Carter lingering at the edge of the crowd, his figure tense and rigid. His eyes, usually so full of mischief, were now heavy with something darker—resentment, perhaps? It was as if he had been waiting for just the right moment to strike. I swallowed hard, feeling a knot tighten in my stomach. What had begun as a night of healing now seemed to teeter on the brink of chaos.

"Hey, are you alright?" Mia, my best friend, nudged me gently, her gaze following mine. She was dressed in a stunning emerald gown that sparkled with every movement, her hair cascading in soft waves. The warmth in her voice grounded me momentarily.

"Yeah, just a bit of a chill," I replied, forcing a smile, though my eyes remained fixed on Carter. The way he stood apart, as if cloaked in darkness, sent shivers down my spine.

Mia raised an eyebrow. "You sure it's just a chill? Because I'm getting the distinct feeling that storm clouds are gathering."

I chuckled, but it came out more like a nervous laugh. "You could say that again."

Before I could ponder the potential repercussions of Carter's presence, he stepped forward, commanding attention like a dark knight emerging from the shadows. The music dimmed, and the laughter subsided, replaced by an uneasy silence. My heart raced. This was not how the night was meant to unfold.

With a theatrical sweep of his hand, Carter called for silence. "Ladies and gentlemen," he began, his voice smooth but laced with venom. "I believe we need to address the elephant in the room. Or rather, the backroom dealings that have been taking place under our noses."

Gasps filled the air, and I felt the heat of embarrassment flush my cheeks. There was a sharpness to his tone that cut deeper than any knife. "What do you mean?" I managed to stammer, though I already feared the answer.

He stepped closer, eyes glinting like shards of glass. "You've all gathered here tonight under the pretense of unity, but it seems a certain someone"—he directed his gaze at me—"is more interested in betrayal than reconciliation. A clandestine plan to merge our families that's been hatched behind our backs."

I felt the weight of disappointment crash around me like a tidal wave, drowning my carefully constructed hopes. It was as if a veil had been ripped away, exposing the festering animosity that had lingered just beneath the surface. I could hear murmurs rippling through the crowd, fingers pointing, eyes narrowing in judgment.

"Carter, you don't know what you're talking about," I shot back, trying to maintain my composure despite the sudden chaos swelling around me. "This was meant to be a night of healing!"

He smirked, a cruel twist of his lips. "Healing? Or perhaps a masquerade, cleverly designed to conceal betrayal? Why should we trust you?"

His words hung heavy in the air, and I glanced at Mia, who looked as stunned as I felt. The fragile connections we had worked so hard to build seemed to crumble before my eyes, swept away by Carter's tempestuous accusations.

Suddenly, a familiar voice cut through the tension. "Enough, Carter!" It was my brother, Jack, stepping forward, his face set with determination. "We've worked too hard for this moment to let you sabotage it with your jealousy."

Carter scoffed, "Jealousy? Is that what you think this is? I'm merely calling out the truth."

A palpable tension crackled between the two men, and I felt as if I were caught in a storm, the winds of conflict swirling around me. I needed to regain control of the narrative before everything I had dreamed of for this night shattered like glass.

"Carter," I said, my voice steady despite the chaos, "let's talk about this privately. There's no need to air our family's dirty laundry in front of everyone."

He paused, a flicker of surprise crossing his features. For a moment, I thought I could reach him, appeal to whatever shred of decency he still possessed. But then he shook his head, a cold laugh escaping his lips.

"No, my dear. You've made your bed, and now everyone deserves to know just how deep the betrayal runs."

With a final glance, he turned away, leaving the crowd buzzing with murmurs and confused glances. The festive atmosphere had soured, and I could feel the excitement from earlier evaporating like the last sip of whiskey in a glass. I felt raw, exposed, and completely unprepared for the fallout of this night.

As I stood there, my heart pounding and cheeks aflame, I realized this wasn't just about family feuds or misunderstandings. This was about reclaiming my narrative, not allowing Carter's darkness to overshadow the light I had fought so hard to cultivate. I had to rally my allies, those who believed in the potential for change, and remind them that unity was still possible—if only we could weather this storm together.

The atmosphere, once bright with laughter, now crackled with tension, an electric charge that seemed to pulse through the crowd. I could sense the unease radiating from every direction, a collective intake of breath as eyes darted between Carter and me. The festive decorations, the carefully chosen music, and the aroma of fine food—all of it suddenly felt like a façade, crumbling under the weight of betrayal. My heart raced, a chaotic rhythm matching the tumult of emotions swirling within me.

"Are you really going to let him get away with this?" Mia leaned closer, her voice barely a whisper, but filled with urgency. She was a pillar of support, but I could see the worry etched on her face.

"I have to try," I replied, my throat dry. "I can't let him twist this into something it's not."

But the fire in Carter's eyes sparked a deeper fear within me, one that threatened to extinguish the flicker of hope I had clung to all night. I stepped forward, determined to reclaim my narrative, to drown out the whispers of doubt that crept through the air.

"Carter," I began, my voice steadying with each syllable, "this isn't about betrayal. This is about healing. Can't you see that?"

He raised an eyebrow, his smirk morphing into a mask of disbelief. "Healing? Please. You think this charade will fix years of animosity? You're delusional."

The crowd seemed to sway, caught between my pleas and his disdain. I could feel the weight of their expectations pressing down on me, and I had to remind myself why I had fought so hard to bring everyone together.

"Look around you, Carter!" I gestured broadly, encompassing the room filled with familiar faces. "People are here tonight because they want to change, to move past the pain. They deserve a chance to rebuild what was broken. But that requires trust. And right now, you're doing everything you can to sabotage that."

He scoffed, crossing his arms in a way that made him seem larger, more imposing. "Trust? From the family who's been planning behind our backs? Spare me."

A heavy silence fell, and I could feel the weight of judgment settle upon me, like a dark cloud obscuring the warmth of the evening. Just when I thought the moment couldn't feel more tense, an unexpected voice piped up from the back of the room.

"Why don't you show us your proof, Carter? Let's see this grand conspiracy you've conjured up." It was Jack, my brother, stepping into the light like a knight ready to defend his kingdom.

Carter turned, surprise flickering across his features for a split second before he sneered. "You want proof? Just look at her! She's trying to win you all over with her sweet words and charm while she plots our downfall."

"Or maybe she's just trying to make amends," Jack shot back, his voice steady and authoritative. "Don't pretend for a second that you're here for anything other than stirring the pot."

A murmur of agreement rippled through the crowd, and I could see a shift—a small yet significant wavering in Carter's confidence.

The laughter that had filled the room moments ago now returned, not as a riotous roar but as a cautious, collective hope.

"Enough with the theatrics," I said, emboldened by Jack's defense. "We all know the history here. It's messy, and it's painful. But if we keep holding on to the past, we'll never move forward. What do you really want, Carter? Do you want this feud to continue, or do you want a chance to start over?"

Carter's expression flickered, the mask of bravado cracking just enough for me to glimpse the uncertainty beneath. "What do I want? I want to protect my family, the one you've taken advantage of for your own gain."

"Protect them from what? Healing?" I stepped closer, feeling the urgency of the moment wrap around us like a tightrope. "You think hiding behind old grudges is protecting anyone? It's not. It's imprisoning you all. Let's tear down the walls, Carter. Let's build something new."

His jaw tightened, and for a moment, I thought he might relent. But then, with a flick of his wrist, he turned away, as if dismissing me like an annoying insect buzzing around his head. "You think it's that easy?"

"Nothing worthwhile ever is," I shot back, my heart pounding with a mix of defiance and desperation.

As the crowd buzzed around us, I could feel the weight of their gazes—some curious, some skeptical, others filled with support. I took a deep breath, grounding myself in the moment. I had come too far to back down now, too invested in the dream of unity to let this night end in despair.

"Let's show them, Carter. Let's prove that we can rise above this. We owe it to ourselves."

He hesitated, a flicker of conflict passing through his eyes. Just then, the crowd began to murmur among themselves, debating the merits of what I had proposed. Laughter resumed, and I could hear snippets of conversation about old grudges and fresh starts.

Mia, sensing the tide turning, chimed in. "Carter, wouldn't it be better to come together than continue this endless cycle of animosity? If we all truly care about our families, we need to be willing to take that leap."

The room felt alive with possibility. The collective energy shifted, wrapping around us like a cocoon, fostering the growth of something new. And as I stood there, facing Carter, I realized this was not just about our families; it was about all of us—about breaking down barriers and healing wounds that had festered for far too long.

Carter shifted, the resolve in his posture wavering just enough for me to sense the shift. "Fine," he muttered, a reluctant admission dripping from his lips. "Let's say I'm willing to consider it. But only if you can convince everyone else."

A spark ignited within me, and I knew this was the opportunity I had been waiting for. "Deal. Let's show them that unity isn't just a dream but something we can achieve together."

As he nodded, albeit grudgingly, the atmosphere in the room transformed again, laughter and chatter flowing like a gentle stream, washing away the remnants of doubt. I glanced around, meeting the hopeful gazes of my friends and family, feeling the swell of possibility rise within me. The night was still young, and while we faced challenges ahead, for the first time in a long while, the weight of the past felt just a little lighter.

As Carter begrudgingly agreed to consider the possibility of unity, the energy in the distillery shifted yet again, transforming from hostile stares to a hesitant but palpable sense of hope. People exchanged glances, their expressions a mix of skepticism and curiosity. It was as if I had thrown a pebble into a still pond, and the ripples were just beginning to form, inching outward with each cautious murmur.

"Okay, what's the plan?" Jack asked, breaking through the haze of uncertainty. He stepped up beside me, his presence a reassuring anchor amid the swirling emotions.

I looked around the room, my mind racing with possibilities. "We can create a roundtable discussion. Open dialogue, where everyone can voice their concerns and share their hopes. Let's make this a collaborative effort."

Carter crossed his arms, a reluctant skepticism lining his features. "You think that'll work? You really believe we can just sit down like adults and hash this out?"

A nervous laugh escaped me. "Well, it's worth a shot. What's the alternative? We let the resentment simmer until it boils over again?"

"Touché," Carter replied, his tone a mix of begrudging admiration and thinly veiled irritation.

"Everyone deserves a voice," I added, glancing at the gathering crowd. "The past doesn't have to dictate our future. We're all in this together."

The murmur of agreement began to spread, an undercurrent of support that started with Mia and quickly enveloped others who had once stood in opposition. I felt a swell of determination, but it was swiftly tinged with anxiety. Would this newfound willingness translate into real change, or were we merely postponing an inevitable confrontation?

Before I could delve too deeply into that thought, Mia raised her glass, a mischievous twinkle in her eye. "Alright, let's toast to new beginnings, then. And to the crazy idea that families can actually get along."

Everyone laughed, the tension in the air easing just a little as we clinked our glasses together. "To new beginnings!" echoed through the room, creating a momentary bubble of unity.

I scanned the faces surrounding me, their features softening as they took a sip of their drinks, slowly allowing the idea to seep into their minds. Maybe, just maybe, this night wasn't destined for disaster after all.

"Let's set a date for our first meeting," I proposed, feeling emboldened. "And I'll make sure we have a neutral location, somewhere comfortable for everyone. No hidden agendas—just a genuine discussion."

"Can I bring snacks?" Mia chimed in with a grin, clearly attempting to lighten the mood further.

"Absolutely! Nothing starts a conversation better than food," I replied, grateful for her infectious optimism.

Yet as the laughter flowed and plans began to take shape, I couldn't shake the feeling that we were walking a tightrope, one wrong move away from falling into chaos. Carter, while seemingly on board, had a glint in his eye that hinted at mischief. I couldn't trust him completely, and my gut twisted with apprehension.

Just then, I felt a sudden chill sweep through the room, like the dark shadow of an incoming storm. I turned, scanning the faces around me, searching for the source of the sudden shift. The laughter faded, the vibrant atmosphere dulling as if someone had pulled the plug on our lively celebration.

At that moment, the door to the distillery swung open, the hinges creaking ominously. A figure stepped inside, silhouetted against the light streaming in from the hallway. My heart dropped as I recognized him. It was my father, his face set with an expression that spoke of secrets and burdens far too heavy to carry alone.

"Dad?" I called, my voice trembling slightly. "What are you doing here?"

His gaze flickered around the room, taking in the assembled guests with a mix of disbelief and apprehension. "I need to talk to you. Now."

Panic rippled through me as I moved toward him, my mind racing. The sight of him here, unannounced and obviously distressed, sent a chill of dread coiling in my stomach. "Is something wrong? Did something happen?"

"It's about your plans," he said, his voice low and grave. "You need to listen to me."

Carter moved in beside me, a protective instinct rising as he narrowed his eyes at my father. "Is this going to be another one of your warnings about staying away from the family? Because—"

"No, Carter. This is serious." My father's voice cut through the air, firm and unwavering. "What you're trying to do—bringing our families together—it's more complicated than you understand."

An uneasy silence settled over the room, each guest shifting their weight as they leaned in to listen. The sense of hope I had cultivated just moments ago threatened to evaporate, replaced by a tangible tension.

"Why? What do you mean?" I pressed, my heart racing. "If we can just have one conversation—"

"Conversations can be dangerous," he interrupted, his expression darkening. "And you don't know the half of what's at stake. There are things in our past, things that could resurface if you're not careful."

"What are you talking about?" I demanded, frustration and fear churning within me. "You can't just drop a bomb like that and not explain."

But he was already shaking his head, glancing nervously around the room as if the walls themselves might be listening. "We need to go somewhere private. I can't say anything here."

The guests, now hanging on every word, exchanged looks of concern. I felt a tightening in my chest as the realization struck me—my father was here to reveal something that could shatter everything we had just built.

"Fine," I said, though my heart raced at the implications of his words. "Let's talk."

As I turned to lead him toward a quieter corner of the distillery, the air felt thick with foreboding. Behind me, Carter watched closely, the tension between us palpable.

Just as I reached the door leading to the back office, I heard the sound of a glass shattering behind me, the sharp crack piercing through the air like a gunshot. Everyone turned, and for a moment, time seemed to freeze.

"What was that?" Mia exclaimed, her eyes wide with alarm.

I whirled around, heart pounding, only to see Carter's expression shift from annoyance to something darker. He took a step forward, his gaze fixed on the chaos erupting in the crowd.

"Get back!" I shouted, instinctively placing myself between my father and the commotion. The room erupted in confusion, people shouting, stumbling backward as panic spread like wildfire.

In that moment, I realized that the night had taken a turn I couldn't have anticipated. Whatever secrets lay buried in our past were clawing their way to the surface, and the fragile bonds I had fought to build were teetering on the brink of destruction.

As I stood there, my heart pounding, I felt the ground beneath me shift, and I knew this night was far from over. Whatever was about to unfold, it would change everything.

Chapter 29: The Fracture

I had always thought of the distillery's garden as a sanctuary—a lush, fragrant retreat where the heady scent of fermenting grapes mingled with the crisp autumn air. Vines hung heavy with ripe, purple clusters, swaying gently in the breeze, while the intricate lattice of leaves overhead danced like playful spirits caught in a moment of glee. But tonight, that idyllic scene felt more like a gilded cage, its beauty a stark contrast to the chaos we'd just escaped. Jason and I pressed against the cold, stone wall of the distillery, our breaths mingling in the cool night air, the weight of our families' wrath hanging over us like a thundercloud.

"I can't believe this is happening," I said, shaking my head, my heart racing as I fought against the rising tide of panic. The shouting had echoed through the hall, each word a sharp dagger aimed at old wounds. The anger had ignited, feeding off years of resentment and misunderstandings, igniting flames that felt impossible to extinguish.

"I know," Jason replied, his voice a low murmur, but the urgency in his tone cut through the stillness like a flash of lightning. "We need to talk—just us. Away from..." He gestured vaguely, frustration curling his lip as he surveyed the chaos we had left behind.

I turned my gaze toward the sprawling estate, the lights flickering inside like distant stars, oblivious to the turmoil outside. "What if they find us?" I asked, a shiver creeping up my spine, the uncertainty wrapping around me like a heavy cloak. My thoughts raced as I remembered the furious faces, the wild accusations. My father's voice had risen above the din, thick with disbelief. How had we let it get this far?

"They won't," he insisted, taking my hand in his, his fingers warm and reassuring. "We can't let them drag us into their mess." The softness in his grip offered a sense of comfort, but the turmoil inside me twisted tighter, a knot of dread that refused to loosen.

The garden was alive with the rustle of leaves and the distant hum of cicadas, a stark contrast to the maelstrom we had just escaped. I could almost forget the shouts, the tears, the look on my mother's face when she had discovered that Jason and I were more than friends. The anger had been instantaneous, a firestorm ignited by a single spark.

"Do you think they'll ever accept us?" I asked, my voice barely a whisper, as if speaking the question aloud might summon some dark answer.

Jason hesitated, his brow furrowing as he searched for the right words. "I don't know, but we have to try." His gaze was intense, the dark pools of his eyes reflecting not just uncertainty but a fierce determination. "I refuse to let them dictate our lives."

In that moment, I felt a wave of affection wash over me. He had always been my anchor, even as the world spun around us like a dizzying carousel. But even anchors can wear thin under pressure, and I could feel the strain tightening between us like a taut wire.

Before I could respond, a loud crash echoed from inside the distillery, the sound of shattering glass piercing through the night. I stiffened, instinctively leaning closer to Jason, who frowned, his expression a mixture of concern and anger. "They're not going to stop, are they?"

"It doesn't seem like it," I replied, a heaviness settling in my chest. My heart raced as I imagined the unfolding scene, families fracturing before my eyes. My own family—rooted in traditions that felt as old as the vines climbing the trellis—was crumbling under the weight of our choices.

Jason stepped closer, his voice low and conspiratorial. "We could just leave. Tonight. Just drive."

The idea was intoxicating, a sweet escape that painted vivid pictures in my mind: open roads stretching endlessly before us, the moon hanging low and bright, the world left far behind. Yet, I could almost hear my father's voice echoing in my head, thick with disappointment, betrayal. "And then what?" I countered, shaking my head. "Run away from our families? From the mess we've made?"

"It's not a mess we've made," he snapped, the edge in his voice startling me. "It's a mess they've created. We can't let their hate spill into our lives." His passion was palpable, a fierce flame igniting within him, but my heart tugged in a different direction.

"It's not just hate, Jason. It's love turned sour, wounds that haven't healed," I said, my voice trembling with the weight of unspoken truths. I felt the familiar sting of tears threatening to spill over, each memory of my family's anger striking like a fresh wound. "If we leave, we may never come back."

He stepped back, the space between us growing. "Maybe that's exactly what we need to do."

The intensity of his words hung heavy in the air, like the sweet scent of fermenting grapes that now felt suffocating. "You don't really mean that," I said, trying to swallow the lump in my throat, my chest tightening as I grasped the gravity of our situation. "What about everything we've worked for?"

He looked away, his jaw set in determination, and I knew I had to make a choice. The weight of our families loomed over us, threatening to crush the fragile bond we had forged. And as I stood there, feeling the pulse of the earth beneath my feet, I realized we were at a crossroads, the air thick with the electric tension of uncertainty.

With a deep breath, I reached out, my fingers brushing against his arm, desperate to bridge the gap that had grown between us. "I don't want to lose you," I said softly, my voice trembling as I fought against the tears. "But I don't know how to fix this."

Jason's expression softened, and he stepped closer again, wrapping an arm around me, pulling me into his warmth. "We'll figure it out. Together."

Together. The word resonated deep within me, stirring hope in the depths of despair. But even as I leaned into him, I could feel the tension simmering beneath the surface, a storm still brewing on the horizon. And in that moment of fragile peace, I couldn't shake the feeling that the battle was only beginning.

The silence in the garden wrapped around us like a thick blanket, muffling the chaos that echoed just beyond the stone walls. The moonlight dripped through the leaves overhead, casting dappled patterns on the ground, illuminating the uncertainty that lay between us. I felt Jason's heartbeat sync with mine, a silent rhythm that pulsed with tension. Yet, in that moment, I couldn't shake the feeling that we were holding onto something fragile, a delicate truce amidst the storm.

"Let's sit," he suggested, gesturing to a weathered wooden bench nestled beneath a canopy of vines. The bench creaked under our weight as we settled in, the night air heavy with the sweetness of overripe fruit. I looked at him, really looked at him, his dark hair tousled and his eyes gleaming with an intensity that both thrilled and terrified me.

"What are we doing, Jason?" I finally asked, my voice breaking the stillness like a twig snapping underfoot. "Is running away really an option?" The thought was seductive, a siren's call tempting me to abandon all that I had known. But the reality of it sent my mind spiraling. Leaving felt like surrendering, a retreat from the very people who had shaped us.

"Sometimes it's the only option," he replied, his voice steady yet layered with unspoken fears. "You know what they're like. They won't let us be happy, not with each other."

"But isn't it worth fighting for?" I countered, my heart racing at the thought of turning my back on everything. The rich history of my family, the roots that tangled deep within the soil of our hometown—they were a part of me, after all. "What about our families? What about us?"

His gaze hardened, and I could see the anger brewing beneath his calm exterior. "They don't see us, Alyssa. They see their expectations, their ideals. We can't keep living in their shadow."

The conviction in his voice stirred something within me, a flicker of courage that pushed against the confines of my apprehension. "But running away doesn't solve anything. It's like putting a Band-Aid on a bullet wound."

Jason sighed, frustration etching lines across his forehead. "You're right, but we can't fix this tonight. All we're doing is prolonging the inevitable."

As he spoke, a breeze whispered through the garden, rustling the leaves and carrying away the heavy atmosphere that had settled over us. I closed my eyes, trying to tune out the noise inside my head. I had always been the peacemaker, the one to smooth over the jagged edges of familial discord. But with Jason, everything felt different, more intense, like a river that surged beneath the surface, ready to burst forth.

"We need a plan," I said, suddenly energized by the prospect of action. "What if we invite them to meet? Just us, with no shouting, no accusations?"

His brow furrowed, and I could see the gears turning in his mind. "And what? Play a game of emotional chess while they throw us under the bus?"

"Maybe," I mused, letting the idea take root. "But it's better than running away and hiding." The thought of facing our families head-on sent a thrill of adrenaline coursing through me. I could picture the scene, the potential for healing mixed with a hefty dose of tension.

"Fine. But if this goes south, I'm holding you responsible," he teased, a reluctant smile breaking through the tension.

"Deal." My heart lifted at the spark of hope igniting between us, the possibility of confronting our families together, standing shoulder to shoulder against the tide.

Just then, a sudden rustling in the bushes startled us, and we turned to see Sarah, my little sister, poking her head through the foliage. "Alyssa! Jason!" she squeaked, her eyes wide with excitement. "You're not going to believe what I heard!"

"What are you doing here?" I hissed, my mind racing. The last thing we needed was more family drama infiltrating our plans.

"Shhh! They're going crazy in there!" she exclaimed, her cheeks flushed with exhilaration. "I overheard Mom and Dad arguing about you two! Mom said she'd never forgive you for this!"

My stomach twisted. I couldn't deny the hurt in my mother's voice from earlier. "What else did you hear?"

"Dad said something about cutting off college funds if you don't come home," she said, biting her lip.

The stakes felt impossibly high. I exchanged a glance with Jason, who looked equally stricken. "They can't do that," he said, his voice low but fierce. "It's blackmail."

"That's not the point, though," I interjected, my heart racing. "They're desperate to keep us apart."

"Not if we get to them first," Jason said, a glimmer of defiance lighting up his expression.

"Right! We have to turn the tables." My pulse quickened at the prospect of seizing control, of wielding our fate instead of being tossed around like leaves in the wind. "If we face them as a united front, maybe we can at least stall their plans."

"You mean we turn this into a family council?" Jason quipped, a grin creeping back onto his face. "We'll need name tags and everything."

"Definitely name tags," I replied, laughing despite the heaviness in my chest. "I'll make mine say 'The Peacemaker' and yours can say 'The Dashing Hero.'"

"Hero? I'm just trying to survive," he shot back, amusement dancing in his eyes. "But I'll take it."

Sarah's laughter filled the air, a sweet sound that broke the tension lingering like smoke. "So you're really going to do this? Face Mom and Dad?"

"Looks like we have no other choice," I said, my resolve hardening like steel. "But we need you on our side, Sarah. We can't let them intimidate us."

"I'm in!" she declared, puffing out her chest with the pride of a tiny warrior. "I'll make sure they hear you. I'll distract Mom with cupcakes!"

I chuckled, my heart swelling with affection for my sister. "Cupcakes? What are you, the dessert fairy?"

"Hey, don't knock it! Everyone loves cupcakes!" she shot back, her confidence unwavering.

As I watched her enthusiasm, the weight on my shoulders began to lighten. It wouldn't be easy, but perhaps together, as an unyielding trio, we could confront the chaos head-on. The moon hung high above us, a witness to our resolve, and I felt a stirring of hope, the dawn of a new chapter blossoming against the backdrop of impending uncertainty. In that moment, I knew I wasn't alone; we were in this together, ready to face whatever storm lay ahead.

The garden seemed to breathe around us, the leaves whispering secrets as if the world beyond could hear the turmoil roiling in our hearts. I could still hear the echoes of our families fighting, their voices like thunder rolling through the hills, filled with years of resentment and unresolved grievances. The moon cast a silvery glow on the vines, illuminating Jason's face, etched with determination and a hint of fear.

"I'm serious about this meeting," I said, breaking the silence that had settled between us. "We need to get everyone together and talk this out. If we don't, it'll only get worse."

Jason leaned back against the bench, crossing his arms as he contemplated my words. "You think they'll listen?" His brow furrowed in doubt, and I could see the wheels turning in his mind.

"Maybe not at first," I conceded. "But if we can show them that we're not backing down, maybe they'll realize how ridiculous this is. I mean, look at us!" I gestured dramatically, feeling the weight of the situation lift just a bit with the absurdity of it all. "Two families at war over two people who are just trying to be happy."

He chuckled, a soft, disbelieving sound. "Happy? More like two people caught in the crossfire."

"Details, details." I waved my hand dismissively, though my heart wasn't as light as my words suggested. "What about your parents? Do you think they'll even show?"

Jason's expression darkened, a shadow creeping into his eyes. "They might. They love a good family drama as much as the next person." He paused, his gaze drifting off into the distance. "But I can't promise they'll be civil."

"Well, at least we're both in this together," I said, a flicker of hope igniting within me. "We just need to make sure our voices are heard."

"I guess we can try," he replied, his tone still laced with uncertainty. "But what if they start throwing things again? I'm not sure I'm ready for a replay of the Christmas dinner incident."

The memory made me smile—a spectacularly disastrous evening where my father had accidentally knocked over a tray of the infamous holiday punch, sending glass shards and sticky liquid everywhere. "True. But you did throw that pie at Uncle Rick. That was pretty impressive."

"I was aiming for the pumpkin spice candles," he protested, a grin breaking through his earlier doubt. "I'd say I succeeded in my own way."

Just then, Sarah appeared again, her little face a mask of enthusiasm. "You guys! I have an idea!"

"What is it now, cupcake fairy?" I asked, amused by her relentless energy.

"What if we made a video? Like a family YouTube video!" she exclaimed, bouncing on her toes. "You know, 'Family Feud: The Real Life Edition.' We could post it online and go viral!"

Jason laughed, shaking his head. "That sounds like the worst idea I've ever heard."

"Yeah, because your family's not known for their stellar behavior on camera," I added, unable to contain my amusement. "That might just guarantee our doom."

"Or we could take bets on who throws the first punch!" Sarah giggled, her laughter bright against the backdrop of our tension.

I ruffled her hair, appreciating her attempts to lighten the mood. "As much as I love the idea of a dramatic family showdown, I think we need to keep this under wraps for now."

"Boring!" she retorted, pouting. "But fine. I'll keep the cameras off... for now."

As we shared a laugh, a glimmer of warmth spread through me, reminding me why I was fighting so hard. Family was chaotic, messy, and sometimes completely insane, but it was mine.

"Okay, so we'll have the meeting," Jason said, finally coming around. "Let's do it tomorrow afternoon, when everyone's cooled off a bit. Maybe we can meet at my parents' place. They'll have to be civil there, right?"

"Right. And if they aren't, we'll just have to threaten them with cupcakes," I joked, a sense of determination rising within me. "I'm pretty sure no one can resist a cupcake."

Jason stood up, brushing off his jeans. "Okay, let's regroup tomorrow then. This will either go spectacularly well or spectacularly wrong."

I felt a mix of excitement and dread churn in my stomach as I nodded. "Can't wait."

We lingered a moment longer in the garden, soaking in the peacefulness of the night, but the weight of our decision hung heavily in the air. As we finally made our way back to the distillery, I could see flickering lights through the windows, shadows moving with frenetic energy inside.

The moment we stepped into the distillery's main hall, the atmosphere hit us like a gust of wind—tension palpable enough to slice through. My parents stood on one side, Jason's on the other, their faces set in grim lines, the previous chaos having morphed into a brewing storm of silence.

"Ah, look who decided to grace us with their presence," my mother said, her voice cool as she crossed her arms.

"Glad to see everyone's still in one piece," Jason quipped, attempting to ease the mood with humor, but it landed like a lead balloon.

"Where have you two been?" My father's tone was sharp, cutting through the air like a knife.

"Just outside, taking a breather," I replied, forcing a smile that felt more like a grimace. "You know, the chaos inside was a little much."

"Don't pretend this is a game," Jason's father interjected, his voice low and tense. "This is serious."

And just as the words settled in, like the lead weight they were, the front door burst open. A gust of wind swept through the hall, bringing with it an unexpected visitor—a figure clad in dark clothing, face obscured by a hood. My heart raced as I caught a glimpse of their piercing eyes, shining like two beacons in the dim light.

"What do you want?" my mother snapped, her composure cracking at the sight.

The figure stepped forward, a sinister smile curling their lips. "I think you all need to hear what I have to say. Things are about to get much more complicated."

Tension thickened like fog rolling in, wrapping around us as I felt the ground shift beneath my feet, reality spiraling into a deeper, darker unknown.

Milton Keynes UK
Ingram Content Group UK Ltd.
UKHW020756231024
450026UK00001B/68